IN DEADLY EARNEST

A Collection of Fiction by New Zealand Women 1870s–1980s

Selected and Introduced by
Trudie McNaughton

CENTURY HUTCHINSON

*I would like to dedicate this book to
Stuart, Sam, Talia, and Harry*

I am very grateful to the two diligent and patient editors who have worked on this book, Chris Price and Harriet Bennett Allan (especially for the latter's work in compiling the Biographical Notes). Librarians at the Auckland Public Library New Zealand Section, the University of Auckland New Zealand Room, and at the Auckland Institute and Museum Library have, as always, been very helpful.

Century Hutchinson New Zealand Ltd
An imprint of the Century Hutchinson Group
187–189 Archers Road, P.O. Box 40-086, Glenfield, Auckland 10.

Century Hutchinson Ltd
62–65 Chandos Place, Covent Garden, London WC2N 4NW

Century Hutchinson Australia Pty Ltd
89–91 Albion Street, Surry Hills, Sydney, N.S.W. 2010

Century Hutchinson South Africa Pty Ltd
P.O. Box 337, Bergvlei 2012, South Africa

First published 1989
Selection and Introduction © Trudie McNaughton, 1989
Stories/Excerpts © the contributors : date of publication

Printed in Singapore

ISBN 1 86941 042 4

CONTENTS

Introduction	v
Biographical Notes	viii
Acknowledgements	xiv
LADY BARKER 'Death in our New Zealand Home — New Zealand Children' Letter IX from *Station Life in New Zealand* (1870)	1
EDITH SEARLE GROSSMANN 'Girlhood' Chapter V from *In Revolt* (1893)	4
EDITH SEARLE GROSSMANN 'Volcanic' Chapter VI from *In Revolt* (1893)	7
EDITH SEARLE GROSSMANN 'Tried by Law' Chapter LVII from *In Revolt* (1893)	11
EDITH SEARLE GROSSMANN 'The Nearest Type of Eternal Damnation' Chapter LIX from *In Revolt* (1893)	13
LADY ANNE GLENNY WILSON Chapter VII from *Alice Lauder* (1895)	17
LOUISA BAKER 'Sowing Seed' An extract from a chapter from *Wheat in the Ear* (1898)	21
CONSTANCE CLYDE (McAdam) 'I Was the Man' An extract from a chapter from *A Pagan's Love* (1905)	25
SUSIE MACTIER An extract from *The Hills of Hauraki* (1908)	30
LOUISA BAKER 'The Woman in the Wilderness' An extract from *The Perfect Union* (1908)	32
LOUISA BAKER 'Twilight of Dawn' An extract from a chapter from *The Perfect Union* (1908)	35
SUSIE MACTIER 'The Angel's Wing' Chapter XII from *Miranda Stanhope* (1911)	37
B. E. BAUGHAN 'Grandmother Speaks' Extracts from a chapter from *Brown Bread From a Colonial Oven* (1912)	40
JANE MANDER An extract from *The Story of a New Zealand River* (1920)	44
KATHERINE MANSFIELD *The Woman at the Store* (1924)	47
ROBIN HYDE 'The Purple Mantle' Chapter Thirteen from *Nor the Years Condemn* (1938)	56
JEAN DEVANNY Chapter XIV from *The Butcher Shop* (1926)	67
GREVILLE TEXIDOR *An Annual Affair* (1944)	76
NGAIO MARSH Prologue from *Died in the Wool* (1945)	85
JANET FRAME *The Day of the Sheep* (1951)	91
MARY SCOTT Chapter I from *Breakfast at Six* (1953)	95

SYLVIA ASHTON-WARNER 'Spring' A chapter from *Spinster* (1958)	101
MARILYN DUCKWORTH Chapter Twenty from *A Gap in the Spectrum* (1959)	104
JANET FRAME Chapter IV from *Faces in the Water* (1961)	107
JANET FRAME *The Mythmaker's Office* (1962)	113
JANET FRAME *A Sense of Proportion* (1963)	117
AMELIA BATISTICH *A Dalmation Woman* (1963)	121
AMELIA BATISTICH *A Place Called Sarajevo* (1963)	125
ARAPERA BLANK *Yielding to the New* (1970)	130
PATRICIA GRACE *A Way of Talking* (1975)	135
BUB BRIDGER *Girl in the River* (1977)	139
MARGARET SUTHERLAND *Codling-Moth* (1977)	143
MARGARET SUTHERLAND *Need* (1977)	153
JEAN WATSON An extract from *the world is an orange and the sun* (1978)	159
FIONA KIDMAN An extract from *A Breed of Women* (1980)	162
YVONNE DU FRESNE *Arts and Crafts* (1980)	168
SUE McCAULEY Chapter six from *Other Halves* (1982)	172
J. C. STURM *Jerusalem, Jerusalem* (1983)	183
J. C. STURM *A Thousand and One Nights* (1983)	193
LAURIS EDMOND Chapter Thirteen from *High Country Weather* (1984)	198
SHONAGH KOEA *Mrs Pratt Goes to China* (1984)	204
JOY COWLEY *The Woman Next Door* (1985)	211
FRANCES CHERRY *Waiting for Jim* (1986)	214
KERI HULME *The Knife and the Stone* (1986)	219
KERI HULME *While my Guitar Gently Sings* (1986)	226

INTRODUCTION

This anthology is a celebration of women's writing in New Zealand. It shows some of the scope, variety, and common concerns of thirty-two women writers whose work spans over a century. It is also a reminder of our debts to earlier writers, for their struggles as feminists, writers, and feminist writers.

Many women have had great difficulty in getting good work published. Remaining in print has been an added difficulty. As a result the work of writers such as Edith Searle Grossmann or Louisa Baker is almost unknown today. With such books long out of print and almost impossible to track down, readers have to rely on critics' assessments of their literary worth.

Most of these critics have been male. Some of them have managed to explain away the successes of women who have been published and read. E. M. Smith in *A History of New Zealand Fiction* (Reed 1939) explained the predominance of women writers after World War I by claiming that many of the young men who might have been writing 'were among *Our Glorious Dead*. So that the principal traits of this period are to be found in the feminist and pro-Labour views of Mrs Devanny, Miss Rees contenting herself with lavish applications of local colour in place of ideas.'

While acknowledging Mansfield as 'the greatest New Zealand-born writer' and that women made up a third of writers, including the most prolific and the authors of best-sellers, Smith claimed that popularity was no criterion for assuming a high standard of women's work — 'far from it. They are responsible for two features — the reforming zeal which has already been noted, and for the fact that many details of everyday life are given which might have escaped the notice of men. Thus, especially in the earlier years, the women's point of view is brought out, and it is especially interesting in the study of pioneering days.'

While admitting women writers have different perspectives from men, he finally rejected their views. He decided 'from a study of our fiction as a whole' that New Zealand is by no means a country of bullying husbands and downtrodden wives. The novels of Searle Grossmann, Devanny, Baker, and Clyde he labelled 'propagandist', regretting that women take things so seriously and are in such 'deadly earnest'. It seems Smith and other critics have accepted women's tales of domestic life in trying colonial conditions amidst beautiful scenery, but not of their personal relationships and roles.

The picture Smith receives of New Zealand women is therefore distorted by such selective viewing; it is of 'eminently practical women, anxious for the welfare of their husbands and families, but willing to leave the management of outside affairs in the hands of their husbands, not because of a lack of confidence in their own capabilities, but because their home interests are sufficient. As a result, they are shown as conservative, having a pathetic faith in everything English, and as being very conscious of the scrutiny and possible criticism of their neighbours.'

We can't dismiss such writing as the quaint views of a fossil. The continued evaluation and ranking of writers too often echoes such standards. Even those critics who appreciated women writers carped at the driving force behind some of their writing. Alan Mulgan, in an obituary for Edith Searle Grossmann, regretted that her militant feminism limited her literary value. Men whose strongly held views, whether about the roles of the sexes, socialism, developing nationalism, or the relationship of New Zealand to Britain, have not been labelled propagandist as quickly as women writers writing about issues important to them.

What have been the concerns of women writing in New Zealand? Readers may be surprised at the shared themes of early and contemporary writers. Domestic violence, the isolation and loneliness women suffer in restricted lives, the choice forced on women between relationships (with partners, children, family) and career, the rejection of a woman's individuality, rebuffing of her imagination, and the limits set on women by narrow education are all vital issues to many of the women represented in this anthology, regardless of when they wrote.

Much of this writing is about rebellion — personal rebellion (often triggered by the desire to help other women), and rebellion against institutions such as marriage, education, the law, and religion. Personal rebellion often centres around a refusal to compartmentalize life, to fulfil one role at the expense of others. Ascot in Constance Clyde's *A Pagan's Love* rejects the narrow view that 'there must be two types of woman — the breadwinner all brain, and the fireside dame all affection'. She condemns the way women are expected 'to endure the greatest strain of all — that of doing without love altogether or yielding to it an absolute surrender'.

Many of the stories in this anthology condemn the roles foisted on women. In the earlier fiction this is often explicit, and seems didactic to contemporary readers. One of the most fiercely rejected roles is that of the victim. Women and girls in much of the writing are abused, physically and emotionally. The violence is particularly damaging and difficult to escape when it occurs within the sanctity of the home. Searle Grossmann, Baughan, and Mactier are among the early writers who focused on such uncomfortable topics. Hulme, Frame, Kidman, Sutherland, and others continue to expose harassment and other abuse. Writers such as Mansfield and Texidor show how women themselves become violent, hitting out in desperation at partners and children.

Women's domestic roles are a major subject in the fiction. They are sometimes treated lightly, as in Mary Scott's popular writing which treats men with a condescending humour, similar to the tone used for children or pets. There is an assumption of shared experience behind this work just as there is behind the very different writing of Texidor, Sturm, Watson, Kidman, and others. This leads to an expectation of sympathy:

> Joy could see there was something wrong, but Mum said it was only her legs.
> They swelled up, generally in the evenings, about the time Dad came home, and she would say to him Just look at my legs again, it's from being on them all day.
> (Texidor, *An Annual Affair*)

Domestic roles of mother, wife, housekeeper, and child often keep women isolated and lonely. The unhappiness of immigrant women comes out in many of the stories, while such writers as Hulme, Blank, and Grace show the extra burdens that Maori women bear, when racism compounds sexism. For women of all cultures the urge to make, to create is strong. Embroidery, storytelling, farming, baking, childrearing, and writing itself are all seen as occupations requiring enormous dedication but offering satisfaction to the women involved.

Women's writing over the last hundred years is honest about the pain women suffer. It also celebrates the triumphs of women as survivors despite the odds. It does so with variety and skill, and deserves to be read, challenged, and valued.

Trudie McNaughton

BIOGRAPHICAL NOTES

SYLVIA ASHTON-WARNER   Born in 1908 in Stratford, New Zealand, and educated at Wairarana College and Auckland Teacher's Training College. She married a teacher and for seventeen years was infant mistress in Maori schools. She developed 'organic teaching' which provoked interest among educationalists here and in other countries. She died in 1984. She published ten books. 'Spring' is an extract from her novel *Spinster* published by Secker and Warburg, London, in 1958, and republished by Virago in 1980.

LOUISA ALICE BAKER (née Dawson)   Born in 1858. She wrote over fifteen novels often under her psuedonymns 'Alien' and 'Rita'. She died in 1929. 'Sowing Seed' is an extract from *Wheat in the Ear* published by Hutchinson, London, in 1898. 'Twilight of Dawn' is from *The Perfect Union* published by Digby, Long, and Co, London, 1908.

LADY MARY ANNE BARKER   Born in Jamaica in 1831 and educated in England. She married in 1852 and accompanied her husband to Simla, India, in 1860. Widowed shortly afterwards, she returned to England where she married again, in 1865. She and her new husband sailed to New Zealand to establish a sheep station. After a severe winter, in which they lost most of their stock, they returned to London in 1868. She later visited Natal, Mauritius, Western Australia, Barbados, and Trinidad. She died in London in 1911. She published twenty books, edited a magazine, and wrote book reviews. *Station Life in New Zealand* was first published in 1870 and reprinted in 1883 by MacMillan and Co, and it was republished by Virago, in 1984.

AMELIA BATISTICH   Born in 1915 in Dargaville. Her parents were immigrants from Dalmatia (now in Yugoslavia). She was educated at Dargaville and Ellerslie Convent Schools, Sacred Heart High School, Pukekohe, and Adult Education classes. She married Aton Batistich in 1935 and has three children. She has written for radio and school publications. 'A Dalmation Woman' and 'A Place Called Sarajevo' were published in *An Olive Tree in Dalmatia and Other Stories* by Paul's Book Arcade in 1963 and republished by Longman Paul 1980.

BLANCHE EDITH BAUGHAN   Born in 1870 in Putney, England, and educated at Brighton High School and Royal Holloway College, London. In 1900 she moved to New Zealand. She was interested in prison reform: in 1921 being the official visitor to Addington reformatory and in 1928 being the honorary secretary of the NZ Howard League for Penal Reform. She died in 1958. She published poetry, short stories, novels, and articles on prison reform. 'Grandmother Speaks' is from *Brown Bread from a Colonial Oven* published by Whitcombe and Tombs, London, in 1912.

ARAPERA HINEIRA BLANK   Born 1932 in Rangitukia and descended from Ngati Porou, Ngati Kahungunu, Rongowhakaata, and Te Aitanga-a-Mahaki.

She was educated at Hukarere College, Wellington Teachers' College, and the University of Auckland. She is a teacher. She has published essays, stories, and poems, and her work has been broadcast by Radio New Zealand. 'Yielding to the New' was published in 1970 in *Contemporary Maori Writing* by A. H. & A. W. Reed, and edited by Margaret Orbell.

BUB BRIDGER   Born 1924 in Napier and descended from Ngati Kahungunu. She has lived in Wellington for most of her life. She began writing in 1974. Her stories and poetry have been published in the *New Zealand Listener*. 'Girl in the River' was published in *Shirley Temple is a Wife and Mother* by Cape Catley in 1977.

FRANCES CHERRY   Born in the 1940s in Wellington, where she grew up and now lives. She works as a tutor in creative writing for a correspondence school. Her parents were well-known Communists in the 1950s and this has influenced her writing significantly. She has five children and began writing when she was pregnant with her fifth child. 'Waiting for Jim' was published in *The Daughter-in-Law and other Stories* by New Women's Press in 1986.

CONSTANCE CLYDE   See Constance McAdam

JOY COWLEY   Born in 1936 in Levin. She has worked as an artist, freelance photographer, builder's labourer, farm worker, pharmaceutical apprentice, newspaper children's page editor, housewife, mother, and writer. She has four children. She has contributed to literary journals, written novels, and children's books. One of her children's books and one novel have been made into films. 'The Woman Next Door' was published in *Heart Attack and Other Stories* by Hodder and Stoughton in 1985.

JEAN DEVANNY (née Jane Brook)   Born in 1894 in Ferntown near Collingwood. She left school at the age of thirteen to help at home. In 1911 she married a miner and with him was involved in the Miner's Union. She had three children. In 1922 she and her family moved to Wellington where she was involved in the Labour Party. In 1929 they moved to Australia and in 1931 she travelled through Russia to Berlin to attend a conference for Workers' International Relief. She was involved in the Communist Party in the 1930s but was expelled in 1940, readmitted in 1944, and resigned, though still loyal, in 1950. She separated from her husband, and in the 1950s moved to Townsville, Queensland, where she died in 1962. *The Butcher Shop* was published by Duckworth in 1926, but was banned in New Zealand, Boston, Australia, and Nazi Germany for its revolutionary ideas about the role of women and for its bold portrayal of the brutality of farm life. The book was reprinted by Auckland University Press in 1981.

MARILYN ROSE DUCKWORTH (née Adcock)   Born in 1935 in Auckland, but grew up in England. She has four daughters and several step-children. She lives in Wellington where she is a full-time writer. She wrote her first novel, *A Gap in the Spectrum* at the age of twenty-three. It was unpublished by New Authors Ltd, London, in 1959 and was reprinted by Oxford University Press in 1985.

YVONNE DONNA DU FRESNE   Born 1929 and brought up in the Danish-French Huguenot Community of the Manawatu. She has a full-time teaching career, including positions as music specialist in primary schools, music lecturer in Wellington Teachers' College, and STJC at various schools. She lives in Wellington. 'Arts and Crafts' was published in *Farvel and Other Stories* by Victoria University Press with Price Milburn in 1980.

LAURIS EDMOND   Born in 1924 in Hawkes Bay and educated at Victoria University. She now lives in Wellington. Her first book was published in 1975. She has since published several plays, nine books of poetry, and one novel *'High Country Weather*, which was published in 1984 by Allen & Unwin/Port Nicholson Press.

JANET FRAME   Born in 1924 in Dunedin. Her family worked in the railways. She spent many years incarcerated in mental hospitals, but emerged as one of New Zealand's most distinguished writers. She has been awarded the CBE, an honorary doctorate in literature by the University of Otago, and is an honorary foreign member of the American Academy of Arts and Letters. She has written eleven novels, four collections of stories, a volume of poetry, and a children's book. *Faces in the Water* was published by Pegasus Press and Braziller, New York, in 1961. 'The Day of the Sheep' was published in *The Lagoon* by Caxton Press in 1951 and reprinted in *You Are Now Entering The Human Heart* by Victoria University Press, 1983. 'The Mythmaker's Office' was published in *Snowman, Snowman* by Braziller in 1962, and 'A Sense of Proportion' was published in *The Reservoir and Other Stories* by Pegasus Press and Braziller in 1963.

PATRICIA GRACE   Born 1937 in Wellington of Ngati Toa, Ngati Ruakawa, and Te Ati Awa descent. She was educated at St Mary's College and Wellington Teachers' College. She is a teacher and a writer. She has published novels, short stories, and a book for children, and her work has been translated into Russian and Swedish. 'A Way of Talking' was published in *Waiariki* in 1975 by Longman Paul and reprinted in 1983 by Penguin. It was the first book of short stories to be published written by a Maori woman writer.

EDITH SEARLE GROSSMANN   Born in 1863 in Beechworth, Victoria, and educated in Invercargill Grammar School and Christchurch Girls' High School. She went to Christchurch College in 1881, graduating with a BA in 1884 and an MA in 1885. She taught at Wellington Girls' College and later took up journalism and civic work. She had an unhappy marriage with Professor Joseph Penfound Grossmann originally from Warsaw, Poland. They lived apart for many years and had one handicapped child. Edith spent may years abroad trying to find treatment for him. *In Revolt* was published by Remington and Co, London, in 1893.

KERI HULME   Born in 1947 in Christchurch, she grew up in Christchurch and Moeraki. She is of Kai Tahu descent and is affiliated to Kati Rakiamioa and Ka Ruahikihiki. She lives in Okarito, Westland, where she fishes and writes. She has written novels, poetry, and short stories. 'The Knife and the Stone' and

'While My Guitar Gently Sings' were published in *Te Kaihau/The Windeater* in 1986 by Victoria University Press.

ROBIN HYDE (née Iris Guiver Wilkinson) Born 1906 in Capetown. Her family moved to New Zealand soon after her birth. She worked as a journalist, but suffered from a severe illness for much of her life. She travelled to China were she was the only woman given a pass to go to the Eastern Front by General Chiang Kai-Shek during the Sino-Japanese War. She had two children, the first dying in infancy. She committed suicide in London in 1939, aged thirty-three. She wrote both novels and poetry. *Nor The Years Condemn* was first published in 1938 by Hurst and Blackett in London and was reprinted by the New Woman's Press, Auckland, in 1986.

FIONA KIDMAN Born in 1940 in Hawera. She has worked as a librarian, columnist, and writer. She now lives in Wellington where she works as a full-time writer. She is married with two children. She has published poetry, novels, and short stories, and has written for television and radio. *A Breed of Women* was published by Harper and Row, Sydney, in 1979 and reprinted by Penguin, Auckland, in 1988.

SHONAGH KOEA Born in 1943 in Taranaki. She has worked as a journalist and a teacher, but now works as a full-time writer in New Plymouth. She has published both short stories and a novel. 'Mrs Pratt Goes to China' was first published in *Listener Short Stories 3* by BCNZ Enterprises in 1984 and was reprinted in *The Woman Who Never Went Home* by Penguin, Auckland, in 1987.

CONSTANCE McADAM Born in 1872. Under the pseudonym of Constance Clyde, she wrote several novels and a book on New Zealand. 'I Was the Man' is an extract from *A Pagan's Love* published in 1905 by T. Fisher Unwin, London.

SUE McCAULEY Born in 1941 in Dannevirke. She has worked as a journalist on several newspapers, and as a freelance writer has contributed reviews, articles, and regular columns to many magazines. Her short stories have been published and broadcast on radio and she has written several plays for both radio and television. *Other Halves* was published by Hodder and Stoughton in 1982 and won New Zealand's two major literary awards. It has been made into a feature film.

SUSIE MACTIER (née Seaman) Very little is known about her life. *The Hills of Hauraki* was published by the Sunday School Union, London, 1908. *Miranda Stanhope* was published by Brett Printing Co, Auckland, 1911.

MARY JANE MANDER Born in 1877 near Auckland. She travelled around the country as a child. She taught in Auckland primary schools, worked in the editorial department of the Northern Advocate, and helped her father's campaign in Parliament. At the age of thirty-five she became a student at Columbia University's School of Journalism. While in America she campaigned for the New York State referendum on women's franchise in 1915. Subsequently she worked for war effort organizations and held a post in the Red Cross. In 1923 she moved to London where she worked in publishing. She returned to Auckland in 1932 where ill health dogged her until her death in 1949. She wrote book reviews, radio scripts, and six novels. *The Story of a New Zealand River* was published by Lane, New York, in 1920 and was reprinted by Whitcombe and Tombs in 1973.

KATHERINE MANSFIELD (née Kathleen Beauchamp) Born in 1888 in Wellington. In 1903 she went to London with her sisters, where she studied at Queen's College. She returned to New Zealand in 1906, but in 1908 managed to persuade her father to pay for her to return to England. In 1912 she began living with John Middleton Murry, and they married in 1918. Her only brother was killed in 1915 and three years later she was diagnosed as having pulmonary tuberculosis. She travelled between England and the Continent trying to improve her health, but died fives years later in 1923. Her stories have never been out of print, and she also wrote poetry, letters, and journals, all of which have also been published. 'The Woman at the Store' written in 1912 first appeared in *Something Childish and Other Stories* published by Constable, London, in 1924 and has been reprinted in several editions subsequently.

EDITH NGAIO MARSH Born in 1899 in Christchurch and educated at St Margaret's College Christchurch and Christchurch College, School of Art. She directed and produced both professional and amateur theatre (particularly Shakespeare) and was producer of the British Theatre Guild. She began writing as a playwright, but turned to detective novels, of which she has written more than thirty. She was awarded the Grand Master, Edgar Allen Poe Award, an Hon. Dr Litt and in 1966 was made Dame of the British Empire. She died in 1982. Her work has been translated into over twelve languages. *Died in the Wool* was published by Collins, London, in 1944.

MARY SCOTT Born in 1888 in Waimate North, Bay of Islands. She was granddaughter of George Clark, the pioneer missionary. She was educated in Napier and Auckland Grammar School and graduated with an MA from Auckland University. She spent two years teaching and then married a farmer, Walter Scott. She lived on their fam in the backblocks in the King Country, where she worked on the farm and wrote. She stayed there with her four children until the death of her husband, when she moved to Howick. She died in 1979. She has written over thirty novels and short stories. *Breakfast at Six* was published by Hurst and Blackett, London, in 1953.

JACQUELINE C. STURM Born in 1927 in Opunake. She has spent most of her life in Wellington where she has spent many years working in Wellington Public Library. She has published short stories, poems, and book reviews. 'Jerusalem, Jerusalem' and 'A Thousand and One Nights' were published in *The House of the Talking Cat* in 1983 by Spiral Collective.

MARGARET SUTHERLAND Born in 1941 in Auckland. She has lived and based some of her novels in Titirangi, but now lives in Australia. She is married with a daughter and two sons. 'Codling-Moth' and 'Need' were published in *Getting Through and Other Stories* by William Heinemann, in 1977.

GREVILLE MARGARET TEXIDOR (née Foster) Born in 1902 in England. She worked as a music hall dancer in England, Paris, New York, and Buenos Aires. She married an Englishman but they were soon divorced, and in 1929 she married Manuel/Manolo Texidor, a Catalan. They had a daughter, but separated around 1934 after they had moved to Catalonia. Greville met her next husband there, a German called Werner Droescher. They fought together in the anarchist militia in the Spanish Civil War. When the Second World War began they went to Britain, but because Droescher was a German who had fought with the Republicans in Spain and associated with a Communist, served with a Wehrmacht Intelligence and Communications Unit for a short time, and had been permitted an exit from Germany, he was imprisoned in Devon and his wife was imprisoned in Holloway. Through the influence of their friends they were released and sailed to New Zealand. She published several stories and left several unpublished after her death in 1964. 'An Annual Affair' was published in 1944 in *New Writing New Zealand* and reprinted in *In Fifteen Minutes You Can Say A Lot*, published by Victoria University Press, 1987.

JEAN WATSON Born in 1933 and brought up on a farm near Whangarei. She lived many years in the country. She has travelled widely and is based in Wellington with her son. She has a deep interest in vedantic philosophy and meditation and has studied religion at university. She has written five novels to date and numerous short stories. *the world is an orange and the sun* was published by Dunmore Press in 1978.

LADY ANNE GLENNY WILSON (née Adams) Born in 1848 in Greenvale, Victoria, and educated in Melbourne. She married a sheep farmer, James Glenny Wilson, in 1874. She wrote poetry which was published in Australia and New Zealand journals and also published a book of poetry which was used in New Zealand Schools for many years. She died in 1930. *Alice Lauder* was published by Osgood, McIlvaine, and Co, London, in 1893.

ACKNOWLEDGEMENTS

For permission to reproduce copyright material the editor and publisher are grateful to the following:

The Story of a New Zealand River — Rangi Cross / Richards Literary Agency; *The Butcher Shop* — Joan Hurd; *Nor the Years Condemn* — Derek Challis / New Women's Press; *An Annual Affair* — Greville Texidor Estate; *Died in the Wool* (Ngaio Marsh) — William Collins; *The Lagoon, Faces in the Water, Snowman, Snowman,* and *The Reservoir and Other Stories* — Curtis Brown (Aust) Pty Ltd, Sydney; *Spinster* — William Heinemann Ltd; *A Gap in the Spectrum* — Oxford University Press; *An Olive Tree in Dalmatia* — Longman Paul; *Yielding to the New* — Arapera Blank; *Waiariki* — Penguin; *Girl in the River* — Bub Bridger; *Getting Through* — William Heinemann Ltd; *the world is an orange and the sun* — Dunmore Press; *A Breed of Women* — Fiona Kidman / Richards Literary Agency; *Farvel and Other Stories* — Victoria University Press; *Other Halves* — Hodder & Stoughton; *The House of the Talking Cat* — Spiral Collective / Hodder & Stoughton; *High Country Weather* — Allen & Unwin / Port Nicholson Press; *The Woman Who Never Went Home* — Penguin; *Heart Attack and Other Stories* — Hodder & Stoughton; *Waiting for Jim* — Frances Cherry / New Women's Press; *Te Kaihau / The Windeater* — Keri Hulme / Victoria University Press.

LADY BARKER

Death in our New Zealand Home — New Zealand Children

Letter IX from
Station Life in New Zealand

Broomielaw, Malvern Hills, May 1866

I do not like to allow the first Panama steamer to go without a line from me: this is the only letter I shall attempt, and it will be but a short and sad one, for we are still in the first bitterness of grief for the loss of our dear little baby. After I last wrote to you he became very ill, but we hoped that his malady was only caused by the unhealthiness of Christchurch during the autumn, and that he would soon revive and get on well in this pure, beautiful mountain air. We consequently hurried here as soon as ever we could get into the house, and whilst the carpenters were still in it. Indeed, there was only one bedroom ready for us when I arrived. The poor little man rallied at first amazingly; the weather was exquisitely bright and sunny, and yet bracing. Baby was to be kept in the open air as much as possible, so F— and I spent our days out on the downs near the house, carrying our little treasure by turns: but all our care was fruitless: he got another and more violent attack about a fortnight ago, and after a few hours of suffering he was taken to the land where pain is unknown. During the last twelve hours of his life, as I sat before the fire with him on my lap poor F— kneeling in a perfect agony of grief by my side, my greatest comfort was in looking at that exquisite photograph from Kehren's picture of the 'Good Shepherd,' which hangs over my bedroom mantelpiece, and thinking that our sweet little lamb would soon be folded in those Divine, all-embracing Arms. It is not a common picture; and the expression of the Saviour's face is most beautiful, full of such immense feminine compassion and tenderness that it makes me feel more vividly, 'In all our sorrows He is afflicted.' In such a grief as this I find the conviction of the reality and depth of the Divine sympathy is my only true comfort; the tenderest human love falls short of the feeling that, without any words to express our sorrow, God knows all about it; that He would not willingly afflict or grieve us, and that therefore the anguish which wrings our hearts is absolutely necessary in some mysterious way for our highest good. I fear I have often thought lightly of others' trouble in the loss of so young a child; but now I know what it is. Does it not seem strange and sad, that this little house in a distant, lonely spot, no sooner becomes a home than it is baptized, as it were, with tears? No doubt there are bright and happy days in store for us yet, but these first ones here have been sadly darkened by this shadow of death. Inanimate things have such a terrible power to wound one: though everything which would remind me of Baby has been carefully removed and hidden away by F—'s orders, still now and then I come across some trifle belonging to him, and, as Miss Ingelow says —

My old sorrow wakes and cries.

Our loss is one too common out here, I am told: infants born in Christchurch during the autumn very often die. Owing to the flatness of the site of the town, it is almost impossible to get a proper system of drainage: and the arrangements seem very bad, if you are to judge from the evil smells which are abroad in the evening. Children who are born on a station, or taken there as soon as possible, almost invariably thrive, but babies are very difficult to rear in the towns. If they get over the first year, they do well; and I cannot really call to mind a single sickly, or even delicate-looking child among the swarms which one sees everywhere.

I cannot say that I think colonial children prepossessing in either manners or appearance, in spite of their ruddy cheeks and sturdy limbs. Even quite little things are pert and independent, and give me the idea of being very much spoiled. When you reflect on the utter absence of any one who can really be called a nurse, this is not to be wondered at. The mothers are thoroughly domestic and devoted to their home duties, far more so than the generality of the same class at home. An English lady, with even an extremely moderate income, would look upon her colonial sister as very hard-worked indeed. The children cannot be entrusted entirely to the care of an ignorant girl, and the poor mother has them with her all day long; if she goes out to pay visits (the only recognized social duty here), she has to take the elder children with her, but this early introduction into society does not appear to polish the young visitors' manners in the least. There is not much rest at night for the materfamilias with the inevitable baby, and it is of course very difficult for her to be correcting small delinquents all day long; so they grow up with what manners nature gives them. There seems to me, however, to be a greater amount of real domestic happiness out here than at home: perhaps the want of places of public amusement may have something to do with this desirable state of affairs, but the homes seem to be thoroughly happy ones. A married man is an object of envy to his less fortunate brethren, and he appears anxious to show that he appreciates his good fortune. As for scandal, in the ordinary acceptation of the word, it is unknown; gossip there is in plenty, but it generally refers to each other's pecuniary arrangements or trifling peculiarities, and is all harmless enough. I really believe that the life most people lead here is as simple and innocent as can well be imagined. Each family is occupied in providing for its own little daily wants and cares, which supplies the mind and body with healthy and legitimate employment, and yet, as my experience tells me, they have plenty of leisure to do a kind turn for a neighbour. This is the bright side of colonial life, and there is more to be said in its praise; but the counterbalancing drawback is, that the people seem gradually to lose the sense of larger and wider interests; they have little time to keep pace with the general questions of the day, and anything like sympathy or intellectual appreciation is very rare. I meet accomplished people, but seldom well-read ones; there is also too much talk about money: 'where the treasure is, there will the heart be also;' and the incessant financial discussions are wearisome, at least to me.

(1870)

EDITH SEARLE GROSSMANN

Girlhood

Chapter V from
In Revolt

O life, O beyond thou are strange thou art sweet.

There followed one of those peaceful periods in Hermione's life to which she looked back afterwards as one on mountain heights looks back on sunlit valleys. At Hawthorne her world was a pure but limited one. The lady principal, Grace Clare, lived in a curious isolation of virtue and birth and breeding. Yet Hermione Howard was her favourite, the girl's beauty and innocence, her proud bearing and good birth outweighed in Miss Clare's eyes her impetuous enthusiasm and carelessness, though everything Miss Clare herself did and said was marked by precision and lady-like dignity. Her government might be called rather spiritual than temporal; the real work of the school was carried on by her sister Lucy, Hermione's dearest friend, a sweet-faced, soft-eyed girl, with something of her sister's nature, but softened and deepened; Lucy, while she greatly influenced Hermione, was in all external matters influenced by her; a few words from Ione would often change Lucy's views entirely, for she had the fault that follows gentleness like its shadow — weakness — as hardness follows strength.

At school Hermione's position was rather different from that of the other girls, as it was understood that she was under Miss Clare's special charge, an arrangement that caused at first much jealousy among the girls, and much unhappiness to herself. But nearly all her leisure time was spent with the Howes.

She kept up unconsciously a certain distance between herself and her schoolfellows, though she was the leader in every game, and at first the ring-leader in every rebellion. But her nature toned down more than might have been expected from the wild little bush girl. To quote Miss Clare's report, 'Miss Howard has shown much improvement in deportment.'

Hermione was still a healthy girl with a fine physique, and consequently a keen love of exercise, though acutely susceptible to pain. Her affection for Lucy Clare was of that demonstrative self-forgetful kind that a passionate spirit often lavishes on a receptive one. Her intellectual sphere was confined by that narrow routine to which it was then the fashion to force young girls, whatever their abilities and natural bent. The girl, however, had some influence over Miss Clare, and had thus gained more freedom than the others enjoyed. At one time she rejected music and singing, for which she had no taste, and replaced them by additional history, Latin, 'mathematics' -- very elementary — and, strange to say, theology. The desire to study mathematics was characteristic of her strong grasp on actualities.

Hermione wrote essays and composed short poems. Her essays were the products of a youthful social reformer, full of interesting projects and suggestions — slightly ambitious perhaps for a girl of fourteen or fifteen.

The subject that touched her most was 'The unfair share of education given to girls.' For as the girl grew up she chafed more and more against the narrow barriers, while she felt within herself widening desires and capacities. Another time she wrote on 'The Future Empire of Victoria', wherein she undertook to show that it was expedient the embryo 'Empire' should immediately be separated from England and left to pursue its own glorious career. This essay was long the glory and triumph of Lucy, and she even showed it to Mr Howe, who, however, only shook his head, and quietly jested with his favourite about her want of loyalty.

Her youthful poems were simple, natural little pieces, the outpourings of her own feelings — 'To the Australian Magpie', 'To the Wild Sarsaparilla', 'Golden Wattle', 'My Friend Lucy', associating her name with Lucy.

After her fourteenth year she passed gradually from childhood to girlhood. She ceased to be content with her childish games and lessons, the living that is for a moment. Her first passion was for knowledge. At Woodville House and the Parsonage she could get this only by reading. She read eagerly the few books within her reach, and for a time overtired herself. But it was a narrow literature, a few standard poets, volumes of sermons, religious records and tales, a translation of 'Utopia' and Newton's 'Principia' being her highest levels. But she loved best 'The Christian Year' and Bernard of Clugny's hymns.

Of the vast many-coloured ocean of literature — its gems from many lands — she had but a vague, longing glimpse. Her spirit was like the wide, beautiful lands that are yet unoccupied — a solitude that yearns for completion.

The earliest beauty that dawned upon her was a simple, childlike nature-worship, unformulated, yet more living than any church-taught dogmas. Sunlight and sunset, the great fresh sea, the far-off, low, blue hills, the little wild flower of the bush — she loved them all even with some poetic consciousness in her first awakening from the mere unconscious inbreathing of beauty that comes in childhood. Religious struggle or deep inward conviction had not come within her experience, for Mr

Howe, a simple Puritan of the gently stoical type, regarded anything approaching conversion or religious ecstasy with peculiar dislike. His notion of religion was to live purely and according to a rigid interpretation of Scripture and the Church Catechism, to take an interest in the poor, to read the Bible and go to church regularly, all of which Hermione could do easily without any conflicts. Sometimes, indeed, when she read the life of Christ, deeper thoughts would be aroused, and vague tears would come into her eyes; but at this time these feelings sank into her mind, and were lost to sight.

Youth came all the more fully to Hermione because unforced. The influences on her had been chiefly of a negative kind. For a Victorian girl her development had been gradual; in her sixteenth year relics of her childhood still lingered. She had none of the conventional manners and superficial worldliness of girls who are taken too soon into 'society,' but a half-trained, childlike nature, innocent of evil, ignorant of the world and its ways, very trustful, and very truthful.

Let me take her portrait on this bright March afternoon of her sixteenth year — a picture of her as she stands on the threshold, with the sunlight and acacia shade moving softly, caressingly, over her. She is going a solitary ramble up the road, but stands a moment self-absorbed, hearing the distant voices of the girls at play. Then the sunlight makes her dreamy as she looks along the shady road, her lips half-stirred by some thought within, her face bright with half-awakened thoughts and dreams.

She feels a sense of vague, unaccomplished happiness. Like a traveller coming through a narrow pass, she sees suddenly before her a new and beautiful scene, stretching far away. She has fallen into a delicious reverie.

Standing on the threshold of her life, looking into the dim, bright future — passing into her girlhood, with a lingering glance backward, the voices of her childhood growing fainter; womanhood, love, the world, life, before her. What unknown regions, what new glories, what infinite knowledge, what sweet and tender passion, what rapture of beauty, in that distant land! Love, a thing blissful, and as yet unseen, lay before her. Sweet to think that this crowning glory must come. Or was it only a dream of poetry? But the thought of love was only a vague unconscious cloud shape that soon floated away through her young heaven. A poem she had read had struck some unknown chord within her — that was all.

Yes, she was passing into her girlhood now — a land of dreams, of sudden, sweet passion, of uncertain instincts, vague, intense longings, ardent aspirations, of youthful misery, of budding love and pure ideals, and infinite hopes — a wondrous land, so utterly incomprehensible to the mere onlooker.

(1893)

EDITH SEARLE GROSSMANN

Volcanic

Chapter VI from
In Revolt

Give me truths
For I am weary of the surfaces
And die of inanition.

When Hermione was fifteen years old the desire for wider life became more intense, and at last took the form of a resolute purpose. She imagined that she might reach this higher sphere if she could only have knowledge. So she set to work with the primitive, imperfect materials around her. Evening after evening, Hermione and Lucy might be seen with their arms around each other, laboriously but enthusiastically making their way through 18th century French classics, working out problems, or puzzling over a yellow old volume of Tacitus.

In the midsummer holidays Charlie Clare came on a visit to his sisters. He had been sent to Cambridge, and managed, by the aid of a tutor, to pass, so they regarded him as a prodigy, though he was nothing more than an ordinary colonial youth. He was by no means loath to display his superiority in a lordly, offhand manner to his gentle sister Lucy, and with a curious mixture of condescension and sheepishness to her stately girlfriend. This visit of Charlie Clare roused ambitious projects in Hermione's mind.

When she and Lucy were together they had a long talk. At night Hermione was so restless that she could not sleep, so she got up and wrote on the spot to her father and aunt:

'DEAR, DARLING FATHER,
'There is something I want to tell you, and I don't know how to put it, I don't think I know exactly what it is myself.

'I do want you to let me do it; I know it is right, too, so I am sure you will let me. I want to have a tutor and study. Then I can get clever and do something in the world. I am going to help you with your great book. Won't that be nice, papa darling? Do say yes. Oh, I will work ever so hard day and night. I will teach in a school at the same time. Of course Miss Clare says it is not feminine, and Aunt Bertha will say it is masculine. But I know you must sympathise with me — you who are so fond of learning. I do hate being so stupid. I hate and detest plain sewing and ugly worsted roses and hideous wax *things* that aren't flowers at all; I can't be always thumping on the piano. I can't draw — it's no good, and Signor Vernelli is *so* cross. And dear Lucy wants to study too. She is six times cleverer than Charlie Clare, yet she has to be drudging away here while Charlie is sent to the University and ever so many pounds spent on *his* education, yet he is younger than Lucy. It is not fair.

'Why shouldn't girls go to Universities too? Oh, papa darling, don't be horrified at me for saying that; I really couldn't help it.

'Dear father, I know this is a horrid, excited scrawl. Do you know I got out of bed to write to you? Please don't let Aunt Bertha see this dreadful letter. Do, do help me, or I don't know what will happen!

'Your loving daughter
'HERMIONE HOWARD'

The note to Miss Howard was briefer.

'DEAR AUNT BERTHA,
'Miss Lucy and I have been talking about what we ought to do, and we intend — at least, if our relations are willing — to get a tutor and some books and begin studying — I mean properly, Latin and things; then we shall be able to do more than most women. I am sorry I have such a dislike to teaching; I never seem to know what the children are doing — I find myself thinking of other things. But if I were better educated there are so many things I could do better suited to me.

'Your affectionate niece,
'HERMIONE HOWARD'

Some time elapsed without an answer, so Hermione wrote again, a clearer statement of her plans and present position. The answers were not satisfactory. Her aunt wrote a short, contemptuous letter, merely referring to Hermione's suggestion as a piece of disgraceful absurdity, and stating that her father and she had decided that Hermione should come to Brooklyn for a few months, and should afterwards go out as a governess. Enclosed was a scrap in her father's handwriting.

'MY DARLING DAUGHTER,
'I am sorry that I must seem not sympathetic with you, but it is clear, as your aunt says, that learning was meant for men and not for women. I trust you entirely into her care, as she takes a strong interest in you, and understands so much more about these matters than I do.

'I trust to see you on your way to Brooklyn, and will meet the coach at Ballarat.

'Do not fret over this disappointment, my little daughter.
'Your loving father,
'ARTHUR HOWARD'

Immediately on receiving her aunt's letter Hermione wrote back in impetuous haste:

'I will not stay here; I am wasting my life. If you *will* not help me I will go out and make my own way in the world.
'HERMIONE HOWARD'

Miss Howard had been in Melbourne when Hermione's first letter came, but hearing that Brooklyn was more lively now she made up her mind to set off for that town. When she received Hermione's second letter she was on a visit to the Rollestons. It alarmed her, for she had always some fear of Hermione's desperation. So she drove over to see her brother.

He was arranging his papers when she came in, and rose slowly, with some embarrassment, to greet her. Her face foreboded a storm.

'My dear Bertha, so glad to see you. How did you come? Nothing wrong I hope?'

'Such nonsense,' said Miss Howard, taking not the slightest notice of his greeting. 'Of course, Arthur, that girl wrote to you?'

'Well, I have been thinking —'

'You are going to let her make a fool of herself. *Well*, indeed!'

Miss Howard sat bolt upright for a few seconds, looking out of the window, as if determined never to speak on that subject again; her brother, however, recognised in this her customary signal for a long tirade.

'A mere child like that — a tutor teach *her*. She'd elope with him in a fortnight.' Mr Howard looked apprehensive. 'If she were *my* daughter — thank heaven she is not! — I would shut her up in her room till she came to her senses. What a masculine idea! I suppose she'd like to be a lawyer or a doctor. The girl has not a grain of common sense. She is just like Beatrix. I always told you what would come of it.' She paused awhile, then took a pathetic strain. 'To think of the interest I have taken in her, paid for her education, and I always looked after her. She has not an inch of gratitude.'

'I am sure Ione would never —' he began.

'Nonsense, Arthur, you are blind about that girl — stone blind. I know she gets these absurd ideas partly from you. And that outlandish Greek name! No human being could bear it,' said Miss Howard, ambiguously, with a martyred look.

Mr Howard suppressed a sigh. His sympathy was with Ione, but girls and women were mysterious beings, not to be managed by men. Bertha was clever — surely she ought to know.

'Of course, Bertha, you understand about these things better than I; but we must be very gentle to the poor child, and I really don't see what she is to do.'

'*Do!*' repeated Miss Howard, contemptuously, 'go out as a governess, of course. She can live with me for a while.'

The fact of having completely vanquished the enemy softened her slightly, and as she got ready to go she said —

'Of course, Arthur, I don't mean to be harsh to Hermione; you know I am as fond of her as you are. But she isn't an ordinary girl — so flighty, and wild, and proud. I hope she will get married soon, and then her husband may manage her; no one else can.'

As she was driving home her own words suggested a new train of thought to her, and she mentally repeated the question, 'What is to be done with Hermione?'

Miss Bertha herself had her house and income, but experience had shown her that she and Hermione could not permanently live together.

'Hermione is such a strange girl,' she thought, 'so chilling and reserved; but she really will be beautiful, and she has something about her quite patrician. She shall stay with me this Christmas. There's Thompson, of course, but he's a snob, and Magistrate Marston's son.'

At this point her rambling thoughts were checked by the sight of the house. But before she had entered Burmapore she had met her question by a mental resolution, 'Hermione must get married.'

(1893)

EDITH SEARLE GROSSMANN

Tried by Law

Chapter LVII from
In Revolt

Plate sin with gold, and the strong lance of justice hurtless falls;
Arm it in rags, a pigmy's straw can break it.

Bradley Carlisle had been at first annoyed that his wife should have to give evidence, but he soon saw that he could turn this to his own advantage.

The morning she was to appear in Court, Hermione was strangely quiet and still, her face colourless, and her eyes dark beneath. But when she left the carriage and passed through the crowded entrance she heard among the murmurs of 'Bradley Carlisle's wife', once 'Old Howard's daughter', and that thrilling upon some hidden chord flushed her face with sudden crimson.

While she waited, Susie Wood, confused and frightened, was being cross-examined. Ellen Pierson and her husband often quarrelled. He had threatened to strike his wife, but had never done so in Susie's presence. She could not tell whether Ellen had been drinking. Ellen did not say Pierson struck her. She only said, 'Pierson.' Ellen was lame, and might have fallen. The Doctor, being asked, said such a fall might be fatal to her. Ben Hardy, the shepherd, had nothing to say, but that Pierson went about complaining of his wife.

Then there was an irrepressible, excited movement and buzz in the Court, for Hermione Carlisle moved slowly into the witness-box. The Court was crowded — mostly with the roughs and low women of Brooklyn, and those who came more to see Bradley Carlisle's wife than to hear the case. A few even there might feel the pathos of her face, so young, so desolate of youthful hope, tranced now with a repressed, devouring passion that lent strange light to the grey, silent eyes, and curved with hopeless scorn the firm-set, sensitive young lips. Bradley Carlisle looked at her before she spoke, a warning glance from under his eyebrows. A cold shiver ran through her, but she made no outward sign, and, turning away her eyes from him, answered the questions put to her with unmoved, proud, patrician composure.

'I knew Ellen Pierson before her marriage. She was the favourite of her family. Last November she spoke to me of her husband's brutality.

She had sent her children away because their life was not safe with him. She once told me Pierson threatened if she did not give him money he would have her life.' Bradley Carlisle started and muttered to himself. 'On the fifth night before her death I was with Ellen Pierson. I made her promise to go to law. She said if Pierson found out he would murder her.' Bradley Carlisle ground his teeth and gave an evil look at his wife. In answer to the prisoner's counsel, she said, 'I heard nothing of Ellen's bad temper except at secondhand, through Pierson, whom I did not consider an authority. She herself told me nothing made him more savage than for her to sit silent and cry. It was he who caused her lameness. Pierson did not strike his wife in my presence. The worst men are not in the habit of striking their wives before witnesses.'

Sentence was postponed, and the Court rose.

When Bradley Carlisle came up to Hermione he gave her one sinister, sneering look, and then resumed his ordinary manner. Coming out of Court, they passed a group of men he knew, one of whom, Neil MacIntyre, was saying —

'But what induced Carlisle to back up Pierson passes my comprehension.'

So Brooklyn knew that his wife defied him.

(1893)

EDITH SEARLE GROSSMANN

'The Nearest Type of Eternal Damnation'

Chapter LIX from
In Revolt

In many cases marriage involves to the weaker party a tyranny so brutal, galling, incessant, and absolutely hopeless, that it forms the nearest earthly type of eternal damnation.

MacKenzie's *History*

When Bradley Carlisle and Forbes went into the bar parlour together Forbes said —

'Your wife is a very clever woman. She has outwitted you, Carlisle.'

His laugh covered a sneer. The words goaded on Bradley Carlisle's rage. *He* would keep Hermione quiet! *He* would make his wife obey him! Now the man to whom he had made his secure boasts turned on him and mocked him. The galling part was that this woman, whom he considered especially his property, had thwarted and over-reached him as no one else had ever dared to. For a moment he lost more of his self-possession than Forbes had ever seen him do before. The evil look was in his eyes before he said, with a forced laugh —

'She will know better next time.'

'I have no mind to manage a case for you instead of Pierson,' replied the lawyer, jestingly; but Bradley Carlisle knew that was a hint, and he laughed more freely.

He had no more intention of murdering Hermione than of burning Moorabool over his own head; besides, he could satiate his cruelty better than by killing her.

The landlady told him Mrs Carlisle had walked towards the creek. 'Though, poor dear, she looked so white and tired, it was no fault of mine she stirred a step,' added Mrs Allen.

Hermione was leaning against a tree by the creek, and looking down into the dark water with a desperate feeling. If it were not for the children, she thought she would have thrown herself in, and ended for ever her wretched existence. A storm was breaking over her. Her nervous energy had been strained to its utmost lately, and now all was over she felt the reaction. She had believed herself hardened, and yet now a mortal terror of him crept over her.

'Do you want to drown yourself?' said Bradley Carlisle, dragging her back roughly by the arm. She started. 'Go to the hotel, idiot that you are, and don't stand staring there. I have something to say to you at home.'

Home! The fear was increasing, and he saw it.

'I'll give you something to be afraid of before I've done with you.'

'I'm afraid of you now, if it is any triumph to you to know that,' she said, lifting her sad, tearless eyes to him.

At the door of the hotel they met Forbes. He admired Mrs Carlisle's courage and presence of mind, but he hated her none the less for her interference.

'You'll be sorry you meddled with your husband's business, my lady, before this day's over, or I'm mistaken in Bradley Carlisle,' he thought, as he watched them coming up. But to her face he smiled and said —

'You nearly floored me to-day, Mrs Carlisle.'

'I simply gave my evidence,' she replied, in a tone of indifference.

'That won't do, Beauty,' said Bradley, affecting to jest. 'You won't be let off that way. The horses are ready. Will you come up, Forbes?'

'No thanks. I have an engagement with Gascoigne.'

Bradley Carlisle helped Hermione into the carriage, seated himself by her, gave the horses the whip, and they started at full speed. He took a peculiar pleasure in lashing them just now, partly because he knew she detested it, and partly to relieve his feelings. They had got some way in silence before he said —

'You fool! I'll make you eat dust tonight.'

Then, as she did not speak or move, he cut her with the whip. 'You had better not defy me.'

She spoke at last.

'I wish I were dead. I wish you would throw me onto the stones and let the horses trample me.'

He laughed savagely; her fear and misery gratified him. The sky was dark and frowning; there was a gloomy lull in the atmosphere preparatory to a storm. Already clouds of dust were sweeping up the road. Bradley drove furiously, and arrived home before the storm broke. Janet came out and helped Mrs Carlisle with her things. In the evening they had a most uncomfortable meal; Bradley Carlisle scarcely took his eyes off Hermione. She silently put by the food he gave her till he said, with a sneer —

'It's not good enough for you, my lady, is it?'

Janet saw that something was wrong, and she tried desperately to help Hermione. After dinner Bradley said —

'Go to my room, and I'll come to you.'

She went up. Janet said —

'Mrs Carlisle looks very ill, Bradley; but perhaps a good night's rest will restore her.'

Bradley Carlisle took no notice, but went to his room. She was standing by the dressing table. He leaned against the mantelpiece and fixed his eyes on her in a way that almost made her wild.

'Did you see Wood about this precious business?'

'No,' she said.

She really did not know what she was saying.

'You liar! I saw Wood myself. That will teach you to lie to me,' and he caught hold of her and struck her on the mouth.

It was only desperation that kept her quiet; a mist was coming before her eyes, and she could hardly stand. He kept his hold of her, and stared at her in a horrible fixed way; in reality he was thinking how he could best have his revenge.

'Are you going to murder me?' she said, but her voice sounded strange to herself. He gave a coarse laugh, and went on staring at her till she covered her face convulsively with her hands. 'You are making me mad,' she said. He tore her hands away, and she tried to scream, but her voice died as in a nightmare, and he struck her again. Then he seized hold of her, shook her as if she had been a wild animal till she was exhausted, then threw her down upon the bed, where she lay quivering. She must have got beyond fear, for she spoke only once, and then in a terrible voice, 'Kill me.'

When Janet got into her own room downstairs she was almost as afraid of murder as Mrs Carlisle herself was, but that with her was a mere reasonless fear, arising from the haunting horror of the recent event on a mind almost childlike in its simplicity. She went to bed, but could not sleep. She thought, 'If I saw her dead in the morning I should never forgive myself to my dying day.'

The suspense became at last too horrible to bear. She got out of bed, put on a dressing-gown and went to the foot of the stairs. There was no sound. It was impossible for her to interfere. Bertha gave a peevish cry. Janet went to the bedroom and called —

'Mrs Carlisle?'

Bradley Carlisle called out —

'What is it?'

Janet's horror increased that only he should answer.

'Mrs Carlisle! Mrs Carlisle — it is I, Janet.'

'Get up and see what the idiot wants,' said Bradley.

'What is it, Janet?' said the young voice, that now sent a thrill through Janet's heart.

Mrs Carlisle was coming to the door, but Bradley said in a rough voice —

'Here, Hermione,' and as she came back, 'get a handkerchief; your lips are bleeding.'

She went to the mirror and tried to wipe the blood away, but found she could not, so came to the door holding the handkerchief to her mouth.

'Bertha is crying for you, Mrs Carlisle.'

'Thank you, Janet.'

They went downstairs, and once she missed her footing and nearly fell, but Janet helped her. As she bent over the child Janet said, in her simple Scotch way —

'I was sore afraid I would never hear your voice again, Mrs Carlisle.'

'Were you? Poor Janet,' said Hermione, touched, putting her hand into her cousin's. 'You need not be afraid; he will not kill me.'

'Have you neuralgia, Mrs Carlisle?'

'Yes — no — you know better. He struck me. It is no good concealing it from you. Don't look troubled, Janet; that makes me feel almost as if I could cry.'

'Oh, Mrs Carlisle,' said Janet, momentarily putting her hand over her eyes.

'Is that dreadful? There are worse things than blows.'

It was the first time Janet had seen marks of Bradley Carlisle's cruelty, and she was deeply moved. At the door of her room Hermione said —

'I should not have told you so much, Janet. I scarcely know what I am saying. Good-night.'

'Good-night, and God help you,' said Janet, sadly.

The first few days after the trial Bradley Carlisle behaved to Hermione with galling and brutal tyranny, ordering her about to wait on him, insulting and sneering at her openly before Nora and before her own children. Once she turned round and said —

'There's an end of it. I can bear it no longer. Do what you like.'

Then he came up to her, clutched hold of her and looked at her as he had done before. He had found a new way of torturing her finely-strung nervous system.

'Look here,' he said, 'if you defy me I'll turn you out this very night, and let you wander about till the morning — that'll teach you how to speak to me. My fine dainty lady, I'll drag your pride through the dust.'

'Do,' she said, momentarily losing her reason, 'it will only be the sooner end of it.'

'You think you will get a separation? Go to the Law Courts and tell them what I did to you if you dare. Do you think I will stick at anything when I've made up my mind to it?'

'No — no, I know,' she said; 'God is helping you, not me; that is religion and morality. Yes, I will do what you tell me. There are the children; I forgot.'

'A precious lot you care about them' he said. 'It is a good thing they have got me to look after them. You forgot, did you? I'll help you to refresh your memory.'

He thought her broken down, little knowing what he had roused within her. Her strength had never been of a passive, enduring kind; it lay in the depth and intensity of her emotions. This was what had mocked her — that he had *the right* to torture her at his brutal will, the right confirmed by law, sanctified by Scripture, and applauded by society.
(1893)

LADY ANNE GLENNY WILSON

Chapter VII from
Alice Lauder

The large empty room in the hotel garden, used occasionally for concerts or dances, looked dim and shady, and as cool as any place could be on that burning afternoon. There was a grand piano at one end, a big punkah which was worked rather intermittently by the bribed but intelligent native outside, a number of dusty wooden forms, and only a narrow gleam of green leaves and white sunshine from the half-open Venetian shutter at one end of the room. One of the white-robed silent-footed natives brought in the tea-tray and placed it on the long table, and Alice made the tea and handed it to Campbell with as calm and domestic a mien as if they had been married ten years, slightly flavoured, however, by the consciousness that not a soul knew where they were — outside the room. They had some fruit, too, mangoustines and bananas, and they talked and laughed and ate together as if it were a child's tea-party. But Campbell had something on his mind to say.

'I know you will be vexed with me, Miss Lauder, but I *do* wish you would give up this stage idea. I don't like it at all, though I've no right to say so.'

Alice wished very much to say something pleasant at parting, but this was a little too much to ask. She considered for a moment or two what she could say.

'Don't think me obstinate. I know you think differently about these things, but I cannot help it — I must go on. I don't talk much about art, like some people, and I've always approached it from the practical side, which makes a difference; but I do love it all the same. What should I do without it? It's my living, in every sense — I can't give it up.'

'But you will marry some day, perhaps.'

'Ah, perhaps; but sufficient to the day is the evil thereof.'

'Then do you think that your husband will like you to appear in public for money? Five shillings box seats, gallery eighteenpence, and that sort of thing! I hope not.'

'As far as that goes,' said Alice, with much dignity, raising her head and showing a spark of fire in her eyes, 'I have acted in public — and for money — already. My father used to go round as a pianist sometimes to a travelling company, and I went with him, and now and then I took a small part. I must say he only did it when he was very hard up, and the companies were not very grand, and we played in all kinds of out-of-the-way halls and theatres — at little up-country diggings, and so on. But it was experience for me, and I got on very well.' She saw that this was rather a blow to her companion, and to soften it she went on talking —

'Amateurs always think that anyone can do the small parts. That's such a mistake. The big parts are comparatively easy — they are all chalked out for you; but the little side-characters are a blank sheet, and you have to make your own sketch. However, they all said I managed it very well. So now I've made a beginning, you see, and I don't think there is any way out of it.'

Campbell got up hastily and walked away to the other end of the room, where the window was open. A storm was brewing out at sea, and the wind began to rise, and rattle the big leaves of the bananas and palms in the garden, and drew out a creepy sort of rustling, like a ghostly flock of mice running over the walls, from the ropy vines and creepers that clothed the roof. He came back to Alice, who was rather sadly looking down, and playing a funereal little tune on the table with her teaspoon, and took her hand up as if to say good-bye.

'There's one way out of it, Miss Lauder. Give it up, and take me instead. I haven't very much to offer you, but it's better than going to a miserable little theatre — And you have no one to take care of you,' he added, in a very gentle tone.

There are some moments in life — moments few and far between, but never to be forgotten in their swift, sudden thrill of mingled joy and pain — when the world does actually seem to stand still, not in a figure of speech, but in a strange reality; moments of vision when we see other skies, other constellations, and gaze on them bewildered, till, before one can say, 'It lightens!' the horizon reels back again, and our old familiar earth wheels away as of old in her star-lighted voyage round the sun. Perhaps it is our own hearts that stand still, and not the solid earth-fields and the immemorial horizon, but the strangeness of the sensation could not be much more perplexing in either case.

Such a momentary experience came to Alice Lauder at these commonplace words, dividing asunder one part of her life from all that had gone before. She was pale and remained standing, silent and immovable, her blue eyes fixed on his with a serious, penetrating gaze. Childish and inexperienced as she was in many ways, she had all the quick perception of the artist-nature when once her thought was thoroughly aroused; and probably she read and understood all that was passing in his mind — the sudden generous impulse, the conflict of old associations and influences, even the want of real passion, better than he understood himself. For more than a moment she wavered, balanced, almost yielded. He looked so manly, so kind, with something noble in his eyes, and he would be pleased if she yielded to his wishes and threw over her own future for his. Should she throw it over? To him this appeared no sacrifice, but a great advantage offered to the untried and friendless girl. And she knew too well the wrong side of the medal — the hard experience of cares and work, and endless struggle with poverty, of small successes and depressing failures, and fond speculations in hope deferred. Even if she succeeded, as she so often promised herself, what would that success be compared with a home and a woman's happiness? . . . But Love must build his house upon a rock.

'No, Mr. Campbell,' she said at last, very softly but decidedly, withdrawing her hand from his — 'it cannot be.'

'Then you won't give anything up? Even for my sake? I am disappointed —'

He walked away, feeling bitter and hurt, and leaned out into the garden. There was a low roll of thunder out at sea, and some big drops of rain fell like bullets here and there on the leaves. The palms in the woods shook and clattered together with a sharp metallic sound, like the clash of men in armour. The storm would be upon them directly. Alice looked at him, and her eyes slowly filled with tears. It was hard to part like this, yet she did not know how to make friends with him again. He looked very gloomy and unapproachable; it never occurred to him he had not said a word about love, and he thought she was foolishly setting her heart on this scheme of hers above everything a woman ought to prize.

She returned to the teaspoon and the 'Funeral March of a Marionette', while in her mind a passage out of a little drawing-room comedy she had once taken part in, kept repeating itself vexatiously, 'If you want to make a man respect you, the best way is to refuse him.' In despair she took up her music and looked over it. She had brought down some of her songs, and on the top was a MS copy of Mendelssohn's 47th Psalm, arranged as a solo, as her father had taught her to sing it. The beautiful music in which a great artist — arrived at the highest point of success in his art, his love, and his genius, while still in the first golden radiance of his honeymoon — poured out the inextinguishable desire of the soul for something higher still, and so wonderfully translated that 'divine despair' into melody, rose to her lips almost involuntarily. She played a few chords, and began the recitative in a low and nervous tone; but by degrees her voice seemed to gain new life from the music, and rose in the soprano part with all the lift and spring of a fountain starting into the sunshine:

> *Oh, for the wings — for the wings of a dove!*
> *Far away — far away — far away would I rove.*

Her higher notes were pure and spontaneous, and there was a dramatic power and intensity in her singing which she had never shown before. The depths were stirred, and her whole mind and soul seemed to seize on the music as a vital instrument to express that inexpressible 'yearning for the lamps of night', which all the poets have striven to reveal, but never so nobly and simply as in the words of the Hebrew shepherd:

> *In the wilderness build me a nest!*
> *And remain there for ever at rest;*
> *In the wilderness build me, build me a nest,*
> *And remain there for ever — for ever at rest.*

Then almost in a whisper, with a deep vibrating intensity, she repeated the beautiful cadences:

> *And remain there for ever, for ever, for ever at rest.*

. . . A blue quiver of lightning hovered over the room tentatively, as if searching for something hidden there; then came the hesitating snap of thunder — the stammering thunder, as the old Greek poets called it — and the storm suddenly fell upon the house with a spinning blow that made it clatter and shake to its foundations. The tropical outburst — almost explosion — of rain followed in a blinding, hissing deluge. Through all this uproar Alice heard Campbell's step — he was coming to say good-bye. He had to bend over her almost to her ear to make himself heard:

'Good-bye again, and thank you. You have made me understand. That was beautiful, and I know now what you mean. Good-bye, and perhaps some day we may meet again.'

'*Auf wiedersehen!*'

The door slammed, the rain swayed past in almost level showers, all the colouring of the room disappeared in the grey muffled atmosphere. Alice stood by the piano and looked out at the raving storm. It was very dim indoors, and very silent and melancholy. She was alone.

(1895)

LOUISA BAKER

Sowing Seed

An extract from a chapter from
Wheat in the Ear

'G. Goodyear, M.A., Principal.'

Miss Goodyear was sitting in her study, in a Russian-leather armchair, resting. The walls of the room were lined with bookcases, the floor overlaid with a thick carpet of a rich crimson colour; curtains of the same hue hung at the windows, the lower panes of which were hand-painted, the panels of the door showing the same design of hand-painted flowers. A bearskin rug was spread before the gas stove on the tiled hearth, another was thrown over a low couch; several deep-seated chairs were scattered about; a few exquisite water-colours stood on ivory easels on the mantel-board, with a few photographs. Near the hearth and Miss Goodyear's chair was a handsome carved oak reading-table. On this a green-shaded reading-lamp was burning. A porcelain vase, filled with red and white roses, stood near the lamp.

Gertrude Goodyear rose, and with an easy, slow movement, crossed to the bookcases, touching a volume here and there with the light, lingering touch of a mother caressing her baby's hair. She was dressed in a black garment — a blending of academical robe and tea-gown. She stood, tall, slender, and square, with a dignity of carriage almost stately. Her age it was impossible to tell; when she smiled she appeared little more than a girl; as she stood now her pale face impassive, her firm mouth closed, three lines of concentration and study showing between her dark, straight brows, she looked thirty at least. Her chief beauty was her hair, which, cut short like a boy's, waved in half curls of purest gold — every separate hair a separate glory — about her broad forehead and small, transparent, shell-like ears. Her eyes were also handsome, or would have been, but for the quizzical glance that shot from their blue-grey depths, and disturbed their grave serenity. Her throat was rounded and statuesque, its beauty set off by a deep point-lace collar. The neck, hair, and ears were so truly feminine that they seemed at variance with the square shoulders and the firm lines of the chin and lips, and the lordly air that fought with charm and grace. In one light she was seductive, and invited caresses; the next her manner signified, 'I pray you have me excused.' It has been said that intellect is aristocratic. Miss Goodyear had the aristocracy of intellect. She had pretensions to learning, combined with some natural wit, and counted those of inequality who were dull and uneducated. She created much amusement among her set by her satires and caricatures of the women of fashion, the purse-proud and commonplace women who darned the stockings and had babies. Of man — Miss Goodyear thought of him with a capital M — she had absolutely nothing to say. She smiled when he was mentioned in the abstract — a slow, deep, lingering smile, and invited him collectively to her lectures and at homes; but admitted individually to her domestic hearth — never, unless he chanced to be a lion or a hero. Perhaps in her fight up from poverty and obscurity, she had found man in the abstract, collectively and individually, her hill difficulty, which having surmounted with considerable toil, she had never forgiven for her aching feet. There might have been a love episode — she never said. She made no complaint whatever; she had won her woman's guerdon, and she smiled her inscrutable smile.

The sound of cab wheels caused Miss Goodyear to lift her head expectantly. Presently the brass knocker shook the door; loud revibrations echoed through the house.

Miss Goodyear turned on the electric light, dispelling the partial darkness of the room.

'Mr, Mrs, and Miss Jefferies,' announced the maid; and Father, Mother, and their only daughter Joan were ushered in.

The brilliant light dazzled Father's eyes; shading them with his hand, as though from the rays of the rising sun, he discerned a lady in the radiance, and bowed with the gravity of a magistrate; then, a sudden impulse of goodwill and admiration breaking through his impressions of polite deportment, held out his hand. Miss Goodyear let her slender, strong hand rest for a moment in the large brown palm, then advanced to greet Janet.

With simple and undisguised satisfaction, Father undertook the introductions:

'Miss G. Goodyear — my wife, Mrs Thomas Jefferies, and Joan John Jefferies of Otira Farm, Canterbury.'

Miss Goodyear bowed. It was a moment before she raised her head; when she did so the sad, grey eyes were sparkling.

'I expected you by tonight's express,' she said quietly, drawing forward a chair for Janet, and at the same time taking in every detail of the Quakerish figure.

Father refused a seat, and stood on the hearth-rug, a tall, bronzed figure demanding attention, his grey tweed suit smelling of new-mown hay. The night was warm, but he wore a knitted comforter of white wool — Janet distrusted the air of cities — and the fringed ends hung almost to the carpet. His massive grey head was lifted proudly, as though conscious of his important part in the bestowal of such a pupil as Joan upon the learned lady. He did not feign a mild interest in the occasion so important to himself and Janet and he was bound already by friendly bonds to the instructress who was to 'rub the rust off' Joan. He smiled benignly, as a generous-hearted person who bestows a favour.

Miss Goodyear felt conscious that the position of recipient, though not the spirit, was being forced upon her. The shadow of authority passed again into her face, the expression of intellectual solitude into her eyes. The gratitude should be theirs, that she had renounced for life sexual and maternal joys, ease and peace, to train other people's children to their fullest responsibilities.

While Tom talked — he never found himself embarrassed in any circumstances, playing his simple part honestly, giving everyone credit for feeling his own identical interest in it — the tragi-comic side of her situation struck Miss Goodyear anew. Here was another uncultivated mind brought to her for culture; later the parents would return for their child and boast of her ability. She would be forsaken and forgotten. The next moment she soared quickly and high away from the hurtful, embittering thought. Her cause was woman's cause; every fresh thinker among women helped forward their emancipation. While she was striving unconsciously to crush down emotion, and see only with her intellect, Mother, who sat watching the grave face attentively, decided, 'No, she didn't much like her. She was neither a natural woman, nor domestic.' Then, her eyes falling upon a volume on the bookshelves, entitled 'Bacon', and another 'Lamb', endeavoured to readjust her first impression.

By a quick, unreasoning intuition, Janet realised that this woman was destined to be her rival in the admiration of her child, for she had caught Joan's look of interest, and seen Miss Goodyear's glance travel slowly from the brown curling head and daintily proportioned figure back to the piquant, sun-tinted face.

'Ah!' she exclaimed enigmatically, and, with a quick movement, stretched out her hand.

Joan placed her small palm in it, and glanced up into the eyes looking down with a gaze as steady.

'Make a scholar of her, ma'am, make a scholar of her!'

Miss Goodyear was very tired. She wished they would go; but she kept her attitude of courteous attention.

Father glanced at Mother, who was struggling to keep her face calm for the parting, then shifted from one foot to the other, and, twirling his wide-awake in his hands, said, with a deprecating glance, and voice of courage:

'With your permission, we will now commit the stranger into safe keeping.'

Miss Goodyear bowed. She gave the great rough man credit for a pretty compliment. Then an unprecedented thing occurred. He drew the little girl into his encircling arms and knelt, Janet beside him. Miss Goodyear, embarrassed, stood, one hand resting lightly upon the reading-desk. She wrestled for a moment with a feeling of vexation, when the meaning of the singular scene came to her. The trio were at their devotions. The littleness of indignation passed when Father spoke. Miss Goodyear's embarrassment changed to attention when, tremulous and shaken with his own petition, the man's voice faltered:

'When we are farthest from home, we are most akin to Thee,' he concluded, 'for Thou wert a wanderer, O Son of Man. Silence an' solitude echo Thy sorrow, for Thou didst dwell in the wilderness.'

'Eloquent!' thought Miss Goodyear.

And when she bowed Tom out there was a subtle change in her demeanour that those who knew her would have pronounced respect. She stood patiently by while the farewells were said.

Father, clearing his throat, for it had grown suddenly hoarse, said: 'Little maid, be a gentleman.'

'I sha'n't tuck you in tonight,' said Mother tremulously. 'Come, Father.'

Father's voice was loud to the gate, and loud for some distance down the quiet street.

When it had died away, Miss Goodyear returned to the study.

Joan had sunk into an easy-chair, and was leaning back among the cushions. Her brows were puckered, and lips compressed, but no sound escaped them.

Miss Goodyear glanced at the small forlorn-looking figure, then crossed to Joan's chair. She noted the paling cheeks and the dark circles beneath the closed eyes, that were made by unshed tears.

'You don't cry,' she said a little wonderingly.

Joan's large eyes opened.

The two stared at one another.

'Do you?' asked the small girl, in a toneless voice.

Miss Goodyear was surprised once more tonight.

'I do — occasionally,' she admitted, as to an equal.

'So do I,' responded Joan, sitting bolt upright; 'but not when I get something I want very much.'

The perplexed expression deepened upon Miss Goodyear's face.

'This,' explained Joan, waving towards the shelves.

'Ah, I understand!' rejoined the woman, with spontaneous interest, a faint flush mounting to her cheeks. She bent forward her body from the waist, and asked eagerly, and yet with slight hesitation, 'You find the exchange of home and parents . . . for books . . . easy?'

'No,' thundered Joan, 'I do not; it is not true; but one must give something always for the thing one wants.'

(1898)

CONSTANCE CLYDE (McADAM)

I Was the Man

An extract from a chapter from

A Pagan's Love

Miss Wingfield had donned her rose silk wrapper, and her hair, loose from its coils, massed itself on each side of her face, falling clear from it, black and shining. Softening the clear intellect of her features was a light of subdued joy and relief. It curved her lips; it flickered in her dark, narrow eyes; it quivered as a faint, red glow in her fine, thin cheek. Ordinarily she was hardly attractive; she was more than handsome now.

'I suppose you heard what I said when I came in and saw —' She shuddered, and the hand raised to turn up the lowered lamp trembled a moment.

Dorothea looked straight into the eyes opposite hers. She, too, was nervous, but not at the recollection of Chrystal's danger.

Ascot seated herself; her glance was cheerful.

'I did hear.' Of the two hearts Dorothea's beat the faster at the moment.

'Well, you heard what I had intended should never be known, not for a certainty that is, certainly not to you, who are young and impressionable. Yet my story, after all, would not prove an incentive to irregular conduct, and then again, one lives one's life for one's own convenience and not to make a picture for one's acquaintances. Chrystal is my child. Her father you will never meet.'

'He deceived you. How could he!'

'*He* deceived *me. Me!*' The glow left Ascot's cheek and concentrated itself in her dark, angry eyes.

Dorothea felt as if the floor were giving way beneath her feet. What a horrible slip to make before this personification of feminine dignity!

'Of course, I should have guessed you had been married,' she faltered.

Ascot laughed, as she leant her elbow on the table, the anger gone, but the light still glittering in her eyes.

'No, you mistake again, Dorothea. I never married; never went through the ceremony, but deceived — never that! I was the *man*, Dorry, *I* was the man. I will tell you about it; you know so much that you may just as well hear more. To me it is so simple; to you it may seem strange, almost wicked. You shall hear.'

She leant her head on one deep-hollowed palm and spoke in an even voice, calmly and slowly —

'I said something to you about my mother this afternoon. As a girl she had been inclined to the intellectual life, but living at a time when the female brain was not appreciated, they promptly put a stop to Lydia's queer ways by marrying her to a middle-aged man who gave her little time for considering anything save the needs of a constantly increasing family.

'My mother was proud of me. In consideration of her natural prejudices, I should not have ruled my life as I did had she not died before I had any serious thought of Chrystal, otherwise no Chrystal!

'When I tried my luck and finally did not fail in Sydney's journalistic scramble, she was proud of me till the day of her death, and glad at heart for one special boon, that I would not need to marry. She recognised only one need — the financial.

'You see she belonged to what was then the new order of woman emancipators, the generation that delighted in the novelty of seeing its girlhood, freed from the tyrannical necessity of marriage, going in for art, literature and university degrees. They had come to recognise, and considered themselves advanced for recognising, that there must be two types of woman, — the breadwinner all brain, and the fireside dame all affection.

'They no longer scoffed at the blue-stocking as unwomanly. She was quite right to go her own way. Thus freed from the trammels of sex, what calm, grand lives brain women would lead! A new era was beginning of woman writers, woman artists, woman philosophers!

'It was taken for granted that these two types of our sex must remain distinct. A man might combine the lives of intellect and affection, but that was never thought of for the woman. She must, in general, abandon all hope of husband or child if she wanted to educate the thinking part of her. It was assumed that she did not want husband or child.

'Strange, is it not? Woman is accounted the weaker sex, the sex most liable to hysteria and emotional strain, yet it is our sex, not the other, that is expected to endure the greatest strain of all — that of doing without love altogether or yielding to it an absolute surrender.

'Yet when we break down under the complete surrender on the one hand, or the unnatural aloofness on the other, they call us hysterical, which is to say, abnormal.

'Would not strength be abnormal under such circumstances?

'When does man, the strong, the wise, the able-to-bear-all-things, put such a yoke on his own shoulders? When does he tie himself down to the one course or the other? For man there is always love — love of any sort. He picks it up and lets it go again just as he pleases. And his brain works the freer for it.

'I felt it, Dorothea; I knew it before I had been in my profession a year; I was not living and loving, and so my life work fell off. I saw what the years were bringing me — a strange, one-sided creature, half-child, half-dwarf. "Your soul," said the Future, presenting it to me; religious hysteria threatening it on one side, mental stagnation menacing it from the other.

'I was twenty then, but old for my years; I had begun life young. Moreover, I was penniless, not good-looking, without time and without inclination for entering the marriage market, such as it is. The only match possible to me was one of those hazardous attempts at double harness which literary women occasionally make (to mutual disaster as a rule) with some brother of the pen. Good enough for me, perhaps, but there was Chrystal to consider.

'I might have married an honest John and a suburban cottage; but that would have meant the finishing of my career; and you see I wanted both Chrystal and the career.

'Oh, it made me angry, Dorry, angry, *angry!* What right had things to be so? Why should the two loves hinge so brutally on each other? A man might deprive me of himself, but of Chrystal?

'You know, Dorry dear,' she bent her shining eyes upon the listening girl, 'I have just a touch of Jewish blood in me; perhaps that explains so much. My grandmother belonged to that red-blooded race, and maybe from her I have inherited this sublime dislike to quitting the world and leaving behind no copy. I felt, of course, the common desire for maternity for its own sake, that desire that is dying out of womankind here through the mixed influences of selfishness and puritanism; but besides this desire there was the craving to live by proxy, this hope that when I drifted away from earth something that would in a sense be me might pass down from generation to far generation. Here my eyes would flash out; here some gesture that I had used would reappear; there again my poor gift of expression growing and growing till a genius might flame out in some distant century, to which this one would be as savage history.

'So by one action I should make this present life more glorious, and likewise link myself forever with eternity.

'Do you ever feel these thoughts, little Dorry? Why do I ask? You will marry, marry as other women do.

'Oh, I have no desire to form a crusade. Not I. I had then, as now, only the strong wish to do with my life as I pleased. To enjoy all; to endure all; to know everything!

'I would not scream from a platform on the rights of my sex: I would simply annex these rights and say nothing.

'How I have laughed at these women; *used* to, mind you; now I am sorrowful a little sometimes, thinking that my Chrystal may be one of them. Oh, little current of life that will flow beyond my guidance!

'I had a dog once. I chained it to its kennel for a whole day, and it sat with its back to the house of bondage, howling. Then I came behind it and untied the chain — and it continued howling. That is woman today, Dorry; she is quite unchained, but she doesn't know it. Sometimes I think she prefers the howl.

'It is beautiful to think of the drama of life, Dorry, and how one can add quaint plots to God's great book of plays. To work for the child that is coming is a common lot, but to lay aside for the child that it may be — to bridge over with hard-earned gold the gulf of time that separates it from your arms. Was it ever done before? I should grieve to find that I was a plagiarist!'

There was another pause, while she gazed thoughtfully at her interlacing fingers. It was seldom that Ascot Wingfield's bright, *alive* face wore an expression of such dreaming spirituality, and it suited the clean-cut, intellectual features as a mist becomes a kingly mountain head.

'I kept Chrystal in Melbourne till she was two years old, and then brought her here as the child of a dead school friend who had left her to my care. It was such a remarkably lame story that no one believed that clever Ascot Wingfield could be guilty of inventing it. What they think is nothing. I have my child. She sleeps beside me at night. I feel the soft pressure of her limbs against mine, hear her voice call Ascot how many times a day; always a surprise. A mother never gets over the surprise of her motherhood, you know. Does it trouble me that she can never call me by that name? I like it best as it is. I have a feeling that when necessity compels the public ignoring of relationship, the tie itself grows all the stronger. So Chrystal is more than ever my very own.'

'Will she ever know?'

It was the recognised stumbling-block at which Dorothea hinted, the *pons asinorum* of the moral world. 'The child will turn against you, even the child,' so Waihoa womanhood would have said.

Ascot laughed, and flicked a withered flower from its companions in the bowl.

'That depends. If she grows up as I hope, then I will tell her, trusting that she will pardon a fault without which she would never have existed. I must teach her logic. But if she grows up a throwback to some conventional ancestor of mine, then Chrystal shall never know, and I trust that she will love me none the less because she bears on her little coat of arms that sign which, even in the days of the deepest religious conviction, knights were not ashamed to acknowledge.

'Especially when the cause was a king.

'And the cause may always be a king — in my way. No woman who elects to tread my path need hand down a hare lip or crass stupidity to the next generation, because the owner of these blessings happens to be the only man who has made her a respectable offer.'

She rose, a little tiredly, her excitement having spent itself, her dark eyes dreamy and languid.

But Dorothea's were now wide awake.

'Did you,' she asked, 'never feel — that you were different — from other women. Did you never — feel — forgive me — that you were outside the pale?'

Ascot was not angry. She mused a moment, her hand upon the open door, her face bent towards the girl.

'No, not once. I quite expected that the centuries of enslavement would have dowered me with a few illogical remorse pangs; but it never did. I am quite surprised at that; but it is true.'

She waited a moment; Dorothea seemed inclined to speak again, but no words came.

(1905)

SUSIE MACTIER

An extract from
The Hills of Hauraki

'Life to me is all sorrow, storm, and distress,' she sobbed bitterly and hopelessly, 'these meetings and these hymns are not for me, sin as well as sorrow has taken possession of me.' She was hopeless and helpless. The cause of her grief was this, and if you blame her just picture yourself placed in a like position and see how *you* would act. Forced as she had been by the will of her husband into a position repugnant to her sensitive nature and opposed to her whole training and religious principles, Chrissie had vowed to herself and to God, that, come what may, she would never touch the accursed drink. But 'a glass of wine' was Mrs. Bailey's panacea for all woes, and often before they left the place had she prescribed it for her daughter-in-law for hysteria, tears, exhaustion, and what not. After the birth of the little boy she had been weak and delicate for a long time, and again had the well-meaning but ignorant old lady pressed brandy or porter or stout upon her. Often had Christina refused to drink these things which were at first so nauseous to her, but at last she grew weary of opposition, and yielded.

Then came Ned's anger at her refusal to drink wine in the bar, which had forced her into an unwilling compliance, and now she was beginning to feel it a necessity; was weak and faint in the morning, until she took a small dose 'just as medicine' from the bottle which Ned always kept in the sitting-room cupboard 'in case of sickness.' In fact, she felt, but did not dare to own it to herself, that she could not do without it. She felt herself on the edge of a precipice, yet knew not how to draw back. Her prayers were lifeless and brought no answer, and she often said in those days despairingly to herself, 'If I regard iniquity in my heart, the Lord will not hear me.'

The visit of the evangelists and the wave of spiritual life which was passing over the place had revealed to her the awful position in which she stood; hence her distress. Yet even now had she confessed her sin to a human friend and sought aid and counsel and the prayers of another to assist her feeble faith, she might have been saved. But a fancied loyalty to her husband and a feeling of shame for both him and herself kept her lips sealed, and the opportunity passed.

Our poor Chrissie dared not seek for counsel or for aid. Had she in her extremity ever laid the *whole* of her burden upon her Saviour and entreated Him to undertake for her that which she could not do for herself, He would have helped her and lifted her up and found a way of escape for her, but the evil lay here. *She had never realised her first wrong step* which lay in her acceptance of and marriage to a man who she *knew* in her inmost heart (though she would not confess it even to herself) was not a child of God at all. That was the root sin which bore such bitter fruit to Christina; and many and many a Christian girl does the same thing today, and suffers for it more or less according to the ordinance of God — suffering pain and loss, sometimes even of life, that they may not lose the life eternal.

(1908)

LOUISA BAKER

The Woman in the Wilderness

An extract from a chapter from
The Perfect Union

'You must not let us be a nuisance, Miss Leslie,' he said in a tone of apology, yet with look and voice that were unconsciously eager. 'What would you like to see? My mother's garden? Or will it tire you? Have you walked enough already this morning?'

Alma liked the tone in which he spoke of his mother, liked too the delicacy in which he made it appear that his mother would have had her so welcomed. He checked his strides to keep pace with her movement beside him, and was surprised to find how tall she was, and how easily she seemed to move over the ground.

'We have no sort of function on just now, even for the backwoods,' he proceeded, when she had assured him that she was by no means tired. 'The shearing is of course over and that's a thing to see. It means the mustering of the whole run. Perhaps in the spring —?' His eyes interrogated, but she gave him no hint that she might be here in the spring — 'But I can show you the shearing sheds and leave you to imagine the scene.'

Alma found the garden delightful. His enthusiasm about his sheep had left her cold — but the garden —!

'This interests you?' He smiled as she exclaimed over the late roses, a faint colour in her cheeks springing to match their pink. 'Oh, you dears!' she said. 'No, no you must not!' as he made to gather them. 'Let them finish their day in the sunshine.' She flitted from bed to bed and along the shady walks in a subdued transport of pleasure. Then it occurred to him with a queer little stab of disappointment that it was not his garden in which she delighted, but in the old English flowers. They had memories for her? She went up and down the paths, all life, all animation for these inanimate things.

He was jealous of those memories which every English bloom recalled and in which he had no part. And she linked herself with the memories of his ideal gentlewoman, the maker of this garden — his mother. Her flowers had bloomed here without sacrilege — bloomed and seeded and flowered again since their mistress had departed.

Today he wanted to gather the choicest for the woman by his side. She had spoken little, but had conveyed much. A score of impressions had moved him — her aloneness — her proud aloofness — her friendliness. Inaccessible, yet accessible. She was worlds away in her interests in life — yet charmed with his mother's flowers.

Before he realised that he was saying it, he expressed his opinion that women were poor pioneers. A man took himself into the desert and subdued and conformed it to his requirements, he re-created. A woman brought her old world with her, and modelled the new on the old. His father had forced the mountains and the plains to yield to his increase; — his mother had brought the flowers of her memory and made a garden 'mid rock and river; — the old flowers of custom, habit, religion —

Alma was seated on a bench under flax trees, the tangled native bush spreading around, the 'home' flowers emphasising the man's simile. She was looking at him intently, and suddenly asked in a curiously suppressed tone, for its eagerness,

'And you call that — weak?'

'Weak? Lord no!' he exclaimed. He sat down beside her on the bench, and for a second time within the hour forgot his shyness of her in the sincerity of himself. 'It is to the woman's tenacity, to the strength by which she clings to her idols, and sets them up in barren places that the world is eternally indebted.'

Alma rose; her manner was distant. The faint colour that had made her face look so girlish had left her cheeks. There was something hostile in her voice —

'Men have their thrones, and enter into the privileges of their dominion with their manhood. A woman takes her self-graven gods with her from old captivity into new. We must renounce progression, and accept law.'

He twirled and pulled at his moustache, his expression changing to bewilderment.

'I didn't mean that,' he said slowly, choosing his words with difficulty. 'I meant something quite different. In this country, you know, women are our legal equals. We don't have any sort of right, they don't have too —'

'Except that of the unwritten law of deciding for yourself your own right and wrong,' she interrupted, 'of being your own moral conscience, and setting the ideal standards for us, by which your verdict is passed. The woman *must* mould her new in the old moulds — Else —!'

Her gesture said the rest.

He was somehow chilled. Their eyes met as Alma turned to him and in their expression was something of defiance. She walked quickly towards the paddocks as though to dismiss the subject, but something in him rose against the barrier between them.

'You're wrong, Miss Leslie,' he said determinedly, keeping by her side. 'There *is* a difference between us — but it's not of man's making. It's a spiritual as well as a natural difference — the essential law of woman's own nature, and can no more be interfered with, without violence, than any other eternal law. The sun will shine by day, and the moon affect the tides, as long as earth is under heaven, Miss Leslie.'

He sprang to let down the rail for her to pass out, and put it up again after her —

'We are your tyrants or your slaves,' he laughed, 'according to our individual and national conception of your deserts. But you are self-bound.'

Alma did not spring to his lighter mood, but resting her arms upon the rail, looked past him, her eyes full of thought. She seemed almost unaware of his personal presence but occupied by what he had said.

'Self-bound?' she queried.

'By your maternity,' he answered quickly, almost eagerly, 'and no cultivation of the intellect can uproot it, it's too deep. That's where the difference lies between us, which no conceded licence or legislation can touch. It's a spiritual as well as a natural difference, as I said. The child is nurtured by the woman. The highest physical accomplishment of woman is the perfect child: her highest religious achievement — moral offspring. In her lap the future is nursed —' He suddenly became aware of his own heat, and dropped his voice as he raised his cap, part in deference to her and part to his thought.

'"Mary the Mother of God —" of Good. Isn't that what the Catholics mean when they worship the woman?'

(1908)

LOUISA BAKER

Twilight of Dawn

An extract from a chapter from
The Perfect Union

But the glory of the morning had paled for Alma; and the glad light had left her face. She turned apart, and looked out over the wide freedom of leaping waters, and before Geoffrey had chosen words from the tumult her repudiation of bondage had raised in his mind, her voice broke in with sad passion —

'Free? After all, are we women ever free? Is there any height, any horizon for us beyond man's passion? Any place for a woman in a man's life except in his arms? Any knowledge or strength she may need of him that she must not pay for with her kiss?'

She reached out the hand on which the glittering ring seemed all the morning to have focused the light to itself. 'You have betrayed me,' she said with a sweeping gesture towards the mountain wilderness. 'I came to you for peace.'

'And I have spoilt it for you?' His eyes were on her quivering face.

'No, not you! My complaint is not of you, it goes further back, to the mandate — "He shall rule over thee." You do, you do! The man was in possession when the first woman was made; he's in possession still.' She turned on him almost fiercely. 'We can't get away from you, go where we may.'

'Because,' he broke in passionately, 'we are not complete without you. It was meant so. We lack just what we covet, in you.'

She would not meet his eyes, or see his seeking hand.

'You talk of worship, and make us slaves,' she went on relentlessly, and yet her resentment was not of him. 'When we refuse our body you ask for our soul, you claim us whether we will or no: "there is no life apart," you plead. "My life is yours." And Jacob's service? Didn't that bind Rachael whether she would or no? If we are not harpies who take your service for what it is worth to ourselves, when we have no passion for you, you hold us by our compassion.'

She turned to the avenue, and he beside her, struggling for the word that should quiet the tumult he had raised in her, struggling to quell the tumult in himself.

'I have made you miserable,' he said at last. 'And I can't retract anything. I do care. I care more to see you happy than what becomes of my life. And you were happy this morning, you have been lately. I've seen the difference in you. And I've spoilt it for you! But don't go away with the thought that I tried to trick you into a false relation.'

His voice broke from its calmness. 'My God! no! I am your debtor for the best experience of my life. I could only imagine what a woman might mean to a man, till you came, now I know. But it is myself I have tricked in thinking I could be with you all these months, and let you go for ever without a sign. I can't. I'd give everything, *everything*, to be near you, to be your slave, your dog.'

'For toll!' She spoke with bitterness, the tone of repudiation bringing the colour to his face and brow. 'We do not accept the service of slaves without responsibility. We feed our dogs. A man's passion has its exactions. I am not personal. I do not blame or mock you. It is so: it has been so since man and woman were. Spite of culture, man is still the savage lord who strips life of its best before he throws the bone to the woman to pick.'

She turned and walked with quick steps as though hurrying from her thoughts. 'We call the bone by big names now, "chivalry" among others. And the woman gnawing it has big names too to account for her scanty meal, a "wife's sacred rights" is one of them. But if we do not love you, and are too honest to flatter and trick you with pretence, where is your chivalry then? Or if you love another woman, where is the wife's right then?'

'Alma, you shall not!' He took her arm almost roughly, his eyes angry and reproachful. 'Who taught you all this bitterness? *Curse* him whoever he may be!' he added under his breath. He was beside himself with rage and jealousy, and terror for her combined! The half-truth of her words filled him with shame that experience had taught this distrust to her immature womanhood. He could hear the hurt cry of her own pure womanliness in every word, in every tone. Some man's passion had tormented her. Oh! to show her the large truth of a man's love; the deep sacredness, the spiritual bond of the union of body and soul!

But he had touched in his blundering impetuosity some tortured nerve of hers, some wound which his restraint had helped to heal. Now —

'Love! Love? Always a man talks of his love, and refuses the woman his friendship. If he cannot bind her to himself alone she is as nothing to him. All that has gone before in her life, all its possibilities apart from him, that have not gone to mould her to his will, are only so much to the bad. He is not her ideal, and she falls from his pedestal; she must grow no higher than that, go no deeper than the man's ideal who elects her. And what of the woman's ideal of the man? She had thought him a good comrade, disinterested, anxious only for her well-being. And when she had grown dependent, he says, "now give me yourself, or you shall have nothing of me." However great her need —'

(1908)

SUSIE MACTIER

The Angel's Wing

Chapter XII from
Miranda Standhope

The secret that was not told that night remained untold for many weeks. Again and again Miranda made an effort to utter the simple words that would have roused all her husband's best feelings and restored him to his wavering allegiance. But there was a barrier between them, which was not easy to bridge, nor was the first offence the last.

Many a lonely evening was spent by Miranda now; but she locked her door and busied herself with her sewing, and strove to shut her ears to the noisy talking and laughing which too often penetrated to her retreat.

Her work was often wet with her tears, and when she rose in the morning weary and unrefreshed, her pale face and listless manner reacted on Charles and made him surly or short-tempered.

At last one day, when he came in to dinner, he found her lying unconscious between the half-laid table and the fireplace. It was the work of a moment to pick up the little form of his wife, to lay her on the bed, and to get water, brandy — any and everything that could revive. She soon unclosed her heavy eyes and put aside the spoon which he was holding to her lips.

'Not that, Charlie,' she gasped. 'Water, please,' and with trembling hand she held the cup he brought her to her mouth. A little revived, she leaned against him for a while, then, fixing her great, sad eyes upon him, she said: 'If I am faint again, dear, never give me brandy. My children shall never know the taste of it, so help me God!' and she buried her face on the pillow and sobbed hysterically.

And thus the secret was told, and another bond established between husband and wife.

Charles confided his hopes and fears to his only friend, Frank Williams, whose good little wife came over and stayed a day or two and cheered Miranda up.

It was a real relief to pour her hopes and fears for the future into the sympathetic ears of Lucy Williams, but not even to her did she mention the blow that had fallen upon her spirit and destroyed her faith in her husband. 'Perhaps,' she thought, 'when he sees his little son, he will feel his new responsibilities and be steadier for his sake.'

In due time the little son so earnestly expected appeared, and so much touched and softened was Charles Stanhope as he knelt beside the couch of his wife and saw the little dark head nestled to her breast, that Miranda ventured to whisper, 'You will keep steady for baby's sake, Charlie dear, won't you? Begin from today, do?'

And he kissed her and promised, and when the men came down that night to drink the health of 'the kid', he refused to pledge them in anything stronger than ginger beer, and got them away as soon as possible.

Miranda soon recovered her strength, and her new duties kept her fully occupied, and gave her little time for repining over the limitations of her lot.

Four years had passed away, and two bonny boys now called her 'Mother', when death came to the Stanhope household for the first time. He laid his icy fingers upon the tiny six-weeks-old girl, who faded away like a snowdrop, and was laid with many tears in a tiny grave.

No clergyman ever came their way, and but for the kindly offices of their good friends, the Williamses, no word of Christian hope would have been read over the grave. As it was, Charles Stanhope held the tiny coffin in his arms, while Frank Williams read in a hushed voice the sublime words of our Burial service.

Miranda stood with drooping head, holding the hands of her wondering boys; but life was dealing hardly with her, and she turned towards home with a feeling almost akin to relief that this little one had been taken in the arms of the Good Shepherd and sheltered from the ills of life.

Her husband was drifting further and further away from her, and, if not absolutely unkind, was neglectful of her, and very capricious in his treatment of the little boys. He was becoming coarsened by his familiar intercourses and drinking habits with the bushmen around, and, though prospering fairly well in business, she felt with many a bitter pang that he was losing in all that made life worth living.

Lucy Williams stayed with her that night, and together they folded and put away the little garments that were no longer needed, put the little boys to bed, and sat down by the fire to have what was a real luxury to both women — a good chat.

A terribly isolated life was led by the wives of the early colonists, and our friends were instances of this.

Months often passed without either of them seeing the face of a white woman, and now they talked on for a long time, and Miranda overcame her natural reserve, and spoke to her friend of the temptations that were assailing her husband.

Lucy looked sorrowfully into the fire. 'I know,' she said. 'Such a change has come over him. Frank and I have noticed it; but did not like to mention it to you unless you spoke of it yourself. It is a shame that drink should have been brought down to a place like this, and it makes the natives so troublesome and quarrelsome. They have been worrying Frank to get a license, too, but he won't do it. He did not see much harm in it till it was started here, but now he sees the mischief it has done nothing would induce him to sell the stuff. We have a pledge page in our old family Bible that my father gave me, and I persuaded him and the boys to sign it the other day. Could you not induce your husband to do the same? though he would find it much harder to carry on business without it now than if he had never started it.'

Miranda sighed and shook her head. She did not tell her friend how she had pleaded with her husband again and again, or that she bore on her delicate breast the mark of a cruel blow struck by him in exasperation when she knelt to implore him to refrain from bringing it into their home.

She dreaded that her innocent boys should become familiar with the sight and smell of it. She rose now and began to prepare for bed. Charles had gone back to the store, 'to make up some accounts', he said, but she knew he would probably seek to drown his sad thoughts, and she could not bear that Lucy should see him thus. So she prepared his couch in the outer room, and withdrew with her friend to the inner room, where the little boys, Harry and Hugh, were sleeping with the tears for their baby sister scarce dry upon their cheeks.

Long, long did she kneel in prayer that night, and though her heart was sad and her arms empty, she thanked the dear Lord who had taken her sweet babe into His tender keeping, removing that delicate flower from the wilderness that must still be trodden by her weary feet.

(1911)

B. E. BAUGHAN

Grandmother Speaks

Extracts from a chapter from
Brown Bread from a Colonial Oven

'Well, father an' mother an' me come out together, as you know, early in the fifties, when I was but seven year old; an' nearly five months we was in comin' by the way; like everythin' else, ships was slower then. Soon almost as we'd a-landed here in port (that was pretty nigh nothin' else then, only tents, mind you), father, he got word for to go down to sawpit work, down along the coast. An' so, down along the coast we went, in a little bit of a cutter; an' all day long it took us, the men sayin' it was a good trip, too; an' by the time we got there, in the evenin', it was a-rainin', an' a-blowin' very cold; an' never will I forget the look upon my poor dear mother's face as she sat in that boat a-gazin' on the land, an' a-seein' what she'd left London town for!

'It was just a little bit of a beach, at the top of a long narrow bay, that looked for all the world like a finger o' water, two or three miles along, stuck up in between the hills, an' a-dintin' of 'em down — but there! *you* know the Bay. It looked a bit different though in them days; for the hills, that's grass all over now an' cocksfoot, was covered then with standing' Bush — there was Bush, and nothin' *but* Bush, for what looked like miles above the sand, as well as miles on either side of it; an' the only other thing to be glimpsed, strain your sight how you would, was three or four funny-lookin' huts, thatched with tussock-grass, an' a-standin' nigh on to the water's edge.

'"Cowsheds, I see," says mother, as they carried us out o' the boat, "but where do the poor things feed?" Poor mother! when they told her all the cows there was in Rakau could go through her weddin'-ring, an' the furthest house was ours, she just up an' dropped herself down upon a lump o' wet seaweed, an' burst out a-cryin'.

'It *was* hard on mother, mind you! In them days it was just about as bad as dyin', in one way, to come out to the Colonies. For you left all your friends behind you, an' you knew you could never get back no more for to see 'em; at leastways, people like mother couldn't. That was why it was best all to come in a family, when you could, fathers an' mothers, an' brothers an' sisters, an' the little children — all together, an' all a-lookin' the same way. But mother, there she'd a-left her own dear mother behind her, an' she'd been livin' in a nice three-storied house down Bermondsey way, with butcher and baker just round the corner, an' chimney-sweeps, an' newsboys an' all, up an' down the street — haven't she 'minded me about it, often and often! An' now here she was, come out to live in a one-roomed hut at this God-forsaken last end o' nowhere, right the other side of the world; an' no way out o' the mess but to go straight through with it. Yes, there she sat an' cried, nor I don't wonder at it — no more I don't; an' couldn't be got even to look towards our hut, much less to go into it, whatever poor father could do; an' I sat there with her, while they got the chests and things out of the boat, an' cried too, for company, at first; only presently there was a two-three children come a-runnin' out o' the other huts, an' them an' me stood a-lookin' at each other.

'An' then, all of a sudden, I give a great start, an' catched hold, *hard*, o' mother's hand; for there, stole up so silent out o' the trees that we hadn't heard him come, an' a-standin' straight up before us, was a great tall Maori man! Mother she looked up, saw him, give one screech that you'd think they could a-heard in Town, an' was off into that there hut of ours, an' me with her, an' the door shut, with both our backs against it, before you could ha' blinked. In them days, you see, a blanket was a native's full dress, an' they mostly didn't trouble to dress full, an' that man hadn't . . .

'Well, but you can get used to pretty much anything, bless you! an' specially when you must. It wasn't very long before the Bay was home to me, an' every day a holiday. Not that I hadn't work to do — everyone in them days had to do their bit, soon as they was born, almost; but there wasn't any school (another thing to tease poor mother, but I know it never did me, not till I was grown up), an' all you did was done out in the open, an' there was the sea, an' the Bush, an' I'd my little mates in the other *whares*; an' young ones always like that; it's as good as a game. We'd no oven, I remember, nor no camp-oven neither, at the start; Mother used to bake in her biggest saucepan. An' we'd no bedsteads; father, he boarded over the floor, first thing, an' mother used to keep it strewn deep with fresh sawdust from the pits (bright reddish-brown it was to look at, an' as *sweet*! for nearly all the trees was pine), and she'd a-brought out her feather-beds with her, an' we spread 'em on the floor an' slept soft. For all chairs an' table, we'd our wooden chests that we brought with us; an' mother, I remember, made curtains of a bit o' print she had, because she couldn't abide the sight of a naked window — it looked so mean, she said. Mother, she got more contented, after a bit, specially after your great-uncle Mat was born; but she never come to like the life as father an' me did. See England again? Poor soul, poor soul, nay, that she never did!

'What did we do all day, an' how did we live? I'll tell you. The men (they was all sorts, from them that lived respectable in the huts alongside ours with their wives an' children, to them as had built themselves little shacks right back in the Bush, an' was mostly Tasmanian ticket-o'-leaf men, an' nothin' for nobody to boast on), they used to work some of 'em at fallin' the Bush, an' some at sawin' the timber in the sawpits. An' then, when they'd got enough cut, one o' the craft 'ud come down for it from Port, an' some o' the men 'ud go away in a whaleboat up to Town with it — plenty o' the wood Town's built of grew green once in the Bay; an' then, with the money it fetched, they'd buy stores an' bring down. So the men wasn't so bad off, you see, for they did get a change, once in a while; an' rare old sprees some of them used to have too, don't I know it! when they found theirselves back among faces again, an' talk, an' news, *an'* liquor! But the women, with all the cookin' an' cleanin' an' clothin' to do an' mostly nothin' to do it with: an' they a-grievin' for them they'd left behind, an' scarce ever a letter: an' all the change ever *they* got, just to look from the Bush to the sea an' then back from the sea to the Bush: an' the little children a-comin' an' a-comin', with never no doctor to call; — well, my word! I didn't think of it then, nor understand, but many's the time since I've thought, an' reckon them women had *pluck*! . . .

'My word, though, didn't some of them sawpit fellows use them poor women bad! There was one of 'em, Roimata (well named, for it means "Tears") used to live with Black Joe. My! he was a bad one! — an' there he'd knock her about, an' carry on all sorts, till the poor soul was fair desperate, an' tried to hang herself with a flax rope. But it broke, so it did, an' cut her throat bad in the breakin'. The tumble, an' the sight of her own blood scared her so as to save her; for a-lookin' up an' around an' all ways for somethin' to help, there she sees the chimney; an' lively wi' fright, she does what she'd never ha' thought, most-like, o' doin', else — she scrambles up that chimney, an' out, an' down the other side, an' comes to mother, all over bruises an' blood (my word! she was a sight), but anyway, safe from Joe. Mother she kep' her till it was evenin' an' she could get away to her own people, an' they smuggled her out o' the Bay, an' Joe never got her again.

'Eh dear! I remember Roimata said a thing that afternoon, though, as must ha' made mother feel a real Christian to help her after. You see, the Maori women's ways wasn't just our ways, nor our men hadn't helped 'em, mostly, to be so; an' while Roimata an' mother was a-talkin' friendly together that afternoon, Roimata, she says, quite innocent, "An' how many men," she says, "*you* had?" "Me? Why, whatever does the woman take me for? Why, one, of course, an' that my own lawful wedded husband!" cries mother, a-bridlin' an' a-bristlin' of herself till she didn't look like the same woman — she was a meek-lookin' woman, mother was, an' pretty too, even to a Maori taste, it seemed; for Roimata, she puts her head on one side, an' lookin' at her kind of sly, "Too much the lie!" says she, quite positive, as if you couldn't hope to take *her* in about it — she knew better than you, if needful. "E! too much the lie!" she says, an' looked so sure, that mother she gave up bein' angry all of a sudden an' just burst out a-laughin'. "The poor heathen!" says mother, as soon as she could speak, an' ever after that she always spoke of Roimata as "that poor heathen".'

(1912)

JANE MANDER

An extract from
The Story of a New Zealand River

Alice and Roland had been married four years. They had met in Christchurch soon after her arrival in New Zealand. In a tragic moment, when she was almost penniless, and sick with dread of the future, he had been kind and helpful. Something told her that he was honest with her, but she had not borrowed money from him without much prayerful consideration. When he suggested that she should come north to Auckland where he lived and knew many people, and where he promised to get her the music pupils she needed, it seemed too much like the finger of the Lord for her to refuse. After many appeals to God to help her, she finally accepted his offer because there was absolutely nothing else between her and starvation.

Roland had done all that he promised, and more. He found her music pupils, and he financed her beginnings. He took her to a quiet boardinghouse kept by a friend of his, where she was comfortable and decently fed. He managed her all along by his frankness, his general decency and his vitality.

He had proposed marriage to her almost without any previous signs of affection. He had been rather blunt about it, but she thought that was due to nervousness. She had taken a week to think about it. Every time she was in danger of refusing she had looked at Asia. Every time she was in danger of accepting she had looked into her own heart. Finally, with her eye on Asia, she had accepted him, but not entirely without feeling for him. She saw that people liked him, and she guessed that he would get on. And she was attracted by his impulsive kindness, and by his sweeping energy.

And so she had married him, determined to do her duty, and hoping to get some happiness by the way. But very soon after the marriage the incompatibilities began to assume those undreamt of proportions that are the despair of those who would do their duty. Before a year was over Alice felt that a good deal of her had died.

Roland's reasons for marrying her had been a curious mixture of impulsive need of affection, and business acumen, and a satisfaction of being benevolent. He saw in her a poor, but beautiful young widow, who would very well fit in with his schemes for future greatness and social recognition. He would never have admitted his class inferiority, but in his secret heart he knew he valued her largely because she belonged to the class that ruled the world. Naturally, he expected a return for his money, and he looked for that when he proposed to her. But at the same time he had a comforting sense of his own goodness in rescuing her from the necessity of making her way slowly by teaching the piano.

There was more heart in it, however, than either he or she suspected. And it was this unsatisfied heart in him that drove him to the other women. To them he went for the stimulus and affection that she could not or would not give, and back to her he came for the logical conclusion that she never refused, because she had contracted to give it.

They had never openly quarrelled. Once or twice, when he had become blustering, she had risen and left the room, afterwards ignoring the breaks. There were times when her calmness nearly drove him mad. But he had extraordinary common sense, and he knew it was useless to rage at her. Within a year he, too, had begun to see that something he had hoped for had gone out of their union, if, indeed, it had ever been in it. The thing that annoyed him most was that he could not make her love him. He felt that something tumultuous lay beneath her calm. It piqued his curiosity. He tried to be good to her. And he wondered why the devil he was always wrong. He was just as determined as she was to do his duty.

Thus far they had drifted when they came to the bay. Ever since learning of the isolation of the bush life, Alice had looked forward, with alternating moments of resolute calm and wild despair, to a future of self-suppression save in so far as she could grow again in her children. The possibility of any other man in her life had never occurred to her.

On this day of the picnic it entered her consciousness for the first time. She had felt before this that something about David Bruce challenged her. Her thoughts had turned to him many times in those three weeks. Now the knowledge that he was a doctor forced her to think of the possibilities arising from his position. If her children met with sudden illness or accident she would have to send for him. Intimacy seemed to be inevitable. And then she had always surrounded doctors with the halo that most women put upon them and curates, and bishops, and reformers, believing them to be the props of mankind.

Seized with a premonition of evil, she stared up at the stars and then at their reflection in the river. She now saw in Bruce the unconscious breaker of her fine scheme of life-long martyrdom. This meant that he was another thing to fight. She must kill her impulses even to think of him. She tried to feel that she had thought of him only because she had treated him badly, that it would be quite easy not to think of him any more. Because of her behaviour to him she knew he would make no advance, and the best thing would be just to go on as she had begun, and let him think her cold and distant. She could be courteous, of course.

But she was secretly afraid of her impulses. She could not understand why any one who hated them as much as she did should have them so violently. She had been taught and she still believed that impulses were monstrous inventions of evil to be fought and suppressed. Her own experiences had already taught her their terrible results. The assurance that 'Whom the Lord loveth He chasteneth' had never filled her with the satisfaction said to be enjoyed by those who believe that God uses them to demonstrate eternal laws.

For years she had lived so apart that she did not realise how in the world about her the impulses and instincts had begun their innings, backed up by biology and the Individualists, as powers to be discussed, lauded, developed, and allowed to run their riotous course unchecked. She did not know that the instincts had now accumulated a cult, along with the eugenists, the feminists, the cremationists, and Bernard Shaw.

New Zealand, even more than any other part of the world, seethed with the atmosphere of social and moral experiments. But, in its boarding-houses, the last stronghold of organised prudery and artificial and anaemic chastity, no wandering vibrations of the Zeitgeist had ever reached her. No thought of having any fun with any other man had ever entered her mind. She did not see any human relation as fun. And the mere thought that she might come to care for David Bruce filled her with alarm.

But, she reflected as she sat there, if nothing ever began there would be nothing to fight. All she had to do was to prevent the beginnings. She began calmly to think of ways and means. Her treatment of David Bruce now seemed like a blessing in disguise. She would go on as she had begun; that is, she would keep him at the distance she had already made inevitable. In any case there was nothing else for her to do. There was no reason for her to like him if she did not wish to. There was no reason why she should openly accept him as anything but a mere acquaintance.

After all, it was simple. Duty always was when you faced it clearly. She realised that above all things she wanted peace. She thought of her compensations. She had Mrs. Brayton and her children; she had her music and her books. She had a home, such as it was. And there was her husband. She knew now that he was a power in the land. He would make money, and perhaps he really meant to do his best for her and the children. She determined that she would try to think better of him. With tears dropping from her cheeks she bowed her head under the stars and prayed to God to help her.

Then she got up and walked calmly and serenely home.

(1920)

KATHERINE MANSFIELD

The Woman at the Store

All that day the heat was terrible. The wind blew close to the ground; it rooted among the tussock grass, slithered along the road, so that the white pumice dust swirled in our faces, settled and sifted over us and was like a dry-skin itching for growth on our bodies. The horses stumbled along, coughing and chuffing. The pack-horse was sick — with a big open sore rubbed under the belly. Now and again she stopped short, threw back her head, looked at us as though she were going to cry, and whinnied. Hundreds of larks shrilled; the sky was slate colour, and the sound of the larks reminded me of slate pencils scraping over its surface. There was nothing to be seen but wave after wave of tussock grass, patched with purple orchids and manuka bushes covered with thick spider webs.

Jo rode ahead. He wore a blue galatea shirt, corduroy trousers and riding boots. A white handkerchief, spotted with red — it looked as though his nose had been bleeding on it — was knotted round his throat. Wisps of white hair straggled from under his wideawake — his moustache and eyebrows were called white — he slouched in the saddle, grunting. Not once that day had he sung

> *I don't care, for don't you see,*
> *My wife's mother was in front of me!*

It was the first day we had been without it for a month, and now there seemed something uncanny in his silence. Jim rode beside me, white as a clown; his black eyes glittered and he kept shooting out his tongue and moistening his lips. He was dressed in a Jaeger vest and a pair of blue duck trousers, fastened round the waist with a plaited leather belt. We had hardly spoken since dawn. At noon we had lunched off fly biscuits and apricots by the side of a swampy creek.

'My stomach feels like the crop of a hen,' said Jo. 'Now then, Jim, you're the bright boy of the party — where's this 'ere store you kep' on talking about. "Oh yes," you says, "I know a fine store, with a paddock for the horses and a creek runnin' through, owned by a friend of mine who'll give yer a bottle of whisky before 'e shakes hands with yer." I'd like ter see that place — merely as a matter of curiosity — not that I'd ever doubt yer word — as yer know very well — but . . .'

Jim laughed. 'Don't forget there's a woman too, Jo, with blue eyes and yellow hair, who'll promise you something else before she shakes hands with you. Put that in your pipe and smoke it.'

'The heat's making you balmy,' said Jo. But he dug his knees into the horse. We shambled on. I half fell asleep and had a sort of uneasy dream that the horses were not moving forward at all — then that I was on a rocking-horse, and my old mother was scolding me for raising such a fearful dust from the drawing-room carpet. 'You've entirely worn off the pattern of the carpet,' I heard her saying, and she gave the reins a tug. I snivelled and woke to find Jim leaning over me, maliciously smiling.

'That was a case of all but,' said he. 'I just caught you. What's up? Been bye-bye?'

'No!' I raised my head. 'Thank the Lord we're arriving somewhere.'

We were on the brow of the hill, and below us there was a whare roofed with corrugated iron. It stood in a garden, rather far back from the road — a big paddock opposite, and a creek and a clump of young willow trees. A thin line of blue smoke stood up straight from the chimney of the whare; and as I looked a woman came out, followed by a child and a sheep dog — the woman carrying what appeared to me a black stick. She made gestures at us. The horses put on a final spurt, Jo took off his wideawake, shouted, threw out his chest, and began singing 'I don't care, for don't you see . . .' The sun pushed through the pale clouds and shed a vivid light over the scene. It gleamed on the woman's yellow hair, over her flapping pinafore and the rifle she was carrying. The child hid behind her, and the yellow dog, a mangy beast, scuttled back into the whare, his tail between his legs. We drew rein and dismounted.

'Hallo,' screamed the woman. 'I thought you was three 'awks. My kid comes runnin' in ter me. "Mumma," says she, "there's three brown things comin' over the 'ill," says she. An' I comes out smart, I can tell yer. "They'll be 'awks," I says to her. Oh, the 'awks about 'ere, yer wouldn't believe.'

The 'kid' gave us the benefit of one eye from behind the woman's pinafore — then retired again.

'Where's your old man?' asked Jim.

The woman blinked rapidly, screwing up her face.

'Away shearin'. Bin away a month. I suppose ye're not goin' to stop, are yer? There's a storm comin' up.'

'You bet we are,' said Jo. 'So you're on your lonely, missus?'

She stood, pleating the frills of her pinafore, and glancing from one to the other of us, like a hungry bird. I smiled at the thought of how Jim had pulled Jo's leg about her. Certainly her eyes were blue, and what hair she had was yellow, but ugly. She was a figure of fun. Looking at her, you felt there was nothing but sticks and wires under that pinafore — her front teeth were knocked out, she had red, pulpy hands and she wore on her feet a pair of dirty Bluchers.

'I'll go and turn out the horses,' said Jim. 'Got any embrocation? Poi's rubbed herself to hell!'

''Arf a mo!' The woman stood silent a moment, her nostrils expanding as she breathed. Then she shouted violently, 'I'd rather you didn't stop . . . You *can't*, and there's the end of it. I don't let out that paddock any more. You'll have to go on; I ain't got nothing!'

'Well, I'm blest!' said Jo heavily. He pulled me aside. 'Gone a bit off 'er dot,' he whispered. 'Too much alone, *you know*,' very significantly. 'Turn the sympathetic tap on 'er, she'll come round all right.'

But there was no need — she had come round by herself.

'Stop if yer like!' she muttered, shrugging her shoulders. To me — 'I'll give yer the embrocation if yer come along.'

'Right-o, I'll take it down to them.' We walked together up the garden path. It was planted on both sides with cabbages. They smelled like stale dish-water. Of flowers there were double poppies and sweet-williams. One little patch was divided off by pawa shells — presumably it belonged to the child — for she ran from her mother and began to grub in it with a broken clothes-peg. The yellow dog lay across the doorstep, biting fleas; the woman kicked him away.

'Gar-r, get away, you beast . . . the place ain't tidy. I 'aven't 'ad time ter fix things today — been ironing. Come right in.'

It was a large room, the walls plastered with old pages of English periodicals. Queen Victoria's Jubilee appeared to be the most recent number. A table with an ironing board and wash-tub on it, some wooden forms, a black horsehair sofa and some broken cane chairs pushed against the walls. The mantelpiece above the stove was draped in pink paper, further ornamented with dried grasses and ferns and a coloured print of Richard Seddon. There were four doors — one, judging from the smell, led into the 'Store', one on to the 'backyard', through a third I saw the bedroom. Flies buzzed in circles round the ceiling, and treacle papers and bundles of dried clover were pinned to the window curtains.

I was alone in the room; she had gone into the store for the embrocation. I heard her stamping about and muttering to herself: 'I got some, now where did I put that bottle? . . . It's behind the pickles . . . no, it ain't.' I cleared a place on the table and sat there, swinging my legs. Down in the paddock I could hear Jo singing and the sound of hammer strokes as Jim drove in the tent pegs. It was sunset. There is no twilight in our New Zealand days, but a curious half-hour when everything appears grotesque — it frightens — as though the savage spirit of the country walked abroad and sneered at what it saw. Sitting alone in the hideous room I grew afraid. The woman next door was a long time finding that stuff. What was she doing in there? Once I thought I heard her bang her hands down on the counter, and once she half moaned, turning it into a cough and clearing her throat. I wanted to shout 'Buck up!' but I kept silent.

'Good Lord, what a life!' I thought. 'Imagine being here day in, day out, with that rat of a child and a mangy dog. Imagine bothering about ironing. *Mad*, of course she's mad! Wonder how long she's been here — wonder if I could get her to talk.'

At that moment she poked her head round the door.

'Wot was it yer wanted?' she asked.

'Embrocation.'

'Oh, I forgot. I got it, it was in front of the pickle jars.'

She handed me the bottle.

'My, you do look tired, you do! Shall I knock yer up a few scones for supper! There's some tongue in the store, too, and I'll cook yer a cabbage if you fancy it.'

'Right-o.' I smiled at her. 'Come down to the paddock and bring the kid for tea.'

She shook her head, pursing up her mouth.

'Oh no. I don't fancy it. I'll send the kid down with the things and a billy of milk. Shall I knock up a few extry scones to take with yer ter-morrow?'

'Thanks.'

She came and stood by the door.

'How old is the kid?'

'Six — come next Christmas. I 'ad a bit of trouble with 'er one way an' another. I 'adn't any milk till a month after she was born and she sickened like a cow.'

'She's not like you — takes after her father?' Just as the woman had shouted her refusal at us before, she shouted at me then.

'No, she don't! She's the dead spit of me. Any fool could see that. Come on in now, Else, you stop messing in the dirt.'

I met Jo climbing over the paddock fence.

'What's the old bitch got in the store?' he asked.

'Don't know — didn't look.'

'Well, of all the fools. Jim's slanging you. What have you been doing all the time?'

'She couldn't find this stuff. Oh, my shakes, you are smart!'

Jo had washed, combed his wet hair in a line across his forehead, and buttoned a coat over his shirt. He grinned.

Jim snatched the embrocation from me. I went to the end of the paddock where the willows grew and bathed in the creek. The water was clear and soft as oil. Along the edges held by the grass and rushes white foam tumbled and bubbled. I lay in the water and looked up at the trees that were still a moment, then quivered lightly and again were still. The air smelt of rain. I forgot about the woman and the kid until I came back to the tent. Jim lay by the fire watching the billy boil.

I asked where Jo was, and if the kid had brought our supper.

'Pooh,' said Jim, rolling over and looking up at the sky. 'Didn't you see how Jo had been titivating? He said to me before he went up to the whare, "Dang it! she'll look better by night light — at any rate, my buck, she's female flesh!"'

'You had Jo about her looks — you had me too.'

'No — look here. I can't make it out. It's four years since I came past this way and I stopped here two days. The husband was a pal of mine once, down the West Coast — a fine, big chap, with a voice on him like a trombone. She's been barmaid down the Coast — as pretty as a wax doll. The coach used to come this way then once a fortnight, that was before they opened the railway up Napier way, and she had no end of a time! Told me once in a confidential moment that she knew one hundred and twenty-five different ways of kissing!'

'Oh, go on, Jim! She isn't the same woman!'

''Course she is . . . I can't make it out. What I think is the old man's cleared out and left her: that's all my eye about shearing. Sweet life! The only people who come through now are Maoris and sundowners!'

Through the dark we saw the gleam of the kid's pinafore. She trailed over to us with a basket in her hand, the milk billy in the other. I unpacked the basket, the child standing by.

'Come over here,' said Jim, snapping his fingers at her.

She went, the lamp from the inside of the tent cast a bright light over her. A mean, undersized brat, with whitish hair and weak eyes. She stood, legs wide apart and her stomach protruding.

'What do you do all day?' asked Jim.

She scraped out one ear with her little finger, looked at the result and said, 'Draw.'

'Huh! What do you draw? Leave your ears alone!'

'Pictures.'

'What on?'

'Bits of butter paper an' a pencil of my Mumma's.'

'Boh! What a lot of words at one time!' Jim rolled his eyes at her. 'Baa-lambs and moo-cows?'

'No, everything. I'll draw all of you when you're gone, and your horses and the tent, and that one' — she pointed to me — 'with no clothes on in the creek. I looked at her where she couldn't see me from.'

'Thanks very much. How ripping of you,' said Jim. 'Where's Dad?'

The kid pouted. 'I won't tell you because I don't like yer face!' She started operations on the other ear.

'Here,' I said. 'Take the basket, get along home and tell the other man supper's ready.'

'I don't want to.'

'I'll give you a box on the ear if you don't,' said Jim savagely.

'Hie! I'll tell Mumma. I'll tell Mumma.' The kid fled.

We ate until we were full, and had arrived at the smoke stage before Jo came back, very flushed and jaunty, a whisky bottle in his hand.

"Ave a drink — you two!' he shouted, carrying off matters with a high hand. "Ere, shove along the cups.'

'One hundred and twenty-five different ways,' I murmured to Jim.

'What's that? Oh! stow it!' said Jo. 'Why 'ave you always got your knife into me. You gas like a kid at a Sunday School beano. She wants us to go there tonight and have a comfortable chat. I' — he waved his hand airily — 'I got 'er round.'

'Trust you for that,' laughed Jim. 'But did she tell you where the old man's got to?'

Jo looked up. 'Shearing! You 'eard 'er, you fool!'

The woman had fixed up the room, even to a light bouquet of sweet-williams on the table. She and I sat one side of the table, Jo and Jim the other. An oil lamp was set between us, the whisky bottle and glasses, and a jug of water. The kid knelt against one of the forms, drawing on butter paper; I wondered, grimly, if she was attempting the creek episode. But Jo had been right about night time. The woman's hair was tumbled — two red spots burned in her cheeks — her eyes shone — and we knew that they were kissing feet under the table. She had changed the blue pinafore for a white calico dressing-jacket and a black skirt — the kid was decorated to the extent of a blue sateen hair ribbon. In the stifling room, with the flies buzzing against the ceiling and dropping on to the table, we got slowly drunk.

'Now listen to me,' shouted the woman, banging her fist on the table. 'It's six years since I was married, and four miscarriages. I says to 'im, I says, what do you think I'm doin' up 'ere? If you was back at the Coast I'd 'ave you lynched for child murder. Over and over I tells 'im — you've broken my spirit and spoiled my looks, and wot for — that's wot I'm driving at.' She clutched her head with her hands and stared round at us. Speaking rapidly, 'Oh, some days — an' months of them — I 'ear them two words knockin' inside me all the time — "Wot for!" but sometimes I'll be cooking the spuds an' I lifts the lid off to give 'em a prong and I 'ears, quite suddin again, "Wot for!" Oh! I don't mean only the spuds and the kid — I mean — I mean,' she hiccoughed — 'you know what I mean, Mr. Jo.'

'I know,' said Jo, scratching his head.

'Trouble with me is,' she leaned across the table, 'he left me too much alone. When the coach stopped coming, sometimes he'd go away days, sometimes he'd go away weeks, and leave me ter look after the store. Back 'e'd come — pleased as Punch. "Oh, 'allo,"'e'd say. "'Ow are you gettin' on? Come and give us a kiss." Sometimes I'd turn a bit nasty, and then 'e'd go off again, and if I took it all right, 'e'd wait till 'e could twist me round 'his finger, then 'e'd say, "Well, so long, I'm off," and do you think I could keep 'im? — not me!'

'Mumma,' bleated the kid, 'I made a picture of them on the 'ill, an' you an' me an' the dog down below.'

'Shut your mouth!' said the woman.

A vivid flash of lightning played over the room — we heard the mutter of thunder.

'Good thing that's broke loose,' said Jo. 'I've 'ad it in me 'ead for three days.'

'Where's your old man now?' asked Jim slowly.

The woman blubbered and dropped her head on to the table. 'Jim, 'e's gone shearin' and left me alone again,' she wailed.

''Ere, look out for the glasses,' said Jo. 'Cheer-o, 'ave another drop. No good cryin' over spilt 'usbands! You, Jim, you blasted cuckoo!'

'Mr. Jo,' said the woman, drying her eyes on her jacket frill, 'you're a gent, an' if I was a secret woman I'd place any confidence in your 'ands. I don't mind if I do 'ave a glass on that.'

Every moment the lightning grew more vivid and the thunder sounded nearer. Jim and I were silent — the kid never moved from her bench. She poked her tongue out and blew on her papers as she drew.

'It's the loneliness,' said the woman, addressing Jo — he made sheep's eyes at her — 'and bein' shut up 'ere like a broody 'en.' He reached his hand across the table and held hers, and though the position looked most uncomfortable when they wanted to pass the water and whisky, their hands stuck together as though glued. I pushed back my chair and went over to the kid, who immediately sat flat down on her artistic achievements and made a face at me.

'You're not to look,' said she.

'Oh, come on, don't be nasty!' Jim came over to us, and we were just drunk enough to wheedle the kid into showing us. And those drawings of hers were extraordinary and repulsively vulgar. The creation of a lunatic with a lunatic's cleverness. There was no doubt about it, the kid's mind was diseased. While she showed them to us, she worked herself up into a mad excitement, laughing and trembling, and shooting out her arms.

'Mumma,' she yelled. 'Now I'm going to draw them what you told me I never was to — now I am.'

The woman rushed from the table and beat the child's head with the flat of her hand.

'I'll smack you with yer clothes turned up if yer dare say that again,' she bawled.

Jo was too drunk to notice, but Jim caught her by the arm. The kid did not utter a cry. She drifted over to the window and began picking flies from the treacle paper.

We returned to the table — Jim and I sitting one side, the woman and Jo, touching shoulders, the other. We listened to the thunder, saying stupidly, 'That was a near one,' 'There it goes again,' and Jo, at a heavy hit, 'Now we're off,' 'Steady on the brake,' until rain began to fall, sharp as cannon shot on the iron roof.

'You'd better doss here for the night,' said the woman.

'That's right,' assented Jo, evidently in the know about this move.

'Bring up yer things from the tent. You two can doss in the store along with the kid — she's used to sleep in there and won't mind you.'

'Oh, Mumma, I never did,' interrupted the kid.

'Shut yer lies! An' Mr. Jo can 'ave this room.'

It sounded a ridiculous arrangement, but it was useless to attempt to cross them, they were too far gone. While the woman sketched the plan of action, Jo sat, abnormally solemn and red, his eyes bulging, and pulling at his moustache.

'Give us a lantern,' said Jim, 'I'll go down to the paddock.' We two went together. Rain whipped in our faces, the land was light as though a bush fire was raging. We behaved like two children let loose in the thick of an adventure, laughed and shouted to each other, and came back to the whare to find the kid already bedded in the counter of the store. The woman brought us a lamp. Jo took his bundle from Jim, the door was shut.

'Good night all,' shouted Jo.

Jim and I sat on two sacks of potatoes. For the life of us we could not stop laughing. Strings of onions and half-hams dangled from the ceiling — wherever we looked there were advertisements for 'Camp Coffee' and tinned meats. We pointed at them, tried to read them aloud — overcome with laughter and hiccoughs. The kid in the counter stared at us. She threw off her blanket and scrambled to the floor, where she stood in her grey flannel night-gown rubbing one leg against the other. We paid no attention to her.

'Wot are you laughing at?' she said uneasily.

'You!' shouted Jim. 'The red tribe of you, my child.'

She flew into a rage and beat herself with her hands. 'I won't be laughed at, you curs — you.' He swooped down upon the child and swung her on to the counter.

'Go to sleep, Miss Smarty — or make a drawing — here's a pencil — you can use Mumma's account book.'

Through the rain we heard Jo creak over the boarding of the next room — the sound of a door being opened — then shut to.

'It's the loneliness,' whispered Jim.

'One hundred and twenty-five different ways — alas! my poor brother!'

The kid tore out a page and flung it at me.

'There you are,' she said. 'Now I done it ter spite Mumma for shutting me up 'ere with you two. I done the one she told me I never ought to. I done the one she told me she'd shoot me if I did. Don't care! Don't care!'

The kid had drawn the picture of the woman shooting at a man with a rook rifle and then digging a hole to bury him in.

She jumped off the counter and squirmed about on the floor biting her nails.

Jim and I sat till dawn with the drawing beside us. The rain ceased, the little kid fell asleep, breathing loudly. We got up, stole out of the whare, down into the paddock. White clouds floated over a pink sky — a chill wind blew; the air smelled of wet grass. Just as we swung into the saddle Jo came out of the whare — he motioned to us to ride on.

'I'll pick you up later,' he shouted.

A bend in the road, and the whole place disappeared.

(1924)

ROBIN HYDE

The Purple Mantle

Chapter Thirteen from
Nor the Years Condemn

Bede Collins (no longer, unless by courtesy, Sister Collins) was attending Anzac Day service in Auckland. There was a church service before the parade and laying of wreaths at the foot of the Cenotaph, which would follow in the Domain grounds, the paths there blocked by streams of civilians, who would be a little ashamed if they groused because their feet were trodden on and their breasts squeezed; also by sailors from the Naval Base, squat and jolly in their flapping trousers; a thin bristling moustache of drawn bayonets; and small boys astride the necks of old cannon that crouched like dilapidated lions, facing seaward over marble steps and the gulf of brown autumnal trees. Somebody would tell the little boys to hop off. The Garland of Flowers would wreathe from the brass lips of a cornet, sweet and high as if those lips blew into the air the very soul of the young player, his taut courage and aspiration. A wind would lay hold on that, floating it down over Grafton gully towards the city.

Army nurses led the parade; Sister Collins was supposed to attend, in mufti and wearing her medal, but she was Bede now, and wasn't going. After the nurses would come the overseas women, ambulance drivers, V.A.D.'s and others, wind cockling their hair. Then the regiments, each proud of its colours, each hailed by the crowd, but the Kilties making the best show, because tartan is tartan, and big bare knees dear to the female heart, especially the ultra-feminine hearts of little girls who wished they could wear a sporran. The most interesting section, if you did not watch with an eye to the spectacular, would be the ex-servicemen in mufti, war medals and ribbons on their breasts; they tried to march better than the men in uniform, but civilian clothes made a drab job of them. There were always a few rows of Boer War veterans, and a number of funny, proud old dodos from obscure museum-piece wars, men like ivory-handled sticks redeemed for the one day from the pawnshops. They were straightest-backed of any; on the way home they hobbled and coughed, most of them pensioners living in single rooms without fires, and a few coming from old men's homes.

The wreaths would be placed, official ones first, gigantic compositions in scarlet cotton poppies and laurel leaves, the dark or the gilded laurel: then several big ones from the women's organisations, home-made, perhaps, but still elaborate and handsome. After that, black-clad women would creep forward like beetles to lay beside the big wreaths their wreaths not a foot across, arranging them carefully so that the memorial cards would show. Standing in thin sunshine, they would salute, most of them quite wrongly, and creep back, dabbing their eyes. Their loss, though keen and ardent in the moment they laid down the wreaths, was normally faded now, and their eyes were scared blue, like skim milk. They wore fabric gloves, the finger-ends neatly sewn up after they had burst, and found it good to be pressed against the crowd-breast, choking: 'I'll be all right in just a moment.' They were kind to one another, so long as they knew it was respectable to be kind.

'There, I know. I'm sure I don't know what we women would do without our cry. The poor dear's broken right down. I always say there's nothing like a good cry, is there? You mustn't go on like that, when everybody's looking to us to be brave.'

(It's like a kind of dialect laid over speech to conceal it, a cipher, thought Bede; the funny things we all say off pat, over and over again. And underneath it, what? People aren't half such fools as they look and sound.)

When they had done, the Cenotaph would be waist-deep in flowers and glossy ribbons; cotton poppies and chrysanthemums, mostly, for this day fell late in autumn, when the curled bronze heads were at their best. Sun glinted, prickling on the bayonets. The little boys fidgeted, very tired, but their minds pranced off, up hill and down dale, riding the horses of the special constables, horses with coats shaved like silk, whose whinnying heads pointed still as still, at one touch on their bridles. What horses! The little boys dreamed of the time they would be riding, quite grown up.

At the sound of the Last Post, men lurched off their hats and caps. Unspent, undefeated, the music bade farewell as the clumsy letters the women had treasured never could say it; ah, such a music. Into the air it spired, and crystallised there above them, crying: 'Remember me, remember me.' Afterwards the crowd would break and hurry; but in their hearts they did remember the Last Post, sounded on a still autumn day, with the faded colours washing back and forth in the air-tides, as quiet men held them erect. Across the gully, coming home, they would see the old mill, with its cinnamon-coloured bricks and its one pitchpine sail, like a one-armed soldier.

But she wished, thought Bede, that one could know for certain if the Garland of Flowers and the Last Post made the wars, or if the wars made the music. That didn't sound much, on the face of it, but meant every-thing. If the Last Post made the wars — that lovely wreathing thing to produce war and the aftermaths — the whole affair was hopeless; that would mean, humanity's talk about a will to peace was mere lip service, a lie and a cheat. But if the lovely wreathing thing were subsidiary, the reply of the human spirit speaking out of its unearned Hell, saying: 'I live on. Listen to me, do not despair, for I live on,' then the case was altered.

She bent her head; a woman sighed and creaked against her. Bede could feel the vast sigh through stay-ribs. On the whole, she thought the latter belief was true. War in its beginnings had no beauty, but was a simple business of eradicating a fear or a rival, getting out of the way something the ancient fathers had wanted out of the way. Very well, then; it grew big and autocratic. Helmets shone, and the unhelmeted, innocently caught up, made their own replies. They replied with systems of chivalry (a Tommy marching-song was a system of chivalry) with carving a vine or a dog's head on the hilt of a dagger, with giving the basic ugliness of war the lie in its throat. They themselves weren't ugly; they themselves weren't carrion. Of course this theory had its obvious danger, because the people were still the unhelmeted, caught up, and they couldn't see how their own kind were trying in music, colour, forlorn meetings, to break free. Always there existed for them a nation of bogies, of frightful people outside the human law, against whom they must protect themselves. Some of the patriots identified the wars with the banners, and as for the rank and file — so many people could talk to them, anyone with the gift of the gab. But the thing carried also the germ of its own salvation. If what people loved was the vine on the hilt, the Last Post, the comradeship — called by them 'the fun of it' — these things were not the proprietary medicines of war. The scientists of peace could work upon them, work like slaves and isolate the instinct for beautiful excitement from the instinct of fear and destruction. They might be doing so now, obscure and intent.

Too late, said a tolling bell in her mind, too late, too late. Another bell answered: Never too late. Too late for you, perhaps, but who are you? I do not know one face from another face. Not too late for the only face I know.

Without turning her head, Bede could see the exact expressions of the people in church; and knowing them for what they were, knowing that they would all die some day, many going through unspeakable boredom and misery on the road, that a fair percentage would die with cancer fingering their breasts, abdomens and throats, she knew they would probably endure another war, but didn't want them committed to a dogma of wars. It was not their death, pain or grief through war which worried her at all; those things had their like in peace. What hurt her throat was the idea that they should be allowed to get just so far, and no further. They were too good for that, and no flourish of trumpets could pardon those who spoke otherwise.

But she thought it would be all right. The more one looked at war, the more one saw it as a separate entity, apart from human wishes. Now that science was dabbling its lean fingers in the dish, giving germ warfare, incendiary bombs, Boy's phosgene, all the other dehumanisers, were the people pleased? Not a bit of it. They were sensationalists, like every other living organisms — how in God's name can you be anything but a sensationalist, when your means of living happen to be by way of your senses? — but they were holding thin little meetings, trying to make war respectable. Thank God for science, for the spectacled men who might accidentally segregate war.

> *Whatever hope is yours*
> *Was my life also. I went hunting wild*
> *After the wildest beauty in the world,*
> *Which lies not calm in eyes or braided hair, . . .*
> *Now men will go content with what we spoiled.*
> *Or, discontent, boil bloody, and be spilled.*
> *They will be swift with the swiftness of the tigress,*
> *None will break ranks, though nations trek from progress. . . .*
> *To miss the march of this retreating world,*
> *Into vain citadels that are not walled . . .*
> *I would have poured my spirit without stint*
> *But not through wounds; not on the cess of war.*
> *Foreheads of men have bled where no wounds were . . .*

Wilfred Owen, twenty-one years old, writing that for the only German he ever killed; and soon afterwards he was shot himself. Not a traitor or a flimsy arm-chair idealist, people couldn't say that, but a boy in the direct tradition of Malory. What could they have done with him, if he had lived? The worst thing of all, perhaps; he might have lived to be petted and flattered by the intellectuals, to become precious.

Bede shut her eyes. 'Oh God,' she prayed, 'I believe we're moving towards them, but there's a hard time first. If we do move, have more than pity; don't let them make the deadly mistake of thinking and calling us soft. The young can talk things over, as a rule, but most of them haven't even got the money to meet one another, and you know what the pride of old men is, how it justifies itself by a million comely things, things so comely that in his age a man begins to think they were righteous after all. How else, he thinks, could the russet tiles slope back so gravely among the russet trees? And it justifies itself by the fact that some things are done and irrevocable; that is a wound, God, a mortal wound which the dying body of a people learns to bear with a fortitude which can become their only pride. And we out here, isolated, we're just the same. Moderately honest, but we can't stand up to too much poverty or mocking, or to the want of excitement. Don't let the others provoke the old men's pride to wrath; or between the very old and the very young, we'll be done, and you couldn't want that, just for a spectacle. For the sake of my little people and their little people, who are honest unless they have to beg or lie or steal a bit, don't let us have arrogance all over again. Some of us have learned the bitterly hard lesson of winning a war. You were supposed to have spared a city once, for the sake of one just man. You might spare a world now, for the sake of a few fools.'

The people in the pews rustled up to sing: 'O God, our help in ages past.' That was a strong hymn, and her favourite once, but now her ears rang with another.

'Pass on to Calvary, O Son of God . . . Pass on to Calvary . . . Pass on . . . I mustn't keep saying it or thinking it.' The woman next to her was looking. Bede saw her tears hit on the dusty yellow wood, which made her laugh inwardly. It showed that she was a little sicker than Dr Currie had thought, though she felt no pain, and no weariness except this intense pity.

Like the meshes of a seine net let down in the blue waters washing between the stained glass windows, her mind swayed against people's faces and the hairy backs of hands, and brought back little judgments. Staring at the high-bridged dark face of a youngish man who looked as if he had been at the war three months, and brought back a medal and a wound, she thought: 'He likes blood because it's such a pretty colour . . . crimson.' And of the minister, a quiet, grey, convincing man, she thought: 'He's good, but he can't understand how Christ would ever have managed without the Apostle Paul to follow on and organise. Discipline and organisation. He's never stopped to imagine what a shoddy little epileptic nobody *Saul* might have become without Christ . . . or how often Paul reverted to Saul. All these years, the one who really loved the world has been obscured by the one who both hated and loved himself so well, the organiser, Saul, Saul, Saul.'

> *Solemn the drums beat; death, august and royal,*
> *Sings sorrow up into immortal spheres.*

Binyon's hymn, which had found its way to the people like nothing else since Kipling — (poor old Kipling, crucified between his own two thieves, Imperialism and 'If') — was the climax to the service. But it wasn't that verse, so much better from the poet's point of view, that the people loved. When the other came, their voices all joined in; men's voices which were merely ordinary became gentle and deep, the women's voices were true.

> *They shall not grow old, as we that are left grow old;*
> *Age shall not weary them, nor the years condemn.*

The voices died, lingering upon 'Remember them.' Bede thought: 'Poetry and music are two of the things we haven't given them since the war. We have taken away from them even that little they had, so they don't care about death august and royal, but only for the things you feel not with your mind but with your bowels — age, weariness, condemnation, the true things they can understand.'

'Are you all right, dear?'

'Yes, thank you; quite all right.'

'You look very sick. Did you lose somebody?'

'Yes, I did lose someone.' She didn't mean Boy, or her brother Nevil, or the young cousin who had been so annoyed when she laughed at him in Cairo . . . poor old Jimmie . . . Whom she had really lost, she couldn't have said. The woman, whose ridged flesh was marked with not unpretty little snailtracks of wet, patted her hand.

'Never you mind, dear, you'll feel better once you get a breath of fresh air. Have you any children?'

'No.'

'I've got three. It's been hard, and it gets no easier, but there you are, you wouldn't be without them once you've got them. Children are a great blessing.'

'You keep them away from the war,' said Bede, and caught herself away from the aisle. The minister who liked St. Paul was shaking hands with people as they went out: very adequate he was, with all these women. Bede brushed past him.

Death august . . . A Caesar with a burning face, sitting on his throne and wearing a purple mantle, whose folds spread over the lands and over the seas. She longed to stoop and bury her face in this, crying, while yet the sweet notes of a bugle broke on the air like the boughs of a young tree offered for sacrifice: 'I submit. That was all I wanted, only to touch your mantle. I never knew how weary I was, until I saw its colour. Some of them like crimson, but the purple is stately. Let me rest now, your mantle in time will cover them over, and besides, they're their own affair, not mine.'

Her eyes felt unsealed as if the lids had been torn apart. She saw a boy walking in the thin brown scurf of poplar leaves, taking delight in kicking them up with the broad toes of his boots. He had a tidy jacket worn at the elbows, and the kind of thick clean hair which bristles up without any parting, brittle and shining like gold-dust at the back of his skull. 'Albie,' said his mother, shaking his elbow, 'how often have I got to tell you? You wear out those boots, and you'll wait a fine time before you get new ones. Stubbing your toes out, indeed.'

'Didn't the Highlanders look great, Mum?' asked the clear voice of the boy, who had seen and heard nothing since. Two others from the parade passed Bede, one in mufti with a row of medals, a good height and grey-blue eyes. The younger man interested her more at the moment; a lanky, pleasant colt, so obviously English, and obviously as happy as the blue sky. His face had burnt in layers, the scarlet still showing beneath the brown on his fair neck. Bede heard him say: 'Come along to the pie-cart, I can hear my belt buckle click against my spine. You'll admire the old sport in the pie-cart, Mac. He's been a sailor, and last night he told me his past. Most of it was bloody well indecent. He's got a curly chest all tattooed with things better hidden in the undergrowth. If he ever shaved he'd be arrested.'

'Did I hear you say "bloody", Homie?'

'You did. Wait till you hear him, and you'll say it too. Come along, you old oyster. What are the chief products of Stewart Island? Oysters, muttonbirds, only nobody but the Maoris can take them, ambergris, only the bottom's dropped out of the market, *paua* shells, only nobody wants them, venison, only that's never sold, and timber, only you think that's so good-looking it mustn't be cut. Oh, and fish, only you get drowned catching those. Prospectus by J. Macnamara. No Company, unless you count me.'

'There's no civilising the English. They've got rude blood, and very rude ideas.'

'And a rude appetite just now.'

'You're cheerful, Homie.'

They passed on; Bede thought it was the first time she had ever heard the word Homie used without a fight starting, or somebody looking sick. Then she forgot them. She started to walk to the Domain by a little bush path which lanced the side of the reserve, coming out near a flagged lily-pond.

Suddenly, magically, the church service was gone; this was one of her good days, and that she had bent down, five minutes ago, to touch the purple mantle was only laughable. Leaves were clear as the sky, the bubbled air touched her eyes and faintly stung her nostrils. She walked light and happy, her senses exquisitely acute, taking every tiny signal of sound or colour flashed to them; afterwards she'd be down. Bede didn't care. She walked with her head back, letting the air stroke her young again. An old sandwichman, off his beat and knocked flat as his own boards by time and weather, smiled at her. Bede beamed back as if he had left her a fortune. Some of her best friendships lasted just one second — a flash of eyes and teeth, one sentence of commonplace. Or little girls, balancing on the edges of gutters like jerseyed fairies walking tightropes (they even shut their eyes, they were so afraid they would fall off), had stopped her by demanding in piercing voices: 'Have you seen my brother Johnnie? He took his trike down the street, and Mum says if he goes out in the traffic he'll get smacked.' Occasionally a very small one, peeping out among wattles whose catkins were still damp from spring's eggshell, said confidently: 'Hullo.' Bede always said 'Hullo,' and then the very small ones, losing the edge of their shyness, thought they had been clever, and screamed: 'Hullo, 'lo, 'lo.' If children asked her questions, she was careful to answer them sensibly and directly, and to say 'I don't know' if she didn't know; and went back to her own place with these things like a basket of herbs, but not for witch's malice. But lately, it seemed that when she smiled at strangers they no longer smiled back, and the children ran too fast, so she knew she was getting old.

She had given up nursing when Dr Currie told her of the spot on her lung, picked up during a few months' nursing at a small country sanatorium. Of course he had wanted her to go into a sanatorium herself, but when he told her that she was non-infectious, and could remain so if she took the right measures to get the bug out of her system, she shook her head. Partly a faint memory of Boy's terror of the cage held her back, but it was more the depression. She didn't want to ride that out at anchor between clean sheets, with everything done for her and nobody telling her any real news.

'Nurses make dreadful patients, Dr Currie. I can look after myself as well as any hospital, so long as there's no chance of my passing it on.'

'No fear at all, if you're sensible and don't let yourself go to the pack. Of course you mustn't share a room.' Bede shook her head, and Dr Currie was vexed with himself. He had forgotten young Paul's suicide.

'Live with your people?'

'I haven't any people. I am the complete solitary. I'll live somewhere quiet, hilly and fresh, and just get better. Then I can work again.'

'Well, monthly visits and a report, remember,' he grumbled. For several months Bede obeyed. Living alone (the first time for years that she had been away from hospital quarters) had its funny side, but sometimes she felt that she was between the edges of a great quicksilver bubble, sea and sky, out of which the air was slowly being sucked. 'That's the bug, fool,' she told herself, and was surprised to remember how cheerful other tubercular cases had always seemed. She rented a one-roomed shack with a balcony, on a hillside facing out to sea. Its silvers and sunrises were really fine, but when the rain came down at night, pelting on its quaint peaky roof of tin, she stared at her lamp, and the lamp stared back. She kept the little place spotless, putting in glass jars the showery white and brown flowers of *manuka*, which grew wild all over her section. Strident ganders and roosters belonging to an old lady up the right-of-way overran the place, but except when their gabble irritated her, she was glad of their company. At times she watched the old lady patiently spudding her back garden, and called over the vacant section between them that she had sour milk or stale bread to spare for the ganders. However little she bought, one person always had scraps left over; this worried her faintly, for she had no income, and a dwindling remnant of savings in the bank, but the silvery sea drew back her eyes, and made money vague. She tried out bypaths in books, and wished she had learned to do something worthwhile with her hands — making chairs, or even dolls. There was a man in a spinal jacket, cheerful little sparrow with a peaky face, who had been doll-making for years, selling them out of his bedroom window. 'But it's no use,' thought Bede. 'If you don't learn to use your hands before you're thirty, you'll be only a technical college effort or another precious hobby-rider; unless you're very exceptional, which I'm not.'

On her good days she didn't care. There was no worry, no clumsiness, no Bede Collins to speak of, only a light unidentifiable body which walked up hills and streets, soaking in what she needed, it seemed by the use of an extra sense. The path to the Domain was raddled with beaten leaves; an old head hung over a fence, the apparently guillotined head of a white mare, and its broad eyes took her in so gravely that she laughed. 'Hullo, Duchess.' Then, in the waste land, a man was chopping a stump of eucalyptus; the tree had no arm left with which to shield itself, but its clean scent reeked into the air, and justified all the days of its youth. The blows rang sweetly. The man grew tired, and piling up brushwood set light to the tree, which with its leakage of resin helped the flames, and blazed up like a young Joan of Arc. The red hair of the fire poured backwards, the mare peered over, and Bede thought: 'How beautiful . . . how beautiful . . .'

She came into the Domain, and balanced on the stone brink of the pond to read again the bronze letters of the inscription, which she already knew by heart. The letters ran round a globe on which a mounted bronze Valkyrie straddled her horse, a horn at her lips.

'When the best of the earth are gathered, to know the Chooser's mind.' That was the inscription; the base of the Valkyrie statue was marble, and round it raced the naked snowy women on thick-buttocked snowy horses, hair and manes blown back to mingle. The water-lilies had sealed their rose and creamy buds, afternoon over them turning cold. One blue lily remained open, its stem flung up like the despairing arm of a suicide. Bede walked across grass rubbled with earth-worm casts, to stare again at marble Cain and Abel, though these too she knew like brothers. Abel, fallen with his head limp, looked such a little boy; Cain, enormous and despairing, towered over him, one wild hand imploring the skies to open and undo the results of a moment's temper. The sculptor had given him a sort of fleece instead of a fig-leaf, and Bede thought: 'Poor old Cain. Anyone so shaggy was bound to get into mischief.' Lichens rode sedately on the marble, green like water, green like old stained clothing, and the blackbirds were fond of Abel for their droppings. It was not very clean; Bede passed a pond where the brown water was wonderfully ruffled by ducks and swans who never dreamed of showing more than one black foot apiece; their bills were eager and used to visitors, and they expected bread. The mother swan hissed so violently that Bede would have bought her stale cakes at the Kiosk, but that cottage building was shut for Anzac Day.

She walked down on a slanting road, just at dusk, which meant that the colours were brown, thin green and blue: blue of mist, brown of those leaves so drily curled at their edges, green of sere grass which hardly patched the earth enough for warmth. The slantwise road became more human, having found houses. A wooden one with attic gables had been deserted so long that banksia rose had a stranglehold on its verandah, and the thick green boughs of its hedge laced the gate like the spears of mistrustful sentries. Inside Bede saw privet run wild, and two little smiling grubby statues, plaster girl and boy. She wished she could have lugged them home, for it must be wildly lonely there at night, much lonelier than her shack, and the children had only petals to kiss at best, or at worst wet slimy leaves.

Things she had always wanted: a rocking-chair, absolutely unlimited firelight playing snakes and ladders, golden processions of Chinese dragons along a wall, a small statue of Persephone (only nobody had made it yet) and some kind of instrument with a delicate voice, perhaps a spinet, or a minor piano with green silk behind its rosewood fretwork. Oh, and a cat: but to keep a cat at her shack, with no fireplace and all those ganders, was asking for scenes. Rather watered-down, vinaigrette tastes, really: but what did one expect, when the senses became too acute for heavier company to be borne?

On a stone wall where red creeper was beaded like strands of coral, the sparrows clung holding with their claws to the vertical face; when the impulse seized them, they did not fly, they fell down, and God saw them as was promised in the Bible, for the little invisible palms of the air cupped under them and bore them up, until with a ruffle of chestnut feathers they were mounted again. Bede wanted to say to a cyclist who had a bread-basket at the rear of his slim machine: 'Look, aren't they like coral beads and walnut shells?' but the youth, who was probably getting depression wages, fifteen shillings a week and find your own bicycle, did not look affable. Over a gate a little further on leaned a girl of perhaps twenty-three, with the most beautiful face Bede had ever seen. Her hair, pale red, waved and was cut to guard her head to the chin, like a helmet. She wore a blue jersey, and her greenish eyes, staring at the houses opposite, had an intensely dreamy expression. Love deluged them, and twilight, and being a young woman, and hearing the fine crack of a twig that reluctantly parts with its leaf.

I know you: I know you. Instead of passing, the others will turn in at your gate, sit down in your parlour, measure your proportions of mind and body, and make themselves comfortable. You will love them for the time, because we've got to eat, haven't we Sister? But will anyone know you as I know you?

Bede passed by, and was in streets ordinarily crowded, but today chastened as if for Sabbath; liked the great calico banner sprawled across one chemist's window: 'Influenza Is Dangerous — Don't Die'; wondered that there should really be a herbalist named Mr. Bottles; saw a polar bear rampant, if a bit decayed, in a furrier's window, and heard behind the shutters of an animal shop the fairy snarling of hundreds of caged-in, cross, tirelessly talkative little shell parrots, Cambridge or Oxford blue, green or pale yellow. They were the same breed as young Captain Burton's Frenchwoman's lovebird. Captain Burton . . . what in the world could have happened to Captain Burton? She didn't know, but saw in an antique shop a quite attractive set of painted wooden Apostles, looking like degenerates from the Balkans, and only five bob the set. Even so, she couldn't afford them.

What had happened to the army nurses she knew. They were mixed in the crowd, some prosperous, some shabby, seedy and anonymous-looking. Twice a year they held a reunion at the Lyceum Club . . . women with funny hats and babies. They looked so tired, so old. Everybody grows old, but Bede didn't want to commit herself to age until she was worn out looking for the man she had lost in the war.

The right-of-way on which her shack bordered was a grass track, in wet weather a sea of mud. She shone her torch on it, going down, and was ever so pleased to see a baby hedgehog. She picked it up before it could curl; instantly its soft paws and belly closed like a sea anemone round her hand, and its underneath was wet from trundling about in the grass.

'I wouldn't hurt you, Joey,' she soothed it. 'Of course you know that. I wouldn't hurt you.' She took it into her shack, but the light froze it stiff. After a moment it uncurled and began to scratch at the wall. She knew it would never burrow back to happiness there, so after spilling a lot of milk on the floor, trying to persuade it to drink from a saucer, she carried it out again. Between one flash of her torch and another, the baby had disappeared. She left the saucer outside, went in, and read the *Communist Manifesto*, with six prefaces by Engels. It convinced and depressed her. The Communists — Brigadier, *vous avez raison*; but what the devil were they going to do with people like herself, riddled with good intentions and emotions, like old ships riddled with rats? Oh, well: she supposed they might sink her for a breakwater somewhere, and anyhow, the individual was not proving so important. Certainly she liked the Communists much better than their opposite extreme.

In the morning the saucer was empty; whether the baby or the old woman's ganders had drunk the milk she did not know. She regretted not having been able to keep the baby.

(1938)

JEAN DEVANNY

Chapter XIV from
The Butcher Shop

Margaret thought a lot about Messenger's return, but without alarm. Not with joyousness, of course, but with loyal fairness she fought away unworthy wishes.

Unlike Glengarry, she felt no regret at the turn affairs had taken, because, unlike him again, she had no thought of depriving Messenger of anything. Truly, the possibility of loss to Messenger because of her love did not occur to her. She would have shrunk with horror from the thought. Barry still ranked supreme in her estimation. This new man was her lover, but his attitude towards their love had at once placed him inferior to Barry. Love, to her simple naturalness, was a transcendent thing brooking no consideration of such things as station 'hands'.

She accepted the fact that the man was of a piece with the world he knew and lived in. She gave his vulgarity contemptuous toleration, even saw the expediency of his attitude; but nevertheless she inevitably made comparisons with the result that Glengarry suffered. Barry and she dwelt together equals. Though Margaret had never consciously told herself of her utter trustworthiness, the whole fabric of her was saturated with the essence of the thing itself. 'To let a person down', as she would have expressed it in her own boyish way, was the unpardonable and unthinkable crime.

Messenger was pure. He was the last word in trustworthiness. In the disagreements the two had had, in the quarrels, hearty enough sometimes, which had embroidered the early years of their married life, neither had failed the other. In the pettiest of things as in the big issues of their life together each had found the other dependable. Disagreement and quarrels there might be, but never even a bordering on the unworthy. Margaret would have veritably staked her life with a laugh on Barry's probity, and, had she considered the matter, she would have known the same of him in regard to her.

But Glengarry had, to her simple though true intuitions, shown a canker at the core. He had done wrong. He had transgressed his own code of honour. Not one carking thought had she had regarding the right or wrong of this love affair of theirs, once her physical weakness had betrayed her into his arms. Her kind was such that had she believed him to have wronged her she would have killed him — or herself. She could not have survived the realisation that she had 'let a man down'. This, to her, was not a question of honour but of nature. Natural laws transcended man's. Why, but for this man's coming she would have gone through life unknowing the ecstasies of love's communion. Men were not so barbarous, surely, that they would deny to a woman that knowledge and experience? Would Barry be so barbarous as to deny her the fullness of life he had known himself?

For she knew that this love and ecstasy she enjoyed with Glengarry was the same emotion she had wondered at in Barry himself in his union with her. She realised the pity of it from Barry's point of view. How wonderful for them both if she had responded to her husband instead of to this new man who resembled Barry so in appearance and manner! But one could only take what life offered. That was, so long as one took without pain to others. Any other acceptance did not occur to her.

The canker she saw in Glengarry impressed her fairly. He was not utterly dependable. His actions could not be anticipated. She saw the possibility in him of 'letting her down', or Barry, which came to the same thing with her.

She thought continually of Barry's return, therefore, even though without alarm. She would not renounce Glengarry. That was too much; it would destroy her. But they must be secretive. She hated that. It was abominable, but Barry must be preserved from pain and the children must be considered. Her bonny bairns must lose nothing whatever to supply their mother's want. She was not gross, this Margaret. Newly awakened to love's fervour, she must necessarily appreciate it, but more than the sex-embrace by far to her was the loved one's presence.

Of course she did not take the man himself enough into account. If necessary, she would content herself with his nearness, with his daily companionship. To have him at her table, within her sight, would satisfy her if necessary, though there would surely arise occasions when they could be alone. (Barry would often travel now.)

She did not think, during these soliloquies of hers, that the man was made of quite different stuff.

She was not *frightened* of Barry knowing. She had no fear of him misunderstanding, though the subject of marital infidelity had never been discussed by them. But instinctively she knew that the knowledge would mean terrible suffering for him. She knew that his only thought would be of self-sacrifice.

The weather held fine day after day, so that it was easy enough for her to meet Glengarry at one or other of the thick copses that were scattered among the hills of Maunganui. The secrecy never became less hateful to her, but so glamorous was her time of love that she pushed all thought of the obnoxious thing away. Her love was all-powerful. She longed to be for ever at his side. She bloomed entrancingly. Love fulfilled its mission and drew out the richness of her personality until she was in love with all mankind. Her health improved. Her pale skin glowed with life. Her strong body took on new vigour. So gracious was her demeanour to all around her that her small world was at her feet.

Glengarry's spirit wilted before her. Instead of exhaustion his love flamed higher, though he learned to keep some sort of control over it. Her attitude towards her children intrigued and maddened him. There seemed no limit to her bounty. He was jealous of the children, of her pride in them and her care and thought for them. She talked to him about the children as though they were his, and decency compelled him to meet her on that ground. Small Margaret added him to her list of heroes, and indeed all the children liked him.

He was torn with conflicting emotions. Margaret never guessed at what the taciturn, dour Scotsman was going through. She suckled her baby each evening before him, most modestly, but still she did it, and at such times the anguish of his spirit, clamouring for fatherhood of her children, almost wrecked him. His health suffered. Matter fell before the onslaughts of the mind; as she gathered physical strength he lost it.

And he knew that Tutaki suspected. He knew that Margaret was too guileless. He was jealous of Tutaki too. At times he thought that he would go mad, and almost hoped for Messenger's return so the thing could be settled one way or the other. Yet he would not allow Margaret to talk of Barry's return. She thought he was boorish when mostly it was fear that bade him tie her tongue.

She saw that the matter must be discussed and some readjustment made. So did he, but he was frightened to face the issue. He could not blind himself to her attitude of mind, thought it was unexpressed. 'By and by,' he would say impatiently when she mentioned it.

Then came a telegram one day. The house party were at tea when Margaret was called to the telephone. Telegrams were always forwarded from Taihape in that manner.

Barry would arrive home on the morrow, which was a Saturday. Margaret bravely pretended to herself that she was glad. She walked back to the dining-room slowly, and on opening the door immediately said: 'Daddy will be home tomorrow, children.'

An outcry of delight from the little ones, especially from small Margaret.

Margaret sat down and for an instant her eyes met Glengarry's. She was shocked. His face was white, his eyes were pitiful. She had a mad impulse to rush to him and comfort him. She half rose. Tutaki, who always sat on her right, leant over and tapped her arm with a finger. 'Some more ham, please, Lady,' he said softly, but his eyes were cold as ice.

She fell back and recovered herself, met his eyes squarely and — lied. 'I left my handkerchief at the phone,' she said, helped him to some ham, and then left the room for an instant, returning with her handkerchief in her hand.

As soon as the meal was finished, Tutaki took up his cap. Usually he played with the children for a while after tea. 'Come for a walk,

Glengarry?' he asked casually.

Margaret looked up, startled. It was the first time Jimmy had evinced any desire for the manager's company.

Glengarry was glad to say 'Yes'. He was in agony. Not until the blow had fallen had he realised what Messenger's return would mean to him. Tomorrow she would be the other man's. That awful tearing flame at his heart! His stomach had turned to water. He felt like a doddering old man. He was sick. He rested his head on his hand, half shielding his face. An excuse to get away! To master that awful sickness in his stomach. 'Yes, I'll come,' he answered Tutaki, and left the room through the window without glancing at the woman.

That upset her. She trembled with dread. What, oh what would happen? Something here she could not fathom. Jealousy? What did she know of jealousy outside the pages of novels? No faintest breath of it had reached her world. She took up her babe, as usual, but her spirits sank lower as the minutes passed by and Glengarry did not return. The last evening, and at ten o'clock he had not returned.

All but she were soundly sleeping at nine. She sat in a big armchair with a book in her lap, trying vainly to read. Surely he would come the last night. Other nights her difficulty had been to restrain him. But he saw her there waiting for him. He stood on the lawn among the shrubs watching her and fighting. His soul had withered before the scorn in Tutaki's voice and bearing; he had writhed before the contempt of the brown man. To be despised by 'a bloody nigger!' The phrase came to his lips repeatedly. He cared nothing for Tutaki's threat. 'Every man on the station loves her. I worship the ground she walks on. Messenger only lives for her, and Messenger is my friend. Keep away. She is only a child, really. I know her. If you bring trouble on her I'll put a bullet through you. By the Holy Christ I swear it!'

So Tutaki had spoken. Bravely, Glengarry knew, for his great strength could have beaten the life from the slim brown man without effort. With the threat Tutaki had left him. They had been standing among the cattle pens.

And he had then walked. Anywhere, everywhere, trying to bring order out of the chaos of his thoughts. He had to decide something. He saw through Tutaki's eyes the unworthiness of the course he had decided on. He laughed grimly at the idea of 'a nigger' influencing him. Really it was not Tutaki, but the conventions and reasons laid bare to him by Tutaki that influenced him. After a time his thoughts became ordered enough for him to realise the bedrock issue and face it. He was conventional. Margaret was not. She was natural. He saw that she would accept what to her was the inevitable, and go on with her life on the station sharing with him whatever luck circumstances might afford them. And she would lose not one jot of her mental and moral beauty. Surely she was the most glorious woman in the world! A wonder woman! He thought of her queenly attitudes, of body and of mind; the exquisite bounty of her love, tendered to him always with the same shy, charming dignity that could emanate only from a sense of righteousness.

But he was conventional, of a pattern with the world of men as he knew it. He saw his own actions as Tutaki and others would see them. The right way for the woman was for him the blackguardly way. He could not blind himself, in those moments of honest self-communion, to the fact that she would never leave the children; would never deprive the other man of them nor them of their father. He knew now how they loved their father; he saw by now how fine the other man must be by his reflection mirrored. in his wife and children. The issue for him was plain. He grasped at it fiercely, to wrestle with it and be done. Once his path was chosen — To give her up entirely and merit his own and Tutaki's respect (unconsciously Tutaki had assumed in his mind the dimensions of the world at large), or carry on in secret with his mind a cesspit of guilt and shame?

He was stumbling back towards the house in the darkness, still undecided, when he again met Tutaki, who had been attending to a sick dog. He lurched up against him. Before he had not replied one word to the brown man's accusation. What prompted him to speak now? Perhaps a desire to excuse himself; perhaps a wild hope that the other man had not understood, and might modify his indictment somewhat. Tutaki had spoken as though believing him to be a common marauder. (Glengarry had forgotten his mad outrage of that first night: he remembered only her freely given embraces since.) He lurched against Tutaki and flung at him: 'She loves me! Do you hear? She loves me as much as I love her. I'm no common seducer!'

The other answered him softly. 'That is all the more reason why you should protect her. She is weak. You must protect her against herself. There are the children to consider.'

Worse still! No help, no escape from that bedrock issue. He stood on the lawn watching her through the uncovered windows and fought it out. He knew that she was waiting for him. Her face was hidden from him, but he could see her restless movements. Until the clock struck ten; thereafter she sat still. At half-past ten she rose from her chair and stood for some time with clasped hands looking down. Her whole aspect betokened profound trouble. The man had moved close to the windows. He saw her clearly. Then she made a slow move to leave the room. He lifted the window catch and pushed one door open. She flung round, radiant on the instant and clasped her hands upon her breast. 'I thought you were not coming,' she breathed. 'Why, oh why were you so long tonight?'

He was merciless. He had to be. Straight to the point he plunged, giving no quarter because he dared not. 'Look here, my dear, Messenger comes home tomorrow, so we are going to cut it.'

Her hands dropped to her sides, her eyelids fluttered. She heard the rush of blood from her head and limbs; she felt it congeal there and become a leaden weight. 'What do you mean?'

'What I say. Your husband returns tomorrow. That's the end of this business.'

She looked around wildly for support. Every word was like a physical blow. He saw she was about to fall, and leapt to her. He lifted her to an armchair. She leaned back with closed eyes trying to think. He dropped on his knees beside her and pressed his face against her. She heard him groan. It revived her. She opened her eyes, ruffled his hair with her fingers, then leant over and crushed him to her. 'Why did you frighten me so? Why say such terrible things? You nearly killed me.'

He drew away from her embrace. 'It is true. It has got to end. I couldn't be such a blackguard.'

She thought quietly. 'I don't understand you, quite. Would you feel a blackguard to love me when Barry was home?'

'Yes, I would be a blackguard. I'll go away as soon as I can decently manage it.'

'Go away! Go away! Oh no, never that! Never that! I should die!'

'Well, what else? Oh, Margaret, come with me! Come away with me! I can't live without you!'

'That is impossible,' she answered quietly. 'You know that. Let me think.'

The woman strove to get his point of view, fought to make him see her own. She succeeded. His conventional reasoning nauseated her. 'According to your reasoning I have no right to have a say in this matter at all. What I think, what I feel, has no claim to consideration with you.'

'You are married,' he urged. 'You have a husband and children.

'I have also a human heart, which is filled with love for you. You think that my married state gives my husband and my children the power of life and death over me. What am I, then? What am I in your eyes, eh? A machine, just the female of the species to be caged up, a breeding animal denied even the right to choose my own mate! Get away! You outrage my womanhood!' She pushed him back.

He rose to his feet and stood looking down on her in perplexed misery. She softened. 'Why, dear, even the courts of law would not be so barbarous. And as for Barry — You don't know Barry.'

'What about Barry? What do you think Barry would say to this affair?' he asked curiously.

'Barry would think only of me. I know it. He would think of nothing but self-sacrifice. And that is why he is not to know.'

'Yes, that is just it. You realise that he could never share you with another man, don't you? He would sacrifice himself for your happiness! What about me? You think you can make love to me and keep Barry in ignorance, but you can't keep me in ignorance of the fact that you are living with him. I can't share you, either.'

She stared at him wide-eyed. 'That is another point of view. That is not what you said before. I don't see why you should mind Barry. He is my husband. (He laughed grimly.) You know my situation. You must make the best of it. You are not very reasonable.'

'Reasonable! Are you a child to talk of reason in relation to things of this kind? I can't make you out, anyhow. How you can go on living with him when you love me as you do beats me.'

She regarded him intently. 'Don't you know?' She leant towards him earnestly. 'If you can't imagine why, I don't think I can make you understand. I'm sure Barry would understand were he in your place.'

He moved impatiently, and his voice was full of jealousy. 'Oh, yes, of course he would. You are always throwing your Barry at me. I wonder you give a thought to me when such a paragon is at your feet.'

Her brows contracted. 'Don't, Glen, that is not fair.' She rose. 'I wish I had not loved you. Now for the first time I wish you had not come here. You are going to make it hard. I can see that you are going to create difficulties where none exist. You know how involved my situation is. Certain duties I must perform or become a bad woman. To place my own happiness before the welfare of my children would be unthinkable, criminal. But I have a right to my happiness if I can get it without harming others. Every woman must have the right to consummate the greatest love of her life.' She paused, thinking. And Glengarry stared at her in wonder at her beauty. She looked virginal, somehow. He knew that her mind was virginal. How many times had she shamed him for his grossness? She turned her eyes on him and asked: 'Am I a bad or a good influence, for you?'

'Good! Good!' he answered quickly. Then took her hand and kissed it. 'Oh, Margaret, I appreciate the honour you have done me. Surely you know that. But now I must play the man. I must protect you in spite of yourself.'

She smiled faintly. 'How protect me, Glen? By killing me? You have the chance to make me happy. You know how happy I have been lately, don't you? And because I have been happy my children and all around me have been happy too. This can continue. Of course we must restrain ourselves. We cannot see much of each other alone, but there will always be the chance to keep us happy, and we can feel secure in each other's love. On the other hand you can "protect" me. You can go away from me; take the sunshine out of my life and leave me a wrecked woman. This love I feel for you is — is all of me. It is the best thing in me, the grandest thing in my life. It would be my pride to keep it clean. And you, Glen, you have many nasty little habits and faults. I hope to eradicate them and make you the cleanest man.'

She smiled at him.

He braced himself unconsciously. Always she had that effect upon him now. His first attitude of 'bossiness' had departed. Once he had told her ruefully that she would make a saint of the devil himself. For mere virtue's sake she had taught him self-control, and he had found his reward in the exquisite bounty of her love when at last given.

'Come, Glen, will you leave me?' She stood smiling into his eyes.

'I feel, Margaret, that I should go.' He spoke very slowly. 'I can't trust myself.' He flung away from her and walked quickly up and down the room, then stopped in front of her again. 'I can't trust myself. I would do anything in the world for you, but —' He finished fiercely — 'if I saw another man fondling you I believe I would kill him.'

She was completely disconcerted. They could only stare at each other hopelessly. Then anger flared up within her. She beat her breasts with her hands. 'Why? Why? Oh, you men! Are you all grossness and brutality and jealousy? What is this jealousy that it makes men mad?' She began to cry.

He was unmanned; against his better judgment he gave in. Her tears drew the very heart out of him. She became submissive. 'If you must go, Glen, I'll try to bear it. I'll try, but I know I'll die.'

What man could have resisted? Reason could not have moved him. Stark naked feeling could refute the results of the finest reasoning but her tears, her submissiveness! His defences crumbled in a twinkling. He was left with none. 'I'll never leave you, Margaret, if you want me. I swear it. But you know that people will guess. There will be talk. Tutaki knows now.'

'But they will be loyal to me, Glen, I'm sure. Oh, Glen, I feel I'm right. I know I'm right. If there is any part of God in me that part is speaking now. We are before all things human beings. My womanhood demands its right. We have only a few years to live. We come on the earth through no wish of our own, and go off it the same. We are such infinitesimal things, we poor little humans, and yet so colossal is our vanity that we even dare to lord it over the instinct of Creation.

'You like to think that you are trying to be good, don't you, dear? You like to think that you are trying to be manly and protect me, when what you are really doing is waging the sex-war; you have tried to conserve the rights of the male over the female; despite your love, you have been taking sides with your sex because, unconsciously, you realised the danger to male prerogatives if the female is allowed to assume the attributes of a human being, of your equal.

'Oh, you need not stare so. I can see it. Your goodness is all a sham, Glen. You are only — only what Jack London calls class-conscious. You love me, but you regard me, nevertheless, as an inferior. Never mind protesting. I know that you don't realise it. You are not too intelligent. I found that out long ago. (She caressed him to take the sting out of her words.) You know that I, the individual, am your equal, but you can't separate the individual from the class. As woman I must submit myself to the man who is my keeper, for the sake of preserving male prerogatives. You, by encroaching upon another man's preserves, felt yourself a traitor to your class. I see; I see. I have learned a lot tonight. Really you are my enemy — All men are my enemies.'

(1926)

GREVILLE TEXIDOR

An Annual Affair

It almost seemed to be blowing up for rain. Every minute or two the wind came across the paddocks, like a lorry changing gears, and round the lonely store corner. The store looked lonely because it was closed for Boxing Day. The orange drinks and weeties in the window and the country scene with stout letters, KEEP FIT, cutting across made you feel sad, as if you had eaten too much. The wallops from the wind made you feel tired. Joy sat on the step of the store.

Come on, get up now, her Mum said. You don't want to dirty your dress before we start.

Joy got up. The wind passed again blowing up dust and rain. It was late. It was nearly nine. Mum reckoned Auntie Laurel was holding them up.

Before the lorry came round the corner, they could hear the kids screeching. It was like a cage of cockatoos on wheels. Uncle Nick was in front with Dad. Behind, besides the kids, there was Auntie Laurel and a flash lady from town. She had brought something for the children for Boxing Day. It was some crackers, but they couldn't pull them because Mum said it wasn't the proper time. Mum didn't think much of crackers.

The Domain in front of the hotel was packed out with cars and lorries. Dad growled because the place near the fence where they always parked, was taken. Mum only said, I thought we were going to be late. The cars looked funny all packed round the hotel because there was plenty of room along the beach. The hotel stood by itself away from the baches. It was tall and a dark red colour like the one in Joy's Granny's picture *The Broad Way*. They didn't have pictures like that in Joy's home. They had one of a bunch of pansies and one of a cathedral. In Granny's picture the hotel had a Union Jack on top and through the windows you could see the people inside, playing cards and dancing. But the real hotel windows were always closed. It looked as if nobody lived there, but round at the side there was a small door and men going in and out.

The old jetty was standing over the mud with only its last two legs in the water. Brian and the boys made a dash for the trolley, that was used for loading timber in the old days, and started to push each other up and down, but Mum yelled to them that they'd fall in the water, and Auntie Laurel said the jetty was dangerous and ought to be seen to.

Mum and Dad and Miss Jenkins, the flash lady, sat down on the step of the lorry. Miss Jenkins had several rows of rolls on top of her head, and slacks which were tight behind, and dark red fingernails. She said how pretty everything looked after the rain.

Dad kept looking hard at Miss Jenkins's fingernails, then looking away.

Everyone seems to think it's nice down here in the summer, Mum said, of course we're used to it.

I suppose you always come here, Miss Jenkins said.

We always manage to get down for the picnic, Dad said. It's an annual affair.

Mum said, It looks as if we've been unlucky with the weather though.

Dad said, It's generally like this round about Christmas.

But anyway, Mum said, it does make a change and the kiddies do enjoy it.

Dad took out his cigarette case and offered Miss Jenkins one but she said, No thanks. She did occasionally, but not just now.

Dad said, Excuse me, he had to meet a chap, and went over towards the hotel.

It began to rain a bit and the wind was chilly. Mum said they might as well go for a walk as it wasn't lunch time yet, and Miss Jenkins could see the view from further up. Everyone always said it was rather nice, only of course the tide was wrong now.

Joy had to fetch Terry and Mavis. Mum was nervous about them falling into the mud. They were right at the end of the jetty pretending to fish. Jim was there too, he had rigged up the lines for them.

Jim didn't come round to Joy's place any more. Dad reckoned that scholarship he won hadn't done him much good. He had just picked up a lot of weird ideas and was always slinging off at everything. Dad would say, Where's the Red Flag? And Jim couldn't be bothered with Dad, so he didn't come round any more.

But the first Christmas Joy could remember he was there, and gave her a bell that was meant to be put on a tree and soon got broken. What she remembered about Christmas was the colour of the bell. Auntie Laurel said that it was a nile green, but it wasn't at all like a nile green dress Joy had. She never could get it with her paints either, so after the bell was broken she never saw that particular colour again.

They had the socials at the station hall then, and Mum and Dad still went out together sometimes, and the imaginary man came at night to keep away danger. He wore historical clothes and was called Mr Charles but he looked very like Jim.

And after that nothing much except the picnics. Jim went away to the town and didn't come home very often. He was saving up for a trip to Europe, he said.

The kids didn't want to stop fishing, and Joy had to promise they could come back later on. I'll be seeing you later on, she said to Jim.

With Terry and Mavis dragging behind they walked along past the baches. The baches were mostly empty, and as they hadn't been painted for years, were greyish-white like the sky.

The Dacres were coming. They talked away to each other looking along the ground, not seeing Mum and her friend till they got quite close. Then they stopped and smiled and were introduced to Miss Jenkins. They said the glass had gone up quite a bit this morning. When the Dacres were out of sight Miss Jenkins said she *would* like a smoke now, so Mum suggested they climb up the bank and sit under the pines where they would be sheltered from the drizzle and not be seen. Mavis slipped down the bank and dirtied herself but Mum was quite calm about it. She had brought another dress and panties for Mavis to change to for afternoon tea.

You keep them so nice, Miss Jenkins said with a smile.

When they got back to the lorry it was lunchtime. Auntie Laurel was there with the rest of the kids, waiting. She said she hadn't seen Uncle Nick all morning. He's always Hail fellow well met, she explained to Miss Jenkins.

They sat on the grass on coats and macs. Mum took off her hat with the felt feather. Whew, isn't it hot, she said. The sun had come out and it was stifling hot between the cars. Mum unpacked the peanut-butter sandwiches, and the date scones she had baked on the Happywork stove Dad gave her for Christmas. Well we might as well start, she said, as Dad hasn't come. She sent Brian off for the hot water from Mrs Withers. Then she passed the scones to Miss Jenkins. I baked them before we started this morning, she said.

Miss Jenkins took one. Oh aren't you clever, she said. I must confess I often pop round to the Cosy Cake Shop for scones and things, you know how it is in the city. She didn't look at all ashamed of it though.

They say our baker bakes a fair fruit cake, Mum said, but I prefer my own. You know what's in it.

I suppose you do, Miss Jenkins said.

Dad came and sat down and started fooling with Terry, turning him over and pretending to smack him. Terry didn't know what to make of it but he laughed till he turned red and hiccoughed. Dad had red patches on his cheeks and his eyes were swimmy.

Brian came back with the teapot. In his other hand he carried the broken off spout wrapped in a handkerchief. Mum couldn't let fly at him with Mrs Jenkins there. Dad took it as a joke.

The tea was terribly strong and Miss Jenkins said, Couldn't we borrow some hot water from the hotel? But Mum said, I don't care about asking favours when we don't know them.

You needn't trouble for me, Dad said. He wouldn't have a scone either. He ate one sandwich quickly, then started telling one of his funny stories to Miss Jenkins. He said he knew some better ones than that, but he didn't think he could tell them. This made Miss Jenkins laugh but Mum was rather quiet. She was handing round some of the Christmas cake. This year it had white water-icing and desiccated coconut, but as Mum said herself it had turned out rather plain. No one took any. Terry was being a bad boy because Dad had been taking notice of him, he was wanting his banana now, but Mum said, No, you know they're for later on. But he howled so loud she had to give him one and then the other kids grabbed bananas too out of Mum's bag, which was bulging with bathing togs and things to change and knitting and Miss Jenkins's *Gone with the Wind*, and other things for later on, and ran off to the shore. Mum called after them not to play in the mud and not to go on the jetty.

Miss Jenkins said she'd had such a lovely lunch and she thought she'd retire to the lorry and have a smoke. Dad offered to go along with her. Only in fun of course.

Pull your skirt down a bit Joy, Mum said. The Reverend Allum was walking over their way. He sat down on the grass beside Joy and smiled all round. He always smiled in a special way as if he were much happier than everyone else. Joy looked away so as not to be hooked with his smile and be asked something. She'd been in his bad books since she let out that she was reading the Bible verses at night. The verses to be read were marked on the card and if you were regular you could get right through the Bible in five years. Only the morning wasn't really a good time, Mum was tired after having done so much before breakfast, and the kids had to be got off to school. But the verses are your armour for the day, the Reverend Allum had said. You wouldn't put on your armour when you lie down to sleep would you now? Whoever heard of such a thing as that?

Do have some tea, Mum said, it's rather thick I'm afraid.

Thanks but I've had a cup with Mrs Withers, people are so hospitable. I only wanted to enquire about your little laddie. The one who wasn't at Sunday School last week.

It was only a cold, Mum said, but they hate to miss. It's nice for the kiddies having the Sunday School so near.

Yes and for Mum and Dad too, Joy was thinking, they can have a lie down on Sunday afternoons.

Miss Jenkins came out of the lorry and was introduced. Dad stretched out his legs on the grass till his foot was touching hers, then said, Oh, beg pardon.

Quite a good crowd down here today, Mum said. But the Reverend Allum's smile was for Miss Jenkins.

I expect you must find it pretty quiet, he said.

Oh no, she said, I love a day in the country.

You're right too, the Reverend Allum said. When she was younger Joy had used to think that when the Reverend Allum said You're right too, she'd hit upon something clever. It always turned out though, when he'd enlarged on it, that it wasn't what she had said after all.

The Reverend Allum took a deep breath in and a long look all round him. Yes, he said, on the out-going breath, when all's said and done nature takes a lot of beating. Jim was walking past, carrying a bottle with a straw stuck in it. They all looked away and pretended they hadn't noticed but Auntie Laurel said quietly to Mum, Fancy bringing it out here, where everyone's having their lunch.

But the Reverend Allum went on as though nothing had happened. We country-dwellers now, I sometimes think we're apt to forget perhaps. He looked all round him again. His all-embracing glance skipped the hotel and threaded its way through the cars to the strip of shore. The tide was nearly out. There was only a grey snake of water in the channel, and the steep mud-slopes were steaming off in the sun.

Yes, it's a pity Muriel and Winnie couldn't get down, Mum said. They've been in hospital with their appendixes, she explained to Miss Jenkins. Doctor thought they might as well have them done together and get it over.

Yes, we only see the sunny side of life over here, the Reverend Allum said. It's difficult to imagine what it must be like over there.

Dad had his eyes closed and a dribble of spit on his chin. Joy gave him a quiet agonised poke and he opened his eyes and smiled, looking like Terry. Mum was getting on with her fancy work. Yes. Quite a good crowd here today, she said, but a lot of them have to leave early for the milking.

I don't know what others' opinions may be, said the Reverend Allum, but personally Miss Jenkins, I like to think of this little affair as a sort of commemoration. The settlers in these parts landed here. Quite near where we are sitting now I believe.

There wasn't anything here then, Mum said, her eyes on the hotel.

The settlers had faith, said the Reverend.

Too right, said Miss Jenkins, putting her hand to a yawn.

Dad had found a pair of pink art silk panties that Mavis had had for Christmas. They had been in Mum's bag for Mavis to change to. Dad kept holding them up and squinting between the legs in a comical way. The Reverend Allum went right on about the settler who had stuck in the mud and they never found the body, but Joy felt hot all over. As if somethink awful might happen. She got up, quietly and walked away to be out of sight of Dad and the lot of them.

She said hello to the Dodds, the Band of Hope Dodds, they always came early and got the best place nearest to the hotel, and went round to the yard. The hotel backed on to the shore and the yard was quiet and secluded, with empty cases to sit on and a nice view over the inlet. Jim was there smoking a cigarette with the cider bottle and the straw beside him.

Hello, she said, what are you doing here?

Oh, nothing, he said.

I thought maybe you had a date.

Who with? he said.

Joy pulled little bits off the straw, wanting to cry. Mum had stuck to it that the navy was just as smart and safer for washing, and the perm she could have next year when she worked at the store. Next year it would be all too late. The other girls had florals, the kind with elastic round the waist that fits almost anyone, and their hair nicely set with steel clips, and invisible hairnets. Merle had blossomed out with lipstick too, but really it didn't look so hot with her pimples.

Cheer up, Jim said. How's old stick in the mud?

As usual, Joy said, he's on the settlers again.

And your Dad and the others?

As usual, she said. Dad's had a few of course. You know what he always says, It's a free country.

The curfew shall not ring, but Dad shall turn the wringer tomorrow. He'll have to take his headache to church as well.

Jim was always making fun of Dad and Mum. It wasn't true either, Dad didn't go to church any more. There was only the wringer. It was always like that with Jim. Just as you were settling for a nice yarn he would start slinging off at Dad, or his Dad, or the capitalist system, so that it never came to anything. Still, of course, there would never be anyone else.

It was sunny and quiet in the yard. The people walking up and down, up and down, between the hotel and jetty, stopped and turned back where the metalled path ended. Joy moved along closer to Jim on the box. The people seemed far away. It had to happen then that Murrey popped his head over the fence, grinning at them, showing his black stumps. A horrible boy Murrey, with filthy tricks.

It's only Murrey, Joy said. He'll be having his new teeth when he leaves school, his mother says.

The big thrill that only comes once in a lifetime. Well, my big thrill will be getting out of this. I might get my trip to Europe after all.

More likely land up in the desert though, Joy said. Why couldn't you help your Dad milking and get exempted? You don't want to go and get killed do you?

Get killed for these stick in the muds? But you have to think of the future. A lot of chaps are relieved to get into camp. It's a change from mowing the lawn and all that. It's going to be more of a change than they think though. A change is going on all over the world. Before the war governments had to make camps because the prisons couldn't hold the political prisoners. It's never happened like that before. The bosses are hoping it will blow over, the war will give people something else to do. It was only the old red spectre walking again, they think. But the change that is coming is rising like the tide. It will reach even this little place one day. But I'm going to be on the spot when the big things happen. You have to think of the future.

Joy was looking at the hills across the inlet, not thinking of the future, thinking the hills looked empty and strange today. She had always meant to go over there some time. It looked lonely, but pretty and peaceful, the grass a soft green, not the metal green of the properly fertilised paddocks, the hills split softly into creeks full of scrub and shadows. There were Maori lands over there. Better than on our side, Dad said, they are dirty and carry diseases. There wouldn't be much to see over there, he said, but Joy had always wanted to go some time.

The sun was bright and a cool wind blew from the coast. It was a lovely day now. Cheer up, Jim said. Joy sat still, for fear of disturbing his hand settled on hers, feeling his cool fingers and the heat inside her hand where the straw was crushed.

A man came out of the hotel back door. He was little and sandy and walked slowly and sadly. He must have lost his way.

He crossed to a box and sat carefully down. Then he remembered something and got up again with a nervous look round the yard. He saw them but it was just too late by then. He took out his false teeth and was sick on the ground.

Joy got up. Jim said he'd have to be getting along too. Outside the yard they ran into the Young Men's Bible Class and the Reverend Allum in bathing togs. They were larking and making funny remarks like a boys' school story. Come along in and have a good swim, they shouted to Jim as they passed, it would do you good.

I'm afraid I haven't been introduced, Miss Jenkins said to Jim when she overtook them, but I've heard such a lot about you. Joy introduced them and she got confidential at once. Rather a queer idea for all the men to go in swimming together, Bible Class or no Bible Class, she said. And it was pretty hard to keep up a conversation with some people, and she asked him, had he read, *Gone with the Wind*?

Jim said, Well, yes, but he had to be going himself now. He started up his motor bike with a bang and rode off up the hill, the bike making scornful explosions.

After that there was nothing much to do. It began to rain again, and Mum sat on a box in the bathing shed with her fancy work, pegging away at the big rose in the middle she had promised herself she was going to finish today. Joy could see there was something wrong but Mum said it was only her legs.

They swelled up, generally in the evenings, about the time Dad came home, and she would say to him, Just look at my legs again, it's from being on them all day.

You must have got up too early, Miss Jenkins said.

Oh no, I always get up at five, Mum said. I like to get things done before breakfast.

It's a puzzle what you find to do all the rest of the day, Miss Jenkins said.

I find plenty to do thank you, Mum said, as if she'd been offered something she didn't like.

You must have a gift for it, Miss Jenkins said. And she laughed.

Like some people have a gift for fooling round with men, Mum said. Joy felt as if something horrid was going to happen. But Mum couldn't have meant Miss Jenkins.

The Bible Class was swimming still in the rain, and the other unmarried men must have been in the pub.

When it cleared up it was time to get Mavis changed and line up for the ice-cream. Mrs Dodds, Murrey's mother, and Mrs Chapman were doing the refreshments this year. Mrs Dodds always got first prize at the show with her sponge surprise, or else with her ginger kisses. But when Mum tasted the ice-cream she said there was nothing in it but those powders, and Auntie Laurel said, Mrs Dodds and Mrs Chapman might have put in a bit more sugar and a drop of cream for the kiddies. And only those cheap soft drinks.

The soft drinks were mixed in two kerosene tins. One of the drinks was red and the other green. There was plenty of it and some of the boys got as many as ten drinks. To end off with there was an orange, but Mum said that was extravagant at the price they were now.

Then Brian was sent to fetch the hot water again, and Mum and Miss Jenkins and Auntie Laurel had afternoon tea again with the rest of the Christmas cake. The kids hung round, pestering to go in swimming and Mum kept saying, No you might get in the current. You know you can't go without Dad.

Mrs Chapman passed with her husband. We're off home, she said.

You've got him well trained, Mum said. That was one of her jokes.

Terry getting sleepy, worrying to be taken notice of, was saying over and over again, Where's Dad?

Now what did you promise me this morning? Mum said. What am I going to tell Dad when he asks if Terry has been a good boy all day?

Daddy's having his tea somewhere, Miss Jenkins said.

But Terry said, I know where he might be. Drinking beer in the hotel.

Mum suddenly gave him such a crack on the side of the head that he couldn't even yell for a minute' or two.

The tide's about right in, Joy said. It made noises like smacking kisses under the banks where the kids were sitting looking down at the water. After a while Mum came over and said as the sun was going and Dad hadn't come yet, they could put on their togs. But they mustn't stay in for long, it was getting chilly. The boys rushed off to the shed to change. Joy and Mavis undressed in the lorry.

Terry stood on the bank and cried while the others were in. He hadn't been allowed to paddle because of his cold. The sun was off the water now but he cried so long that Mum undressed him and put on his bathing pants, but when he got down to the water he wouldn't go in.

Joy rubbed down Mavis and dressed herself quickly and walked away along the shore as if she were meeting someone. Passing the Withers she saw the dinghy tied to a post by the beach, and got in and let it drift into the mangroves. The wind had died down. It felt like a warm damp hand across her hair. The ugly old twisted mangrove trunks were all covered up and only the branches with dark green leaves were showing. The water made roads between the tops of the trees. Joy moved along the roads and little lanes till a branch scraped the bottom of the boat. Then it was not a road but only all that water underneath, enough to cover a tree.

She began to row out across the inlet. The sun had set and the valleys and creeks on the other side were smoothed out. The hills were black and flat, like the advertisement letters across the picture, painted across the sky for some reason.

When the boat swung in the current she turned. The kids had stopped shouting on the jetty and everything was quiet, and over towards the sea a crack in the sky opened into a still shiny lake, exactly the colour of the Christmas bell.

When Joy got back Brian and Mavis were sitting in the lorry because it was getting chilly, playing I Spy. Terry was asleep on the floor. He had a blue mark down the side of his face. Mum was walking up and down inside. She said Auntie Laurel and Miss Jenkins had gone home hours ago with somebody else.

It was quite dark when Dad came out at last. He said he had had to stay for Uncle Nick who was not feeling too good. Mum wanted to have it out with him but he only smiled. Might as well be the wind blowing, she said. But perhaps you'll be feeling differently tomorrow.

Mr Chapman, who hadn't gone home after all, sat in front with Dad. Uncle Nick was inside. He was carrying on about his kidneys, how bad they were, they didn't seem to get any better, he was sure he wouldn't pass the medical test, and everyone ought to do their bit, and the loved ones at home. He got so worked up about it he started to cry.

The kids feeling a bit awkward, piped up, *Roll out the Barrel, We'll have a Jolly Good Time*, just to change the subject. I wish it was next year, Brian said, for the picnic.

Joy said nothing, Brian was such a kid. He never stopped to think that everything might be different next year.

(1944)

NGAIO MARSH

Prologue from
Died in the Wool

1939

'I am Mrs Rubrick of Mount Moon,' said the golden-headed lady. 'And I should like to come in.'

The man at the stage-door looked down into her face. Its nose and eyes thrust out at him, pale, all of them, and flecked with brown. Seen at close quarters these features appeared to be slightly out of perspective. The rest of the face receded from them, fell away to insignificance. Even the mouth with its slightly projecting, its never quite hidden teeth, was forgotten in favour of that acquisitive nose, those protuberant exacting eyes. 'I should like to come in,' Flossie Rubrick repeated.

The man glanced over his shoulder into the hall. 'There are seats at the back,' he said. 'Behind the buyers' benches.'

'I know there are. But I don't want to see the backs of the buyers. I want to watch their faces. I'm Mrs Rubrick ôf Mount Moon and my wool clip should be coming up in the next half-hour. I want to sit up here somewhere.' She looked beyond the man at the door, through a pair of scenic book-wings to the stage where an auctioneer in shirt-sleeves sat at a high rostrum, gabbling. 'Just there,' said Flossie Rubrick, 'on that chair by those painted things. That will do quite well.' She moved past the man at the door. 'How do you do?' she said piercingly as she came face to face with a second figure. 'You don't mind if I come in, do you? I'm Mrs Arthur Rubrick. May I sit down?'

She settled herself on a chair she had chosen, pulling it forward until she could look through an open door in the proscenium and down into the front of the house. She was a tiny creature and it was a tall chair. Her feet scarcely reached the floor. The auctioneer's clerks, who sat below his rostrum, glanced up curiously from their papers.

'Lot one seven six,' gabbled the auctioneer. 'Mount Silver.'

'Eleven,' a voice shouted.

In the auditorium two men, their arms stretched rigid, sprang to their feet and screamed. 'Three!' Flossie settled her furs and looked at them with interest. 'Eleven-three,' said the auctioneer.

The chairs proper to the front of the hall had been replaced by rows of desks, each of which was labelled with the name of its occupant's firm. Van Huys. Riven Bros. Dubois. Yen. Steiner. James Ogden. Hartz. Ormerod. Rhodes. Markino. James Barnett. Dressed in businessmen's suits woven from good wool, the buyers had come in from the four corners of the world for the summer wool sales. They might have been carefully selected types, so eloquently did they display their nationality. Van Huys's buyer with his round wooden head and soft hat. Dubois's sleek, with a thin moustache and heavy grooves running from his nostrils to the corners of his mouth, old Jimmy Ormerod who bought for himself, screamed like a stallion, and turned purple in the face. Hartz with horn-rimmed glasses who barked, and Mr Kurata Kan or Markino's with his falsetto yelp. Each buyer held printed lists before him, and from time to time, like a well-trained chorus-ensemble, they would all turn a page. The auctioneer's recital was uninflected, and monotonous; yet, as if the buyers were marionettes and he their puppet-master, they would twitch into violent action and as suddenly return to their nervously intent immobility. Some holding the papers before their eyes, stood waiting for a particular wool-clip to come up. Others wrote at their desks. Each had trained himself to jerk in a flash from watchful relaxation into spread-eagled yelling urgency. Many of them smoked continuously and Flossie Rubrick saw them through drifts of blue tobacco clouds.

In the open doorways and under the gallery stood groups of men whose faces and hands were raddled and creased by the sun and whose clothes were those of the countryman in town. They were the wool-growers, the run-holders, the sheep-cockies, the back-countrymen. Upon the behaviour of the buyers their manner of living for the next twelve months would depend. The wool sale was what it all amounted to; long musters over high country, nights spent by shepherds in tin huts on mountain sides, late snows that came down into lambing paddocks, noisy rituals of dipping, crutching, shearing; the final down-country journey of the wool-bales — this was the brief and final comment on the sheep-man's working year.

Flossie saw her husband, Arthur Rubrick, standing in a doorway. She waved vigorously. The men who were with Arthur pointed her out. He gave her a dubious nod and began to make his way along a side aisle towards her. As soon as he reached the steps that led from the auditorium up to her doorway she called out in a sprightly manner. 'Look where I've got to! Come up and join me!' He did so but without enthusiasm.

'What are you doing up here, Floss?' he said, 'You ought to have gone down below.'

'Down below wouldn't suit me at all.'

'Everyone's looking at you.'

'That doesn't embarrass me,' she said loudly. 'When will he get to us, darling. Show me.'

'Ssh!' said her husband unhappily and handed her his catalogue. Flossie made play with her lorgnette. She flicked it open modishly with white-gloved hand and looked through it at the lists. There was a simultaneous flutter of white paper throughout the hall. 'Over we go, I see,' said Flossie and turned a page. 'Now, where are we?'

Her husband grunted urgently and jerked up his head.

'Lot one-eighty,' gabbled the auctioneer.

'Thirteen.'

'Half!' yelled old Ormerod.

'Three!'

'Fourteen!'

The spectacled Mr Kurata Kan was on his feet, yelping, a fraction of a second quicker than Ormerod.

'Top price,' cried Flossie shrilly. 'Top price! Isn't it, darling? We've got top price, haven't we? That dear little Jap!'

A ripple of laughter ran through the hall. The auctioneer grinned. The two men near the stage-door moved away, their hands over their mouths. Arthur Rubrick's face, habitually cyanosed, deepened to a richer purple. Flossie clapped her white gloves together and rose excitedly. 'Isn't he too sweet,' she demanded. 'Arthur, isn't he a pet?'

'Flossie, for God's sake,' Arthur Rubrick muttered.

But Flossie made a series of crisp little nods in the direction of Mr Kurata Kan and at last succeeded in attracting his attention. His eyelids creased, his upper lip lifted in a crescent over his long teeth and he bowed.

'There!' said Flossie in triumph as she swept out at the stage-door, followed by her discomforted husband. 'Isn't that splendid?'

He piloted her into a narrow yard. 'I wish you wouldn't make me quite so conspicuous, my dear,' he said. 'I mean, waving to that Jap. We don't know him or anything.'

'No,' cried Flossie. 'But we're going to. You're going to call on him, darling, and we shall ask him to Mount Moon for the weekend.'

'Oh, no, Flossie. Why? Why on earth?'

'I'm all for promoting friendly relations. Besides he's paid top price for my wool. He's a sensible man. I want to meet him.'

'Grinning little pip-squeak. I don't like 'em, Floss. Do you in the eye for tuppence, the Japs would. Any day. They're our natural enemies.'

'Darling, you're absolutely antediluvian. Before we know where we are you'll be talking about The Yellow Peril.'

She tossed her head and a lock of hair, dyed a brilliant gold, slipped down her forehead. 'Do remember this is 1939,' said Flossie.

1942

On a summer's day in February, 1942, Mr Sammy Joseph, buyer for Riven Brothers Textile Manufactory, was going through their wool stores with the storeman. The windows had been blacked out with paint, and the storeman, as they entered, switched on a solitary lamp. This had the effect of throwing into strong relief the square hessian bales immediately under the lamp. Farther down the store they dissolved in shadow. The lamp was high and encrusted with dust; the faces of the two men looked cadaverous. Their voices sounded stifled: there is no echo in a building lined with wool. The air was stuffy and smelt of hessian.

'When did we start buying dead wool, Mr Joseph?' asked the storeman.

'We never buy dead wool,' Joseph said sharply. 'What are you talking about?'

'There's a bale of it down at the far end.'

'Not in this store.'

'I'm good for a bet on it.'

'What's biting you? Why d'you say it's dead?'

'Gawd, Mr Joseph, I've been in the game long enough, haven't I? Don't I know dead wool when I smell it? It pongs.'

'Here!' said Sammy Joseph. 'Where is this bale?'

'Come and see.'

They walked down the aisle between ranks of baled wool. The storeman at intervals switched on more lights and the aisle was extended before them. At the far end he paused and jerked his thumb at the last bale. 'Take a sniff, Mr Joseph,' he said.

Sammy Joseph bent towards the bale. His shadow was thrown up on the surface, across stencilled letters, a number and a rough crescent.

'That's from the Mount Moon clip,' he said.

'I know it is.' The storeman's voice rose nervously. 'Stinks, doesn't it?'

'Yes,' said Joseph. 'It does.'

'Dead wool.'

'I've never bought dead wool in my life. Least of all from Mount Moon. And the smell of dead wool goes off after it's plucked. You know that as well as I do. Dead Rat, more likely. Have you looked?'

'Yes, I have looked, Mr Joseph. I shifted her out the other day. It's in the bale. You can tell.'

'Split her up,' Mr Joseph commanded.

The storeman pulled out a clasp knife, opened it, and dug the blade into the front of the bale. Sammy Joseph watched him in a silence that was broken only by the uneasy sighing of the rafters above their heads.

'It's hot in here,' said Sammy Joseph. 'There's a nor'-west gale blowing outside. I hate a hot wind.'

'Oppressive,' said the storeman. He drew the blade of his knife downwards, sawing at the bale. The strands of sacking parted in a series of tiny explosions. Through the fissure bulged a ridge of white wool.

'Get a lung full of that,' said the storeman, straightening himself. 'It's something chronic. Try.'

Mr Joseph said: 'I get it from here, thanks. I can't understand it. It's not bellies in that pack, either. Bellies smell a bit but nothing to touch this.' He opened his cigarette case. 'Have one?'

'Ta, Mr Joseph, I don't mind if I do. It's not so good, this pong, is it?'

'It's coming from inside, all right. They must have baled up something in the press. A rat.'

'You will have your rat, sir, won't you?'

'Let's have some of that wool out.' Mr Joseph glanced at his neat worsted suit. 'You're in your working clothes,' he added.

The storeman pulled at a tuft of wool. 'Half a sec, Mr Joseph. She's packed too solid.' He moved away to the end wall. Sammy Joseph looked at the rent in the bale, reached out his hand and drew it back again. The storeman returned wearing a gauntleted canvas glove on his right hand and carrying one of the iron hooks used for shifting wool bales. He worked it into the fissure and began to drag out lumps of fleece.

'Phew!' whispered Sammy Joseph.

'I'll have to hand it to you in one respect, sir. She's not dead wool.'

Mr Joseph picked a lock from the floor, looked at it, and dropped it. He turned away and wiped his hand vigorously on a bale. 'It's frightful,' he said. 'It's a god-almighty stench. What the hell's wrong with you?'

The storeman had sworn with violence and extreme obscenity. Joseph turned to look at him. His gloved hand had disappeared inside the fissure. The edge of the gauntlet showed and no more. His face was turned towards Joseph. The eyes and mouth were wide open.

'I'm touching something.'

'With the hook?'

The storeman nodded. 'I won't look any more,' he said loudly.

'Why not?'

'I won't look.'

'Why the hell?'

'It's the Mount Moon clip.'

'I know that. What of it?'

'Don't you read the papers?'

Sammy Joseph changed colour. 'You're mad,' he said. 'God, you're crazy.'

'It's three weeks, isn't it, and they can't find her? I was in the last war. I know what that stink reminds me of. Flanders.'

'Go to hell,' said Mr Joseph, incredulous but violent. 'What do you think you are? A radio play or what?'

The storeman plucked his arm from the bale. Locks of fleece were sticking to the canvas glove. With a violent movement he jerked them free and they lay on the floor, rust coloured and wet.

'You've left the hook in the bale.'

'— the hook.'

'Get it out, Alf.'

'—!'

'Come on. What's wrong with you. Get it out.'

The storeman looked at Sammy Joseph as if he hated him. A loose sheet of galvanised iron on the roof rattled in the wind and the store was filled momentarily with a vague soughing.

'Come on,' Sammy Joseph said again. 'It's only a rat.'

The storeman plunged his hand into the fissure. His bare arm twisted and worked. He braced the palm of his left hand against the bale and wrenched out the hook. With an air of incredulity he held the hook out, displaying it.

'Look!' he said. With an imperative gesture he waved Mr Joseph aside. The iron hook fell at Sammy Joseph's feet. A strand of metallic-gold hair was twisted about it.

(1944)

JANET FRAME

The Day of the Sheep

It should not have rained. The clothes should have been slapped warm and dry with wind and sun and the day not have been a leafless cloudy secret hard to understand. It is always nice to understand the coming and going of a day. Tell her, blackbird that pirrup-pirruped and rainwater that trickled down the kitchen window-pane and dirty backyard that oozed mud and housed puddles, tell her though the language be something she cannot construe having no grammar of journeys.

Why is the backyard so small and suffocating and untidy? On the rope clothesline the washing hangs limp and wet. Tom's underpants and the sheets and my best tablecloth. We'll go away from here, Tom and me, we'll go some other place, the country perhaps, he likes the country but he's going on and on to a prize in Tatts and a new home, flat-roofed with blinds down in the front room and a piano with curved legs, though Tom's in the Dye Works just now, bringing home handkerchiefs at the end of each week, from the coats with no names on.

'Isn't it stealing Tom?'

'Stealing my foot, I tell you I've worked two years without a holiday.' You see? Tom striving for his rights and getting them even if they turn out to be only a small anonymous pile of men's handkerchiefs, but life is funny and people are funny, laugh and the world laughs with you.

She opens the wash-house door to let the blue water out of the tubs, she forgot all about the blue water, and then of all the surprises in the world there's a sheep in the wash-house, a poor sheep not knowing which way to turn, fat and blundering with the shy anxious look sheep have.

'Shoo Shoo.'

Sheep are silly animals they're so scared and stupid, they either stand still and do nothing or else go round and round getting nowhere, when they're in they want out and when they're out they sneak in, they don't stay in places, they get lost in bogs and creeks and down cliffs, if only they stayed where they're put.

'Shoo Shoo.'

Scared and muddy and heavy the sheep lumbers from the wash-house and then bolts up the path, out the half-open gate onto the street and then round the corner out of sight, with the people stopping to stare and say well I declare for you never see sheep in the street, only people.

It should not have rained, the washing should have been dry and why did the sheep come and where did it come from to here in the middle of the city?

A long time ago there were sheep (she remembers, pulling out the plug so the dirty blue water can gurgle away, what slime I must wash more often why is everything always dirty) sheep, and I walked behind them with bare feet on a hot dusty road, with the warm steamy nobbles of sheep dirt getting crushed between my toes and my Father close by me powerful and careless, and the dogs padding along the spit dribbling from the loose corners of their mouths, Mac and Jock and Rover waiting for my Father to cry Way Back Out, Way Back Out. Tom and me will go some other place I think. Tom and me will get out of here.

She dries her hands on the corner of her sack apron. That's that. A flat-roofed house and beds with shiny covers, and polished fire-tongs, and a picture of moonlight on a lake.

She crosses the backyard, brushing aside the wet clothes to pass. My best tablecloth. If visitors come tonight I am sunk.

But no visitors only Tom bringing cousin Nora, while the rain goes off, she has to catch the six o'clock bus at the end of the road. I must hurry I must be quick it is terrible to miss something. Cousin Nora widowed remarried separated and anxious to tell. Cousin Nora living everywhere and nowhere chained to number fifty Toon Street it is somewhere you must have somewhere even if you know you haven't got anywhere. And what about Tom tied up to a little pile of handkerchiefs and the prize that happens tomorrow, and Nance, look at her, the washing's still out and wet, she is tired and flurried, bound by the fearful chain of time and the burning sun and sheep and day that are nowhere.

'But of course Nance I won't have any dinner, you go on dishing up for Tom while I sit here on the sofa.'

'Wait, I'll move those newspapers, excuse the muddle, we seem to be in a fearful muddle.'

'Oh is that today's paper, no it's Tuesday's, just think on Tuesday Peter and I were up in the north island. He wanted me to sell my house you know, just fancy, he demanded that I sell it and I said not on your life did you marry me for myself or for my house and he said of course he married me for myself but would I sell the house, why I said, well you don't need it now he said, we can live up north, but I do need it I've lived in it nearly all of my life, it's my home, I live there.'

Cousin Nora, dressed in navy, her fleecy dark hair and long soft wobbly face like a horse.

'Yes I've lived there all my life, so of course I said quite definitely no. Is that boiled bacon, there's nothing I like better, well if you insist, just the tiniest bit on a plate, over here will do, no no fuss, thank you. Don't you think I was right about the house? I live there.'

What does Tom think? His mouth busies itself with boiled bacon while his fingers search an envelope for the pink sheet that means Tatts results, ten thousand pounds first prize, a flat-roofed house and statues in the garden. No prize but first prize will do, Tom is clever and earnest, the other fellows have tickets in Tatts, why not I the other fellows take handkerchiefs home and stray coats sometimes why not I and Bill Tent has a modern house one of those new ones you can never be too interested in where you live. Tom is go-ahead. In the front bedroom there's an orange coloured bed-lamp, it's scorched a bit now but it was lovely when it came, he won it with a question for a radio quiz, his name over the air and all —

Name the planets and their distance from the sun.

Name the planets.

Oh the sun is terribly far away but of course there's only been rain today, pirrup-pirruping blackbirds, how it rains and the sheep why I must tell them about the sheep.

Nora leans forward, 'Nance, you are dreaming, what *do* you think about the house?'

'Oh, always let your conscience be your guide.'

(Wear wise saws and modern instances like a false skin a Jiminy Cricket overcoat.)

'That's what I say too, your conscience, and that's why we separated, you heard of course?'

Yes Nance knows, from Nora herself as soon as it happened Dear Nance and Tom you'll hardly believe it but Peter and I have decided to go our own ways, you and Tom are lucky you get on so well together no fuss about where to live you don't know how lucky you are.

No fuss but lost, look at the house look at the kitchen, and me going backwards and forwards carrying dishes and picking up newspapers and dirty clothes, muddling backwards and forwards in little irrelevant journeys, but going backwards always, to the time of the sun and the hot dusty road and a powerful father crying Way Back Out Way Back Out.

'Oh, Oh I must tell you, there was a sheep today in the wash-house.'

'A what?'

'A sheep. I don't know where he lived but I chased him away.'

'Oh I say, really, ha ha, it's a good job we've got somewhere to live, I in my house (even though I had to break with Peter) and you and Tom in yours.

'We *have* got somewhere to live haven't we, not like a lost sheep ha ha. What's the matter Tom?'

'74898, not a win.'

The pink ticket thrust back quickly into the envelope and put on the stand beside the wireless, beside the half-open packet of matches and the sheaf of bills and the pile of race-books.

'Well, I'm damned, let's turn on the news, it's almost six.'

'Oh it's almost six and my bus!'

'So it is Nora.'

Quick it is terrible to lose something for the something you miss may be something you have looked for all your life, in the north island and the south island and number fifty Toon Street.

'Goodbye and thank you for the little eat and you must come and see me sometime and for goodness sake Nance get a perm or one of those cold waves, your hair's at the end of its tether.'

Here is the news.

Quick goodbye then.

Why am I small and cramped and helpless why are there newspapers on the floor and why didn't I remember to gather up the dirt, where am I living that I'm not neat and tidy with a perm. Oh if only the whole of being were blued and washed and hung out in the far away sun. Nora has travelled she knows about things, it would be nice to travel if you knew where you were going and where you would live at the end or do we ever know, do we ever live where we live, we're always in other places, lost, like sheep, and I cannot understand the leafless cloudy secret and the sun of any day.

(1951)

MARY SCOTT

Chapter I from
Breakfast at Six

Paul said: 'You won't need any trousseau. Just shorts and some slacks. And something to ride in. Best have jodhpurs. Slacks work up. But not a lot of clothes. You won't use them.'

Mother looked tragic, Father relieved. But I was firm.

'Of course I'm going to have a trousseau. Like other girls. Clothes last for years. Why not have plenty?'

It seemed reasonable, though Paul didn't look convinced.

Mother showed a lot of spirit over the wedding. She said there were certain things owing to one's position, though I've never quite understood what that means.

'She's to have a beautiful wedding. After all, she's your eldest daughter.'

'Weddings are damned expensive — and she's got two sisters.'

There was the usual implied reproach in this, and Mother rose to its injustice as to a clarion call, striking back smartly with, 'Well, you *would* have a family.'

That always settled Father, who retired into gloom and the *Listener* crossword, muttering that women always lose their heads over weddings.

All this discussion was the natural end to what any girls who disliked me made a point of calling 'The Pinching of Paul'. The men called it 'The Stealing of Susan'. It was all in the point of view.

Paul had come to our city to visit another returned soldier in hospital. Someone persuaded him to go to a dance and there we met. We were engaged by the end of the week, though Mother mourned a little.

'I feel you could have done better. Think of Your Writing.'

She always spoke in capitals about the three short stories I'd written. Father was worse. He'd a way of saying, 'This little girl scribbles a bit, you know. Quite the budding author.'

Luckily he hadn't a chance to say it to Paul. I saw to that and kept them apart until we were safely engaged. When the Awful Truth came out, Paul took it stoically. He didn't seem impressed. He said he'd a cousin who wrote monologues, but she'd got over it.

'Anyway,' he conceded generously, 'if she does want to, there's plenty of material in the backblocks. Plenty of time, too.'

The first claim may have been true, but I only hope Paul may be forgiven for the second.

In private Mother was inclined to harp.

'Not that I've a word to say against Paul. Of course he's nice and looks a little like Gary Cooper. But he says he's poor and it's just a rough little farm, miles from anywhere. Think of the hardships.'

'Best thing for young people,' said Father, settling a little more deeply into his armchair and reaching for the dictionary. 'What's another word for demagogue? . . . Hardships never did anyone any harm. Pioneering and all that.'

But Mother had a one-track mind.

'And it won't be of any help to the younger girls. No one eligible in a place like that. You're being rather selfish, Susan.'

I meant to be. Paul was just what I'd been waiting for. I was twenty-two and very sure of myself.

When he came down for the wedding Paul broached the subject of a honeymoon.

'Afraid we can't stay away long. I've been in town a lot since I met you. First, that week's holiday. Then twice for a weekend.'

Twice in six months. And he didn't think I needed a trousseau. This made me think. It didn't make me pause. At twenty-two I felt I knew my world — and men. As for the life — well, I could take it.

Of course Mother had her way and Paul and I were married with the usual paragraphs in the papers and some perfectly horrible photographs. Paul said afterwards that the wedding was a merciful blur, and was surprised when I complained that he might have put it more enthusiastically. But he behaved beautifully. As he helped me cut the cake with every appearance of absorption, I whispered, 'What are you thinking about?'

'Wondering if the farm's all right,' he grunted back.

But even his speech, though very short, was adequate. While they were singing 'Jolly good fellows', I caught him looking at me, and his expression encouraged me to mutter, 'Still thinking of the farm?'

'Yes, and you there. On horseback. Riding round the sheep. By the fire at night.'

This was better, but even then I wondered if he had also an inspired vision of me at the wash-tubs. Darning socks by that fire.

Everyone was very witty about Susan in the backblocks, but the woman who'd taught me English was at least original.

'I'll watch for the book you're going to publish. I haven't forgotten all your essay prizes. You'll have plenty of opportunity to write.'

We drove away in Paul's ancient but honourable car. Mother looked a little self-conscious. She had suggested a taxi as far as the city boundary. Paul couldn't see any sense in that, and I thought the car was part of the fun. We were going somewhere, anywhere. It was February and the hotels wouldn't be crowded. I said how lucky this was as we drew up before a wayside pub that evening.

'We had to be married in February,' replied Paul briefly.

I snuggled closer, sleepy with champagne and happiness. I loved his impatience. It had to be February.

'No time in January,' the bridegroom continued earnestly. 'Lamb-shearing and sales then. And in March there's dipping and so on. So it had to be February, you see.'

I saw. It almost woke me up.

It was a good honeymoon, casual and economical. My sisters had given me a picnic-basket, so we lunched in paddocks or by the side of the road, and put up at any little hotel for the night. We had to be careful of our shillings and pence. This was fun too, but new to me. As a family we'd never had much spare money, but we'd spent pretty freely. Now I was keen to learn economy. To learn anything — with Paul.

Afterwards I used to wonder how Paul lasted out the whole week of honeymooning. It might even have been longer if we hadn't struck market-day in one small town. We didn't expect it — just turned a corner into a cloud of dust that resolved itself into a mob of sheep being driven to the sale next day — and that was the end of the honeymoon.

Next morning Paul said: 'Don't wait lunch for me. I might as well take a look at this sale.'

I ate alone and we left that afternoon for the farm.

It was a long drive — towards the west, right away from my part of the world. We reached the hills about five o'clock — wilder hills and wilder, fewer farms, more bush. Worse roads and hairpin bends with steep drops that took my breath away. It was dusk when we got to the top of the last hill — the last in the world, it seemed to me. Paul pulled up the roaring, rattling car and flung out one arm in an expansive gesture.

'We're coming to our part now. Like it?'

There were half-a-dozen ranges of hills, falling to the sea-line. A glow of pink on the horizon was the Tasman. It was strange and very beautiful. Yes, I liked it, and said so. Paul hugged me briefly.

This gave me courage to say faintly, 'But where are the farms?'

'Here and there. This block's a Soldiers' Settlement. You know the sort of thing. Under Rehab.'

I didn't know till he explained. Rehab meant the Rehabilitation of Returned Soldiers, a Government department. It advanced money to buy farms and was generous to suitable men.

'Our land's on the left.'

'Is there much of it?'

'It's all economic units. When it's sheep, that means about a thousand acres of this sort of land. But the houses are quite near each other. Some of them are only a mile or so apart. A regular settlement.'

'Almost a crowd.'

Presently we came to a cattle-stop. Beyond it a narrow clay road with two ribbons of metal ran up a steep hill. Paul bumped noisily across.

'Don't like gates. The hill's steep and the brakes aren't much good. Awkward to have to stop for a gate. Now we're on our own land, darling.'

I was immensely impressed. Not by the land but by the 'darling'. This was the eleventh time Paul had called me that. I'd kept count. Eleven times in six and a half months. He must be terrifically excited. Also there'd been both a subject and a verb in that last sentence. Yes, this was a great occasion.

I was excited too. This was my new life. No suburban streets with a wireless each side of you, one opposite, friends in the next block, a milk-bar at the corner, a picture theatre at the bus stop. This was elemental, immense.

So this was the last hill. The car was hot and tired and just made it. I wondered what happened if your wheels got off the metal ribbon on a wet day. I never had a straight eye and the metal was very narrow. Paul was being positively garrulous.

'Hope you like the house. Most of the chaps have new ones. Convenient, but I like space. Ours was the original homestead before they cut up the place. It's old.'

Ours. I said: 'I'll like it.'

The light was almost gone as we drove up to the door. There was actually an attempt at a garden. Some dahlias and chrysanthemums and a lot of Michaelmas daisies. Somehow this seemed pathetic to me. How had Paul found time for beauty in these busy, lonely years?

'I'll take over the garden,' I murmured lovingly.

He didn't seem impressed; just nodded and pulled up the car.

'Front steps a bit wobbly, but I won't drop you. Lucky you're a light-weight.'

I realised that he was solemnly preparing to observe the ritual, and shut my eyes, almost dizzy with happiness. At heart he was a romantic too. He picked me up and carried me over the threshold and I couldn't help noticing that the steps were distinctly wobbly.

'I'll mend them the first wet day,' he volunteered, and I was satisfied, not realising then that there were at least nine hundred and ninety-nine odd jobs waiting for that wet day. This would make the thousandth.

There was a wide verandah, sagging a little, a front door, and several french windows on to the verandah. He took me into a high square room that was certainly large enough. I couldn't see any more in the half-dark. Paul took a big lamp down from a shelf and lit a match.

'Pity there's no electricity,' he said, 'but it's promised in three years.'

Later I found that it was promised pretty well everywhere in the Dominion in three years. But it seemed comforting at the time.

The lamp was patent and very temperamental. I came to terms with it eventually, but not before it had singed my hair, my eye-lashes, and a sampler worked by my great-great-grandmother. Tonight it was sulky and flared to the ceiling, then sank to a dull glow. Its reluctant gleams showed me a linoleum-covered floor, a square table, four hard chairs and two wicker ones. Also, some shelves piled with books and papers and odd bits of machinery. On the mantel was my own photograph, looking resignedly out on four blank walls papered with large pink roses.

I felt glad I'd acted sensibly when Father said, 'What do you want for a wedding present? I'll give you a decent cheque if you don't fritter it away on a lot of nonsense.'

Father is the most generous of men, but he is apt to call us fritterers when we buy anything he doesn't happen to want himself — like nylons or tennis rackets. He glared affectionately at me and grunted: 'What about something useful? A solid thing like furniture.'

When I consulted Paul he said defensively that the place was furnished already, but of course I might like something different. Treading delicately, I suggested that it would be rather fun to choose our own things — together. Paul was mollified at the magic word and we had a good time in the furniture shops — new and second-hand. To Father I said that it was so clever of him to think of furniture and thank you very much — and he winked at me in that disconcerting way he has when you thought you'd managed him nicely. Anyway, the cheque was as solid as the advice.

The furniture would transform this room, which already had space and possibilities.

Paul was lighting the primus in the kitchen and the lamp had stopped sulking and was burning brightly. Now I could see on the table a lovely pottery bowl filled with splendid chrysanthemums. They were perfectly arranged and amongst them was a slip of paper which read, 'Welcome home, Susan and Paul. With love from Larry and Sam.'

For the first time I felt that warm glow that contact with Larry was to induce so often. Sometimes it was a glow of affection; sometimes of shame. I'd tried to get Paul to talk about Larry, who was the wife of his closest friend, but he always just grinned and said, 'I think you'll like her. Larry's the limit, but she's a good kid.' Not very enlightening. Pressed for details of her appearance, her age, her character, he just said, 'Oh, you'll find all that out in time. She's a bit Irish, of course — but you'll see for yourself.'

Looking at the flowers and the bowl that held them, I felt that I should like what I saw.

I wandered down the wide passage and opened a door or two. No luck. A bathroom, nothing more. Paul, I had realised, was slightly proper with women. Well, one Victorian was enough in any family. So I went and asked him where he had hidden the lavatory.

He looked rather stricken. 'I meant to tell you about that, but somehow I didn't get round to it. Fact is, there's no septic tank. Can't get the cement. But I'll put one in some day.'

I said that would be fine, but meantime I didn't feel like waiting. So what exactly . . .?

Paul began to babble. 'It's perfectly sanitary really, but a good way off. I hate that sort of thing near a house . . . I'll show you from here. You take that path and go up the hill.'

Dimly I made out the outline of a four-by-four with a definite slant on the sky-line, and said with a sigh that I wished I'd brought my bicycle. Paul looked dignified and I added hurriedly, 'I mean it must be rather tiring . . . And what happens if you're ill?'

This ridiculous and far-fetched notion had evidently not occurred to my husband. He dismissed it airily by saying that he always kept a torch handy on the scullery window-sill, and I went off submissively on the long, long trek.

My eyes were still bulging when I returned. 'It's marvellous,' I gasped. 'I'm going to call it the Leaning Tower. And it's positively subterranean. Quite fifty feet, I guess, I never saw anything like it. But all the same, some day . . . Well, what happens? I mean it must . . . Perhaps not in our time, or in our children's, but in our children's children's.'

Paul took me firmly by the arm. 'Stop showing off and come and see the house,' he said briefly.

I realised then that it was the end of the honeymoon.

(1953)

SYLVIA ASHTON-WARNER

Spring

A chapter from
Spinster

'What is it, what is it, Little One?'

I kneel to his level and tip his chin. Tears break from the large brown eyes and set off down his face.

'That's why somebodies they tread my sore leg for notheen. Somebodies.'

I sit on my low chair and take him on my knee and tuck his black head beneath my chin.

'There . . . there . . . look at my pretty boy.'

But at night when I am in my slim bed, away from the chaos and hilarity of my infant-room, it is I who am the Little One. Before I turn out the light above me and open the window behind I take out my photo. It is pillow-worn, finger-worn and tear-worn, yet the face of the man is alive. I read into it all the expressions I have known; and the attention my spinster heart craves. But memory only loosens the tears. No longer does Eugene take me on his knee, tuck my black head beneath his chin and say, 'There . . . there . . . look at my pretty girl.'

Not for many long virgin years.

But here is the spring again with its new life, and as I walked down my back steps ready for school in the morning I notice the delphiniums. They make me think of men. The way they bloom so hotly in the summer, then die right out of sight in the winter, only to push up mercilessly again when the growth starts, is like my memory of love. They're only shoots so far but I can't help recalling how like the intense blue of the flowers is distilled passion. Living the frugal life that I do I am shocked at the glamour they bring to my wild garden and at the promise of blue to come. With no trouble at all I break apart into sobbing. What luxury is self-pity! How blessed to weep in the spring!

But you can't get this sort of thing to last and soon there is only sniffing left. And confound it, here's my face to wash and powder again. Also I'd better take some brandy to make my legs go. Yet as I come down the back steps for the second time these tender shoots are still hard to pass. They've got so much to say. There's something so mature about them, as if there was little they didn't know.

However, you don't drink half a tumbler of brandy for nothing and soon I'm severely immune. I walk out and away from the garden, singing an orderly tune.

Yet, when I have crossed the paddock between the rambling old house and the school and reach the cabbage trees that divide them, and when the pre-fab where I teach comes into view, I run into something that does more than renew life in a garden. It is something you find on your shoulders with the tight legs clasping your neck. I thought I had forgotten Guilt. I thought he was gone for good, and not merely into hiding for the winter. But oh, these precarious springs! Is there nothing that does not resume life?

My song stops. So does my step. I lurk among the trunks like one of my five-year-old newcomers. If only I had done all that inspectors had told me in the past — whenever they wanted me to, in the way they wanted me to and for the reason! If only I had been a good teacher, an obedient teacher and submissive! If only I could have remained in the safety of numbers that I knew when I was young! But no, I've always been wrong.

Yet it can't be too late. True, the mistakes have all been mine, but this is the ground I'll build on. Plainly the inspectors are all good men and all I need to do is to co-operate. What could be easier or more profitable? Slowly I will recover my lagging professional status and prove myself a thoroughly useful force in the service. Then maybe this Old Man Guilt will release my throat and I'll be one with others at last. How fortunate to have these chances! After all everything else comes up new in the spring: flowers and guilt and love. Why not my teaching? With a new courage, not wholly originating in my plans, I walk forward again.

. . . or try to, through the clusterings and questionings and greetings of my Little Ones.

'Miss Vorontosov,' inquires Mohi, 'how old do you weigh?'

I can see that I'm not going to like this young Vercoe who has been appointed temporarily to the school: a teacher-in-training fresh from the Emergency Course in which teachers are trained in half the time to meet twice the difficulties of the staff shortages since the war. How he comes to be selected at all can only be put down to the desperate shortage of teachers. Where has he come from, anyway? From what strange soil of life has evolved that mixture of culture and gutter in his voice? Why has he chosen children? Why isn't he married, with a surplus of women after the war? Why hasn't that face taken him to the front line of a chorus on a New York stage? He's young but he's still had time to try and fail in other things. Yet, as I emerge from the trees between my house and the school and see him standing uncertainly there by the Big School steps, the sun touching his hair and outlining his story-book features, my general dislike for bachelors does not wholly take over. I can't help feeling touched at his youth, and his strangeness to the world about him.

So that as I make my way across the frost to the pre-fab where I teach, through the greeting hands of my Little Ones, and their dark upturning eyes, I still see him in mind. And although it is far from comfortable for me to think of men, I cannot escape the interest they bring. The faultless blue of his eyes reminds me of the delphiniums and the glamour of my garden in spring.

'Miss Vorontosov,' cries Whareparita from the Big School, running gaily up to me as I mount the dingy steps of the pre-fab, 'how old are you?'

'Good God!'

'It's my turn to take the quizz sessions in class this morning and it would do for one of my questions.'

I plough through all my talking, laughing, pulling Little Ones . . . the brown, the few white and the brown-white of the New Race . . . across the spare pre-fab to the piano the Head has bought with his last Show-Day funds and unlock it for the day. If you don't lock it you'll find apple-juice on the precious keys and crumbs of biscuits and lolly papers. Next I put my pen-box on the table. Then I unlock the storeroom where I keep the guitar, away from boys who can't play it, and reach down my box of pre-war chalk from behind some books where I hide it. I stoke the fire which has been lit previously by a boy. Then I tuck up my sleeves, damp the sand in the container, send Blossom and Bleeding Heart out for a bucket of water for the trough, tie the flared fullness of my short red smock behind me in a business-like knot, pull on a sack apron and get to work on preparing the clay. No. I'll mix the paints first before I wet my hands.

'Matawhero, get out the pencils. Waiwini, put out the books. Little Brother, use your handkerchief. Reremoana, go and tell Mr Reardon the wood boy has not brought the wood. One-Pint, get out of the sand. Hine, put the papers on the easel. Who's got my . . . where's my . . . who is this dear wee boy? Did you come to see Miss Vorontosov? Here. Patchy, show this wee new boy a picture book. Sit him by the fire. Where's my . . .? What are you laughing at, Bleeding Heart? You mustn't laugh at my little New One. Who's got my . . .? Are you big enough to open the windows, little Dennis? Look at the big long legs and arms Dennis has got! Ani, tidy my . . . I mean dust my table. Who's got my . . .? Tuck in your shirt, Matawhero . . . Seven! Don't you frighten that little boy! Look, who's got my . . .?

'Miss Vorontosov,' inquires Bleeding Heart, 'what for those smell by your breff?'

'Aa . . . hair-oil.'

(1958)

MARILYN DUCKWORTH

Chapter Twenty from
A Gap in the Spectrum

Every day I grew more frightened. Stephen was indifferent and sulky. I found myself talking a lot, especially late at night, and I would ask Stephen questions at intervals to see whether he was listening. He was always able to make satisfactory replies, and yet I suspected him of not paying much attention to the things I was telling him. I was obsessed by the idea of his going away. He couldn't go away and leave me in this awful world! And yet, I didn't want to go back to Micald. Before long, this became an obsession with me, too. I terrified myself with the thought that one night I may go to sleep and wake up in Micald. I dreaded each night as it approached. Darkness was a good breeding ground for my dread, and the room in shadow would grow sinister as I watched it over the fold of the sheet. I told Stephen I had been having nightmares, but he refused to take me seriously.

One evening I was really afraid to go to sleep — so afraid, that I wouldn't go to bed. I was convinced that when I woke up it would be in a world without Stephen.

'Let's go to the pictures,' I urged him.

'But it's half past eight. Why didn't you think of it sooner?'

'It's supposed to be funny,' I persisted.

'Oh, I don't want to go out now.' He sounded martyred.

'Please, darling. I want to forget everything for a while.'

'Read a book or something,' he suggested.

'No. That doesn't work. Oh, all right, I'll go on my own.'

'No, you won't.'

We argued about it for half an hour, by which time it was too late to go, anyway. Saying I was going for a walk, I slammed the door and ran down the stairs to the street. The evening was cold on my bare arms and the darkness crept over me in chilling waves. I walked quickly on the even pavements, hearing my footsteps echo on the other side of the street. I didn't know where I was going — I didn't know Reigate very well. I half expected Stephen to follow me, but the street behind me was still empty when I turned the corner.

I had walked for some distance when I came to a church — a small building with the door opening on to the street. The heavy, round catch squeaked as I turned and pushed it away from me. Inside it was almost colder than the street outside. The shadowed pews filed away from me to a simple little altar. It seemed strangely naked. The whole place was bare in comparison to the church near Cadogan Square. Even the smell was absent — the funny, mysterious smell. But the atmosphere was there. I could hear it breathing about me like some big, invisible animal. As I stood there it seemed to grow louder, heavier, as if it were waiting to pounce. Goose pimples ran over my arms and I leapt for the door. I was running up the street, crying and coughing, and I could feel my face drawn up tight with terror.

Under a railway bridge I stopped, panting, and leant against the damp bricks. A train was passing noisily overhead, and by the time it had passed, I had stopped crying. I began to walk home.

I hurried, suddenly afraid that I was lost, but it seemed no time before I reached the familiar concrete gateposts. Stephen was asleep. I crossed to the table, rubbing my cold arms, and switched the table-lamp on. Still he didn't wake. He had been reading a mystery thriller, *The Golden Eye*, and it was lying under the lamp. I sat down and began to read where he had left the book open. It was a story of sordid, perverted crime, and I turned the pages in fascinated horror. I was still reading, the lamp growing pale against the daylight, when Stephen woke up.

'What the hell? Haven't you been to bed?'

'No. I was reading.'

'You've got to go on duty this afternoon.'

'I know.'

'You'd better get some sleep instead. Maureen'll ring up and say you're not well.'

'Oh no. I'll go. I don't feel tired.'

We had a silent breakfast, and Stephen left to catch his bus. I lay for a moment on the unmade bed to finish my book. The rag-and-bone man was calling in the street below. A funny, eerie call, it sounded to me, in my sleepless state. I listened harder to make out his exact words.

It didn't seem long before I woke. I sat up smiling rather foolishly. My head was heavy, but at least I had had some sleep and was still in this large, untidy bed. I opened the cupboard door and lifted out the breadboard to make myself some lunch. I felt a sudden peculiar affection for all the now familiar objects in our large, shabby room. Then I noticed the time. It was after three o'clock — too late for me to go to the hospital. I remembered Stephen's suggestion and took some pennies down to the hall, to telephone. Maureen was quite concerned.

'Are you getting the 'flu or something?'

'No, I'm just worn out. I couldn't face going on duty today,' I told her. I could see the landlady listening at the end of the hall and turned to stare at her defiantly. She went away.

'Perhaps you'd better have tomorrow off, too,' Maureen suggested.

After a moment I agreed.

Stephen made me take two A.P. Codeines that night. I swallowed them with a strange feeling of fatalism. One half of me was convinced

I had signed my death warrant in this world. The other half was relieved that the question of sleep was out of my hands.

I was still sleeping when Stephen left in the morning, and I woke to an empty room, buzzing with flies. I remember the flies particularly. They were all part of the horrible, brooding atmosphere. My mind had grown dark with apprehension, and I felt as if I was looking out on to the sunlight from somewhere deep and a long way off. I wandered about, touching objects in the room and handling them absently. My finger-tips seemed especially sensitive, and so did my tongue. I could feel it in my mouth, curled tight as if waiting for something.

Suddenly terror gripped me. I was aware of a feeling of compulsion. I was going to be forced to do something against my will! The feeling was so strong and stayed with me long enough for me to wonder about it. Fantastic ideas leaped into my brain. Was I going to jump out of the window? Throw the breadboard into the glass doors of the sideboard? I stood still in the middle of the room, looking round suspiciously.

Then I had my idea. There was a chemist's shop on the corner, at the end of the High Street. I chose a henna rinse carefully. The chemist glanced at my hair inquisitively and I stared back in irritable defiance as I handed across the money. I almost danced through the gateposts and up the dim stairway. With red hair — if it was as red as the girl's on the packet — I couldn't return to Micald. There I would be more than a freak. I would be an impossibility. There was just no such colour in the spectrum. I lit the geyser in the bathroom with trembling fingers. The darkness had gone out of my mind and it was burning with a bright, white light. I turned the rinse into the cup and stirred it viciously with the end of the wooden spoon. The powder burst into startling colour, intoxicating in its very ugliness. Then a paler scum gathered on the surface, hiding it momentarily.

I sat by the window with my hair bound in one of Stephen's bright beach towels, and watched the street below. I looked contemptuously at the passers by — frowning or complacent, but always hurrying as if they were important enough to be needed anywhere. I laughed out loud and turned up the radio. The Critics shouted at me, then laughed drily and intellectually among themselves. I snapped off the switch and went to the mirror. There were fly spots on the glass and I removed them carefully with the edge of the lace duchess set before beginning to unravel my turban.

The hair fell out about me, damp and still streaked with uneven moisture — but red! A horrible, wonderful red! The room sang! And then I heard Stephen's voice in my head. 'I've gone off red — it's been getting on my nerves lately — it made me feel quite sick.'

My face tightened defiantly. I arranged myself on the sofa facing the door and waited for him to come home.

(1959)

JANET FRAME

Chapter IV from
Faces in the Water

It is said that when a prisoner is condemned to die all clocks in the neighbourhood of the death cell are stopped; as if the removal of the clock will cut off the flow of time and maroon the prisoner on a coast of timelessness where the moments, like breakers, rise and surge near but never touch the shore.

But no death of an oceanographer ever stopped the sea flowing; and a condition of sea is its meeting with the land. And in the death cell time flows in as if all the cuckoo clocks grandfather clocks alarm clocks were striking simultaneously in the ears of the prisoner.

Again and again when I think of Cliffhaven I play the time game, as if I have been condemned to die and the signals have been removed yet I hear them striking in my ears, warning me that nine o'clock, the time of treatment, is approaching and that I must find myself a pair of woollen socks in order that I shall not die. Or it is eleven o'clock and treatment is over and it is the early hours or years of my dream when I was not yet sitting in rainbow puddles in Ward Two Yard or tramping the shorn park inside the tall picket fence with its rusty nails sprouting from the top, their points to the sky.

Eleven o'clock. I remember eleven o'clock, the pleasant agony of trying to decide when plump pale-faced Mrs Pilling ready with the laundry basket with the cheese-smelling tablecloth inside would ask me, 'Will you come for the bread with me?'

And at the same time anxious Mrs Everett who was detained in hospital, as they say, 'at the sovereign's pleasure' would appear with an empty milk jug and ask 'Will you come with me to collect the cream for the specials?'

The prospect of two journeys at the same time beyond the locked doors was so full of delight that I dallied to savour the pleasure and to hold a debate with myself on the merits of bakery and separator room. Bread or cream? The bakery with Andy shovelling the trays of loaves like yeasted molars into the yawning oven, slicing our ward bread and trying to sing above the slicer a duet for baker and bread machine with incidental crusts, or perhaps inviting me into the back room to give me a pastry left over from the Superintendent's party, or an advance chunk of the currant-filled Sunday Borstal cake.

Or the walk up the hill to the farm, past the deserted dung-smelling cowsheds into the separator room where Ted had arranged the cream cans in order of importance the way we used as children to arrange cups — first in the class, second in the class, and so on, when we played school with them.

First, the Superintendent's can, well polished with no dents and no ridge of old cream inside the shoulders. Next, the can for the doctors, also cleaned. Then for the Chief Clerk the farm manager and his family the engineer matrons and head attendant the attendants and nurses. Finally, the special patients who were too frail or suffered from tuberculosis and whose names appeared on a list pinned to the dining room wall. From a ward of one hundred women only ten or fifteen could be 'special' enough to have cream. I remember my amazement and gratitude when for some weeks my name appeared on the list of 'specials' and I sat smugly at dinner while the nurse poured cream on my tapioca or rice or farina or bread pudding (Mondays) or (Thursdays in season) baked apple.

You know that I have been pretending; you know that it is eleven o'clock and I am not allowed to go for the bread or up the hill past the poplar trees and the broom bushes and the wattle to fetch the cream; that I am hiding in the linen cupboard, sitting on an apple box of firewood and crying and afraid to be seen crying in case I am written up for E.S.T. The linen cupboard is my favourite hiding place. It is scrubbed every morning by the T.B. nurse and the floor looks like the deck of a ship. From here I listen to Margaret who has T.B. and whose hoarse whisper tells continually of the First World War. She pleads with anyone who passes in the corridor to help her to evict the enemy from her room. She has lived for many years in this room, seeing the sun only for a few hours on a summer afternoon when shafts of light manoeuvre their way through the rusted wire netting of the window to shine and set the motes dancing on the wall. Sometimes on an afternoon walk with the nurse you can see Margaret standing in the sunlit corner of her room; the sun seems to shine through her as if the texture of her bones were gossamer. Her face is without colour, even without the two familiar fever spots on her cheeks, and her body is like a skeleton. Looking at her you think, She is dying. Yet she goes on living, year after year, while other consumptives more robust on appearance — Effie, Jane, die and their bodies are hastily and antiseptically dispatched to the mortuary which is at the back of the laundry, facing the greenhouse, surrounded by rows of flowers and vegetables, the hardy plants outside and, inside, the sensitive begonias in pots used for surrounding the piano when the blind man from the city comes to play.

The mortuary is faceless.

If it were built in proportion, to really house the dead, its size would swallow the greenhouse and the laundry and the boiler house and the Big Kitchen, perhaps the entire hospital. But it is small, unobtrusive, and begs that patients conform to the rule of loneliness by dying one at a time.

In spite of the scrubbed appearance of the linen cupboard the smell pervading it is of floor polish boot polish (from the little-used caked tins of black and brown kept inside the large dented biscuit tin which bears on its lid the earnest profile of George the Sixth); wet-stained chipped wood whose smell leaves a parched blocked taste in the mouth; clinging wet linen; and the muffled ironed smell of fresh linen on the shelves labelled Drawers Chemises Nightgowns Sheets Counterpanes (with their scrolled patriotic design *Ake Ake*, Onward Onward). Here are kept the T.B. masks and dishes and the cardboard sputum boxes as they are procured, unfolded, from the stores. The T.B.'s, as part of their realistic occupational therapy, spend some of their time folding the boxes tucking in the flaps setting them upright with the ounces clearly marked on the side; like a kindergarten class engaged in constructing do-it-yourself coffins. Here are the cut-down kerosene tins where the used T.B. dishes are put to be boiled, for there is yet no steriliser for them, on the open fire in the dining room.

This process is supervised by Mrs Everett and Mrs Pilling who share control of kitchen affairs and are responsible for the fire. It is Mrs Pilling (the most trusted patient in the ward) who also arranges the making of toast over the open fire in the morning, the collecting of bread and cream, the carrying out to the side door of the full pig-tin ready for the golden-haired pig-boy to pick up on his way to the farm driving the leisurely old cart horse. When the tin has been loaded on the back he rummages through the food, bypassing the cold skilly bog of leftover porridge and reaching for the more appetizing dainties of discarded toast and sodden pieces of currant bun, all of which he stuffs hungrily in his mouth and, chewing contentedly, climbs again to the front of the cart and with a tug of the reins and a 'Gee-up' sets the morose but patient horse on his way. Mrs Pilling in her undemonstrative silent manner has an understanding with the pig-boy and though she recoils from his habits she has a stolid tolerance and respect for other people's peculiarities and is inclined to act out of character herself in order to preserve someone else's individuality.

She sometimes leaves a slice of staff cake on the pig-tin. It seems that she has no husband no children no relatives. She never has visitors. She never speaks of her personal concerns; one is seldom aware that she has any. She has lived for many years in the hospital and has a small room at the end of the T.B. corridor; one is surprised on passing it to notice that it has a cosy appearance as far as that is possible in a room in a mental hospital. She is allowed to keep her overcoat. It hangs behind the door. There is a feminine smell of powder and clothes. At one time someone must have given her a potted plant; it now stands on a chair in one corner, and an old calendar of five years ago, presumably kept for its old-fashioned English country scene, hangs over the hole in the centre of the door so that the nurses may not peep in at her in the night. She is allowed that privacy.

Her sobriety, her apparent acceptance of a way of life that will continue until she dies — these frighten me. She seems like someone who could set up camp in a graveyard and continue to boil the billy, eat and sleep soundly and perhaps spend the day polishing the tombstones or weeding the graves. One watches her for a ripple of herself as one watches an eternally calm lake for evidence of the rumoured creature inhabiting perhaps 'deeper than ever plummet sounded'. One needs a machine like a bathysphere to find Mrs Pilling. A bathysphere of fear? Of love?

In the beginning and the end her life is bread cream building the dining room fire; making sure with Mrs Everett, who also has a passion for polishing, that the copper tea-urn is given its daily shine; setting out the Private Cupboard food. Fruit sweets cakes biscuits brought by visitors and not eaten during the Saturday and Sunday visiting hours are taken from the patients and locked in the Private Cupboard and at teatime, depending on how much food has been stored for you, you find beside your place at the table a dish with your name on it containing perhaps two or three wrapped chocolates an orange an apple. Sometimes, because I seldom have visitors, I contrive to help Mrs Pilling and the nurse and wait greedily for the expected moment when the nurse arranging on a plate a glittering still life of chocolates says suddenly, 'Here, have one.'

I protest, 'Oh no. They do not belong to me.'

The nurse answers according to plan, 'No, this patient has bags and bags of food; it's going to waste.'

Guiltily I seize the chocolate unwrap it slowly smoothe the wrinkles from the silver paper take a small bite testing for hardness then, like a thief, like the cunning scrounger that I am, I eat it. In the same way after visitors leave and the patients depressed and agitated talking about husband home children are wandering around clutching their only visible and palpable remnants of visiting hour, their small collection of biscuits sweets fruit, then I, with nothing in my hand and trying calmly to answer the question 'Who came to see you?' will 'happen' to appear in the most crowded corner of the dayroom where I know I will be offered an orange or a peppermint or a biscuit.

'You should keep them for yourself,' I protest, greedily holding out my hand.

There is no past present or future. Using tenses to divide time is like making chalk marks on water. I do not know if my experiences at Cliffhaven happened years ago, are happening now, or lie in wait for me in what is called the future.

I know that the linen room was very often my sanctuary. I looked through its little dusty window upon the lower park and the lawns and trees and the distant blue strip of sea like sticky paper pasted edge to edge with the sky. I wept and wondered and dreamed the abiding dream of most mental patients — The World, Outside, Freedom; and foretasted too vividly the occasions I most feared — electric shock treatment, being shut in a single room at night, being sent to Ward Two, the disturbed ward. I dreamed of the world because it seemed the accepted thing to do, because I could not bear to face the thought that not all prisoners dream of freedom; the prospect of the world terrified me: a morass of despair violence death with a thin layer of glass spread upon the surface where Love, a tiny crab with pincers and rainbow shell, walked delicately ever sideways but getting nowhere, while the sun — like one of those woolly balls we made at occupational therapy by winding orange wool on a circle of cardboard — rose higher in the sky its tassels dropping with flame threatening every moment to melt the precarious highway of glass. And the people: giant patchworks of colour with limbs missing and parts of their mind snipped off to fit them into the outline of the free pattern.

I could not find my way from the dream; I had no means to escape from it; I was like a surgeon who at the moment of a delicate operation finds that his tray of instruments has been stolen, or, worse, twisted into unfamiliar shapes so that only he can realise their unfamiliarity while the team around the table, suspecting nothing, wait for him to make the first incision. How can he explain to them what they cannot understand because it is visible only to him? Dutifully I thought of The World because I was beyond it — who else will dream of it with longing? And at times I murmured the token phrase to the doctor, 'When can I go home?' knowing that home was the place where I least desired to be. There they would watch me for signs of abnormality, like ferrets around a rabbit burrow waiting for the rabbit to appear.

I feared the prospect of a single room. Although all the small rooms were 'single' rooms the use of the phrase *single room* served to make a threat more terrifying. During my stay in Ward Four I slept first in the Observation Dormitory and later in the dormitory 'down the other end' where the beds had floral bedspreads and where, because of the lack of space, there was an overflow of beds into the corridor. I liked the observation dormitory at night with the night nurse sitting in the armchair brought in from the mess-room, knitting an endless number of cardigans and poring over pull-out pattern supplements in the women's magazines, and snatching a quick nap with her feet up on the fireguard and the fire pleasantly warming her bottom. I liked the ritual of going to bed, with the faithful Mrs Pilling sending in a tray of hot milk drinks, and one of the patients marching in balancing like a waitress a high pile of dun-coloured chambers. I liked the beds side by side and the reassurance of other people's soft breathing mingled with the irritation of their snoring and their secret conversations and the tinkle-tinkle and warm smell like a cow byre when they used their chambers in the night. I dreaded that one day Matron Glass hearing that I had been 'difficult' or 'uncooperative' would address me sharply, 'Right. Single room for you, my lady.'

Hearing other people threatened so often made me more afraid, and seeing that a patient, in the act of being taken to a single room, always struggled and screamed, made me morbidly curious about what the room contained that, overnight, it could change people who screamed and disobeyed into people who sat, withdrawn, and obeyed listlessly when ordered Dayroom, Dining room, Bed. Yet not all people changed; and those who did not respond to the four-square shuttered influence of the room, who could not be taught what Matron Glass or Sister Honey decreed to be 'a lesson', were removed to Ward Two.

And Ward Two was my fear. They sent you there if you were 'uncooperative' or if persistent doses of E.S.T. did not produce in you an improvement which was judged largely by your submission and prompt obedience to orders — Dayroom Ladies, Rise Ladies, Bed Ladies.

You learned with earnest dedication to 'fit in'; you learned not to cry in company but to smile and pronounce yourself pleased, and to ask from time to time if you could go home, as proof that you were getting better and therefore in no need of being smuggled in the night to Ward Two. You learned the chores, to make your bed with the government motto facing the correct way and the corners of the counterpane neatly angled; to 'rub up' the dormitory and the corridor, working the heavy bumper on the piece of torn blanket smeared with skittery yellow polish that distributed its energetic soaking smell from the first day it was fetched with the weekly stores in the basket beside the tins of jam jars of vinegar and the huge blocks of cheese and butter which Mrs Pilling and Mrs Everett quarried with a knife specially unlocked from the knife box. You learned the routine, that it 'was so', that bath night was Wednesday, but that those who could be trusted to wash further than their wrists were allowed to bathe any night in the large bathroom where the roof soared like in a railway station and three deep tubs lay side by side each with its locked box containing the taps. In small print so that one might mistake it for a railway timetable the list of bathing rules was pasted on the wall. It was an old list, issued at the beginning of the century, and contained fourteen rules which stated, for example, that no patient might take a bath unless an attendant were present, that six inches only of water should be run into the bath, the cold water first, that no brush of any kind should be employed in bathing a patient . . . So we bathed, one in each bath, without screens, gazing curiously at one another's bodies, the pendulous bellies and tired breasts, the faded wisps of body hair, the unwieldy and the supple shapes that form to women the nagging and perpetual 'withness' of their flesh.

(1961)

JANET FRAME

The Mythmaker's Office

'The sun,' they said, 'is unmentionable. You must never refer to it.'

But that ruse did not work. People referred to the sun, wrote poems about it, suffered under it, lying beneath the chariot wheels, and their eyes were pierced by the sapphire needles jabbing in the groove of light. The sun lolled in the sky. The sun twitched like an extra nerve in the mind. And the sunflowers turned their heads, watching the ceremony, like patient ladies at a tennis match.

So that ruse did not work.

But the people in charge persisted, especially the Minister of Mythmaking who sat all day in his empty office beating his head with a gold-mounted stick in order to send up a cloud of ideas from underneath his wall-to-wall carpet of skin. Alas, when the ideas flew up they arrived like motes in other people's eyes and the Minister of Mythmaking as an habitually polite occupier of his ceiling-to-floor glass ministry did not care to remove ideas from the eyes of other people.

Instead, he went outside and threw coloured stones against the Office of Mythmaking.

'What are you doing, my good chap?' the Prime Minister asked, on his way to a conference.

'Playing fictional fives,' the Minister of Mythmaking replied, after searching for an explanation.

'You would be better occupied,' the Prime Minister told him, 'in performing the correct duties of your office.'

Dazed, shoulders drooping with care, the Minister of Mythmaking returned to his office where once again he sat alone, staring at the big empty room and seeing his face four times in the glass walls. Once more he took his gold-mounted stick and, beating his head, he sent up another cloud of ideas which had a stored musty smell for they had been swept under the carpet years ago and had never been removed or disturbed until now. One idea pierced the Minister in the eye.

'Ah,' he said. 'Death. Death is unmentionable. Surely that will please all concerned. Death is obscene, unpublishable. We must ban all reference to it, delete the death notices from the newspapers, make it an indecent offence to be seen congregating at funerals, drive Death underground.

'Yes,' the Minister of Mythmaking said to himself. 'This will surely please the public, the majority, and prove the ultimate value of Democracy. All will cooperate in the denial of Death.' Accordingly he drafted an appropriate bill which passed swiftly with averted eyes through the House of Parliament and joined its forebears in the worm-eaten paper territories in panelled rooms.

Death notices disappeared from the newspapers. Periodical raids were carried out by the police upon undertakers' premises and crematoria to ensure that no indecent activities were in progress. Death became relegated to a Resistance Movement, a Black Market, and furtive shovellings on the outskirts of the city.

For people did not stop dying. Although it was now against the law, obscene, subversive, Death remained an intense part of the lives of every inhabitant of the kingdom. In the pubs and clubs after work the citizens gathered to exchange stories which began, 'Do you know the one about . . . ?' and which were punctuated with whispered references to Death, the Dead, Cemeteries, Mortuaries. Often you could hear smothered laughter and observe expressions of shame and guilt as ribaldry placed its fear-releasing hand simultaneously upon Death and Conscience. At other times arguments broke out, fights began, the police were called in, and the next day people were summoned to court on charges relating to indecent behaviour and language, with the witness for the prosecution exclaiming, 'He openly uttered the word . . . the word . . . well I shall write it upon a piece of paper and show it to the learned judge . . .' And when the judge read the words 'Death', 'the dead' upon the paper his expression would become severe, he would pronounce the need for a heavy penalty, citizens must learn to behave as normal citizens, and not flout the laws of common decency by referring to Death and the practices of burial . . .

In books the offending five-letter word was no longer written in full; letters other than the first and last were replaced by dots or a dash. When one writer boldly used the word Death several times, and gave detailed descriptions of the ceremonies attending death and burial, there followed such an outcry that his publishers were prosecuted for issuing an indecent work.

But the prosecutors did not win their case, for witnesses convinced the jury that the references to death and its ceremonies were of unusual beauty and power, and should be read by all citizens.

'In the end', a witness reminded the court, 'each one of us is involved in dying, and though we are forbidden by law to acknowledge this, surely it is necessary for us to learn the facts of death and burial?'

'What!' the public in court said. 'And corrupt the rising generation!' You should have seen the letters to the paper after the court's decision was made known!

The book in question sold many millions of copies; its relevant passages were marked and thumbed; but people placed it on their bookshelves with its title facing the wall.

Soon, however, the outcry and publicity which attended the case were forgotten and the city of the kingdom reverted to its former habits of secrecy. People died in secret, were buried in secret. At one time there was a wave of righteous public anger (which is a dangerous form of anger) against the existence of buildings such as hospitals which in some ways cater to the indecencies of death and are thus an insult to the pure-minded. So effective had been the work of the Mythmaker's Office that the presence of a hospital, its evil suggestiveness, made one close one's eyes in disgust. Many of the buildings were deliberately burned to the ground, during occasions of night-long uninhibited feasting and revelry where people rejoiced, naked, dancing, making love while the Watch Committee, also naked, but with pencils and notebooks, maintained their vigilance by recording instances of behaviour which stated or implied reference to the indecencies of Death.

People found dying in a public place were buried in secrecy and shame. Furtive obscene songs were sung about road accidents, immodesties such as influenza, bronchitis, and the gross facts of the sickroom. Doctors, in spite of their vowed alliance with the living, became unmentionable evils, and were forced to advertise in glass cabinets outside tobacconists and night clubs in the seedier districts of the kingdom.

The avoidance of Death, like the avoidance of all inevitability, overflowed into the surrounding areas of living, like a river laying waste the land which it had formerly nourished and made fertile.

The denial of Death became also a denial of life and growth.

'Well,' said the Prime Minister surrounded by last week's wrapped, sliced, crumbling policies, 'Well,' he said proudly to the Minister of Mythmaking, 'you have accomplished your purpose. You have done good work. You may either retire on a substantial pension or take a holiday in the South of France, at the kingdom's expense. We have abolished Death. We are now immortal. Prepare the country for thousands of years of green happiness.'

And leaning forward he took a bite of a new policy, which had just been delivered to him. It was warm and doughy, with bubbles of air inside to give it lightness.

'New policies, eaten quickly, are indigestible,' the Minister of Mythmaking advised, wishing to be of service, before he retired to the South of France.

The Prime Minister frowned. 'I have remedies,' he said coldly. Then he smiled. 'Thousands of years of green happiness.'

Yet by the end of that year the whole kingdom except for one man and one woman had committed suicide. Death, birth, life had been abolished. People arrived from the moon, rubbing their hands with glee and sucking lozenges which were laid in rows, in tins, and dusted with sugar.

In a hollow upon dead grass, and dead leaves the one human couple left alive on earth said, 'Let's make Death.'

And the invalid sun opened in the sky, erupting its contagious boils of light, pouring down the golden matter upon the waste places of the earth.

(1962)

JANET FRAME

A Sense of Proportion

The sun's hair stood on end. The sky accommodated all visiting darkness and light. Leaves were glossy green, gold, brown, dried, dead and bleached in drifts beneath the trees. Snow fell in all seasons, white hyphens dropping evenly, linking syllables of sky and earth. Flowers bloomed forever, spinning their petal-spokes like golden wheels, sucking the sun like whirlpools. Black-polished, brick-dusted, spotted ladybirds big as airplanes with pleated wings like sky-wide curtains parting, flew home to flame and cinders.

Houses had painted roofs of red and yellow with tall chimneys emitting scribbles of pale blue smoke. All houses had gardens around them, paths with parallel sides enclosing pebbles; gates were five-barred, with children swinging from them. The children wore red stockings. They had ribbons tied in their hair. Their eyes were round and blue, their eyebrows were arched, their lips were rosy. Their hands displayed five fingers for all to see, their feet pointed the same way, left or right, in gaudy shoes with high heels. The ocean was filled with sailing boats, the sky was filled with rainbows, suns, scalloped clouds.

Coats had many buttons, intricate collars with lace edges. The bricks of houses were carefully outlined. Front doors had four panels and a knocker in its exact position.

Winds were visible, fat men or witches with puffed cheeks in the four corners of the sky. The trees leaned with their skirts up over their heads.

The streets were full of painted rubber balls divided carefully into bright colours.

Men wore hats placed firmly upon their heads.

Dogs walked, their tails like masts in the air.

Cats had mile-long whiskers, like rays of the sun. They sat, their tails curled about them, containing them. Their ears were pricked, forever listening.

The moon, like the sun, had a face, a smile, eyes, teeth. The moon journeyed on a cloud convoyed by elaborately five-pointed stars.

There was no distance or shade in our infant drawing. Everything loomed close to the eye; rainbows in the heavens could be clutched as securely as the few blades of bright green grass (the colour of strong lemonade) growing symmetrically in the lower right-hand corner of the picture.

Some years passed during which we learned to draw and paint from a small tin of Reeve's Water Colours: Chinese White, Gamboge Tint, Indigo, Yellow Ochre (which I pronounced and believed to be *Yellow Ogre*), Burnt Sienna: the names gave excitement, pain, wonder. We were shown how to paint a sunset in the exact gradations of colour, to make blue water-colour sky, a scientific rainbow (Read Over Your Greek Book In Verse) receding into the distance. The teacher placed an apple and a pear in a glass bowl upon the table. We drew them, making careful shading, painstakingly colouring the autumn tints of the apple.

We did not paint the worm inside it.

We drew vases of flowers, autumn scenes, furniture which existed merely to cast a perfect shadow to be portrayed by a B.B. pencil. The Art lessons were long and tedious. I could never get my shadow or my distance correct. My rainbows and paths would not recede, and my furniture, my boats at anchor, my buildings stood flat upon the page, all in a total clamour of foreground.

'You must draw things,' said Miss Collins the Art Teacher, 'as they seem. Notice the way the path narrows as it approaches the foothills.'

'But it is the same breadth all the way!'

'No,' Miss Collins insisted. 'You must learn to draw these tricks of the eye. You must learn to think in terms of them.'

I never learned to draw tricks of the eye. My paint refused to wash in the correct proportion when I was trying to fill the paper sky with sunrises, sunsets, and rainbows. My garden spades were without strength or shape; their shadows stayed unowned, apart, incredible, more like stray tatters shed from a profusion of dark remnants of objects. My vases had no depth, and their flowers withered in their laborious journey from the table to the page of my scholastic Drawing Book Number Three.

The classroom was dusty and hot and there was the soft buzz of talking, and people walking to and fro getting fresh water and washing brushes; and Miss Collins touring the aisles, giving gentle but insistent advice about colours and shadows. Her hair was in plaits, wound close to her head. In moments of calm or boredom the fact or fancy rippled about the classroom, lapping at our curiosity, Miss Collins wears a wig. Once, long ago, in the days of the Spartans and Athenians, someone had observed Miss Collins in the act of removing her wig.

'She is quite bald,' the rumour went.

Like so many of the other teachers Miss Collins lived with her mother in a little house, a woven spider's nest with the leaves and rain closing in, just at the edge of town. She cherished a reputation as a local painter and at most exhibitions you would see her poplar trees, tussock scenes, mountains, lakes, all in faded colours, with sometimes in the corner, or looking out of the window of a decayed farmhouse, the tiny fierce black lines that were the shape of people.

Every term she gave us examinations which were days of flurry and anxiety when we filed into the Art Room and took our places at the bare desks and gazed with respectful awe at the incongruous display on the table — fruit, a vase of flowers, perhaps a kettle or similar utensil whose shape would strain our ability to 'match sides'. And for the next forty minutes our attention would be fixed upon the clutter of objects, the submissive Still Life which yet huddled powerfully before us, preying upon us with its overlapping corners and sides and deceptive shadows.

How I envied Leila Smith! Leila Smith could draw perfect kettles, rainbows, cupboards. Her pictures always showed the exact number of strokes of rain, when rain fell, and snowflakes when the scene required them. By instinct Leila Smith *knew*. On those days when the gods attended the classroom, penetrating the dust-layered windows hung with knotted cords so complicated that a special Window Monitor was needed to operate them, and the window sills ranged with dead flowers and beans in water — when the gods walked up and down the aisles at our Art Examination they showed extra care for Leila Smith, they guided her hand across the page. When they passed my desk, alas, they vindictively jogged my elbow. Miss Collins despaired of ever teaching me.

'How's your drawing?' my Father would say, who had spent the winter evenings painting in oils from a tiny cigarette card the ship that carried him to the First World War. His sisters painted as well; their work hung in the passage — roses, dogs, clouded ladies, and one storm at sea.

'I can't draw,' I said. 'I can't paint.'

Miss Collins readily agreed with me. 'Your perspective and proportion are well below average. Your shading is poor.'

The obsession with shading fascinated me. All things, even kettles and fire shovels, stood under the sun complete and unique with their shadows, fighting to preserve them. It was an act of charity for us to draw the shadow with as much love (frustration, despair) as we gave to drawing the shape itself. In the world of Miss Collins, morning and evening were perpetual, with the shadows spread beautifully alongside each object, their contours matching perfectly, a mirror image of the body. Why was it that in my world the sun stood everlastingly at noon; objects were stripped of their shadows, forced to stand in brilliant light, alone?

In the end Miss Collins gave up trying to teach me to draw and paint. She spent her time giving hints to Leila Smith. Oh how wonderful were Leila's flowers and fire shovels, garden spades and kettles!

Sometimes Miss Collins would ask us to paint things 'out of our head.'

It showed, she said, whether we had any imagination.

I had no imagination. My poverty could not even provide shadows or proportionate rainbows. The paths in my head stayed the same width right to the foothills and over the mountains which were no obstacles to vision, as mountains are agreed to be; they were transparent mountains, and there was the path, the same width as before, annihilating distance, at last disappearing only at the boundary of the picture.

Distance did not cloud the outline of objects; trees were not blurred; you could count the leaves upon the trees, even on the slopes of the mountain you could count the pine needles hanging in their green brushes.

Yes, it was true; I had no sense of proportion.

When I last saw Miss Collins she had been taken to the hospital after a stroke, and was lying quietly in the hospital bed. She was dying. The torment of the unshaded world lay before her, the sun in her sky stood resolutely at noon, her life was out of proportion, there was no distance, the foreground blazed with looming and light.

She closed her eyes and died.

Her life, in its spider's web, had absorbed her. She had been aided, comforted, made less lonely, by acknowledging and yielding to a trick of the eye. How does one learn to accept that trick and its blessings before it is too late, before the shadows are razed and the sun stands pitiless at perpetual noon?

(1963)

AMELIA BATISTICH

A Dalmatian Woman

When the boat came into Auckland she was at the ship rail with the other proxy brides, all of them waiting to see their husbands for the first time, all looking down anxiously at the crowd of faces on the wharf, trying to pick the one face out. She looked at the unfamiliar scene, listened to the noise of the people chattering in the strange English tongue all around them, and wondered suddenly what madness had possessed her to marry a man she had never seen, knew only from his photograph and the letters he had written, all for the chance to come to New Zealand. It felt like the end of a life, not the beginning. The others were younger. They chattered like starlings, pointing to people down on the wharf. 'What is wrong, Lucia!' they said. 'Don't you feel excited? You are going to see your husband!'

They had not long to wait. The ship's officer who had looked after them on the way out so kindly came towards them with another man, a fussy little man with a ginger moustache and yellow teeth. He was holding a handful of papers. A little behind him were the husbands. She decided that was who they must be. They looked so shy and clumsy and eager. She scanned their faces, looking for hers, and found him easily enough. He was older than he looked in the photograph, big and awkward.

The little man took charge. He called out their names, fussed over the papers. She felt like a bought thing. One after another the husbands came forward to be introduced to the wives. She waited for hers. He came forward, put out his hand, changed his mind and kissed her clumsily. She felt his mouth, wet and awkward on her face. She put up her hand to brush the kiss away, then remembered it was her husband who had kissed her.

They went to a Dalmatian boardinghouse for dinner. There had been one in Sydney where they had stayed a day and talked with their fellow countrymen. It was good to hear your own speech around you. It made New Zealand seem not so frightening. It even seemed like home. But it was not home. That afternoon she said goodbye to the others, all of them going, like her, to face a life as strange. Her trunk and her cane hamper were put on the train and with Toma she went out to find her new home.

Toma was not a man to speak easily. Words came slowly as if he had to think hard for them. He looked at her and smiled and put out a hand hardened from work on her own. She felt a revulsion to this stranger, and would have pulled her hand away but something in his eyes made her keep it there. Perhaps it was because she had always thought herself a little above the other girls in the village at home that she felt like this. But this rough stranger, with his shy eyes, and his groping hands, how would she ever get to know him?

She did not know that he was awkward because he did not feel like himself in the new suit he was wearing. The collar was tight and the coat held him like a straitjacket. He was not used to sitting and doing nothing, unused to having a woman by his side. Later, when he had time, he would tell her of the great loneliness of life without a woman of your own, not even a mother or a sister. Later, but now he had no words.

As they sped through the country she marvelled at the greenness of this land. The vastness of the fields. The fat cattle. It was nothing like home. 'It will be good here,' he said. 'A few years and we will be rich. Wait and see.' But when they came to Waiotira, and he told her to carry the hamper while he took the trunk, all she could see was emptiness. He hoisted the box on to his shoulders and they set off, leaving the little station to its desolation. The road was dusty and the dust covered the vegetation on the side of it. She couldn't see a house anywhere.

'Where is our home?' she asked.

'There!' he said, pointing to something that looked like a matchbox.

She was too tired to walk, too tired to think even. All she wanted was to get to the matchbox, to sit down and take off her shoes and to cry her heart out. But he trudged stolidly on, never complaining about the heavy trunk, shifting it patiently from one shoulder to the other and back again.

'There!' he said, when they had walked a million miles, and she looked to where his finger pointed and there was a hut no bigger than the place they had for the goats at home. Only it wasn't made of stone, but of rough, unpainted wood, with a tin chimney on the outside wall. They went inside. The door hung drunkenly on one hinge. There was a smell of smoke. The rough wooden walls were hung with cobwebs. The one window had a sack for a curtain. She looked for a place to sit down. He pulled a box from under the table. She sat down and kicked off her shoes. Her hat fell off when she bent down and the red flowers on it made a splash of brightness on the floor.

'It will be better when we light the fire,' he said. She looked round for the stove. He lit the fire in a well of stones on an open hearth. A heavy black iron pot swung from a chain over it. It was her first sight of a camp oven. She put her hands to her aching head. 'I would like some coffee,' she said.

'Coffee!' He shook his head. There was none.

No coffee! What did they drink in this New Zealand?

He took down a tin and showed her what was in it. 'Tea,' he said.

'That is what you drink in New Zealand.' Already she was beginning to think that New Zealand was a place where the world stood on its head. But she drank the tea when he made it and it wasn't too bad, smoke and all. She drank it from a mug made of a condensed-milk tin with the edges beaten down. She was too numbed by now even to question it. If everything else was as it was, then you had to accept the tin cup.

Revived a little by the tea, she looked with dull curiosity about her again. Boxes for chairs, a table made of boxes, a stove that was a pot hanging over an open fire. Floor of caked earth, a window with no glass in it, the bed — where was the bed? And then she saw that one end of the room was curtained off with sacking. She got up and went to look behind it. There was the bed. Four posts dug into the floor. Sacking nailed across it. One black woollen blanket. Two pillows, one old, one new. The bridal bed. She thought of the finely-embroidered linen in her trunk. Then she wept.

The man looked at her dumbly. He wanted to say things to her. How lonely the years had been. How hard he had worked to buy this first piece of land. Now at least the loneliness would be gone. She would be there to warm his days and nights.

'Wait,' he said, 'a year, two, three like this, then we will be on our feet. The land needs money, all the money I can get working outside. If I feed it the money now, it will return to us later on.' But all she could say was that she had not thought New Zealand would be like this. When he had written why did he not tell her? Why did everyone believe it was so different? 'And I am from a good house,' she said. 'It is harder for me.' But when she looked down at her hands there was the wedding ring, solid and gold and binding.

They went to sleep in the marriage bed. Long after he had drowsed off she lay awake. It was cold and the one blanket hardly warmed the two. She got up and dressed in her clothes and lay down beside her sleeping man.

Before he went off to his work the next day he showed her the paddock he had prepared for potato planting. He showed her the seed. It was cut and ready. 'You plant them like this,' he said, beginning the first row. 'But I have never worked in the fields!' she wanted to cry out, but she didn't. Instead she watched what he was doing and followed the row to its end. Another and another. Her back ached, but there was something in the feel of earth in her hands. Generations of peasant blood warmed to it. Earth! And it belonged to her and her husband. Her hands stung, the skin broke and she sucked the blood from it, but she worked on.

That night she was too tired to complain about the bed. The man wanted to talk, to keep her awake, but she only wanted sleep. He wanted to tell her all about his dreams for the farm, the shed he would build, the fences he would put up, the ditches he would dig . . . 'You and your farm,' she said, and shut her eyes and the sound of him out.

And the funny thing was that she was soon used to it all. The rough kindness of the man, his clumsy love-making. The hard days and harder nights on the sack bed. The old country faded from her thoughts. She began to feel herself part of something in the making. The acres of land became an obsession with her as with him, and, when their first child was born and she brought it home from the hospital, she held it up to the land and said:

'See what we are making for you!'

(1963)

AMELIA BATISTICH

A Place Called Sarajevo

The launch chugged up the river. Mrs Zelich sat on a coil of rope in the prow, but Ketty stayed in the cabin with Mr Zelich. He kept his eyes on the river and said little, but once he let her take hold of the steering-wheel and showed her how to guide it. The river was still, except for the swish-swash of the launch's wake. The shore seemed far away — already it was becoming shadowy with evening.

They came to Paroa. The launch slowed down and Mr Zelich jumped out and called to his wife to throw down the rope. She tossed it over and he caught it expertly and tied it to the jetty with a loose knot. He called to Ketty to jump and he would catch her. Mrs Zelich gathered up the parcels she had bought and told her not to be frightened. It would be all right. She climbed on to the rails, shut her eyes and jumped. Mrs Zelich did the same, only when Mr Zelich held out his hand she didn't take it.

They made their way down a track through rushes and toetoe, and when they came to a clearing, there was the house. It wasn't much of a house. It wanted paint and bright curtains and the grass around it cut. Then it might have been all right. But it had a kind of mystery, sitting there in a hump with the cabbage trees ringing it round and a huge lump of flax at the door.

They went inside. Mr Zelich put down the sack he was carrying and lit the lamp. The wick flickered palely in the half dark, throwing out huge shadows that made the walls seem alive and menacing. Ketty found herself wishing for the comfort and security of the gas mantle glowing in the rooms at home. Mrs Zelich had taken off her coat and hat and hung them on a nail. 'Take yours off too,' she said to Ketty, 'and I will show you where you are to sleep.' She came close to her and smiled and stroked her face. 'It is nice to have someone here to talk to,' she said slowly. 'It is so lonely on the farm.' She spoke in the old-country language. Ketty followed her to a room that led off the kitchen. It was small and dark and the paper hung dankly from the walls. There was a bed in one corner and a dressing-table. Mrs Zelich brought in some sheets and made up the bed. They were fine linen and embroidered with red initials.

They went back to the kitchen. Mr Zelich had lit the fire. It burned brightly, and Ketty felt more cheerful when she saw it. A kettle was boiling on the stove and there was some soup heating in a big iron pot. It smelt good. She was hungry and hoped they'd have tea soon.

Mrs Zelich spread out a newspaper on the table, took some knives and forks and spoons from a box and put them down with a plate for each place and a loaf of bread on a board. She lifted the lid of the pot and looked at the soup. It must have been ready, for she then took out three deep plates with green leaves on the rims, and ladled the soup into them. 'You sit there,' she told Ketty and gave her the one chair in the place. She and Mr Zelich sat on boxes.

The soup was good. It was cabbage with a flavour of bacon. Mr Zelich drank his noisily and held out his plate for more. Mrs Zelich took sips at hers, but she couldn't have liked it because she soon pushed it away. Ketty finished all hers. Then they had some boiled meat with tomato sauce.

When the meal was finished, Mr Zelich stretched out his legs and lit a pipe. He asked Ketty if she had had enough. She nodded. Mrs Zelich gathered up the plates and washed them with a clatter in the tin bowl. Ketty found a tea towel made from a flour bag. She dried the dishes and stacked them up on the bench. Mrs Zelich smiled at her all the time to let her know she was glad she was there. But Mr Zelich said nothing to anyone.

Outside, the quiet had taken hold of the farm. Once a morepork called, 'More pork', and another answered. The quietness outside and the quietness inside made Ketty feel frightened again. Why had her mother let her come? This was a funny place. At home the house would be blazing with lights and full of people talking and laughing but it didn't seem as if anyone ever talked or laughed here. She tried to say something herself, just so it wouldn't be so quiet, but no words came. So the stillness stayed, broken only by the un-human clatter of the dishes on the tin bowl.

When they had finished the dishes Mrs Zelich sat down on a box by the stove. She moved the chair over for Ketty and told her to sit down. She smiled gently and took some needlework from a carved box by the fireplace. The box was finely made. When it was opened, Ketty saw that it was filled with linen and bright silks. Mrs Zelich took out a cloth — a beautiful cloth, the work on it half-finished, bright reds and blues and greens in a symmetrical design. Mr Zelich had fallen asleep. The pipe lay smoking in a tin beside him. He began to snore and Ketty felt that even the snoring was some company. It was better than the silence.

Mrs Zelich looked disdainful, but she didn't say anything. She threaded the needle and began to sew, her long fingers drawing the red thread and the green thread into the pattern; her face had a calm beauty bent over the sewing. Her eyes were very dark and her hair was black as the night outside. It was wonderful hair, thick plaits wound round and round the head.

She must have seen Ketty looking at it for she smiled and put up her hand and stroked the hair from her face. Little tendrils had escaped and they made her look young, and somehow tender. Then she spoke. 'You like my hair?' And from the way she said it, you could see that it was a vanity of hers.

'It is lovely,' Ketty answered. 'It must be very long.' And Mrs Zelich took out the pins that held it up, and the plaits fell down and they came almost to the hem of her dress. She twined one hand through a plait, and the black hair and the white arm were beautiful.

Mrs Zelich bent towards her as if she had something to tell that she did not want her husband to hear. 'In Sarajevo they called me "Kossara Dyevoyka", the girl with the long hair. I would sit at my window, at the full moon, and passers-by would look up and call to me from the street. "Kossara Dyevoyka, come down!"'

She put down the fancywork and her eyes were far away. 'Now I dream about it at night; in the daytime, it is lost in here' — she put her hand to her head vaguely — 'but in my dreams, my house of white stone with the oleanders growing at the door . . . and the nights smelling of musk . . . and the minarets picked out by the white moon!' Only she didn't say 'minarets' but *djamiye*, but Ketty knew what they were because her mother often said the word in the songs about the Turkish Begs (noblemen).

'Sometimes I wonder if there is such a place at all.' Then she began to cry softly and unhappily. She looked around the room, hating everything that was in it. 'The Muezzins call in Sarajevo, but the pukeko and the morepork, they are my muezzins here!' And her eyes became wild and her hands tore at the fancywork and the tears fell down till it looked as if it had been left outside in the rain.

Ketty remembered all she had heard her mother and the other women saying about Mrs Zelich being strange. Their voices died to whispers there. She remembered the story of the quick courtship and the hasty marriage, the disapproval of the women when they heard that Steve Zelich had come back from his visit home with a Bosnian wife. 'He should have married one of his own.' That was what her mother had said. 'A Bosnian is half a Turk!' It could have come from the pages of a book, not something that happened really. Steven Zelich walking through a street in Sarajevo and the girl, seeing him from the window and knowing him for a stranger by his dress, and calling to him: 'Young man, where are you from?' And when he answered, 'New Zealand', calling back: 'Marry me and take me there!' And Steven finding himself quickly married to the beautiful girl before he knew what had happened to him.

'Poor Steve,' her mother said when she spoke of Mr Zelich. 'A big, plain, clumsy man, but good.' Those were her mother's judgments. It was too much for a child to understand, but she looked at Mrs Zelich crying and wished she had words to comfort her.

But the tears passed and the woman took up the fancywork as if nothing had happened, and she laughed a little and said would Ketty help her set the dough for the morning's baking. And when they went into the kitchen Mr Zelich woke up and said it was time for bed. 'You go,' Mrs Zelich said. 'I have company for tonight.'

They heard his clumsy movements about the bedroom and the creak of the bed when he got into it. Mrs Zelich took out the flour and the yeast and mixed them in a big pan. She stirred the dough, mixing it gently with her hand, as if she loved it. When it was ready she broke off two pieces. One she twisted into a *kolach* (ring-shaped roll). 'For you,' she said, smiling, 'and this is for me.' Her long fingers shaped the dough, and Ketty saw that it was a manikin she was making — legs, arms, head and all of a man. She set him beside the bread and covered it all with a blanket, the *kolach* too. 'Now we will go to bed,' she said briskly and gave Ketty a candle and told her to be careful and put it out before she went to sleep.

In the middle of the night Ketty wakened. She heard voices from the kitchen — quarrelling voices. She lay listening for a while, then she got up and peeped through the door. It was the littlest bit open. She saw Mrs Zelich standing in her nightdress with her arms held out to something. Mr Zelich was telling her to come to bed. 'You will catch cold — you will catch cold,' he kept saying to her, but Mrs Zelich took no notice. She kept saying the angry things and started to laugh and laugh and her husband told her to be quiet, she would wake the child, but she wouldn't stop. He hit her on the face and her nose began to bleed. The blood ran down her chin and on to her nightgown.

The fancywork was lying where she left it and he picked it up and wiped off the blood and threw it on the floor, and there was the beautiful work, with the bright red stains jagging across the red and the green already there, crumpled as if it were a rag. But Mrs Zelich didn't see or care about it. She just stood there, crying in great gulps, her arms held out to the darkened room.

Ketty climbed back into bed and pulled the blankets over her head. There was a world she knew nothing of and this was it. She fell asleep thinking, and when she got up Mrs Zelich was standing by the stove getting the breakfast. Mr Zelich came in from the shed and sat down at the table that still had last night's newspaper on it. Everything looked so ordinary she began to think it had been a dream last night, but when she looked, there was the fancywork lying on the floor with the blood on it. She tried not to see it, but it stayed there accusing the room.

During the meal she said she was sick and wanted to go home. Mr Zelich looked up quietly. 'Are you unhappy here?' he asked, but she shook her head quickly.

'No . . . no . . .'

'Mrs Zelich is so lonely,' he said. 'It would be nice for her if you stayed.' But Mrs Zelich broke in quickly.

'It is lonely here for a child, there is not much for anyone . . . sometimes I think God himself does not know this place.' She said it thoughtfully, not wildly at all. It was just something that she knew.

When Mr Zelich had gone back to the sheds they went to look at the dough to see if it was ready. The bread was a soft, humped roundness, and the *kolach* had risen too. The manikin lay in bloated caricature beside them.

It was all put to bake. When it was done Mrs Zelich opened the oven and took out the tray. There were the loaves all golden with baking, the *kolach* and the manikin beside them. 'You have your *kolach*,' said Mrs Zelich. She laid the loaves on a cloth. The manikin she put by himself. He lay spread out on the cloth, grotesque and sad.

Ketty wondered who would eat him, but she wasn't left wondering long. Mrs Zelich picked him up in her long fingers and stroked him, then she began to eat him, legs, arms, head and all — each part separately and slowly. Ketty shuddered. It was like eating somebody she knew.

There was none of last night's strangeness about the woman now. She was gay and even laughed once: 'I will come to see your mother soon,' she said.

But when the cream launch drew up at the jetty and Mr Zelich called out that there would be a passenger, she took hold of Ketty hard, and looked closely into her face and said:

'There *is* a place called Sarajevo, isn't there? Look in your books and tell me when I come.'

(1963)

ARAPERA BLANK

Yielding to the New

And the restless fingers of the city beckoned and Marama went forth to learn a little more. The parting was sad but her parents understood. 'It is good that you go,' said her father. 'If you stay here you will end up like your cousins. All they can talk about is babies — plenty of time for that. You are young. You have had a little education. Go to the city and learn a little more. Come home during the holidays to help us out. Don't you dare marry one of the village boys! Find someone who is worthy of your intelligence.'

'Find someone who will look after you first! Brains aren't everything,' sniffed her mother.

In the New Year, the service car was always crowded with exuberant youth on the way to the city: some already wearing the outward trimmings of urban sophistication, apparent in the nonchalance of straight skirts, slick high heels and two-tone jackets of brilliant hue; some like Marama, carsick already at the thought of travelling and a little fearful of what the city might hold.

Parents were there for the parting and as usual some of them echoed what Marama's people said. 'Come home with good husbands. We're tired of paying your fares.'

Others said. 'Get married first before you get babies.'

An uncle of Marama guffawed knowingly. 'I'll give you two years, Marama, to find a husband.'

Her father bade her farewell and the service car pulled out before her uncle could say more.

The first year in the city was not so bad after all. Marama went to the university. She took a subject called anthropology: a study in human relations. Marama was lost in the multitudinous flow of how man was first discovered, of the inevitable descent of man from the ape, and of the different ways of life of different peoples.

Now some of the students said that the subject was easy. But Marama understood little of what was said. She remembered only isolated phrases . . . 'the Maori with lipstick looks like the pukeko' . . . Goodness, thought Marama, why does he say that? What connection has this with human relations? . . . and the lecturer's voice droned on . . . 'half-way down the page, underline the following statement . . . "we have to rely on the arboreal theory . . ."' 'Oh dear! I cannot follow what he is saying. I'll have to read it up tonight.'

And Marama was miserable and longed to go home to the security of the village where thinking was easy. In the city the Maori was being flayed by the Pakeha pen.

Marama was soon caught up in the whirlwind of speculation on the meaning of Maoritanga. She forgot her misery for she thought she could contribute to the controversy and enlighten the Pakeha on her rich cultural heritage. But alas! They asked her point-blank. 'Can you tell us what Maoritanga is?' And she could not answer what it was.

'All my life I have lived in my village: I have eaten and slept on a raupo mat: I have been rubbed in mud to cure my sores: yet I cannot tell these Pakehas what Maoritanga is.'

And her misery within her grew strong for her ignorance was greater than she had dreamed and the raupo whispered, 'Come home — come home.'

A year went by and there were more Maori students. All were restless in the deep waters of learning and all insecure in a Pakeha world. They banded together for a little laughter and then felt a little better in the cold atmosphere of European learning.

One person had the high ambition of educating her people. She took her studies seriously and did not waste time. Another was a lad from the backblocks, breathing the scent of the native fern and as rich in his cultural heritage as he was poor in his adaptation to a Pakeha tradition. All had one thing in common and that was generosity. 'I'll lend you a few bob,' would say a lucky member, and there was no embarrassment at all.

Marama fitted in with the pleasant flow of Maori company and the university was a good place after all. The yearning to go home grew less and less and the Maoris at the university increased in number. Some were passing their exams with flying colours; the majority joined with the fifty per cent of failures. Each one however acquired a little learning — one by accident and another by hard toil.

They were all concerned with keeping alive their Maoritanga. It was their strength at the university. Yet no one could really say what it was. Many of the Pakehas felt that Maoritanga symbolised a picture of Maori characteristics of a century's standing — easy going, good-natured, lacking in stability. But most of the Maoris felt that true Maoritanga was reflected in their own language. 'If we lose our language we lose our culture.'

Perhaps that was the closest answer. But Marama had not made a decision. She had Maori friends in the city who spoke no Maori and yet were as much Maori as she although they differed just a little in that they were far more at home with Pakeha students. And yet their home was just like any other Maori home.

Christmas was near and Marama came home. The service car was packed with expectant people who were excited about the prospect of spending a holiday at home. As you drew nearer, the picture you envisaged of the waiting people proved right. Ah yes! They were there to greet the bus and to do their Christmas shopping. The shop was a great meeting place for the people. They were proud of it. It was a milestone in their history. On its concrete veranda, generous in size, nearly everyone gathered to meet and greet and a few just came to lick ice-cream till they well-nigh busted.

The city slickers descended from the bus to the quips and quirks of Maori humour. 'Tena koe! Kia ora! Kei te aha!' There was handshaking, nose-rubbing, and the modern greeting with the Pakeha kiss, and all went hand-in-hand in confusion.

'Good-day Heni. What have they been doing to you in the city? You been eating raw meat?' (in allusion to her painted lips).

'You shut up!' says Heni, feeling embarrassed.

'Kia ora Mate! What's that you are wearing?' Mate teeters out on her pointed high-heels, wearing a skirt with slits on either side which revealed enough of her beautiful legs.

'Why don't you tear them right up so we see them much better!' suggested one of the local boys.

Marama's father was there to greet her. In his slow, ponderous way he put her bags into a waiting taxi.

'The boys are all home,' he says. 'It's good to have you back. Mum and I could do with a hand in the garden.'

Yes, they were all home for the holidays. Her nine brothers and two sisters filled the house with laughter over much exchange of news. 'Your uncle's got a new contract,' says father. 'He carts all the kumaras to town. We're selling them now you know. They're worth their weight in gold.'

'Old Ben's got a new house,' says her brother. 'He got it under the Maori Affairs. Jim and I have just finished building it for him.'

The village was to all appearances as Marama had left it. There was the wide flowing river to the right of her home. The same green-brown-grey hill lay behind it, looking as though it were a whale resting its body in the placid flow. At night you could hear the swish swish of the corn outside her window. No, the place hadn't changed. During the day people trekked to and from their gardens, weeding, weeding: just like the people of any of the other villages along the coast. Half asleep was her village except on Fridays. That was when her brothers dashed off to the public bar, as all the other men did, to drink away their sweat and to talk with friends.

'You hear everybody's business there,' said the local men.

Marama walked down the road to visit her numerous relatives. It was the thing to do, otherwise you were called a 'whakahihi'. She noticed a lot of the new houses along the way. Things were certainly looking up. Ah! There were a few changes. Here and there were a few neat lawns.

Those of her relations who were among the proud owners said: 'You know Marama, it was all right living in an old shack. Not so much work to do. But we're glad we've got a nice house with running water. No more going down to the river to wash clothes. It's all right when you're young, but when you start getting babies by the dozen. Not too good. Besides, our children can bring any of the friends home from the city and we're not ashamed of ourselves any more.'

There were other new acquisitions in the village. There was electricity at the hall and a feature film every Friday. People were selling their kumaras to pay for their new commitments. And most of the young people were going to work in the freezing works because there wasn't enough land to hold them.

Marama forgot to ask her father for the meaning of Maoritanga. There was no need to ask once you got home. Besides, time was short and soon she would go back to the city. She listened to her father's tales about Maori heroes. She practised the tribal hakas with him.

'Listen to the pair of them,' her mother would say. 'Fancy being interested in those cannibal dances after her good education. That's all she can do when she comes out to weed kumaras with us. All I see is arms waving and little else.'

Everyone went to church on Sundays. Marama could not feel that fervent flow of faith any more. She had picked up some nonsensical ideas in the city. She had told her father in one of her preambles that part of her course in anthropology had been the study of man's origin.

'You know Dad,' she said, 'man is said to be descended from the ape, but they can't find the missing link.'

'Stuff and nonsense!' replied father. 'Man was made by God and that's that. Don't you come home with these Pakeha ideas. The Pakeha taught us that man was made by God and now he tells us that man descended from a monkey.'

Her father was a little afraid of what she was learning. She had some queer tales to tell. He was glad that she was still entranced by their tribal dances. It will keep her sane, he thought.

But church was still a good place to go. There were always babies to be christened. The mothers laughed at their numerous progeny. The singing of the hymns was always moving. The people sang lustily and the organ couldn't be heard.

There was that little old man. He was still part of the congregation, Marama was very fond of him. He sang heartily though out of key. Her brothers said he sang like an old tin can, and that he would never do well in a church choir because he hung on to his notes too long.

Her mother excused him. 'He thinks he's still singing one of our waiatas. That's why he drags those last notes.'

Some of her relations would stand at the back to watch the congregation giving during the collection of money for the church.

'Now you watch Hori. He's sure to put only threepence in the plate.'

Her father on his way round to take up the collection would glare at the miserable offering, but this would have no effect on the reluctant giver.

It was good to be home. It was easy to fit in with the flow of conversation. Besides, Marama's people had a deep respect for a little education. One didn't feel as ignorant as one did in the city. You knew tribal history. You could join in with the hakas. You could enjoy a waiata.

The other people home from the city were always restless for lots of entertainment. For Marama and a few others it wasn't as bad. They could always read books. But the trouble was you couldn't find anyone to talk to about some of your ideas and this made Marama restless. All sorts of ideas went through her head. Some she had picked up during her studies ... What did it matter if girls got babies before they were married? What did it matter if you didn't go to church on Sundays? Why couldn't Dad see that the Pakeha wasn't so bad?

And the green house where Marama lived faded from sight, and she passed the red and yellow school and the red and yellow hall, and she saw the shop where the people waited. And the restless fingers of the city beckoned.

I am growing away from my parents. I am going back to the turbulent flow thought Marama, and she grew very sad.

(1970)

PATRICIA GRACE

A Way of Talking

Rose came back yesterday; we went down to the bus to meet her. She's just the same as ever Rose. Talks all the time flat out and makes us laugh with her way of talking. On the way home we kept saying, 'E Rohe, you're just the same as ever.' It's good having my sister back and knowing she hasn't changed. Rose is the hard-case one in the family, the kamakama one, and the one with the brains.

Last night we stayed up talking till all hours, even Dad and Nanny who usually go to bed after tea. Rose made us laugh telling us about the people she knows, and taking off professor this and professor that from varsity. Nanny, Mum, and I had tears running down from laughing; e ta Rose we laughed all night.

At last Nanny got out of her chair and said, 'Time for sleeping. The mouths steal the time of the eyes.' That's the lovely way she has of talking. Nanny, when she speaks in English. So we went to bed and Rose and I kept our mouths going for another hour or so before falling asleep.

This morning I said to Rose that we'd better go and get her measured for the dress up at Mrs Frazer's. Rose wanted to wait a day or two but I reminded her the wedding was only two weeks away and that Mrs Frazer had three frocks to finish.

'Who's Mrs Frazer anyway,' she asked. Then I remembered Rose hadn't met these neighbours though they'd been in the district a few years. Rose had been away at school.

'She's a dressmaker,' I looked for words. 'She's nice.'

'What sort of nice?' asked Rose.

'Rose, don't you say anything funny when we go up there,' I said. I know Rose, she's smart. 'Don't you get smart.' I'm older than Rose but she's the one that speaks out when something doesn't please her. Mum used to say, Rohe you've got the brains but you look to your sister for the sense. I started to feel funny about taking Rose up to Jane Frazer's because Jane often says the wrong thing without knowing.

We got our work done, had a bath and changed, and when Dad came back from the shed we took the station wagon to drive over to Jane's. Before we left we called out to Mum, 'Don't forget to make us a Maori bread for when we get back.'

'What's wrong with your own hands,' Mum said, but she was only joking. Always when one of us comes home one of the first things she does is make a big Maori bread.

Rose made a good impression with her kamakama ways, and Jane's two nuisance kids took a liking to her straight away. They kept jumping up and down on the sofa to get Rose's attention and I kept thinking what a waste of a good sofa it was, what a waste of a good house for those two nuisance things. I hope when I have kids they won't be so hoha.

I was pleased about Jane and Rose. Jane was asking Rose all sorts of questions about her life in Auckland. About varsity and did Rose join in the marches and demonstrations. Then they went on to talking about fashions and social life in the city, and Jane seemed deeply interested. Almost as though she was jealous of Rose and the way she lived, as though she felt Rose had something better than a lovely house and clothes and everything she needed to make life good for her. I was pleased to see that Jane liked my sister so much, and proud of my sister and her entertaining and friendly ways.

Jane made a cup of coffee when she'd finished measuring Rose for the frock, then packed the two kids outside with a piece of chocolate cake each. We were sitting having coffee when we heard a truck turn in at the bottom of Frazers' drive.

Jane said, 'That's Alan. He's been down the road getting the Maoris for scrub cutting.'

I felt my face get hot. I was angry. At the same time I was hoping Rose would let the remark pass. I tried hard to think of something to say to cover Jane's words though I'd hardly said a thing all morning. But my tongue seemed to thicken and all I could think of was Rohe don't.

Rose was calm. Not all red and flustered like me. She took a big pull on the cigarette she had lit, squinted her eyes up and blew the smoke out gently. I knew something was coming.

'Don't they have names?'

'What. Who?' Jane was surprised and her face was getting pink.

'The people from down the road whom your husband is employing to cut scrub.' Rose the stink thing, she was talking all Pakehafied.

'I don't know any of their names.'

I was glaring at Rose because I wanted her to stop but she was avoiding my looks and pretending to concentrate on her cigarette.

'Do they know yours?'

'Mine?'

'Your name.'

'Well . . . Yes.'

'Yet you have never bothered to find out their names or to wonder whether or not they have any.'

The silence seemed to bang around in my head for ages and ages. Then I think Jane muttered something about difficulty, but that touchy sister of mine stood up and said, 'Come on Hera.' And I with my red face and shut mouth followed her out to the station wagon without a goodbye or anything.

I was so wild with Rose. I was wild. I was determined to blow her up about what she had done, I was determined. But now that we were alone together I couldn't think what to say. Instead I felt an awful big sulk coming on. It has always been my trouble, sulking. Whenever I don't feel sure about something I go into a big fat sulk. We had a teacher at school who used to say to some of us girls, 'Speak, don't sulk.' She'd say. 'You only sulk because you haven't learned how and when to say your minds.'

She was right that teacher, yet here I am a young woman about to be married and haven't learned yet how to get the words out. Dad used to say to me, 'Look out girlie, you'll stand on your lip.'

At last I said, 'Rose, you're a stink thing.' Tears were on the way. 'Gee Rohe, you made me embarrassed.' Then Rose said, 'Don't worry Honey she's got a thick hide.'

These words of Rose's took me by surprise and I realised something about Rose then. What she said made all my anger go away and I felt very sad because it's not our way of talking to each other. Usually we'd say, 'Never mind Sis,' if we wanted something to be forgotten. But when Rose said, 'Don't worry Honey she's got a thick hide,' it made her seem a lot older than me, and tougher, and as though she knew much more than me about the world. It made me realise too that underneath her jolly and forthright ways Rose is very hurt. I remembered back to when we were both little and Rose used to play up at school if she didn't like the teacher. She'd get smart and I used to be ashamed and tell Mum on her when we got home, because although she had the brains I was always the well behaved one.

Rose was speaking to me in a new way now. It made me feel sorry for her and for myself. All my life I had been sitting back and letting her do the objecting. Not only me, but Mum and Dad and the rest of the family too. All of us too scared to make known when we had been hurt or slighted. And how can the likes of Jane know when we go round pretending all is well. How can Jane know us?

But then I tried to put another thought into words. I said to Rose, 'We do it too. We say, "the Pakeha doctor", or "the Pakeha at the post office", and sometimes we mean it in a bad way.'

'Except that we talk like this to each other only. It's not so much what is said, but when and where and in whose presence. Besides, you and I don't speak in this way now, not since we were little. It's the older ones: Mum, Dad, Nanny who have this habit.'

Then Rose said something else. 'Jane Frazer will still want to be your friend and mine in spite of my embarrassing her today; we're in the fashion.'

'What do you mean?'

'It's fashionable for a Pakeha to have a Maori for a friend.' Suddenly Rose grinned. Then I heard Jane's voice coming out of that Rohe's mouth and felt a grin of my own coming. 'I have friends who are Maoris. They're lovely people. The eldest girl was married recently and I did the frocks. The other girl is at varsity. They're all so *friendly* and so *natural* and their house is absolutely *spotless*.'

I stopped the wagon in the drive and when we'd got out Rose started strutting up the path. I saw Jane's way of walking and felt a giggle coming on. Rose walked up Mum's scrubbed steps, 'Absolutely spotless.' She left her shoes in the porch and bounced into the kitchen. 'What did I tell you? Absolutely spotless. And a friendly natural woman taking new bread from the oven.'

Mum looked at Rose then at me. 'What have you two been up to? Rohe I hope you behaved yourself at that Pakeha place?' But Rose was setting the table. At the sight of Mum's bread she'd forgotten all about Jane and the events of the morning.

When Dad, Heke, and Matiu came in for lunch, Rose, Mum, Nanny and I were already into the bread and the big bowl of hot corn.

'E ta,' Dad said. 'Let your hardworking father and your two hard-working brothers starve. Eat up.'

'The bread's terrible. You men better go down to the shop and get you a shop bread,' said Rose.

'Be the day,' said Heke.

'Come on my fat Rohe. Move over and make room for your Daddy. Come on my baby shift over.'

Dad squeezed himself round behind the table next to Rose. He picked up the bread Rose had buttered for herself and started eating. 'The bread's terrible all right,' he said. Then Mat and Heke started going on about how awful the corn was and who cooked it and who grew it, who watered it all summer and who pulled out the weeds.

So I joined in the carrying on and forgot about Rose and Jane for the meantime. But I'm not leaving it at that. I'll find some way of letting Rose know I understand and I know it will be difficult for me because I'm not clever the way she is. I can't say things the same and I've never learnt to stick up for myself.

But my sister won't have to be alone again. I'll let her know that.

(1975)

BUB BRIDGER

Girl in the River

She stood knee-deep in grey mud. Water lapped to her waist. She wore an old woollen pullover and brief colourless shorts. Her face and arms were streaked with mud and bits of shining green river weed clung to her hair. She had long strong hands with fingernails painted bright coral. On the bank behind her purple violets and irises blossomed in little clumps and against a huge old plum tree rested a big garden fork and wheelbarrow.

She pulled the weed from the water, reaching into it up to her elbows, dragging the heavy mass against her. She held it there, squeezing out the water and then she braced her legs in the mud and swivelled to heave it up on to the bank behind her. The stench was sickening. She kept rubbing her nose and forehead into her shoulder then throwing back her head gulping the clear cold air above her.

Across the river, hidden by dense lupins, a man watched her. He had been watching her for weeks. He had seen her scything the rank grass that reached the first branches of the plum tree. Clumsily at first, wielding the heavy wooden handle with chopping strokes and then gradually getting the rhythm of it and swinging the curved blade. He saw her mow the stubble so that from the plum tree at the edge of the river there was a stretch of smooth unbroken green up to the cottage. She planted orange and lemon trees, and silver birches and wattles and nectarines and apples. She grew flaxes and toetoes down by the river and in the little dips and hollows of the bank she put the violets and irises. He saw her long arms and legs turn gold in the sun and her hair burn.

At first the man discussed her with his wife. He spoke of the 'brazen bitch across the river going about half-naked'. His wife went down to the river to see for herself and was shocked and angry. She wondered if there were some way they could complain about the way the girl flaunted herself. She talked it over with friends and neighbours and took a group of them down through the garden to the river.

The girl saw them standing on the far bank in a forbidding line and for a moment she was startled, then she stood up and waved to them. They saw her long legs in the faded shorts and the shape of her breasts under the tight shirt that stopped some inches above her waist, showing the bare golden flesh. They stared at her and then they turned and filed through the lupins back to the house. She watched them, leaning against the plum tree, frowning at their retreating backs.

The women decided to sign a petition and send it to the Mayor. They strongly requested that he inform the police of the girl's shameless exposure of herself in an area where they had all lived quietly and decently for years. They mentioned her two small children. That they should be taken from her and given a chance to grow up as good citizens in a Christian atmosphere. But the Mayor didn't answer the petition and they wondered whether he had ever actually received it.

After that the women never went near the river and when they heard the girl laughing and shouting with the children they would go indoors and close the windows.

The river was small and slow moving so that logs and branches and discarded plastic containers got caught in the strong weed and stayed there lining the banks. The summer had been long and the water dropped several feet. The branches and weeds trapped the water at the river's edge and turned stagnant and sour. The winter was cold but it brought little rain and the girl hated the still, stinking mess below the bank. She would stand under the plum tree watching the growing tangle encroaching a little further into the stream and one spring day she brought the wheelbarrow and the fork down to the bank.

The man watched her step down into the water. Her summer skin had paled but the long legs and high breasts were still as arrogant as ever. He saw her cringe as her feet sank in the soft mud.

Downstream a dozen or so mallard ducks observed her. She and the children had been feeding them for months and now they swam closer, quack-chattering hopefully for stale bread. She smiled at them and the man in the lupins heard her talking and swearing happily at them as she plunged bright painted nails into the river weed. The cold water didn't worry her. After a long time he could see the sweat gleaming on her forehead and the pile of weed on the bank grew so high she had to start another.

The children played behind her on the long sloping lawn. Now and then they came to watch and they poked the pile of weed with enquiring fingers.

'Don't touch it,' she warned. 'It stinks.'

Around midday she climbed out of the water and went up to the cottage with the children.

The man rose from the lupins and groaned with pain. The knees of his trousers were wet and his face and hands were blue with cold.

His wife had prepared lunch and when he came inside she stared at him.

'Good God, are you ill?' she asked.

He shook his head without looking at her.

'I've been weeding.'

'Well, don't do any more — you look dreadful.' She served him hot soup and watched him with concern. The soup warmed him and his hands stopped trembling. After lunch, his wife said, 'I'm going over to Doreen's. I wish you'd come with me — you haven't seen the kiddies for ages.'

'No,' he said, 'you go on over. I'll see them at the weekend.'

'Well then,' she hesitated — 'Don't go back to the garden. Stay here in the warm and watch telly.'

When he heard the car start he went through the house and watched from the window for the girl. She came out of the cottage with the children. They were playing with a big yellow ball and halfway down the lawn she drop-kicked it high in the air. They screamed and raced to catch it.

'Don't kick it down here,' she called, 'you'll lose it in the river.'

She had cleared several yards and she stood on the bank with her hands on her hips, smiling and humming her satisfaction.

At the window, the man stood with clenched hands, whispering softly and rapidly. When the girl was back in the river, he slipped out of the house and ran crouching and crab-like to the damp hollow in the lupins.

She moved carefully out into deeper water, lifting each leg with difficulty from the mud. When she reached the mesh of logs and branches, the water covered her breasts. She was suddenly frightened of the oozing slime gripping her legs and in panic she lunged, kicking powerfully to release them. She fell face down into sharp twigs that ripped her face and arms. For a moment she lay there. The branches sank beneath her and the weed gripped her hands and legs. She pushed her head and shoulders back out of the water and then slammed forward in a frenzy, out into the middle of the river. The water ran smoothly about her and she floated with it, gasping and whimpering her relief. The man in the lupins rose and started forward.

She drifted limply down the stream for several yards and then she turned and swam back with long easy strokes. The children still played with the ball. She felt a great surge of joy to see them safe and laughing and unaware. She called to them and they came running, squealing their surprise and delight to see her swimming.

'Can we come in? Please? Can we come in too?' They danced about on the bank waving their arms, yelling at her.

'No! No it's too cold — stay up there.' She blew kisses to them.

She tackled the branches and weed from midstream, completely at ease now. She pulled logs free and pushed them into the current. A tangle of weed broke away. She worked steadily, treading water, tearing the branches apart and guiding them into the stream. She loosened big clumps of weed, dragging them into the flow, swimming back again and again for more. And finally she was aware that the smell had gone. The water ran clear and clean past her bank. She swam up and down, searching the riverbed for snags that might give anchor to floating ribbons of weed from upstream and tossing them up on the bank.

At the moment when the girl made up her mind to brave the mud and get out of the river, the woman found her husband in the lupins. He heard her gasp and he cowered at her feet, unable to look at her. Then his head sank to the damp ground and he began to cry.

The girl pulled herself up on to the bank and lay there, exhausted. Her face was bleeding and her arms and legs were criss-crossed with scratches. Her coral nails were broken and filthy. She rolled over with an effort and saw the fork and the wheelbarrow.

'Tomorrow I'll cart that weed away,' she said.

(1977)

MARGARET SUTHERLAND

Codling-Moth

We talk about it a lot. It is as unattainable, as desirable as beauty. In secret we crave it; cynics, we talk about it as we sit together under the gum trees at lunchtime, eating peanut butter sandwiches.

'It's ridiculous, the way they go on about it all the time,' says Mel, tossing her crusts to the predatory gulls. We aren't supposed to feed them but we do. 'I mean, it's one thing in the pictures and books and poetry and that stuff, but take real life. Take my parents. Or yours. They love each other but you don't see them slopping all over each other and going on as though that's all there is to think about. Do you?'

'No, you don't,' I say. When my father comes home he kisses my mother, or rather he kisses the air by my mother's cheek, and if he's late, as he often is when shift work or his mates at the pub delay him, my mother, rattling plates, says "Your dinner's in the oven and if you don't hurry up and eat it it'll be dried up to nothing." I suppose they love each other.

'Of course they have been married a long time,' Mel says, thinking. You know when she is thinking. Her eyes go away from you, like a blind person who, in following the direction of your voice, misses and looks past your shoulder. 'It's probably different when you're married. Romeo and Juliet never got married did they.'

I think of Romeo coming in late from work and Juliet rattling plates and saying 'Your dinner's in the oven.' It makes me feel sad. Mel and I saw the film. I cried at the end. Mel's more sensible than I am. She doesn't believe in crying, as a rule, but she didn't want to look at me when we came out.

'It's different, being married,' I say, to bring her back to sitting under the trees and feeding the seagulls. 'It must be. I've never seen any married people who love each other so they'd rather die than stay alive if the other one died.'

Mel bites into an apple — glossy, red, perfect. 'Ughff, look at that,' she says, spitting out the words and the apple together, and showing me the core. A dull greyish powder spreads from where the worm has tunnelled.

'Codling-moth,' I say. Mel has a quick look round and shies the apple at the bossiest gull, which lumbers into the air, settles a few feet away, and regards us with the icy outrage of our headmistress objecting to complaints of behaviour on the buses with the boys from St Pat's.

A thought has just occurred to me. 'Maybe they make it up,' I suggest. 'I bet there's no such thing as love. That kind anyway. Maybe people know there isn't and wish there was, so they make it up and write books and compose songs and all the time it isn't true.'

That makes us silent. I wish I hadn't had that thought. I hope I'm wrong.

'I think you're right,' Mel says suddenly. When she's finished thinking, she's back with you, snap; quite startling if you've gone away into your own thoughts while you've been waiting for her. 'There's no such thing. Jolly good thing too. Who wants to go all sloppy and slushy about some idiot with sweaty hands and pimples. It's absolutely disgusting when you think about it. It makes you sick.'

'But they're not all like that,' I say quickly, trying to unthink my thought. 'What about Jolyon Townsend?'

'You certainly see a lot like him,' says Mel, who can be sarcastic. 'At the school ball the floor was littered with boys like him, wasn't it. You tripped over them at every step. Or they tripped over you more likely.'

'Well . . .' I say.

'Well?' she says. Mel likes to be sure she's won the point.

'Well,' I say, 'they can't help it. They might look better when they're older.'

'Like twenty years older.'

'Anyway what about us?' I've remembered the photo of Mel and me, in flocked nylon dance frocks and long mittens, standing in front of the artificial gladioli. 'What about that photo of us?' There is nothing to say.

I try again. 'How about Mr Krassmann then?' I ask in a very insinuating way. I think Mel has a crush on Mr Krassmann, who tutors her privately on Saturday mornings in German. When she came round to my place after her lesson last week her face was quite pink, and *Heute and Abend* isn't the sort of thing to put roses in anybody's cheeks. Mel is giving nothing away.

'Mr Krassmann?' she says, drawing it out as though I've suggested old Harry, the school caretaker, who is about seventy and smells of tobacco. He spits too. 'You must be joking.'

In *The Importance of Being Earnest*, our play for English Lit. this term, Mel has the part of Lady Bracknell. I concede. 'Okay,' I say. 'Love's an illusion.' I've heard that somewhere. To agree with Mel is the best way to call her bluff, sometimes. She looks at me. It's her other look, the opposite of her far-away one. She has unusual eyes — flecked, the iris blue and green and grey and gold and each colour distinct; the white part is very white. Mel's eyes are her best feature. But when she looks at you this way you stop noticing her eyes, as though you can see past them to a small secret place where the real Mel lives. She doesn't let you in very often, which is only natural.

'Gabriel? You don't really think that's true, do you?'

'I hope it isn't true,' I tell her honestly.

'I hope it isn't too,' she says. The game is over. We're in agreement, which we usually are though we like to pretend. We go down to the pool for a swim.

The pool is new. For two years we've had raffles and class fund-raising contests and limp fudge cake from the school tuck-shop, sixpence the piece. And now we have a swimming pool. Mel and I stand beside the steps that lead down to the water, eau-de-nil water that reminds me of polar seas, lapping on smooth tiles white as ice floes. My bathing-suit is regulation black and my skin is very pale.

I tried to tan last year when Mel and I went camping with her cousins. The tan stayed for two days and peeled away, like dirt. All that stayed in my skin was the smell of sunshine when I breathed on my arm. We kept to ourselves in our ten-by-ten canvas world and waited for sunburnt boys to pay court. We wore eyeshadow, and four changes of beachwear every day. The boys went by our tent and we noticed that the girls beside them looked like Ann, who never wore eyeshadow, and said 'something'. We were not grateful to Ann for taking us camping, in the same way that we were not grateful to our parents for conceiving us in their middle age. We did not think about it. Mel and I did not talk about the boys. We bought chocolate-dipped ice-creams, and walked along the beach with our heads close together to hear over the wind and surf.

The light went quickly one evening when we were still on the beach. The two boys came silently out of the sandhills so that at first we were startled. We walked, the four of us, towards the rocks at the end of the beach, together at first, later in pairs, Mel and her boy ahead. His walk was almost a shamble; his arms, before he put one round her shoulders, swung loosely. Smugly, I felt sorry for Mel. The boy beside me was tall and his hand felt firm and warm. It grew dark, and I could have walked on to the rocks for ever.

Mel and her boy drew further ahead as we turned back and went towards the dunes. I wished that Mel was following to notice that my boy didn't shamble and was tall. The juice of the succulent plants, closed now against night, ran out between my toes as he turned me to him and kissed me. His lips, like his palms, were dry and warm. But then his tongue was terrible, slithering wet, strong, a dark eel belonging under stones in the river. He held me tightly but I pulled away and ran back, on and on, to the camp, to the tent. My chest hurt with fright and running. I waited for Mel and was angry because she hadn't stayed with me.

She came back soon. I was curious to know if she had been kissed by her boy but she didn't say and I didn't like to ask. Nor did I tell her about the kiss that had made me afraid. I knew I had not behaved with sophistication, although my eyeshadow was silver and glistened under light. We went to bed soon, on the double mattress that Ann had brought on the trailer for us. Mel's warmth, her solidity, the faint spicy smell of her hair near my face comforted me and I fell asleep against her.

Holidays end; school brings back the pleasure of challenge, approval, Mel's company. We vie in class. While other girls form friendly circles at lunchtime, Mel and I sit apart. In wet weather the shelter sheds smell of sour milk and sandshoes, and wasps hang around the overflowing rubbish tins. When it's fine we sit under the gum trees, and sometimes after lunch we go for a swim.

I look at the pale water, and think that I'm not a good swimmer, that I don't like cold water, that I don't want to go in. Mel, beside me, reaches out and touches a finger behind my shoulders. 'You have such a smooth back,' she says, sounding surprised as though she's just noticed something. Compliments are unusual: from adults who are watchful of praise, from Mel, who tries as I do to be adult. Her words sink like smooth pebbles to the bottom of my thoughts; later I will take them out, turn them over, fondle them. I am flattered. I am happy. I leap suddenly into the water and without a single rest I swim a full width of the pool.

After school we catch the bus to town. It is Friday afternoon, the first Friday of the month. Mel and I are making the Nine First Fridays, in honour of the Sacred Heart. When we have finished we shall be certain of going to heaven; as promised to St Margaret-Mary by the Lord Himself we shall be allowed the grace of final repentance on our deathbeds. Death seems beyond us, as impossible as the committing of horrible, mortal sin, but then one never knows. The Nine First Fridays may save us in the final count. Mass and Communion for nine consecutive First Fridays of the month is a little price to pay for heaven. Besides, before Mass at seven o'clock, there's afternoon tea and a five o'clock session of the pictures. We never see the end of the film because we can't be late for Mass. It doesn't matter a lot. We make up our own endings.

Mel's watch is fast. We are early for Mass. Men and women tread quietly past the confessional boxes into the great cave of the church. Confessional doors open and close; voices too muted to understand exchange private words as Mel and I, kneeling together, examine our consciences. Hail HolyQueen. HailOurLifeOurSweetnessAndHope. ToTheeDoWeCome. BeforeTheeWeStand. SinfulAndSorrowful. Sinful. Even the just man falls seven times daily. Why so hard to put together a respectable list for Father who waits gravely in there, in the small cave smelling so strongly of old planed wood? His profile beneath the dim bulb appears as the window slides back. Latin phrases of absolution switch suddenly, like light, to the patient, 'Yes, my child?' My child? Can he see me? How does he know this is not an old woman, a murderer, a sinner come to repentance after thirty years? Oh, to have the choice of thirty years' wickedness from which to pick sins like cans from a supermarket shelf; oh, how disappointing a display of sin. Disobeyed Mother. Several times. Told lies twice. No. Not harmful to anyone. Not calumny. One about the music practice. One about the chocolates. Mother knew anyway. 'And anything else?' Anything else, anything else . . . Surely, surely, *something*? Answered back, but she deserved that. I answered back. Father. Impure thoughts? Had an impure thought. 'Yes, my child, I see. And anything else now?' Anything else anything else Father I'm almost wetting my pants because it's so dark and there's nothing else so please give me my penance — a thought only, unspoken. Would that be a sin, to do that in Confession? Surely not, not even there. Has anyone ever? . . . dear child, pray for help, Our Blessed Mother, temptation is no sin, remember that the Devil tempted Christ Himself in the desert . . . Yes Father. Pray my child. Yes Father. You do remember your prayers always? Mostly Father. 'I see, my child. And nothing else?'

When I was small I used to clutch when I felt I couldn't wait and Mother would say don't, Gabriel, don't do that. Nice little girls don't do that. I do it now, praying that Father can't see, praying there won't be a little trail of wetness left behind on the brown linoleum when I emerge, absolved, into the light.

For your penance three Hail Marys, and now a good Act of Contrition. OhMyGodIAmVerySorryThatIHaveSinnedAgainstThee. BecauseThouArtSoGood. AndIWillNotSinAgain. Amen. *Te absolvo*. Thank you, Father. The window closes.

I open the door, go back to the church and the faces looking up from their conscience-stricken hunting. Have I been a long time? Too long? Fall gratefully, blushing, into any pew. Disappear. A light-headed feeling of freedom like the last day of term. Sin all gone. Sorrowful? Happy. Bury eyes down on to clasped hands. Three Hail Marys, one, two, three. A soul now, round and white as a peppermint, the smuts of sin rubbed out Gabriel shriven.

Most people leave as soon as Mass is over. Mel and I stay behind kneeling side by side. The church is a great high cave where we are together, lost, alone. The candles sparkling on the side altar remind me of glowworms high up on the caves at Waitomo, cold caves, dark, with lapping black water sensed more than seen. 'My, now *this* is *something*!' the American woman says, impressed again. I think of black sky, no moon, the death of a star, and I am glad to climb the rickety wooden steps up to the light again. Caves are sinister places, running back to no-exits of darkness and dripping water. Mel isn't afraid of caves. She is practical. She will be saying the fourth decade of the rosary and planning her weekend essay. Her beads move, tapping lightly the polished pew cut with the initials J.B., rayed round with lines like a child's sun.

The church smells warmly of flowers and incense. I ease my weight to one knee, to the other, and rest my face against my bent arms. It's no good. I give in and sit down, tracing through the lisle stockings the deep indentations that mark each knee. Mel's back rises straight and rigid as the brown-robed St Joseph who gazes past us from his niche. His head does not wear a beret, but clustered curls and a plaster beard, set stiffly on his chin like old spaghetti. Looking at Mel I am ashamed. I kneel down again, notice the blunt renewed ache in my knees and the warmth of Mel beside me. Her blazer filters a musky smell like faded incense. HailHoly QueenMotherOfMercy. HailOurLifeOurSweetnessAndOurHope. To TheeDoWeCome, BeforeTheeWeStand. SinfulAndSorrowful.

Grateful when Mel's nudge comes, I stand up stiffly, like the old women who wear headscarves and chew on their prayers without caring who listens in to their conversations with the Lord. How sad, I think, how impossible to ever be old like that. I follow Mel down the side aisle, my legs forgetting their stiffness, my callous soul ignoring the sad dimmed oil paintings of the Way of the Cross. Dip, splash, the holy water font an ivory shell. Catholic Truth Society pamphlets, red, blue, purple, on the rack in the church porch. *Have you a vocation? Sacramental Grace. Youth and Problems of Purity.* I cannot go and take that title out of the rack, not with Mel or somebody to see me and wonder why I'm buying that one; but it sounds more interesting than *Fallacies of Jansenism.* We pass the pamphlets and go outside. It is March and by eight o'clock night has settled down cosily. I was sleepy in the warm church. Now, feeling the thin cold air trickle through my nose, I am suddenly wide awake, and pleased with myself.

'Well that's eight,' I say.

'Eight what? Oh, you mean Fridays.'

'Only one to go. Did you think we'd really do it, Mel?'

'We haven't yet. There's one more, remember.'

Sometimes I find Mel's precision annoying, but I don't mind tonight. What does it matter? Mel is coming to stay the night and I am happy.

We have never been less tired than we are now, at bedtime.

'Straight off to sleep now,' Mother says firmly, hopefully. In the darkness I sense Mel in the other bed. We talk in whispers, muffling giggles in our pillows.

'Mel? You know when we were up at the beach last summer, and you went down to the rocks with that boy?'

'The one with the acne? The friendly monster from outer space?'

'He wasn't *that* bad.'

'He was. You were jolly pleased the other one picked you.'

'I was not.'

'Yes, you were. He was a crumb.'

'Yes, but did he . . . did you . . .?'

'What?'

'Oh *you* know.'
'For heaven's sake!'
'Did you, well, kiss him?'
'*He* did. I didn't.'
'Didn't you like it?'
'No. I don't think so. It was wet.'
'Was it? So was mine. All sloppy. He just about stuck his tongue down my throat.'
'Mine didn't do that. He kind of chewed, like those old men who don't wear their teeth.'
'Ugh.'
'Yuck.'
Exquisitely funny. We scream silently into our pillows.
'Licking ice cream.'
'Slurping soup.'
'Gob-stoppers in your mouth. *Two.*'
Excruciating. We roll on our stomachs, hysterical. We have forgotten that Mother, in the next room, is tired and is trying to have an early night. Bang on the wall. Bangbang. Stop that noise, girls. Off to sleep. At once.
Silence.
'Gabriel?'
'Ssshh! She'll hear. Come over here.'
Mel in blue pyjamas brings her incense smell into my bed. We arrange ourselves together, bump to hollow, hollow to bump. 'Gabriel? What do you think about it? You know what I mean. Did your mother tell you or what?'
'She told me. Did your mother?'
'She gave me a book. Last year.'
A whole book! My information had been received in the five minutes between rosary and night prayers.
'What was it like?'
'Awful drawings.'
'Like biology class?'
'Worse. There wasn't much about it. The actual part. It had a lot about getting pregnant and how not to and diseases and that.'
Disappointing. I thought there might be something Mother had forgotten about. What she had told me had seemed really rather pointless.
'Mel? Didn't you think it sounded silly? I mean, don't you wonder why people *do* it?'
'It sounds mad, I think. Don't ask me. You'd think they'd have a better system, wouldn't you? An incubator plant or something.'
'Yes. I think it sounds awful.'
'Well I'm not going to do it anyway. Ever.'
'Neither am I.'

Is it incense, powder, faint sun-on-skin perspiration, this special warm smell that is Mel? The winceyette cloth of her pyjama coat has rubbed into tiny balls under my fingers. I am alive, I quicken with awareness like the vibration of a single hair when we sit, heads not quite touching, in the pictures. I will change my mind and be embarrassed, so I say it quickly before I have time to think. 'Mel,' I say, 'I do like you.'

She turns her head back as though she hasn't heard me. The toothpaste on her breath reminds me of the pink smokers we buy in cellophane packets as she answers.

'Well I like you,' she says. I am happy. I find her lowest rib and tickle. We have forgotten again. Bang. Bangbangbang.

'Get to SLEEP!'

Silence.

'Mel?'
'What?'
'I thought you were asleep.'
'No.'
'Oh.'

At the back of her neck, in the hollow, the hair is fine, like a baby's. I feel it for an instant, lighter than a touch on my lips, and wonder if I imagine its softness.

'G'night, Mel.'
'Mmhmm. G'night.'

Then it is morning and Mother is standing by the bed, wearing her least-pleased expression. We stumble up from sleep; and go in dressing-gowns to the kitchen for breakfast. The air is thick with Mother's bad mood and fumes from the kerosene heater. Our plates are whisked away, dealt ferociously into the sink. The silence trembles with crashes. I ask with guilt if I can dry.

'Don't bother yourself,' Mother says, passing tea-towel to me. 'You go and enjoy yourself with your friend. Don't think of your mother.'

'Didn't you have a good night?' I ask foolishly. Mother snatches her trump.

'Good night? Good *night*! The pair of you talking and giggling half the night ... My word, wait till you're my age. Young people are selfish today. Very selfish.' I dry in silence.

'Is it all right if Mel and I do some homework now?'

'Do as you like. Don't bother to ask me what you can do or can't do. You'll do what you please. You're just like your father.'

I go back to the bedroom. Mel is dressed. 'What's the matter with your mother. Isn't she feeling well?'

'Oh,' I say vaguely, 'she gets like that. She didn't have a very good night or something.' It does not seem reasonable that Mother's sleep is dependent on my own. A heavy burden.

Homework is done. Mother is ironing.

'Mel wants me to go over to her place. Can I?' I ask.

'You and that girl are always in each other's pocket,' Mother says with resentment. 'If it's not her coming to our place it's you wanting to go there. I don't know what her mother thinks, I'm sure.' It hasn't occurred to me that Mel's mother thinks at all. She is a doing person, never still, always washing, ironing, busy in the kitchen. She uses the weekends to catch up on the week when she's away at work.

'We have to finish this project on pollution by Monday, and Mel's got a book about it.' (BlessMeFather, I told one lie.)

'Go if you must,' says Mother, branding Father's shirt with a vicious stab. 'Please yourself. If her mother can put up with your nonsense and carrying on, go. It makes no difference to me. What I'd like to know is, where are all those nice little friends you used to have to your birthdays, that nice little what's-her-name, Rosemary, Mary Rose, what's happened to her?'

I am patient. 'Mother, that was years ago. Absolute ages. She's gone all stupid now. All she talks about is boys.'

'There's worse than boys,' says my mother, thumping the iron fast. 'A lot worse. You want to think about that, my girl.'

'What d'you mean?' I ask. The damping-bottle flies, sprinkling me with drops, like holy water from the Benediction procession.

'I'll tell you what I'm talking about; you see far too much of that girl, that's what I'm talking about. In case you don't know it there are some funny people about, very funny men, and funny women too, and no girl of mine is growing up into one of them. That's what I'm talking about.'

'I don't know what you mean,' I say. 'I don't understand you.'

'I hope you don't,' she says, and says no more, for she has looked at me and seen my face and I think she is sorry that she let her tiredness and her oldness make her say that, that way. But I think also that she is glad it has been said. At least that is what I decide, later on. As I turn and run away out of the kitchen, into the bathroom, lock the door, sit on the ledge of the bath, let the hot hot tears run down, I understand nothing, and everything, and I feel sick to my heart. A grey web of guilt is spinning itself about me. For the first time in my life I learn what it is to be quite alone.

Mel and I go to town. We have afternoon tea. We go to the pictures. We go to church, and kneel side by side. The doors of the confessionals open, close; inaudible words murmur a thread of melody. Mel leaves me and closes the door behind her.

Bless me, Father, for I have sinned. Anything else, my child? Anything else? Sin unspoken makes a worse sin, the sin of deceit, for the priest is the ear of God. Have I sinned? I remember the softness of old winceyette, the fineness of young hair at the back of the neck, in the hollow.

Mel comes out, composed as always. 'I'm not going,' I say. And I turn my back on her surprised face and walk up the church away from the confessionals.

The Ninth Friday. Nine consecutive First Fridays and nine communions and heaven is a promise. This is My Body. And This is My Blood. Mel goes up to receive communion. I do not go. I stay in my seat, kneeling very straight, and I try to concentrate on the pain in my knees and not think of the other pain. I have not made the Nine Fridays and I am trying not to cry.

(1977)

MARGARET SUTHERLAND

Need

The opening of Matahoe's first supermarket was for Julie a vindication of faith. Julie believed . . . in God, Cities, America, True Love. The supermarket, its turnstiles and trundlers, gave substance to hopes as desirable and distant as heaven. As with heaven, and without imagining that a girl like herself would qualify for such a place, Julie, beside a gum-chewing boy in the Matahoe bug-house, liked to sit and marvel at the American way of life where everything was new and big and glittered. Ten-thirty of a week night the main street of Matahoe was, after that experience, something of a come-down. When the same or another boy led her past the fish shop, past the Co-op, down by the bridge where young people sought privacy from the headlights of night drivers passing through, Julie had to adjust the scale. She managed. Born of need, her particular faith allowed her to understand intuitively the essence of others' needs. She hadn't the heart, that was it, to refuse. And there were moments, there on the bank of the Matahoe stream: on clear nights you could look up at the stars. Afterwards the boy might see her home, and her father, if awake, would look up from *Best Bets* to remind her that girls who stopped out till all hours were headed for trouble. And Julie, sighing, would say 'Oh, *Dad*', and go off to the tongue-and-groove walled bathroom to have a wash before bed.

They advertised in the *Matahoe Gazette* for staff. Julie washed her hair and put on her red mini and went for the interview. Jim Blundell, manager, ex-corner-grocer, asked her if she understood the responsibility of the position she was applying for. He looked so serious that Julie wondered privately whether she'd overreached herself. But he gave her the job. She went home and told her father she had a job on the checkout and, while he didn't say much, she could see he was impressed. She loved the job. Mr Blundell taught her about prices and the adding-machine and how to cash up; and sometimes, after hours, she learnt from him that married men too were subject to the need. Surprising, you'd have thought . . . But Julie never pursued thought past that point; instead counted the pyramided baked bean cans, hoped they wouldn't come tumbling down. Afterwards she would stroke through damp striped cotton those plaintive spasms of bone, Jim Blundell's shoulder blades.

The sickness took her one day, in the middle of Mrs Judd's order. She had to make an excuse. She was sick in the lavatory. Mrs Judd said she looked something awful when she came back. Julie said she was all right, and finished ringing up the bill. The next morning she felt sick again. Mr Blundell was none too pleased when she telephoned, she could tell; but he said she should stay in bed, and get back to work as soon as she was better. She went to bed. It seemed a waste; she wasn't sick, only felt she wanted to be. She rang her sister Jocelyn, six years older and a different sort from Julie.

'I've got the washing-machine filling,' Jocelyn said.

Julie hung on.

'What's up then?'

'I don't know. I'm at home. I threw up yesterday, right in the middle of Mrs Judd, and I keep feeling like I'm going to be sick.'

'That's this bug then,' said Jocelyn. 'Minnie's got it. She rung up the doctor and he said just boiled water.'

'I couldn't come over I suppose, Jossie?'

'It's not a very good idea. The twins might catch it. I've just got them over the mumps. Say in a couple of weeks.'

'Okay,' Julie agreed, now very cheerful. 'How long do you think, before I can go back to work?'

'You'll be right as the bank in a day or so.'

'I hope so. Oh, well. Anyway. S'long then.'

'So long,' Jocelyn said.

Her father found out when she kept being sick every morning. Once he knew, Julie realised she'd have to go. She wondered about Jocelyn. In town she bought an Auckland paper and searched the personal columns. She had to make the toll call from the post office in case her father overheard. She bought a suitcase on the way home. Catching the bus next day, she could not feel regret, not about Dad, not about Matahoe. At the bus terminal she had a cup of coffee, an iced bun. The suitcase was heavy, she wasn't feeling well again, she had to give up the idea of seeing the sights. Julie consoled herself with the thought that you couldn't drink in a city in one swallow.

On a blue bus she rode out from the city. A long way. It cost her thirty cents. The inner suburban houses, old, packed in, made her think of home. She felt better further on, where the houses were new and painted the colours she liked, where the gardens weren't cluttered with trees shedding leaves all over the lawns. There was the supermarket, splendidly lettered on a spring sky, FOODTOWN, a building big enough to house a whole city of packets and tins and bottles and special offers. Thinking of the Matahoe supermarket, Julie couldn't help it, she had to smile. But it was only when she stepped down into Silver Birch Grove that she saw the actual extent of her luck. Splendid the houses here, the ranchsliders, concrete patios, double garages under. And, unlike Matahoe where people had nothing better to do than lean at fences, on gates, hardly a person. A toddler came at a trot down a driveway. His mother hurried after, carried him inside like a parcel tucked under one arm.

Mrs Jackson wore her hair in a French roll, offered coffee, a cigarette. Julie said she didn't; wished she did. Mrs Jackson looked altogether experienced, inhaling as though being made love to. Intimates already, Julie and Mrs Jackson inspected Julie's bedroom from the doorway, Mrs Jackson confiding, 'I'm so glad you're such a nice girl; my *dear*, the *stories* you hear!' She laughed, and Julie laughed too.

There were the two little girls who went to school and learnt the violin, and the baby who crawled about and pulled things off tables, all the time chuckling his approval of the world. Julie's duties ran mainly to babysitting. The Jacksons had to go out often. A dreadful bore, said Mrs Jackson, but all in the call of. A new concept to Julie, this was one of the attitudes pointing up that distance, reassuring, between the Jacksons' life and her own. For distance, always necessary to Julie's faith, now permitted a shift from the abstract Hollywood happiness to the particular Jackson kind. You couldn't doubt that happiness. It overflowed from the state of Mr and Mrs Jackson and the two little girls and the baby; it touched Julie. At first not taken with Mr Jackson (he wasn't at all modern — if you took Jim Blundell and fattened him out, put him in a suit, added glasses, there wouldn't have been much to pick), she quite soon changed her mind. He was polite to her, asking about her day. He had a nice voice, deep and serious. She liked him best less in relation to herself than when he came home in a good mood, bounced the children up and down, called Mrs Jackson 'Pussycat'. But if he looked worried, said over dinner that the only way to get things done in a big office was to do them yourself, Julie would look as sympathetic as Mrs Jackson, would think how unfair it was that Mr Jackson had to do not only his own work but everyone else's too. Somehow, without a word being said, Julie and Mrs Jackson had a pact at such times. Julie would take away the dishes and stack them in the dishwasher, and Mrs Jackson would bring out one of the many bottles from the mirror-backed liquor cabinet, and within half an hour there would be Mr Jackson, happier, more cheerful altogether, bouncing the baby on his knee.

Uncomfortable in case she might intrude on the Jackson happiness Julie, in the first weeks, would say she felt tired, would go to the room with the striped bedspread and Mrs Jackson's fashion and decorating magazines. But the Jacksons drew her into their conversations, included her, though she blushed when Mr Jackson turned upon her his slow kind gaze to ask, 'And what do *you* think, Julie?'

They were always asking her advice. Mr Jackson was building a sundeck, and Julie's opinions were sought on whether they should have a miniature pool, with or without a circulating pump, or a waterfall as well, or whether it might not be better if they simply settled for goldfish or water-lilies. Julie would answer as well as she could. Mr Jackson might look to Mrs Jackson with a nod of thoughtful surprise and say, 'I really think Julie's got a point there.' Embarrassed, Julie would turn her pride to the macramé-work that Mrs Jackson had taught her how to do.

Shopping, the highlight of Julie's days, had little to do with the outlay of money; enough for her to gaze, touch, consider through plate glass. She could scent promise in those drifts of leatheriness, ripe fruit, the soapy pungency of supermarket aisles. When Mrs Jackson on her way to the fitting-room would ask, beguiling, 'Julie, love? Mind baby for me?' she would go to the courtyard where there were flowerbeds and vending machines, and the sparrows came for crumbs. A sculpture was set there; the ponderous indifference of cement used by children as a crawling tunnel, look-out, perch. 'Environmental art,' explained Mrs Jackson. 'Contemporary.' But such a definition, associated by Julie with fashion, with curtain prints, added nothing to her understanding of the impassive bulk engraved with the letters WOMAN scratched frail as stick writing in dry sand. Amid scented eddies of petunias, hot peanuts, Julie sat through summer discovering, here, a weight of shoulder and, there, a planted curve of knee. She felt an alliance with the sculpture. Swelling, her own body was drawn nearer to the earth. People hurried past — mothers, children, babies pushed in prams. The shops no longer called. If, as in fairy tales, someone had come to offer her three wishes, even one, she would have answered, 'Nothing. I don't want anything, there's nothing I can think of.'

Julie's labour began at night. Not wanting to be a nuisance, she got up, walked around, leant against the bench each time a contraction came. Mrs Jackson heard her and came to keep her company. Julie wanted to be by herself; she couldn't say so, not with Mrs Jackson trying to help. She woke Mr Jackson and Julie felt worse. He looked tired, his striped pyjamas crumpled, his hair sticking up. Driving her to the hospital, he looked so worried she felt she ought to comfort him, except that there was another pain and Mr Jackson was driving through red lights, which was against the law but didn't matter so much perhaps at two in the morning. She had to hold on to his arm on the entrance ramp. He smiled at her, said, 'Bear up, Julie.' All through the rest of the night, whenever she felt miserable, she thought of the smile and felt a bit better.

She didn't keep the baby. Holding her and nursing her, looked into her eyes, crying — that was one part of it. The sisters and nurses who talked to her, kindly, were the other. They asked her things. What was she qualified for? How would she earn enough to keep them both? Who would mind her while Julie went to work? You couldn't take a baby with you to the checkout every day. Julie said she'd like to have the baby adopted. Once she had decided, it was easier. The baby no longer felt a part of her; until the last time, when Julie walked down the polished corridor and stood at the nursery window. There she was, the baby, scarlet with crying, wrapped in that puckered misery, flailing fist of the new-born in distress. Julie would have chosen to remember her daughter asleep, at peace. The outraged clutch of fist reached her, squeezed tight. Julie cried on her hospital bed, and cried and cried to escape the claim of those tiny potent hands. Later she stopped feeling; the pain went away. But not then, not walking alone down the ramp into the autumn sunshine. Julie wished like anything that Mr Jackson could have come to drive her. There was only the suitcase, so light; she'd have liked something stronger to hold on to. She went into town. She signed the papers. She took the blue bus out to the suburbs.

Life was not so different. She was slim again, her old clothes fitted. Mr and Mrs Jackson said she was a brave girl, they didn't know how . . .
  Mrs Jackson still trailed perfume, read horoscopes with Julie on the patio, shared handcream, handed over the toddler with her breathless, 'I'm late as usual. Hold baby for me, Julie love?' They went shopping together. Mr Jackson still turned his gentle eyes towards her, asking, 'All right, Julie? Not too tired?' Julie could imagine that she belonged to him then, like the house, like the children. She could see herself in the kitchen, making his favourite lemon meringue pie which Mrs Jackson never had time to make. There are people who would rather dream of lotteries than win them. Illusion was Julie's comfort, and she needed comfort; the Jacksons and their happiness were her port. They told her to stay, as long as she liked. She nodded, mute. She did not know where else to go. Matahoe, Dad, Jocelyn had receded to the substance of characters in childhood fable.

Mrs Jackson went to the badminton trophy presentations. Mr Jackson and Julie watched television — Gallery, not a programme Julie fancied, but Mr Jackson was interested in current affairs. A funny sort of thing to put on the telly, thought Julie, listening to the discussion on whether prostitution should be legalised. She went to make a cup of tea for Mr Jackson and Milo for herself.
  'I'm off to bed,' she said; and Mr Jackson thanked her for the tea.
  He came to her room, a while later. She was half asleep, thought his coming something to do with the small wage he owed, on Thursdays, and which she always took with guilt. His mouth pressed. She saw the action as a sequence of motion; angle, line selected, a correct enough pressure. She was paralysed with obedience, distaste; no less offended than if her own father had familiarly slipped his hand on to her knee.
  'Mr Jackson,' said Julie, breaking free, 'honest, I don't . . .' She looked at him. And now, without his glasses, he was . . . he seemed to need . . . She felt, almost, the flow of compassion, as a mother called to her

baby's cries does not stand and watch but bends and gathers up. Between Julie and pity moved the remembrance of minute searching fists. Pity solidified, to rock, to a sculptured woman amongst whose crevices children sheltered, against whose strength assault slid off like water.

'No,' said Julie. 'No, Mr Jackson.'

He went queer then; saying things like, forgive, I didn't mean, I'll never know what, Julie, I'm sorry. She lay, growing irritated, growing fed up with him. As if it mattered.

'It's all right,' she said. 'You'd better go.'

He did not go.

'Go on,' she said, impatience rising. 'Best get off to the other room before Mrs Jackson comes.'

He went.

Funny, thought Julie. She'd forgotten the need.

Not the doing of it; what they did. But their need, filling her now with strength, power. She stretched her body, luxuriating; in the darkness held herself tight, hugging close the possibilities of giving and not giving, of taking back.

She felt strong, felt that, on her own, she would be all right.

(1977)

JEAN WATSON

An extract from
The world is an orange and the sun

I am surprised and excited by an experience I had suddenly, perhaps you could call it an optical illusion. It happened, strangely enough, during a time of frustration — the breakfast dishes, the porridge pot, Baby crying and Freddie under my feet, dissatisfied and grizzling. So I got an orange from the shelf and halved it, one half for Freddie, the other in quarters for Baby. I picked Baby up and sat him out in the sun with his orange quarters, and before his tears had dried he smiled and sighed with happiness. This is when I had the illusion — I saw everything as he would have seen it; there was just the warm sun and the taste and smell of orange in the world. Nothing else, just a warm green grassy circle of world with nothing but sun and orange.

So this is an interesting new thing — I hope it will happen again. It should be easiest through the children, to try and see things exactly as they are seeing them. Baby in particular, he sees so much more sharply and clearly than I do. There is more immediacy in his vision, no interception of words, memories and thoughts.

ONE

'You haven't seen the front of the house yet, have you?' says Dale.

We are having coffee in her long narrow kitchen, a jungle of trellis covered by climbing plants, cactus plants on ledges and window sills as well as trailing wall plants. Scattered among the greenery are mock birds, home-made ones with real feathers, but on the kitchen bench there are four birdcages, each one containing a real bird — a budgie, a canary, a thrush that Dale rescued from a flood and a magpie with one leg.

'Freddie, will you please leave those birds alone!' I say.

On the stove a blackened pot of barley is cooking slowly, a meal for the horses. She has five horses. One of them is a small, dainty, dapple grey stallion called 'Prince of Twilight'. It seems that horses are her life and yet you couldn't call her a horsey woman. She has intense blue eyes and long black hair without a single strand of grey. Her body is supple and brown. She never needs to wear stockings with her best dress when she goes into town. I envy her that. In hot weather she works about the place in a bikini; digging drains, milking the cow, carrying water to the horses.

She is saying: 'I cured and spun the wool for this, it matches the jersey. And this monkey is made from rabbit skins. Cute, isn't he? I love monkeys. This is Cressida's room — as you can see we've got no lining on the walls yet. This is Priscilla's room . . . and this is the spare room. I might use it for sewing and handwork one day . . . I cured this sheepskin for a rug. This one is made out of old stockings; it's so easy to wash and it only takes a few minutes to dry. I made this too and . . . I haven't done any for a long time, I lose interest after a while. My main interest is outdoors with the animals. Not much to see, really.'

I decided that this must have been when Dale accepted me as a friend — when she showed me 'the front of the house'.

I am impressed with the water colour paintings of horses which she has in an old school exercise book. 'I was in my twenties when I did these . . . I haven't done any for years.' I don't know much about art, but I would say she has a wonderful sense of colour and I resolve to encourage her to start again. The one called *Thunder* is a pattern of undulating curves and cloud shapes, white fading to pale, fading to grey, fading to darker grey, then almost black. Swirling shapes with the form of horses — rearing, thundering, pounding horses. So this is how she visualises thunder. More than any of the others, one titled *Sunrise* catches the eye. This time, the horses are in sunrise colours, violent shades of orange and yellow, a halo-ringed explosion of horses in the middle of the page.

How easily they move, those horses of Dale's. I can understand how the feeling of control over or love for something powerful can give a shining sense of consolation when one is at odds with the world.

Often I have heard Dale say, 'Oh how I despise the human race!'

We have been having trouble with the water lately. It comes from a spring up the hill behind our house and flows into a creek which follows the ruts, grooves and hollows down the hill and into the river. A polythene pipe sucks the water from the creek a few hundred yards below the spring and into a collecting tank which stands on the level halfway down the hill. From there two pipes run on, one to our place and one to Dale's. After this long dry summer the pipe has begun to suck the water out more quickly than the spring can fill the creek. We have had a couple of air blocks that stopped the water altogether, so we go up daily to check it.

Everyday, our feet slipping on the dry grass, we trudge up the hill. I call Dale when I am ready to go because I have to wait for Baby's sleep before I can leave the house. Usually we find the water running so slowly that it spurts from the pipe to the tank in rhythmic splashes.

'This is what causes an air block in the pipe,' says Dale. 'When it's running and stopping and running and stopping. It should run in a steady stream.'

So we go up the creek and dig a little. The water runs stronger. We dig a bit here, we shift a stone there. Today we are making a mud dam to build up a reserve of water where the mouth of the pipe rests. Dale's dog is scratching and sniffing around for rabbits and Freddie is picking up bits of smooth driftwood from the creek.

As we work she says, 'He hasn't spoken to me for a whole week now, not a word. I'm seriously thinking of shifting onto the couch in the living room. Not that he'd notice!'

'I thought you weren't looking too happy,' I reply. 'How did it start, anyway?'

As well as listening and talking to Dale while I work, I am worrying that Baby might wake and notice that I have gone. We are too far from the house to hear him if he cries.

'I can't remember for the life of me how it started. Over the kids probably. Cressida was home late the other night, only eleven o'clock, mind you, but he's old fashioned . . . The tension's beginning to get me down, never knowing when he's going to speak and what he'll say if he does.'

'Do you say anything to him?'

'I did at first, but I've given up now. I'm not crawling to him, that's for sure . . . last night he took off because tea wasn't on the table.'

I tell her I think it's just as well we have to fix the water because water is supposed to ease tension. It's recommended for nervous or tired children, being soothing for them to play in. And so we laugh and talk together. A sheep has trodden the bank in here; a stick has fallen across this miniature waterfall; we cut a few channels through this bog; now at last the water is running free. We know it will only last an hour or two, but at least it will help the tank to fill a bit more.

'Freddie, don't throw those sticks into the tank, for heavens sake!'

'But these are my *fish*!'

For a few minutes we stand watching the muddy water flow into the tank.

'I bet those townies would squirm if they saw this water!' says Dale, with a hint of superiority in her voice. I have noticed before she uses the word 'townie' in a derogatory manner when referring to people who live in the city, although it is only a few miles away.

'What would you think of me?' I ask her. 'In the country I'm a "townie" and in the city I'm a "country bumpkin"!'

Finished for the day, we slide and skid down the steep hill, hopefully watching the sky for clouds. As I say goodbye to Dale and she crosses the road to her place I sense she has been dreading the end of this distraction. I feel that she is lonely. She crosses the road reluctantly. I have not yet met her husband Des. The only time I see him is if I happen to be looking across the road when he drives off to work in the mornings or returns in the evenings.

(1978)

FIONA KIDMAN

An extract from
A Breed of Women

When the term ended, she and her parents moved to a remote valley further south, called Ohaka.

Harriet had been loading the trucks for an hour preparatory to departure when she realised that something was wrong. Her dress was too short, and made of thin cotton and in the front was a tiny stain of blood.

She searched her hands for cuts, but there were none that she could see. Next she examined her legs, and with growing horror realised that the time had come; there was a small trickle of blood down the inside of her leg.

'Mary, Mary,' shouted her father. 'Up higher, put it on the top.'

'I'm trying, Gerald,' her mother replied, perched precariously on the edge of the truck's tray, and holding a chair above her head.

Harriet looked at her cautiously. To her astonishment she saw her mother, unable to wipe her face, suck a trail of mucus from her nose down to her top lip with her bottom one. Harriet had never seen her cry before. At least, that's what she thought her mother was doing, though the tears were being whipped away in the wind; only the telltale undignified dribble from her nose told Harriet that she really had been crying. With a dull ache for her mother she wondered whether the prospect of another change to another small, hard farm was more than she could bear.

It did not seem an auspicious moment to relay the information that she had just received admission to the sisterhood of women.

She knew that the bandages would have been packed, and she would have to extract them somehow. With everything now piled on the truck, it was hard to work out which case they might be in. A mental stocktaking added up to the possibility that they were with her mother's underwear, which was in one of the first boxes that had gone on the truck. There was no way that her father would agree to any unpacking — besides, what possible convincing explanation could she give?

When you had your periods, all sorts of taboos had to be observed, apparently. One should not go swimming, take a bath or run fast races — not that this was a problem for Harriet. A girl should certainly not let any male know that she was afflicted by this rare and passing malady.

'Mary,' shouted her father. 'The boys'll want a cuppa. Time to put the billy on.' He normally never spoke like this, but he used the colloquialisms to help the Maori workmen understand that they were about to receive the milk of human kindness.

Everyone trooped inside and the trucks were abandoned.

Gingerly Harriet started to climb up over the boxes. To get to the cases at the back, she had to stand on the chicken crate. It was made of thin plywood. Harriet studied it and decided that it would hold; after all, she was small for her age. If she balanced carefully with one foot on the crate and the other on her mother's sewing machine case, the latter would almost certainly balance out her weight.

While she was in this position, just as she had reached the precious suitcase containing her mother's underwear, her father emerged from the house.

'What in the hell d'you think you're doing?' he roared behind her. 'You stupid, thick-skulled, little cow,' he added, as she collapsed through the chicken crate with a shriek. A pullet flew straight out above her head, showering feathers on her, and the birds in the box set up a fearsome cackling. Looking down she saw that she had broken the leg of one of them.

When her father had killed the injured bird and boarded up the crate again, he turned on her and said venomously that it was about time she started to earn her meal ticket. There'd be plenty for her to do on the new farm, he'd see to that. There had been a time when he had thought she had possibilities, that she might go somewhere. After all, look what he had done for her, leaving behind the old country, and all they held most dear and working themselves to the bone so that she could have a 'decent chance'. (As if, Harriet thought years later, he had analysed his sperm count years before and got on nodding terms with her years prior to her conception.)

And just look where it had got them all. A moron of a daughter who let dirty old men play around with her, a schizophrenic to boot if he could believe half of her reports. A girl, too, which was unjust when one considered that he'd put his life into building up a good farming background for a son. Now it seemed she was a bumbling sneak thief as well.

Harriet stood before this tirade without replying. She'd heard versions of several of the points before, but never delivered with quite such fury. At last he asked, 'What have you done to your leg?'

She looked down at the trickle of blood. 'Scratched it on the chicken crate, I think. When I fell through.'

Gerald Wallace turned away in disgust. 'Go and wash yourself at the tap,' he told her. 'We'll be ready to go soon.'

So it was that Harriet rode to the new farm with the outer edges of her vagina thoroughly packed with a wad of the *New Zealand Herald*.

The day they arrived, she was sitting squeezed up in the cab of the second truck with her mother. After they had been travelling for nearly three hours, the truck in front had slowed down and stopped. Gerald got out of it and came down the road to them. 'That's it, Mary,' he'd said, indicating a clump of bush.

'Where?' asked Harriet's mother, straining her eyes around the hot dry landscape.

'There,' he repeated, pointing. 'That's our boundary line. From here on its our bit of country. We'll be at the house in a few minutes.'

'Thank you Gerald,' she said bowing her head.

The trucks rolled forward again, and Harriet watched, her eyes darting from her mother's face to the passing landscape. It occurred to her that her father had bought the farm without her mother seeing it. When the purchase had first been announced, it had seemed natural enough, the sort of things fathers did. Now she was not so sure.

Clouds of dust rose round them. They seemed to be in a valley, a burnt-out bowl dried to a tinder by the bright North Auckland sun. The trees and scrub growing across what Gerald had described as their country looked as if they would pack up and leave if they could. Harriet was glad that she hadn't bothered her mother with other matters and hoped that her father had said nothing about the chicken crate episode. From her mother's distracted air, it seemed that her misdoings were quite the least important thing on her mind.

One last corner and they were at the farmhouse. Nobody had lived in it for some time and the burnt brown grass was up to the window sills. The trucks pulled up, and they all climbed out.

'Well,' said Mary feigning brightness, 'shall we go in?'

'You'll like it,' said Gerald, but even he looked uncertain.

The truck drivers hung back, sensing that this was not their moment. Gerald motioned for Mary to go in; Harriet decided that the invitation included her too.

The house consisted of four small rooms of the same size, each exactly square — the kitchen (a free-standing sink and a coal range), the lounge, as Gerald grandly called it (an open fireplace), her parents' bedroom and her bedroom. At the back was a lean-to containing a copper and a tin bath. They walked around, silently inspecting it.

In the room that was to be hers, Harriet stood and wondered why it seemed different to the others. She looked to the window and outside there was a plum tree, thick and leafy and laden with ripening plums, casting deep cool shadows into her room.

'Oh,' she exclaimed on an indrawn breath. 'Oh, thank you,' she said, inside herself.

She went through to her mother. Gerald had gone outside to supervise the unloading of the trucks. She touched Mary's arm.

'It's better than the last place, Mum.'

'Yes,' said Mary bleakly. 'It's better than the last place.'

'Don't you like it, Mum?'

'It's going to be a lot of work,' said Mary. 'Still, that's what life's all about.' She shook herself briskly. 'I'd better set to.'

'Come and look in my room,' Harriet said.

'It's just the same as mine, isn't it?'

'Just come and look,' Harriet urged.

She took Mary in and showed her the plum tree. For a long moment Mary stood there looking at it. For the second time that day, Harriet saw the glint of tears in her mother's eyes.

'Mum . . . would you like this room?'

'Oh my dear,' said Mary, 'I'm so glad. So glad for you.'

'I'll help with the work, Mum. Honest I will. I'm older now.'

'Yes, I know you will.'

'And I'll try not to make Dad mad at me. And I'll watch that I don't get a . . . a colonial accent.'

'You're a good girl,' said Mary.

'Shall I help you now?'

'Why don't you go and have a look round?'

'But I really do want to help. And Dad'll think I'm being lazy again.'

That was one of the best and closest moments of the summer between Harriet and her mother. For the rest of the time, Mary was working hard, distracted or fretful when she did think about Harriet, raising her concerns about her possible loneliness, things which seemed impossibly silly in view of the world that was waiting outside.

Mary Wallace worried about her daughter that summer. Here she was, having left her old school without knowing a soul, and the whole summer holidays stretching before her. To Harriet, there seemed no point in explaining to her mother that she had shed the old place like a dirty dress, and that a whole summer on her own was the nicest thing she could imagine. Surely her mother could see that she had been unhappy right through primary.

Still, it was nice that her mother cared. It seemed possible that she had always been an ally, and Harriet simply hadn't noticed. It was odd, this new feeling between her and her mother. She guessed it was to do with the fact that she was now 'a little woman', as her mother put it. She searched diligently through the histories of Amy, Beth, Jo and Meg to see if they could shed any light on the situation, but there seemed to be an entire lack of information about the process by which they arrived at little womenhood.

Her father also seemed to like her considerably less than before, but perhaps she noticed him more.

The farm itself held some unexpected treasures. On that first day, Harriet made some bright and beautiful discoveries.

At first she didn't know where to begin, and for a moment she was engulfed by a blank dark terror that if she went away she would return to nothingness — the trucks would have gone away, her parents would have disappeared, and the house would have vanished, leaving the breeze rippling through a paddock of brown grass. She began to walk timidly down a track leading away from the house, through dusty lawsonianas. In front of it there was a gentle slope. At the bottom she found that she was on the floor of the valley, and it was quite different from the rest of the farm that she had seen so far.

The breeze did ripple through the grass, but what grass! Long and smooth like green silk, dotted with clover in flower, smelling strongly and sweetly, the scent of summer itself. Harriet dropped forward on her knees and spreadeagled out on the grass. Here was a scent, she thought, that she would never forget in all her life.

The sun, hovering on the brink of late afternoon, had become a friend again. The long dusty ride, the pain in her mother's face, her father's early morning anger had all gone away. This was her country all right.

She got to her feet, and started walking again. The flat plain was bounded by a river, dark with shadow, yet clear. Along its edge were thick trees, some native, as well as willows and poplars, hawthorns and wild roses. The hawthorns and roses were thick with flowers and she recognised honeysuckle among them too, its flowers were part of the patterns of fragrance around her.

Harriet was sure she would burst with joy. Only a short distance along the river bank, she came to a half-fallen poplar tree that had re-established its growth after it had fallen, so that it formed a verandah across the river. It was easy to climb up and along it, to a crook formed by a branch and the trunk, a naturally comfortable hollow for a small person to lie and look at the sky through the tangle of leaves and flowers above. There could be no more beautiful place in the world.

Time passed and Harriet had no idea how long she stayed there. At last, when she realised that she was chilled, she climbed down from her perch. Before she left the river, she waded into it and washed, disposing of the shameful pieces of newspaper under a rock. The bleeding appeared to have almost stopped. She thought then that she would never need the bandages, and that it might spare her mother some worry if she didn't tell her about it at all. It didn't seem absolutely necessary for her to be like everyone else, and it was quite obvious that she was not going to have to endure her illness to the same extent that some women had done, if they needed such a wad of bandage when it happened to them.

When she got back to the house the trucks had gone, and she couldn't see anyone about. For a moment her panic returned; it was as if her vision had come true. In a few minutes, though, she heard voices calling, and realised guiltily that by now her parents would be out looking for her.

Her father sent her to bed early as a punishment for being out late, which was no great hardship, for the day had caught up with her and she was engulfed by the most profound exhaustion. She fell almost immediately into a heavy sleep and woke only when the sun, filtered by the plum tree, broke through her uncurtained window the following morning. A blackbird's singing streamed around her as he hung on the bough of the tree.

Was it a summer of waking or sleeping? It passed like dreams and rarely did the world outside intrude, from then until the beginning of school. Afterwards, when she was older, she sensed that the summer had been a time of wakefulness before the long sleep of conventional life began.

(1980)

YVONNE DU FRESNE

Arts and Crafts

There was always somebody doing something with thread in our house. Wool, linen-thread, gold and silver cord, cotton. Fingers flashed and stabbed at the knitting. Faces looked up at me and smiled while the fingers went on knitting.

'Kom, sit!' said my Moder, Tante Helga, Bedstemoder. I sat by them. 'Once a great King rode forth . . .' they started.

Why did the knitting and the stories commence together? From the weaving huts of Jutland. That was where the women went for the weaving, the spinning, the knitting. And while they did those things — the rhythm of their moving fingers made the old stories come. For hundreds of years they told the old stories of Denmark in the weaving huts. That is how I learned them. While I listened to the stories I watched the fingers. They knitted, they pulled threads out of linen for the drawn-thread designs, their needles flashed in and out of linen, embroidering field flowers, with their names beside them in single thread. Sometimes the flowers were Danish — but more and more, New Zealand flowers crept in. Wildflowers, flax and grass. I would go with them on the flower expeditions. 'Ah,' they would sigh, eyes intent, pulling here a shivery grass, there a spray of wild fuchsia. They would put their finds in a vase and watch them with narrowed eyes while they were baking, while they were drying dishes. '*Ah*,' they would say, eyes gleaming. Then they would sit down, and snip, snap, on the tablecloth, on the sampler, would come the same grass and flowers. Their embroideries changed. Nets of fine thread were woven to make a cobweb on the flowers and grass. Raindrops shone coldly in beads and sequins.

And my Bedstemoder made the river. Oh yes, she brought the river to life on fine linen. She made the raupo reeds, toetoe, waves, foam, long grass, and stones glittering on the banks. We found the stones, my Bedstemoder and I, with our kerchiefs tied over our heads, fluttering in the river wind under the great summer sun baking the Manawatu Plains. We found little shells on the beach not far away, at Foxton. The long fingers of my Bedstemoder found them in the glittering sand and turned them over and over.

'The sea,' said my Bedstemoder. 'The sea!'

Her eyes turned a deeper blue as she looked at the long rollers streaming in. The family knew the ocean — they had come from it, they said. From Denmark. I looked for the hundredth time to see the fishtails on them of the Mer-Kings, the Sea-Folk. But that was when I was too young to know better. My Bedstemoder embroidered a ship on her river. She wove the rigging, spider-fingered. Shells winked in it.

'Look,' she said, 'the ship we came in. We danced and sang on that ship.'

I could see it all.

One day my Moder and my Bedstemoder gave me my first embroidery. A bunch of cherries on an apron for me. While I was making the cherries with needle and thread we had the winter floods. My Bedstemoder turned into a warrior queen when the floods came. She continually measured the rising water with her dressmaking ruler.

'Three feet!' she would shout, 'and still rising.'

The cherries came to life under my fingers on the day of the flood. I crouched over them in a patch of cold winter sunlight coming through a window. My needle flashed in the cold light as if it lived. It winked at me as it worked.

'You and I — and the cherries, eh?' it said.

I sewed the scarlet thread under and over to give an impression of plumpness. The cherries grew round and fat. I changed to green thread, and leaves and stalks grew like lightning. They shook in a Spring wind.

At nightfall the flood water dropped.

'Two-feet-six!' screamed my Bedstemoder. 'This house is saved!'

I cut the last thread and held up the apron. Living cherries grew on it. My Bedstemoder, restless with excitement, snatched up my work and held it to the light. Then she became very intent.

'Ha!' she said to my Moder. My Moder's cheeks flushed. She carried the cherry apron around with her.

'Look at my daughter's work!' she said to everybody — over and over again.

We draped it artistically over the sideboard while we ate our dinner and the flood water ran secretly away to the river where it truly belonged. We watched the apron as we ate. My cherries and leaves shook in Spring winds.

At school I sat in my iron desk with a brand new pastel book open in front of me. Miss Gore held up a three-cornered stick, coloured brown.

'This is a pastel!' chanted Miss Gore.

'This is a pastel!' we chanted back.

Then we commenced the drawing. It was a castle. A difficult castle. You drew softly with the brown, the black, the white pastels. You worried it with grey pastel for the shadowing. Well, you want to know what my pastel castle looked like? A lump — flattened by siege — smashed by cannon fire. It was blackened with tears, it fell off the page. Miss Gore closed the tissue page over my pastel-coloured lump.

'No eye for drawing I can see,' she said.

'I can make cherries with the thread,' I said.

'No doubt,' said Miss Gore, and shut the book.

She gave us little sticks. They were the sticks the fierce visiting school doctor had poked down our throats. Spatula sticks.

'Now,' said Miss Gore, 'we are going to have a Parents' Day. We are going to make stick mats.' And she made one, in and out.

I struggled with my spatula mat. It fell to pieces. It was not thread — it was wood — too hard for the fingers to weave. In the end my mat was anchored with drawing pins.

My Moder came to the Parents' Day in her three-piece suit, the hat over one eye. She looked in silence at my spatula mat.

'Dearest God,' she said under her breath in Danish.

At home that night she gave me some crayons. Her cheeks shone pink with love and anxiety.

'We are going to draw an English garden for Miss Gore,' she said, 'to make up for that mat.'

We spent hours on that picture — copied from a lovely photograph in *The New Idea*. Larkspur, hollyhocks and crazy paving. A cottage garden.

'It will remind her of England,' said my Moder. 'It will remind her of her far-away homelands.'

The next morning I took the English-garden drawing, and the cherry apron, in a cardboard box to school. I laid the picture softly on the table where Miss Gore was sitting. 'An English-garden for you,' I said.

Miss Gore looked affronted.

'An English *hus* from your lost homelands,' I said. Miss Gore picked up the picture between finger and thumb. Miss Gore was what we called an Ice-Maiden. No heart. She rejected her homelands.

'I think your Mother has drawn this for you, Astrid,' she said.

I shut her out of my life for ever. I left the cherry apron in its box.

Later that morning we were pushed into a line, with all our school books in our cases. We marched to another part of the school into an old, old classroom, that was built like a garden shed. That was the first classroom of all to be built, when children had not left the grass, the trees, the sky behind them. The windows rattled in the wind, but you could look out and see the world. In the room stood a young black-haired woman with an orange dress on. On the orange dress were printed pink tulips. I knew that orange dress, those pink tulips. It was my Russian doll, come to life. 'Children, this is your new teacher!' said Miss Gore in a voice as cold as Winter.

'My name is Miss Martin,' said the new teacher, my Russian doll come to life. 'Sit down — sit down!' We sat at wooden tables. No iron anywhere. Miss Gore marched back to fresh wars.

You know what happened in that room? Oh, kind God, it was a new world You gave us that day. I showed Miss Martin my cherry apron, my English *hus*. Miss Martin held up the English-garden picture, the cherry apron, for all to see. For the first time, my people were honoured.

'Look at the stitches in those cherries!' said Miss Martin. 'The Danish are famous for their needlework. Astrid is learning all this!'

Oh, Miss Martin, Miss Martin, before somebody snatched you away in marriage, you made us see the world. Air, trees, flowers, grass rushed in upon our senses. We took deep breaths, we laughed, we talked. And the first Art and Craft we did for you was that model farm. Do you remember the model farmyard we made? Do you remember the sticky yellow raffia we cut into little lengths with our blunt scissors for the straw in the farmyard? And when I forgot myself, and called out 'Strå-strå!' you got everybody to listen and said for all to hear 'Can you hear the English word "straw" in that Danish word? The Danes came to England long ago. They gave us many words. You can still hear them if you listen carefully!'

How did she know that secret?

Oh — the Danes and the English were one people that day! One people!

(1980)

SUE McCAULEY

Chapter Six from
Other Halves

Tug chose to remain in bed, where he had spent the whole day, and declined to eat. Over the steak Liz told Jim about the homeless boy she had met at Valleyview and now taken in. Sitting across from Jim, watching him scrape aside his mushrooms (of course, she ought to have asked) with a delicacy which proclaimed pedigree, she could believe it was that straightforward. Jim found her story unremarkable. He was accustomed to the dispensing of good deeds. His mother, he told Liz a little wearily, used to do Meals on Wheels.

He showed more enthusiasm over the discovery that she had been a psychiatric inmate. From his questions she realised that the possibility of madness lent, for him, an edge of mystique.

When they had eaten and were sitting in separate chairs in front of the fire, Tug breezed through the room and into the kitchen to slice and butter himself a piece of bread. She had earlier put his grimy clothes to soak and now he was wrapped jauntily in Liz's pink chenille dressing grown. On his return trip she introduced him to Jim who extended his hand with a conspicuously affable hello. Tug paused, glowered and moved on, slamming the bedroom door behind him.

'What did I do?'

'Nothing. I have a feeling that was aimed at me.'

'Are you sure you know what you're doing. I mean, is it safe for you . . .?'

'He's only a child,' she said.

'He looks capable of looking after himself to me.'

'Did you look after yourself at sixteen?'

'That's hardly the point, Liz. How long's he going to stay?'

'I don't know. I suppose until he finds somewhere.' She felt defensive. Good causes ought to manifest themselves as cherubic waifs pale with gratitude.

'You know,' said Jim, conversationally, changing the subject, 'I've never really known any Maoris. Not personally. There just never were any in my particular circle of friends and acquaintances.'

'Then I wouldn't take Tug as representative. They come in all shapes and moods.' She had meant it to sound wry but it came out tart, a rebuke. Jim, she thought, looks at Tug and sees not Tug but a Maori. Tug looks at Jim and sees not Jim but a dick-head. Obviously it simplified things greatly for both of them. Were the complications simply her own invention?

She tried to retrieve the thread of earlier conversations, but an uneasiness remained. It was as if, Liz thought, they were being watched. Then she realised with dismay that this was possibly true. The house was old and the door to Tug's room had a keyhole. As if in defiance of the same possibility Jim moved his chair closer to Liz and took her hand onto his lap.

Tug appeared on cue. He swayed across the room, purposefully nonchalant, and positioned himself in front of the bookcase. Jim's voice detailed off limply in the middle of a memory of boarding-school humiliations. Tug studied the book titles.

'Are you looking for something in particular?' She asked him brightly, a nervous student teacher.

Tug turned to look at them. 'One with screwing in it.'

Liz felt herself, absurdly, blushing. 'Try Henry Miller,' she said, not looking at Jim. 'Second shelf to your left. The black cover.'

He found the book and thumbed through the pages sourly. 'Bet it's slack.' But he took it with him back to the bedroom.

Jim suddenly remembered his need for an early night.

'I'm sorry about . . .' Liz nodded towards Tug's door.

Jim shrugged. 'I just wonder if you know what you're letting yourself in for.'

She walked to the gate with him. He invited her to go with him to an exhibition opening on the following Saturday, and brushed her lips in a dry kiss.

She confronted Tug in his bedroom. 'This is my home and I won't have you being rude to my friends.'

'Whaddid I do?' Looking up at her in injured innocence.

'You know.'

'Aren't I allowed to read your books or something? Is that it? Stink book anyway.' He tossed it onto the floor. She left it where it was.

'You're a toad,' she said, but no longer angry. 'And I don't think you'll make it to a prince.'

'What's that mean?'

'I'm too tired,' she said, 'to explain.'

Tug spent almost all of that week in bed. When Liz left in the mornings he would be asleep and when she got home from work he would still be in bed, listlessly thumbing through a magazine or simply staring up at the ceiling. If he got up for dinner — and he had little appetite — they'd talk in a polite and almost formal fashion. His manner wasn't so much guarded as apathetic. After a few attempts at jollying him Liz let him be, telling herself that such apparently bleak inactivity must be fulfilling some need in him. And, even lying listless and silent in bed, he provided a certain reassurance, was a bulwark against the mindless panic. Someone to come home to.

On the Friday Ken drove her, in her lunch-break, to the lawyer's office where their separation was to be made official. She was allotted a third of the proceeds from the sale of their house if and when it was sold. A generous agreement, the solicitor said, the courts would probably have allowed her less.

'I gather this is an amicable separation? Good. And there is no problem about access? No? Right. If you wish to attempt a reconciliation and renew conjugal relationships but then resume living apart that will not be considered a breach of legal separation.'

So still nothing was final. The game went on. Did she want or didn't she want? This pretence that people had a choice.

She let Ken do the talking, suspecting anyway that he and the solicitor had some kind of prior understanding from which she was excluded. She signed the papers thinking ruefully of the Treaty of Waitangi. How could you ever know the magnitude of what you were signing away?

'Perhaps we've got time for a celebratory drink,' Ken suggested, back in the car.

'I don't exactly feel like celebrating.'

'I still can't understand you.' He edged the car out of its parking space. 'I never did, all those years.'

She was tempted to say sourly, You never tried, but she knew it took two, and how hard had *she* tried? Besides, she felt an absolute need to have the whole marriage parcelled up nicely and prettily.

'I'm not sorry, Ken,' she said. 'I mean I don't regret all those years. I did love you.'

Ken was watching the car ahead. It had a sticker which said JESUS OUR ONLY HOPE. 'I've thought about that quite a lot. The truth is I didn't love you, Liz. I don't think I ever did.' He was still watching the car with the sticker.

Liz felt numbed with the pain of it. Eleven years of her life flushed down a toilet bowl. 'What a pity you didn't think to tell me sooner,' she said limply, looking at the people on the footpath who could not know that she had just been stabbed in the conjugal back.

'I think it's best to be honest about it,' he said.

'Oh yes,' she said, 'much the best.' She thought about people who died laughing.

'I mean what sort of shit is he? Maybe he's just bitter, d'you think? But he really seemed to mean it. It must be true then? All those years. I was just the cook and the cleaner and the bloody laundrymaid. Very convenient. Oh, it must have been more than that. No it probably wasn't. He didn't lose. He's got Michael. He's got his fancy women. But what was the point of saying it? Why couldn't he have just pretended at the end. Oh God.'

Tug jerked her wrist savagely towards him. 'Shut up,' he roared. 'For fucksake shut up. It's over, okay? There's no point in stirring it round and round. You're screwed in the head I reckon.'

Liz tried with her left hand to prise his fingers from her wrist. 'At least,' she said venomously, 'I manage to get out of bed.'

Tug rolled his eyes sardonically, but released her arm. 'If you don't mind leaving the room,' he said, 'I'd like to get dressed.'

She lay on her own bed, afraid that he would leave her, listening to his footsteps. He came to the doorway sniffing at his armpits. 'Even smells clean,' he said of his jersey, pleased. He tossed her wallet onto the bed. 'I've taken some money.'

'Help yourself.' As sarcasm it was indifferent.

'Thanks, I have.'

She heard him slam the back door and pad down the path.

She lay on the bed and thought about mental cruelty and degrees of mental cruelty and whether there was something about her that invited it, and why. Then she heard him come back, knowing it was Tug for who else on these bleak winter nights travelled in bare feet?

He came straight to her bedroom and spread a feast beside her. Fish and chips steaming, a bottle of sherry, a bottle of whisky. He beamed as he opened the packets.

'Tug,' she protested, 'we couldn't afford whisky.'

'Only paid for the sherry. And the greasies. Here's your change. Go on, count it.'

'We'll take the whisky back. Later. I'll come with you.'

'Fuck off. It's a present. I got it for you.'

'But you didn't pay for it.'

'So what? Maybe I did and maybe I didn't.'

'I know you didn't.'

'If we take it back they'll book me.'

'I don't think so.'

'Jesus. Don't be thick. I got a record. Jus' say thank you and take it.'

She took it. He went for glasses and she prepared a speech.

'Tug, while you live here no more stealing, okay? It's just not on.'

He poured them each a sherry. 'Liz, while I live here no more crying and moaning your arse off, okay?'

'You need some shoes,' she said. 'We'll have to get you some shoes. Your feet must be freezing.' She reached to touch them. 'They are.'

'Last winter I had gumboots. I kept them on all the time so's they wouldn't get nicked and there wasn't nowhere to take a bath and when in the end I took them off I had weedy feet.'

She laughed. 'What do you mean, weedy?'

'There was weeds growing on them. Fungus stuff. True.'

They wrapped themselves in rugs against the cold and kept refilling the glasses until Ken no longer mattered. Raking out memories of his mother Tug said, matter-of-fact, 'Since she died you're the only person who's loved me.'

She was astonished. 'How do you know I love you?'

'But you do, don't you?'

'I suppose so.' Hedging it even then and amazed that anyone could expose himself so incautiously to rejection. With a certain shame she sifted his words for motive. Were they as innocent and trusting as it seemed? Was he trying to trap her into some kind of emotional obligation?

Later, he asked, 'Why do you stare at me so much?'

She was embarrassed. 'Do I?'

'You're always staring at me.'

She said, truthfully, 'Then it's because I think you're pretty. I mean I like looking at you. I suppose I envy you. Brown skin looks so much better than white skin. That's a fact, whatever people may say. It seems a bit unfair really.' She registered the unintended pun, but it didn't seem worth spelling out.

Tug studied the colour of the back of his hand judiciously. 'Yeah, you're right. That's why I only look at you when I really have to.'

The lady artist wore gold satin pants and high leather boots, her hair was straight, glossy black, her husband wealthy and old. She overshadowed her paintings which were abstracts in blues and purples and splotches of brown. If you joined them all together the paintings would have looked almost identical to the material of a dress Liz had bought from Kirkcaldies when she was nineteen. She had loved that dress, and at nineteen she would also have loved the exhibition opening and the party which followed when a selected few of them adjourned to the home of the lady artist.

At nineteen Liz had been a devoted admirer of the world and its people. She was continuously delighted by her amazing good fortune in knowing and meeting so many entertaining, talented and charming individuals. And here she was, deja-vuing in the same circles. But the familiarity lacked pleasure, she stood awkward in her black dress, remote and disengaged. She was not overlooked; her association with Jim lent her prestige and besides she was a new face and a fresh audience.

A plump little man with fleshy lips proffered a bowl of peanuts.

'I'm a criminal lawyer. You can take that however you like.'

'I believe you,' she said.

He laughed with his teeth protruding like a horse and gave a sweep of his hand. 'Did you ever see so much intellectual wankery?'

She smiled dutifully. He thrust his face towards hers. 'You wouldn't like a quick fumble in the spare bedroom I don't suppose?'

'No thanks.'

'Then you won't mind if I try elsewhere?'

She shook her head. He bowed and moved away.

Jim was in a corner being whispered at by the lady artist. A young woman warned Liz that there was a lot of bad acid being circulated these days, a young reporter boasted that he had never set foot on a rugby field, then a middle-aged man recited a poem about manuka bushes to the whole room. Leonard Cohen gloomed from the stereo speakers, joints passed from hand to hand.

A toothy woman in a caftan complained piercingly about the increasing number of louts in the city square, and Liz wondered if Tug was at home or out louting. The little lawyer was put in mind of a party he was once at where loutish males forced one of their women to lie on the table amid the beer flagons while they removed her knickers and shoved a saveloy up her. Then the men shared the saveloy. It was a most successful story. The toothy woman proclaimed it epitomised the average New Zealander. Someone else asked the lawyer if he liked saveloys and he smiled enigmatically. 'That's nothing compared to their gang initiation rites,' said another.

Liz moved away, less in disgust than anger. She felt, obscurely and drunkenly, defiled on Tug's behalf. She had a picture of herself standing, immobilised, with each foot on a separate iceberg and those icebergs incompatible and drifting apart. At some point, she warned herself, she would have to choose.

Jim was still wedged in the corner with the booted lady. He was tracing shapes on his hand, explaining something, with a frown of concentration. The artist's hand was nestled in Jim's crotch. She was smiling. Liz made her way quietly up the sumptuous passage and rang for a cab.

Tug was in bed. Checking on that, she stumbled against the doorpost.
'You're drunk.'
'A bit. Were you asleep? Shall I put the light on?'
'If you want. How was the party?'
'Awful. Full of stupid people.'
'Dick-head bring you home?'
'No. I got a taxi.'
'You left him there?'
'He seemed quite happy.'
'You left before it finished?'
She wanted to explain that she had chosen her iceberg and that the choosing had opened up another dimension of possibility which had seemed both shocking and inevitable. Coming home in the taxi she had made herself an unthinkable promise. Now she took a deep breath and dragged back the words that were cowardly fleeing from her mind.
'Tug, I'd like to sleep with you.'
He just looked at her, eyes widened.
'Well?' she snapped it out. The waiting was unendurable.
He squirmed beneath the blankets. 'I'm not sure what you mean.'
'Oh God,' she pleaded. 'I mean what you think I mean. Just say yes or no.' Her courage had abandoned her, she wanted to retract, deny, pass out.

He pulled the blankets up to his eyes and said something muffled from beneath them.

'I couldn't hear,' she said helplessly.

He lowered the blankets to chin level. 'No,' he said clearly.

The embarrassment was smothered in relief and a sudden sobriety. 'I'm sorry Tug. I'm really sorry. I should never have said it. You're quite right. We'll forget it. Okay? Everything just like it was.'

He nodded with conviction.

At breakfast Tug was polite and watchful. Liz was polite and regretful.

'Are you hungry?'

'No thank you.'

'There's some bacon?'

'No. Really, I'm not hungry.'

'But you'll have a cup of tea? I'm just making one.'

'A cup of tea. All right. If you're making one.'

'Michael's coming today. I thought he'd be here before now.'

'Might go out for a while. See some of the boys.'

'That's a good idea. You haven't been out for days. Shall I keep dinner for you?'

'Don't worry. I'm not sure what time I'll be back.'

I've frightened him away, she thought. I've betrayed his trust.

In the bathroom mirror she reminded her reflection that she was old. Her gums were receding, her skin was loosening. There were furrows and crow's-feet. She was old enough, as he'd once pointed out, to be his mother.

She wanted her times with Michael to be gentle with shared laughter and affectionate gestures, but there was an awkwardness between them. She wanted to explain, atone, be forgiven, but Michael watched her with veiled eyes remembering (she thought) her weeping past.

She walked with him to the park, aware that Ken had the car and access to more exciting diversions. He told her about the air-force bomber he had under construction at home; his hardest model yet. She listened but did not comprehend. Michael was a small encyclopaedia of weaponry and warfare.

At home again they made gingerbread men and he talked about their plans to move north. 'Won't you miss me?' she pleaded. 'I s'pose so,' he said, looking down at the table. After tea he watched out the window for Ken's car coming to take him home.

At midnight she was woken from a dream about Toothless Neddy in a soldier's uniform crouching injured in a barn. She went to answer the 'phone. Did she wish, the operator asked, to accept a collect call from a Mr Morton in Dunedin? *Dunedin?*

'Liz?' He sounded anxious. 'Liz, I'm in . . . hangon . . .' She heard him open a door and ask, 'Hey, whassa name of this place?'

'Dunedin,' she said when he returned.

'Yeah, that's right. Always forget names.'
'What are you doing in Dunedin?'
'Nothing much. Standing in a 'phone box.'
'I meant . . . well how did you get there?'
'Drove down. Me and some of the boys. In this Holden. I drove from Timaru.'
'Whose car is it?'
'One of the boys.'
'He owns it?'
'He found it. Finders keepers doncha know?' He laughed. 'Mightn't be home for a few days so I's ringing to let you know.'
'Like how many days?' Wishing she didn't need to ask, wondering if in Dunedin it emerged as a plea or a threat.
'Not too many.' He was being reassuring, paternal. 'I'll be home by next weekend, okay? You won't give my bed to anyone?'
A whole week.
'I might,' she said off-handedly. 'It depends.'
An instant reaction. 'Go ahead then. I probably won't be coming back anyway.'
'As you like.' But she allowed him the satisfaction of being first to hang up.

'I was really tired so I just thought I'd slip away on the quiet. I didn't want to mess up your evening. It just didn't occur to me that you'd be upset about it.'
Sitting in the Grand Hotel with its red leather upholstery and mahogany-stained tables Liz thought how easy it was to be sophisticated when you didn't really care.
On Monday she had decided there was little point in her continuing to see Jim. But this was Thursday and Tug had not come home and her resolve seemed perhaps a little hasty. Jim had been attending an Indigenous Culture seminar in Palmerston North. He had told her about it, he said, though she had no recollection and would she have forgotten something as portentous as an Indigenous Culture seminar? Anyway here he was buying her drinks and almost nervously explaining that his association with Elly, painter of blue and purple abstracts, was a matter of ambition on her side and reluctance on his.
'You don't need to explain,' Liz told him. 'I don't own you. I don't want that kind of involvement.'
She could see that he was impressed, that her indifference attracted him. She felt ashamed of herself, yet after he had called at the coffee bar that morning to invite her for drinks she had made a deliberate decision to be encouraging. Jim was politeness, conversation, *normality*. When (if) Tug returned her role would be more clearly defined if Jim was around. No more embarrassing lapses.

She watched him walk across to the bar to refill their glasses. He walked with such confidence. Her mother would like him. From across the room the plump lawyer caught Liz's eye and waved. Liz waved back, smiling. It was so easy to be acceptable.

She'd been home an hour when the 'phone went. She ran to answer it. A wrong number. But it was natural to be worried, she thought. He could have been arrested. The car might have crashed. Both seemed more probabilities than possibilities.

If he was dead she wouldn't be notified — they'd track down some next-of-kin. For her he would just have disappeared.

She switched on the radio and waited for the hourly news bulletin and the names of road fatality victims. There were none.

Friday night. A car slowed down on the street; all evening, cars had been passing and slowing, but this one had no muffler. Liz went on reading but the words were just words on their own and would not link into sentences. The car stopped. Definitely it had stopped. There were shouts and a slamming of doors, then the car drove off again. She began again at the beginning of the sentence; the street was full of houses expecting visitors.

The door was locked and he hammered on it with unnecessary force. Liz got out of bed and went to open it, remembering how much he could irritate her.

'You was in bed?' He smelt of beer.

'It's quite late.'

She went back to the bedroom, he followed her and stood leaning against the wall.

'You're glad I'm back?'

'Well, I'm glad you're still alive anyway.'

'You was worried?'

'I suppose the car was stolen?'

'It was and it wasn't. Fat Boy paid the deposit. Only under another name.'

'What did you do down there?'

'Nothing much. Just mucked about. They wouldn't let us in at the prison.'

'But you had a good time?'

'Not really,' he said. 'I's homesick.'

She was going to laugh, but she saw he meant it. 'Well, you're home now,' she said.

He looked past her at the window with its curtains drawn and she knew in a curdling instant what he was about to say.

'You remember the other night, what you said . . . Did you mean it?'

'I was drunk.' Her cowardliness shamed her. 'Yes, I meant it.'

He was crouching beside the bed holding her hand. The whole of her was a hand being held. His face was hidden against the bedspread; when he raised it his eyes seemed huge. Blue eyes, she thought, were intrusive, they invaded you. Brown eyes looked inward; they went deep, you could float in them. Possibly drown.

At eleven Liz had been religious. She had planned to be a missionary in some dark tropical land tending the sparrow-legged bulbous-bellied children who had eyes like Tug's eyes. She longed for selfless dedication and righteous anger. She wrote to Trevor Huddleston, care of his publishers, but he was no doubt too busy to reply.

Her mother sang in the Anglican church choir on Sundays, but Liz was privately scornful of her mother's style of religion — social introductions, descant harmony and a Sunday spiritual inoculation. The daughter waited to be overcome by some dark, tumultuous force; she longed for surrender and dedication and intensity. The feeling was strong in her that she had been Chosen, yet she hesitated, wanting confirmation; a sign; however small. She created opportunities for this to happen beyond the bounds of coincidence, but when no bushes burned, no telegraph poles split in two and the messages of the clouds remained obscure she finally lost interest.

She committed herself then to Ralph and his various successors — stray cats and broken birds. A few died but most of them recovered. The birds flew away or stayed around the home as semi-pets; the cats she took eventually to the S.P.C.A. where they were probably destroyed. Liz was aware of this likelihood but remained committed to tending her ailing strays.

After a time her spiritual aspirations began to seem nothing more than a childish phase. Watching her battered birds flap off awkwardly into the suburban skies she would tell herself that if there was some infinite truth this was it and it was beyond question or comprehension — just *there* like the hillside, like the sea.

And sometimes when she was alone, out riding Delilah, entranced by the shape of her horse's ears and the fall of her mane, she would get a sensation of pure happiness. Although the feeling itself was beyond description it was accompanied by a vague sensation of thirst. For herself she defined it as rapture. She had no doubt it had something to do with that infinite truth.

And now, absurdly, with Tug's hands and mouth moving over her body she thought of religion. She remembered the sharpness of her longing for intensity and surrender and she recognised that incomparably exquisite thirst. *Of course*, she thought. *Of course.*

He was shameless. He presented his body as a chef might present his finest cuisine, confident that every morsel — every hair, every pucker and crevice — was delicious and desirable. And gradually, as he explored her own body without permission or hesitation she felt three decades of caution and apprehension crumble and fall away. For the first time in her life she felt unreservedly — well, *almost* unreservedly — lovable.

They lay tight in each other's arms.

'What are you thinking?' She whispered, feeling that dull thirstiness all through her.

'I's thinking what a lot of time we wasted.'

'That was your fault; you turned me down.'

'I's scared. I mean you're sort of . . .'

'Like your mother?'

'Not now you're not.'

She laughed. 'So what happens now?'

'We start again.'

'I meant . . . I won't regret it,' she told him. 'Whatever happens I could never regret it.'

She woke at eight, exultant. She felt as she had felt after the birth of her children — permanently, cataclysmically altered. She had looked at the clock before she fell asleep and it said half-past five. Tug had fallen asleep about an hour before her, his arms still tight around her. When she slid a hand down over his buttocks he had thrust against her even in his sleep. Now, remembering that, she grinned to herself wanting him to wake so she could tell him.

He was buried beneath the bedclothes. She pulled them down carefully, wanting to look at his face. Unveiling it like a national treasure. His eyes flickered then opened wide and he grabbed at the bedclothes and pulled them back over his head.

'Tug?'

'I thought it was a dream,' muffled through the blankets.

'It wasn't, and you can't stay under there forever.'

He lowered the blankets slowly, fearfully, to make her laugh.

'What happens now?' he asked when they reached his chin.

'I guess we make the most of it while it lasts.'

'How long d'y' reckon we'll last?'

She thought about it. In her experience euphoria had never been more than momentary. 'Two weeks?' she ventured in wild optimism.

'I'd say nearer two months.'

She shook her head.

'Two months,' he repeated. 'D'you wanna bet? Two dollars, ay?'

'I don't want to bet.'

'Come on,' he urged, grinning already at his own joke. 'Make it a bit interesting.'

She cuffed at his head but he ducked. His face grew solemn. 'You wanna know something?'

'What?' Anxiety welled.

'It wasn't me who had the weedy feet. It was Bones.'

(1982)

J. C. STURM

Jerusalem, Jerusalem

If my date hadn't been late that Friday night I wouldn't be telling you this, because I wouldn't have met Olive instead and found out what I did. A brisk southerly had been hosing down the city all day, leaving it brighter and darker and taller and wider than it ever really is, and excited in a shivery jittery kind of way, like a dog that has just had a bath it didn't want. It certainly wasn't the night for a leisurely stroll down town or to be loitering in shop doorways, and yet a surprising number of the city's population were doing just that. There were the usual pub leftovers and the picture crowd and the ones who like eating late in Chinese restaurants and the others who would later take up residence in the coffee shops if they hadn't managed to gate-crash a party. And there were exhausted housewives, weighed down with the weekend shopping and drooping on tram stops, while bright young things, all eye-shadow and stiffened petticoats, clung to their Valentinos and hastened towards Romance. Some of the shops had closed already, hustling their customers and assistants outside where husbands waited with pale-faced children and boy friends shuffled impatiently and dropped half finished cigarettes and stood on them. And as though the natives weren't more than enough, two American ships had berthed that afternoon, and the pavements were awash with sailors and girls like gaudy tropical fish. I was afraid of missing my date in that crowd, so worked my way round the traffic lights twice, just in case, hopping from one side of the road to the other whenever the greens gave me the chance, as a child jumps from rock to rock when the waves suck back and wait, and trying to gain a foothold on each corner was worse than landing on a slippery ledge with someone standing in the way. In the end I gave up, and elbowed myself into the doorway of Madame's exclusive gown salon. I wriggled into the black satin cocoon in the window and went to the party and had a fabulous time and came back on the stroke, like Cinderella, to find a little fox terrier man thumping a newspaper tail against his thigh and snapping at my legs, have a drink have a drink come and have a drink. The last corner, which was also the first, proved to be the best. I backed up against a wall of marcasite and New Zealand souvenirs, wondering how much pressure plate glass can take to the square inch, and then I saw Olive. I never know why some faces stand out in a crowd, but they do, and the shifting shapeless mass suddenly becomes a background to one small oval of meaning, and the shock of recognition is so great, you hail a mere acquaintance as though he were a beloved uncle, and then you have to turn away quickly to hide your excitement while you try to remember his name. Olive had such a face, and my heart leapt and flipped over and went through all the gymnastics hearts are supposed to be capable of, when I saw it. Not that she was a close friend of mine or ever had been, even in the old days, but she belonged to the brightest of my childhood, and who can stand on a street corner and not tremble as the past walks out of a crowd?

I don't know how long the Kellys had been at the Bay before I first saw them. A public works camp had come from nowhere and dug itself in on the outskirts of our small community, and it was hard to keep track of all the new faces. The 'permanent residents', as they called themselves, didn't like the invasion one bit. I think they feared deep down it was the beginning of the End, and in a way, I suppose it was. They used to go to the local store in twos and threes and pretend they couldn't think what they wanted and turn to the nearest stranger and say, 'I'm not in a hurry, you go first,' and then stand back and watch while their victim blushed and stammered and the woman behind the counter who didn't want to lose any old custom on account of the new because you can't depend on PWCs, would go to the fridge at the other end of the room and call out, 'did you say *half* a pound of butter?' One of these sessions was in full swing the afternoon I found Billy and Ken sitting on the ground beside the store door with their backs against the wall. Now that tickled me. We local kids used to get up to all kinds like turning somersaults on the rail at the top of the steps and accidentally kicking people as they came out, and dressing up a dog and taking it for a walk in a borrowed pram, and leaving dead wetas beside the seat in the Ladies. But we never, not ever, sat on the ground outside the store and put our backs to the wall. So I sauntered past them and back again, humming carelessly to myself, and stopped to look at the view, and turned a somersault or two, and I liked them. I liked the way they sat and grinned and nudged each other and whispered in something like Maori, but it wasn't and I even liked the way they soon lost interest and ignored me. And then the woman came out, and it was my turn to lose interest in them. She was tall and dark and thin, and had a thing like a bright cotton curtain wrapped around her somehow and hanging right down to her large bare feet — I looked again, *bare feet* — and her toes sort of spread out and flapped a bit as she walked away. I was goggling after her open-mouthed, and wondering if she really walked differently from us or if it was only because of the curtain thing round her legs, when Billy and Ken scrambled up and raced after her, laughing and shoving each other as they went. Inside the store the post-mortem had already begun, and everyone was fairly clamouring to get her knife in. *What a get up have you ever never in my whole life they say he's white can you imagine what next.* And the woman behind the counter who had her shoes specially made (glacé kid, you know) because of her bunions, and always wore corsets for her weak back (you could see where they stuck into her middle when she bent over), fanned the air in front of her as though some one had made a bad smell, and vowed she had never, *never*, had such a — such a *creature* inside her shop before.

When Billy and Ken came to school, and that was some time after the store, they brought two sisters with them. Mary was olive and pink and very shy and had her mother's straight blue-black hair. Judy was brown and round and curly and her teeth were appalling. The four of them had enormous black eyes and could use them like gimlets when they wanted to. Our school was one room with a porch for coats and two teachers and a paddock with pine trees at the far end, and whatever we did, we did it together, because there weren't enough of us to split up into gangs. So when some brought bags of marbles, they'd be shared out, and at playtime the whole school would play, and the little ones who were too young, like Mary and Judy, would yell and jump about and get in the way. Billy and Ken were very good at marbles. They would crouch in the dust like cats and open their eyes wide and let fly, and whenever they scored a hit and they nearly always did, you'd wonder the glass could stand it. But our favourite game was rounders. Every lunchtime, unless it rained and sometimes even then, the man teacher, who was young and liked to keep fit, would come out swinging the round bat and divide us into teams and toss for it and scatter the fielders round the paddock. Then he would tuck his trousers into his socks, like plus-fours, and lead the batting side and tear round the field roaring like a bull, 'out of my way out of my way', and we'd fall over ourselves laughing and roll in the grass and laugh and laugh because we loved it and he looked so funny. And on very wet days, after we'd finished our sandwiches, we'd sit round the old stove in the corner and have a community sing, and the woman teacher would warble, 'D'ye ken John Peel', and if we didn't, she'd shout the words at us, stamping on the beat till she was red in the face and her fronts flopped up and down. There were a few lunchtimes when both teachers were too busy to keep an eye on us, and we'd sneak down to the out-of-bounds pine-trees and play apes, and Billy and Ken would swing the farthest and hang the longest and make the worst faces, till someone thought they heard the bell, and then it was *slither* and torn clothes and hands and a race across the paddock not to be the last one in. I don't know how those two teachers stood that job, because, in the class-room, even more than in the play-ground, whatever we did, we *had* to do it together. There wasn't anywhere else to do it. But they stood it, all right, and if the new ones, and there were several besides the Kellys, had hopes that they wouldn't be noticed in the confusion that was us working, they didn't have them for long. Mary and Judy had practically no English and the boys were loath to use what little they had preferring expressive grunts instead, but they were all extremely quick in the uptake, only they didn't let on. If that teacher had realised what was going on behind the grunts and solemn eyes, she might have saved herself many patient painstaking hours, or taught them more than she did. On the other hand, she might have given up the job altogether. I was on the other side of the room and didn't see much of them during classes, but every afternoon I found out what they had absorbed during the day, because as soon as we were clear of the school gate they started to chant it, finding the rhythm in it and stamping it all the way down the hill to the beach. And Ken, who was a wicked mimic, would caper before us, and *be* that poor teacher.

Although Tom Kelly had a public works job like most of the newcomers to the Bay, the family lived down on the beach instead of up at the camp. It might have been that there weren't enough army huts to go round, or it might have had something to do with what happened at the store. Or perhaps he was just trying to make his wife and children feel at home in their new country, though I shouldn't imagine that the Bay, even the beach part of it, would have much in common with Apia. Anyway, whatever the reason, he had taken a house at the foot of the big hill, and Mrs Kelly had used all she had to make it into a home. The all consisted of several finely plaited mats, a few beautifully polished coconut bowls, a table and chairs, some crockery and cooking utensils, nearly enough beds and bedding to go round, and the old gramophone. After these had been arranged in the living-room facing the sea and the three bedrooms and the dummy kitchen, there was still plenty of room to move about. No matter what time of day I went to that house, and I practically lived there, Mrs Kelly was nearly always out the back preparing food. The kitchen was a dummy one because it didn't have any of the things you'd expect to find in it, like a stove and water and cupboards, so she had made herself a cook-house with some corrugated iron and a fireplace of stones from the beach, and if we couldn't find her inside when we came in from school, she was bound to be out there in the space between the side of the house and the tin fence, sitting on her haunches and poking and stirring and wiping her eyes with the back of her hand when the fire smoked. She could sit like that, on her haunches with the long skirt wrapped around her thighs, for hours. I don't know what she did for company when we weren't there because she never went out, not even to the store after the first time, and didn't have any visitors because her English wasn't good enough. But she had plenty to keep her busy. There were the mats to shake and water to fetch and clothes to wash and driftwood to be gathered. We used to do what we could to help, like going messages and sweeping the path with a manuka broom, but it wasn't much, and Olive, who was much older than us, had to leave first thing in the morning for the factory in town and didn't get back till late. We hardly saw her except at the weekends, and then if she was in a good mood, she would call us to her bedroom and rub coconut oil into our scalps and whack them with a brush till it hurt, and let us play with her nail polish and powder till we got silly and made a mess, and then we were bundled out and the door closed. And sometimes when we were tired of the beach or it was raining and we didn't know what to do with ourselves, Mrs Kelly would line us up in the living-room and show us how to do the siva, gliding and turning and dipping before us like a bird, and her hands were flowers folding and unfolding and folding again. We used to giggle at first and push each other and pretend we were shy, but the bird and the flowers went on beckoning beckoning, and slowly, one by one, we would follow, gliding and turning and dipping and folding, till we weren't us any more, only birds and flowers. Then Mrs Kelly would snap her fingers and stop and smile at us, and the boys would whoop and fall on their backs and kick their legs in the air while we thumped them and thumped them. But of all things we did in that house, the boys liked playing the old gramophone best. They would pull it out from the corner and crank the handle and put on 'Jerusalem, Jerusalem', and while it was playing, they'd sit cross-legged on the floor like stone images and gaze out the window and gaze out the window, with wide darkening eyes. And when it was finished, they'd crank again and put on the 'Hawaiian War Chant' and leap about the room and shake themselves as though they wanted to get rid of their arms and legs. Then they'd go back to 'Jerusalem'. I used to feel uncomfortable about this at first. Hymns meant standing up in church in your hat and gloves, and not knowing the meaning of the words half the time, and watching the choir move their mouths about as though they had toffee sticking to their back teeth. Or they could be your mother trilling in the kitchen like a canary as she prepared breakfast on the mornings she felt good. But they didn't have anything to do with cranky old gramophones and Hawaiian war chants and sitting cross-legged on the floor and listening. Nothing at all. It took me quite a while to get the hang of it.

We played in the house, but we lived on the beach. And we did the kinds of things all children do on beaches, like playing french cricket with a bit of old fruit-case for a bat, and writing our names and the date in the damp sand with a stick, and skimming flat stones on the water and counting the hops, and throwing seaweed and old fish heads at one another. But we used to get tired of these, and then we'd really *do* something, like making a Map or a Plan and going on a Hunt. We often went on a Hunt, because if we were lucky, it would end up being a Feast. There were small purple crabs under the rocks nearest the house and big red ones in the deep channels further out and pauas at low tide and sea-eggs if you knew where to look. The biggest crab we ever caught was a real red whopper, like a small cray, but we didn't eat him. We had been hunting all afternoon and made a good haul and taken it up to the cook-house, and Mrs Kelly poked our prize catch among the glowing embers and we squatted behind her and smelled the lovely smell and hugged our knees against our chests and grinned at one another. She had raked him out to one side to cool and we were saying who'd have which part, when Tom Kelly looked round the corner of the house. He hardly ever came home till well after our bed-time, but there he was, looking at us without a word, and then he walked over to our Feast and picked him up and took off the back and crammed it all into his mouth at once. And the red legs dangled below his yellow moustache and wiggled up and down as he munched and munched. So we had the sea-eggs instead, and I bolted seven, because of the crab, and was sick all that night. But he never found out about our Plan. The Bay was really three small bays, and we had explored every rock and pool of it except the ones we couldn't reach, and sometimes we would sit in the sand and screw up our eyes against the sea glare and gaze at the part we didn't know and wonder what it was like, out there. And one day we couldn't stand it any longer and that's when we made our canoe. We built it with corrugated iron and the ends of fruit-cases and bits of old sacking, and Mary and Judy kept a lookout for grown-ups because they were bound to say I don't think that's a very good idea, and we used to be careful about hiding it under branches and clumps of seaweed, though no grown-up who was really grown-up would have guessed it was any kind of a boat. Early one good calm morning when we had the beach to ourselves, we launched her, and she floated away from our proud hands like a log. She could take only one of us at a time, so our Plan was for the first one to sail out the first bay and round into the second, and the second one to sail out the second bay and round into the third, and to come back the same way and do it again, till each one of us had sailed round all the bays. And that's what we did, only we didn't sail, we paddled. The one whose turn it was would get in gingerly and the others steadied her and handed him the fruit-case paddles and gave him a bit of a push in the right direction and clambered over the rocks trying to keep level with him, just in case, and shouted look out mind the seaweed, while he paddled like mad to get round before she filled up. So we found out what it was like, out there, and the Great Octopus who lived in the Deep Water beyond the Last Rock, jerked and writhed and bulged his eyes with rage, as we slopped and wobbled by.

That was Summer. Winter brought the bulldozers and the rain and the mud, in that order, and then a repeat of the same. One afternoon when I came home from the Kellys, I found the first of the bulldozers had removed a bank that just happened to be in its way, and half our front lawn and path that just happened to be on top of the bank, had gone too. A slab of concrete was still hanging on and jutted out from the new cliff edge like a diving-board, but the next morning it wasn't hanging on any longer, and slab by slab our path was turned into diving-boards that slipped away and lay like tumbled tombstones in the ruined clay below. And the bulldozers moved on. The ladies went in a morning and the tennis courts that afternoon. The store was picked up and dumped down in the manuka a hundred yards off the road, and the woman behind the counter vowed she had never, *never* been handled so roughly by anyone before.

Some of the 'permanent residents' had left already, shutting windows and locking doors and making sure the power was turned off, after it had dawned on them that the new road was going to be put through their privacy and not over the hills behind. The shrewdest of the PWCs, who had no memories to muddle them like us, and found it easier to imagine what the new Bay would be like when the road was finished and the bulldozers carted away, said, good riddance, to the 'permanent residents'' backs, and left their army huts smartly and moved into the vacant houses. But they made some bad mistakes, for all their shrewdness, and had to pay for them. There was the bloke who went nosing in the gully that was supposed to be an old Maori burial ground, because someone had told him there was so much greenstone down there you couldn't help tripping over it. Well, he tripped over all right and broke his leg and couldn't climb out, and when they found him two days later he was gone in the head and had to be taken away. And there was the drunk who got lost the night of the storm and went down the hill instead of up and passed out on the second zig-zag and was dead of exposure by morning. That was the night our canoe disappeared. And up at the camp someone's baby died of diphtheria before they realised what it was. But while the 'permanent residents' who were trying to stick it out, worried about compensation, and the PWCs were busy getting themselves into trouble, we kids had the time of our lives, at least in the beginning. The bulldozers were hard at it when we went to school and we used to crowd round the big shovel, watching the polished teeth bite into a bank and jerk and strain till the clay cracked and gave at last, and was caught up by the grab and dropped into the trays of the waiting trucks. And if we went too close, the drivers would shout and wave us back and you could tell they were swearing, though no one could make himself heard above the roar and growling of machines. We were late for school more often than not but it didn't matter, we could always say the road was blocked, and the teachers were so afraid one of us would get bulldozed along with everything else, they never said a word. At three o'clock it was a race to be first through the new cutting, and the smoothed clay was all pale blues and greens and golds running into one another and thick and quiet under our feet like A.I. linoleum, and you could walk over it and look back and not see a mark anywhere. Then one of the big boys who did geography, said they find diamonds in pale blue stuff, and we used to clamber up the terraced banks and dig with sticks till they snapped and claw with fingers instead and lift the lumps above our heads and dash them open on the ground in case the diamonds were hidden inside, and our nails were always pale blue. Sometimes a machine broke down and was left behind by the others, and we would perch all over it like seagulls and the boys narrowed their eyes and moved their hands about and made the noises just right, only not so loud. But the bulldozers moved on, and we were left with the rain and the lorries churning our A.I. linoleum into grey porridge, and there weren't any diamonds, and we didn't like the mess that used to be the Bay, any more than the grown-ups did. It was *change* when you got there and *change* when you got back and having to go the long way round, and those of us who had gumboots and slippers were always getting them mixed up in the school porch and going home with two lefts or none at all and not being able to explain why. And some of the mothers made the boys come to school with their heads wrapped in newspaper, like cabbages, because they were sick and tired of buying a new sou'wester every week. By the time the 'flu came, the grown-ups were so fed-up with everything, they couldn't crawl into bed fast enough and turn their faces to the wall, and didn't we kids have to get off our tails then. If we weren't fetching and carrying and trying to cook for our own family, we were doing it for someone else's and no one bothered to say *change* or cared if we lost all our clothes. What with the diving-boards slipping faster than ever and my mother in bed, the Kellys had been away from school several days before I had a chance to go down to the beach. And when I did go, I almost wished I hadn't, it was so awful. Olive was staying in town and came home only at the weekend because the new road made it harder to get to the factory on time, and Tom Kelly had moved on with the bulldozers but Mrs Kelly and the four children were there and even I could see they were very sick indeed. They had dragged their beds into the corners to try and keep dry, because the roof didn't leak, it simply let the rain in, and the water was up to my ankles in the dummy kitchen. I couldn't get round to the cook-house because the bank behind the house had slipped and blocked the back door, but even if there had been some food out there it probably wouldn't have been the right kind for 'flu. I sat on the end of Mrs Kelly's bed and talked about the weather, but I wasn't sure she understood, her eyes were so bright and strange. And the children didn't want to play even being sick-in-bed games, like I spy. They just shivered and shivered and put their heads under the thin damp blankets. My mother was too sick herself to do anything, but she gave me lemons and honey and aspirins and cooked food to take down every day. And they recovered slowly, like everyone else, but most of the mats were ruined and the cook-house was a shambles. Before the children were well enough to go back to school, I went down with chicken-pox and complications, and by the time I could be wrapped in a chair and put out in the pale Spring sunshine, the diving-boards had slipped away right up to our front door and my mother said it was time to go. So we left the Bay, and the Kellys, and moved north.

'How many years is it?' asked Olive. I smiled down at the two little girls sharing the handle of her shopping basket, because they were very like Mary and Judy.

'I'm not sure,' I replied, pretending to count them, 'but too many, anyway.' We had stumbled over the awkward preliminaries, the crowds pressing about us and the noise of the traffic, making them even more awkward, and now there was nothing left to talk about except the memories we had in common.

'And how is your mother?' The question had been waiting impatiently on the tip of my tongue all the time. Olive looked at me sharply with surprise, and away again.

'She's dead. It's a wonder you didn't hear about it.'

'Oh,' I said, and it was my turn to look away, 'I'm so sorry,' as though I had just trodden on her toe. And my date could have whistled in my ear then, and I wouldn't have known.

'Yes, she died soon after we left the Bay. We moved not long after you, and went north too. But she never really recovered from the 'flu and that house, especially that house.' She made a small grimace at me, and I nodded. 'They pulled it down as soon as they got rid of us, and about time too. It was condemned, you know, even before we took it, but Dad was prepared to pay the rent they wanted, so they stretched a point.' I leaned against my plate glass, hardly hearing what she said. People had a habit of dying, they were doing it all the time, and it didn't do to forget it.

'And the children,' I asked, looking down at the two little girls, 'how are the children?' She smiled and put her arm round them.

'You're getting mixed up, aren't you? They aren't like this any more. Judy's got a baby, and Mary,' she hesitated, and the smile faded, 'well, Mary's been in the san. for a while, but she'll be out soon.' The children had been listening and watching us with bright dark eyes, and the one like Judy suddenly piped up.

'And Uncle Billy knows all about jail and tells us, and so does Uncle Ken, but he's only been there once.' Olive shook the child by the shoulder and frowned, and she looked up at her mother, bewildered.

'That's right, Mummy, Uncle Ken's —'

'That's *enough*,' snapped Olive, and nearly jerked her off her feet. There was a long pause, and Olive tilted her chin away from me and watched the sailors and the girls on the other side of the street. The traffic lights blinked and blurred, blinked and blurred.

'What could I do?' she suddenly burst out, facing me furiously though I hadn't said a word, 'what would you expect me to do? Dad went back on the public works, and I had my life to live too, didn't I? And a good job at the factory at last.'

'Of course,' I managed to put in, but she hadn't finished.

'And I used to go out and see them at the orphanage every week, and when they left there I thought they were old enough to look after themselves. And I married a Yank,' she fumbled among the parcels in her basket and looked across the street again, 'I married a Yank, and he didn't come back.' She lifted her shoulders with a deep breath and let it out quickly. 'And by that time it was too late. So there's just the three of us,' and she looked down at her children. They had been watching us uncertainly since something had gone wrong with the conversation, but now they brightened up again and smiled at their mother hopefully, and Olive smiled at me in spite of herself, and I smiled at the three of them. And one or two people glanced at us curiously as they pushed past, we all looked so happy.

'Well, bed-time at the zoo,' said Olive briskly, and the two little girls shook her arm and jigged up and down, crying no, no.

'Yes, I'd better be off too,' I said forgetting all about my date, 'it's not the night for hanging around, is it?' And Olive smiled again as she turned away from me for the last time, and half waved before she crossed with the green. And the little girls went hopping and skipping on either side of her, like children on a beach.

(1983)

J. C. STURM

A Thousand and One Nights

They spent the afternoon on the small front lawn under the gum tree overlooking the harbour. It was more sheltered on the side lawn but the grass round there was stiff and prickly and you couldn't see the harbour, so the woman spread the rug at the foot of the gum tree and sat with her back against the trunk and her knitting in her lap. And all afternoon she pretended they were simply warming themselves in the gentle autumn sun in front of an old house hidden away in bush with a harbour to look at, and all afternoon she knew they were simply pretending and none of it was real, not even the wanting and willing and pretending, nothing except the waiting. The little girl squatted on her haunches at the edge of a garden shabby with withered summer flowers and talked to herself and mixed mud pies in an old enamel bowl and put in gravel for sultanas and baked them in tin lids and iced them with daisy petals and laid them beside the woman on the rug. Are they cooked yet, Mummy? And the women felt each one with a finger and said, what pretty daisy cakes, yes, I think they're cooked, but we won't eat them, they're too pretty to eat.

And when it was three o'clock and time to waken the toddler, they hid the daisy cakes first, just in case, and went up the gravel path and wooden front steps and down the long linoleum passage past the mirror in the old coat-stand that wasn't theirs, past the white china door knobs of the bedroom, sitting-room, breakfast-room, past the old ship's bell on a fretwork bracket hanging at the end of the passage, and round the corner and through the door that always stuck and had to be pushed. And there was the toddler pulling himself up by the bars of the cot and his cheeks were plump and pink and his eyes blank with sleep. They changed him and put on rompers and jersey and carried him out to the gum tree and he blinked and blinked in the gentle sunlight till his eyes were as round and as blue as the harbour, and the little girl laughed and rolled on the rug against the woman's legs and laughed, he's Hunca Munca, Mummy, he's turned into Hunca Munca.

They made a pretend picnic with orange drinks and biscuits and pieces of apple and the toddler rubbed his in his hair and got it mixed up with bits of grass and stones till it looked like a piece of daisy cake and the little girl watched him and said, aren't toddlers silly, Mummy, and ate hers carefully like a tea party lady. And then she pulled off the little white boots she wore to make her ankles grow straight and strong and galloped around the lawn like the horse she was and stopped at the far end where the bush began and held up her arms like branches. Look I'm a tree, you can't get me now, I'm a tree. And the toddler dropped his daisy cake and staggered and gurgled and fell and crawled and dribbled across the lawn. But when he got there the tree turned into a bird and flew away. The woman leaned against the gum tree and watched them and pretended it was all real, but the sun slipped behind the tallest trees in the bush and the shadows crept across the corner of the rug and it was four o'clock.

They gathered everything up except the daisy cakes and put them on the side verandah and went round to the clothes line on the back lawn where the sun still shone and the little girl said, we don't have to go in yet, do we Mummy, it's still warm and sunny here, but the woman shook her head, no, it's getting late, it's time to light the fire and put the dinner on, and she gathered an armful of soft fluffy napkins and dropped the pegs for the little girl to pick up and gave the toddler a nappy to carry. And while they were picking up pegs and folding napkins and the toddler got his tangled round his legs and fell over and had to be untangled and picked up too — while they were busy dawdling in the last of the sun, the cold crept out of the bush on the other side of the house and hid in the darkened rooms waiting for them.

The little girl squatted on her haunches outside the woolshed and peered in the corners for wetas, and the woman poked about inside the shed turning the wood over and feeling it to see if it was dry and keeping a lookout for wetas too, and the toddler climbed up and down the concrete steps and looked at them upside down between his legs like Eeyore. And when they had carried the wood into the sitting-room and filled up the wood-box and the coal-scuttle and found the matches, the woman stuffed newspaper in the grate and jumbled dry sticks on top of it and covered them up with the heavier stuff and lumps of coal and held a burning match to the paper at each corner and dropped it in the middle. But the wood wasn't dry enough and smoked, so the woman covered the fireplace with another newspaper and pressed the edges hard against the bricks and the little girl looked stern, now you Mr Fire, you just burn up that nice wood my Mummy's given you, and don't be silly. And the toddler sat very still and watched the newspaper and waited. And when they heard a low roaring behind the paper and something began sucking its middle inwards the woman pulled it away quickly because she never knew what to do with it when it caught alight, but there was only a small flame after all struggling against the smoke and the heavy damp wood.

By five o'clock the children were in the bath and while the little girl was showing the toddler how to make waves for the boats to float over and the ducks to swim over and how to spread your flannel out flat on your knees like this to rub the soap on, the woman set about cooking the meal. She cooked enough for four. And then she carried the children into the sitting-room in big fluffy towels and rubbed them down in front of the fire and put on their warmed pyjamas and dressing-gowns and slippers. The little girl struggled to do up her own buttons and pushed and pulled at them and pulled her face down to see them properly and asked the woman is Daddy coming home for dinner, and the woman turned away to look at the clock and shook her head slowly, no dinner's ready now, so he can't be. Can't we wait for him? He might be very late. Do all Daddies come home *after* dinner? Some do and some don't, and if they do, they can't help it. If my bunny slippers had teeth they could bite. And she moved her toes to make the ears wiggle and the toddler gurgled and tried to make his wriggle too. Don't forget to pull the blind down, Mummy. And the woman went over to the window and tried not to think of the face that had been there once, a terrible dead white face with everything dragged down — hair, eyes, nose, mouth — pressing to reach them through the glass, till the toddler covered his eyes with his hands and the little girl screamed and screamed and hid herself in her Daddy's coat when he came in soon after. The Daddy laughed and said it must have been the moon come down to see them, but the toddler wouldn't take his hands away till they played peep-bo with him. So the woman pulled the blind down carefully right below the sill and picked up the towels and went out to the kitchen. And when she had served up four dinners and put the biggest one on top of a pot of hot water on the stove and covered it with a plate, she took the other three into the sitting-room and they had their dinner round the fire, the little girl sitting on a cushion with her red table across her knees and her bunnies wiggling at her on the other side, the toddler safe in his low chair with a feeder, and the woman beside him, just in case, with her plate in her lap.

And when they had had enough and drunk their milk, the woman stoked up the fire and dragged up the biggest chair in the room and the little girl brought her favourite book and the three of them squeezed into the big chair and made themselves comfortable for the story of Tom Thumb and his wife Hunca Munca. The little girl liked the story so much she knew what was coming over the page and said it out loud with the woman, and the toddler wanted to pat the pictures and dribble on them and got so excited his cheeks puffed out and his eyes were as round and as dark as Hunca Munca's. And when they had finished the last page they read it again slowly and loudly because they liked it so much and the toddler didn't know it was finished and went on puffing and patting and the little girl gave a great big sigh and stared into the fire. But what was the use of Tom Thumb putting a crooked sixpence into the doll's stocking and Hunca Munca sweeping the doll's house every morning, Mummy, when they'd smashed everything up. Weren't they silly mice to smash up the doll's house just because some of the things weren't real. And the woman said, yes, very silly, but perhaps they didn't know any better, being just mice. She carried the toddler into his cot and tucked them both up as snug as a bug in a rug and the little girl said night-night, Mummy, and say night-night to Daddy when he comes home, and the woman said, yes, I will, night-night and sleep tight. And it was nearly seven o'clock.

She washed the dishes and put the things away and turned off the stove under the pot with the dinner on top and went back to the sitting-room and turned the radio on and settled down with her knitting. But that wasn't any good because she couldn't hear anything except the noise it was making even when it was turned down low. So she found a book and settled down to read but that wasn't any good either because when she'd read a page twice carefully she still didn't know what she'd been reading. So she found a pencil and tried again, underlining bits here and there and writing things in the margin and this time it worked — she could read and underline and write things and *listen* at the same time. And the later it grew the easier she felt because if he hadn't come by eight o'clock it would probably be midnight or the early hours of the morning, that's if he came at all. So the reading got easier and she didn't write so much or listen so hard, but by ten o'clock the fire had burnt right down and the wood-box and coal-scuttle were empty and she couldn't be bothered going out to the woodshed because of the wetas. She thought of having a bath but it seemed a bit risky — a bath wasn't a good place to be caught in — so she made some supper instead and filled her hot water bottle and got ready for bed.

But she didn't want to go to bed in case it happened again. She put her book and knitting away and straightened the chairs and cushions in the sitting-room and straightened the towels in the bathroom and swept the hearth and made sure there were enough aired napkins for tomorrow and picked up the children's toys and put them in the box on the side verandah. And when there weren't any more things to do, she tip-toed down the passage and round the corner, and lifted the handle so the door wouldn't stick and jar and crept in, but there wasn't anything to do there either except gaze at the children so pink and plump and easy in their sleep. So she crept out again and stood in the passage and didn't know what to do. If she went to bed it might happen again, and if she stayed up she might be caught. She stared at the old ship's bell and wondered what would happen if she took it down and stood on the front steps and shut her eyes and swung it up and down up and down with both hands as hard as she could — no, that wouldn't do because the children might wake up, and they mustn't find out — then suppose she ran through the bush with it and stood in the middle of the road and rang it and rang it till she couldn't hear anything couldn't listen to anything except the ringing. Would the people in the brown house with the white facings and the sunken garden and the people in the one next to it with the tennis court and the people in the new two-storied home with the sun-deck and the people who lived at the end of the long wide drive, would they look at one another and say, listen, isn't that someone ringing a bell? Why would anyone want to ring a bell in the middle of the night? And if they left their houses and came out to her, cautiously, in the middle of the road and asked, what are you doing, what is the matter, and she told them, this is an old ship's bell that hangs at the end of the passage. It doesn't belong to me, but I'm ringing it now because I've been waiting a long time and I'm still waiting and *I can't wait any longer* — the woman put a hand to her mouth — what would they say then, what would they do with her then? She turned away from the bell and got into bed and waited and listened.

And some time later, she didn't know what time and it didn't matter because the waiting was over, she felt the footsteps thudding through her sleep, down the steps from the road into the bush, under the macrocarpa trees, past the giant fuschia peeling its brown paper bark in the dark, between the bamboos in the dip beside the stream, into the tree-tunnel that led to the house. She slipped out of bed and crept across the passage into the sitting-room and hid behind the door, and the footsteps thundered around the house and into the house and up the passage and stopped suddenly outside the door. *You don't know I'm here, go to bed, I'm not here.* But the door swung open and the foot-steps came in and closed it and stood there for a time and when they turned round it was the face at the window, dead white and terrible and all dragged down, pressing to reach her and there wasn't any glass *there wasn't any glass*. And the woman covered her eyes with her hands and screamed and screamed and tried to hide herself in the wall, and woke with the screams choking her and the bedclothes pressing her down and her body shaking and clammy with the thudding of her heart.

And then she heard the footsteps again coming through the tree-tunnel, heavy and uncertain at the same time, and then she couldn't hear them at all. Perhaps he's making water against the gum tree, perhaps he's gone off the lawn and fallen down the bank — no, not the bank, I can't do it, it's too far down and too far up and the pungas get in the way, please not the bank — let it be the gum tree. And she waited and listened and the foot-steps came back on to the path and around the house and into the house and tried to be quiet up the passage. And she lay like someone hiding behind a door and shut her eyes and breathed deeply and slowly, I'm asleep, I'm asleep, and listened to the fumblings on the other side of the bed and the clothes dropping and the hands groping and felt the pull of the bedclothes and the mattress sag and listened till the breathing beside her was slower and deeper than her own. And she lay for a long time in the small space between one waiting and next and felt everything but the tiredness drain away from her, and listened to the small night noises and the night wind and watched the gum tree through the window, moving its branches like arms against the pale night sky — if you could turn into a bird, you could fly away — and she watched the gum tree, waiting for the miracle, till her eyes ached and closed and it was over.

(1983)

LAURIS EDMOND

Chapter Thirteen from
High Country Weather

The holidays ended, school began again. The winter term. Mornings were darker, snow on the mountain lower down. Every shower of rain was snow or sleet up there; soon the first fall would come to Arawa itself, everyone said.

Again Louise walked into town every day. Again she glared at the dreary little shops, again was exhilarated by the splendour of the mountain. On cloudy days when it was hidden she felt as though the whole world had turned away from her. She had forgotten her resolution to leave for good, made that day in the Murdochs' hay barn. This, simply, was where she lived. Winter came towards them, a great menacing presence, and drew everyone closer. In the street, outside the post office, in the dim shelved shadows of Mr Drury's draper's shop, people talked of it. The rain last year just as the sprouts were ready . . . the broken pipes . . . that dry spell, tanks low . . .

High country weather, how sharply I recall it. In 1954 there was a daily average, recorded in the *Wanganui Chronicle*, of fifty-nine degrees daily minimum average, in winter thirty-five degrees, three above freezing point. Average minimum in July (just over a month after the beginning of the schools' second term) was twenty degrees, twelve below freezing point.

There were ninety-nine days in the year when there were ground frosts. The year before there had been a fourteen degree frost in mid summer, on December 31st, New Year's Eve. Ten separate falls of snow were likely in any one year, fifty-four inches of rain (a yard and a half!).

Walking along the street, loitering here and there, was now slightly different. People knew she'd been away. Nobody asked where, or why, but everyone — Mr Dumfries, the jaunty girl in the post office, Mr Drury the sober draper — all of them said Oh you're back, that's nice. Did you know that Miss Westmoreland . . . that the older Mr Murdoch . . . yes, awful isn't it? of course you could see Polly'd leave him, but so soon . . . Reg Smith, having failed to get himself elected Chairman of the Parent Teachers, was leaving teaching and buying a market garden. (So much for Eileen Murdoch's threats.) And Mr Mackintosh's girl's coming to school . . . yes, this term, chose the uniform . . . tribute to your husband. Shows the Chairman of the Board has confidence in him . . .

The third day, Louise saw the Chairman of the Board. With his lady.

Turned her head, quite casually, from one of these conversations — with Mr Dumfries in fact — and there they were at the corner, not fifty yards away. They'd come downstairs from his office and into the street and stood there together for a moment. Muriel had said something — stupid? irrelevant? — Nigel turned away and walked a few steps from her, Louise knew his mask-like composure, guessed at the anger or disappointment it concealed; but no disguise can hide the body's habitual actions. He bent his head, hunched his shoulders, put his hands in his pockets, the very shape of misery and dejection. She could have wept.

And then — it was all in a strange kind of slow motion, with Mr Dumfries burbling on at her elbow as she watched — a car came round the corner and drew up to the kerb and Dorothy Highsmith jumped out. Instantly Nigel stood up, assumed that careful courtliness she had first observed the day under the beech tree. He talked, nodded, laughed — indeed in a moment he lifted his head and laughed loudly in delight. Louise had never seen him so whole, so unreserved. It was wonderful. It was incomprehensible.

— I must really go. It's time for the children to be home from school.
— She's so vague isn't she, Mrs West I mean? Mr Dumfries remarked to his next customer, who was Maryanne. Do you think she will ever fit into Arawa? Her mind is always somewhere else, it seems to me.

When she got home Peter and Terry were already there. Not inside though; the afternoon was clear, though cold, and they were out on the lawn. Backs to the gate, they did not see their mother who watched them for a moment without touching the latch. Some kind of performance was going on. Terry, with an absurd mincing walk, was tripping past his bigger brother, swaying from side to side and flapping his hands in a parody of elaborate femininity.

— Oh deah, oh deah, he was twittering, what a *smarshing* piece of work mah deah boy! Quate perfect! That *remarrkable* ruling off!

It was Rupert to the life. Languid, drooping, every word given its ridiculous ironical emphasis. The naughty child even had the moustache and patted it with elegant little smoothing gestures. Peter was doubled up with delight. Louise herself smiled, and was at once as furious with herself as with them.

— How dare you! she raged, bursting through the gate. You little — toads. That nice man — new here — hasn't any friends yet probably, and you — you — you think you can make jokes about him. Who do you think you are?

She stormed inside; righteous indignation in full flood. But there was something worrying about it. Rupert's effeminate and cultivated artificiality wouldn't remain a children's sport for long. What could Arawa do with Rupert? Would it, secretly and in horror, utter the word that would describe his physical oddities, and make him a figure of fear and loathing . . . She remembered him at the end of the fabulous party, a slack puppet, grotesque and helpless. And she thought of the Murdochs, efficiently demolishing a harmless school bus driver; she shivered.

Gossip, gossip. Chief character on the Arawa stage. Powerful, exciting, ripe with surprise. Brisk with informativeness. Bill Murdoch with time to ruminate out on the hills up the North Road . . . Mrs Reid drinking tea in Mrs Masters' kitchen, firing up her speculations with the heat of her neighbour's guessing . . . Mr Dumfries putting out *Superman* and *Flash Gordon* for the kids coming home from school, *House and Garden* the day Dorothy Highsmith came in, *McCalls* for Muriel Mackintosh . . . Bloss Harrison washing dishes three nights a week in the Railway Refreshment rooms . . . Toddy Illingworth prancing about at some sparse gathering in the Scout Hall . . . All gave something to the great central figure that gossip was. The lift of an eyebrow, lowered tone in the voice, a small smile, some pursing of the lips — each contributed to its style, its richness, its colour.

At the same time none were immune from its contagion. Secret as rheumatics, deadly as typhoid, it could recur like malaria, irritate as much as hay fever. Louise mysteriously protected from it before, was now just as mysteriously exposed; indeed she felt at times positively enveloped by its intimate infections.

Wilfrid Murdoch, with Polly gone, was always at the RSA quarrelling with everyone, full of whisky; what did he *think* would happen, the old goat? Imagine him without his — oh you couldn't!

As for Mr Dumfries without his poor old mother, all her life in Arawa, sadly missed — just as well she couldn't see him now, that black sock thing on his withered arm — did he *ever* change it? If you got too close you knew the answer to *that* one — holding your nose was all you could do —

And everyone must know that Dr Patel had quarrelled with his family in Ceylon, or wherever it was, and they'd cut him off so he'd have to stay in New Zealand for ever —

Some news was old — everyone knew years ago that Miss Westmoreland's mother didn't die in Wanganui (as though anyone would go *there* to do it) but drowned herself in the Mangawhero because she was broken-hearted about Mr Westmoreland and Mrs Peacock. Oh that's a bit strong — well, what else is that little cottage in the bush but a you-know-what — and her swanky clothes and all that. I mean who ever saw Mrs Peacock at work? Work! My God — just see your old man doesn't go up there after dark, that's all —

It was true too that Mrs Mackintosh had all the money in *that* family — owned three hotels, her old man did. Or had. It wasn't clear where he was actually. Some said he'd gone to Australia to squander it, others that he'd gone bankrupt and was all sold up. The most likely was that he just went on being rich; that's what the rich are like.

But nothing was said about Rupert, at least not to Louise. She got to know him a lot better though, because he decided to produce his play, chose one and asked her to be in it.

— I so *adore* this place, little outpost that it is — so much more exciting than London. In all my thirty-eight years no one has ever come to my door at eight o'clock in the morning with half a dozen *bantam's eggs* — can you believe it? No one has brought me fresh-cut kindling after a week's rain, no one has come into my back yard and brought my two shirts and three pairs of underpants in off the line before a shower — not that I *had* a back yard. It was a furnished room in Clapham with a gas ring, and a laundry across the street.

— I hope you tell every Arawa resident you see that it's more interesting here than in London, said Louise.

— Oh I do, I *do!*

They were at the school gate. It was a fine afternoon, the snow on the mountain dazzling. The beginning of June, first day of winter.

Rupert swayed, cavorted, caressed his moustache.

— But the play? Louise asked.

— You will be my ally, my support, my inspiration. You and I will bring all our city sophistication to the Arawa stage — our style, that *je ne sais quoi* of the great theatrical venture —

— I've never been in a play.

— Doesn't make a scrap of difference, not a scrap. You will be divine —

— And Wellington isn't London — any more than Arawa is.

— Thank God. But we will take the town by storm. Listen —

When he got down to business Rupert was quite different. He had chosen something of Priestley's — fascinating mixture of the real and the surreal. The what? Well, it all happens, then it all begins again and turns out differently. People say 'If I had my time again . . .' and these people do. In the play. But first, there's all the dirt in their lives . . . *Dangerous Corner* . . . Listen . . .

Louise got away in the end, and took Peter and Terry to buy the new gumboots they needed for slushy walks to school in the winter.

— Rupert's going to do a play. One of Priestley's time plays, she said to Tom with great casualness. He wants me to be in it.

— But you've never acted before.

— Nobody else will have either. Only Rupert. You could be in it if you like.

— Good Lord no. But you go ahead. I've been trying to find something you could do. I thought of the Parents' Association committee actually. That would make more sense. What about it?

— No thanks.

— Oh it wouldn't be me that would decide. You'd have to campaign a bit, get yourself elected.

After all they were poles apart.

About eleven o'clock the next morning there was a knock at the door. I'll tell her I can't . . . not a minute to spare today . . . Louise dragged herself to the door anticipating Miss Westmoreland's wispy, insistent presence. She opened it slowly.

The person who stood on the little verandah was Nigel Mackintosh. Louise turned a bright pink; she could say nothing except Oh I thought — and Whatever brings —

But almost at once it became an occasion. An adventure, even. Nigel had, he said 'dealt with' the neighbours. Really? Exterminated them? Not exactly — but it was a wonderful excuse to come, and completely watertight. Minutes of a Board meeting — Tom couldn't come himself but had said exactly where to find them — there was a visit in an hour or so by a Departmental inspector interested in a plan to build a gym.

So it was a safe guilt they enjoyed, sitting in the warm, slightly smoky kitchen together, drinking tea. Looking back, I am struck by the excitement on their faces and in their low, quick talk — but also by the caution in their actions, their very lack of adventurousness, even while the air all around them was humming with a surprised bravado.

They were alone, these two who had everything to say to each other, and who were prevented by Arawa's neighbourly watchfulness from ever being alone together to say it. Suddenly they were not in the street, not in a shop or the post office, not at school — they were securely concealed inside a house, and very unlikely to be interrupted.

Did they decide to have a glass of wine, say? Impossible. Nobody in Arawa in 1954 would have thought of drinking wine at such a time; it would not have occurred to them that one could. Did they move closer, lean, touch, finally embrace, as they would so acutely have liked to do? And after a while drift towards the bedroom and slowly undress behind drawn curtains . . .

Of course not. They sipped their tea, avoided all mention of Tom, Muriel or each other, but explored in unnecessary detail the reasons why everyone else might have chosen to live in Arawa. That benighted little outpost of what passed for civilisation. Toddy was doing his duty, perhaps furthering his career; the Highsmiths belonged. There was Wilfrid and his child wife — and, recently and remarkably, there was Rupert. And Rupert brought them to speak of the play and, at last, to the forbidden subject of themselves.

— I want you to be in it, Louise said.

— But I'm not an actor.

— Neither am I. Nobody is. Let's try.

— *Let's*? You and me? *Let* us? Oh yes, let's. But wait a minute, is it a dialogue, a rhapsody for two? Won't there at least be a producer there, Rupert himself?

— There may be dozens of characters, I don't know. Haven't read it yet. Oh Nigel do try it, with me. I think I'm going to go mad in this place

if *something* doesn't happen.
— You know people say here that living in the country is good for you because you learn to make your own fun?
— I know, I know. Somehow I think it might be different if it *was* the country. It's the awful in-between-ness. Looks as though it's meant to be a town, yet it's not one. It's not — oh think of all the things Arawa isn't!
— And you're saying let's change that, at least for ourselves?
— Perhaps I am.
— There are other ways.

And then, surprisingly, he did lean over and kiss her; a slow, still kiss. She stood up, stepped back, took a breath. Her eyes opened wide.
— I'll go, shall I?

She couldn't answer. They were both helpless for a moment, drawn together and held apart by tensions of exactly equal tautness. Then Louise turned away.
— Yes, go. But the play —
— I will. I promise I will.

As soon as he'd gone she went back to the kitchen, picked up his cup and hurled it across the room. It smashed against the mantelpiece. Drips of tea splashed on to the hearth.
— Mouse . . . she muttered — me too. Both — bloody mice! and she threw the saucer as well.

But by the afternoon she had cheered up. She exulted, pranced almost, as she wandered about her small plain house and garden. Why should she be so pleased, even proud? It's obvious of course that Rupert's play was tempting simply because it had nothing to do with Arawa, nothing to do with Tom. It was all her own. An assertion of independence. The very thing Arawa could never offer, never impose. I'll show them! She was like a snubbed child banished from the adults' party, planning revenge.

(1984)

SHONAGH KOEA

Mrs Pratt Goes to China

After Arnold's funeral some of them came back to the house to say their piece or have their say, depending on which was longer.

His sisters all said that Arnold had not looked well for years.

'Whenever we saw poor Arn we said, "Arn's not looking so hot," we said, didn't we?'

A cousin chimed in.

'I saw Arnie last Tuesday. No, I tell a lie. Wednesday it must of been because Wednesday was the day Mavis said to me, she said, "Ron, that car's making a funny noise, a sort of pop in the motor, Ron," she said, and on the way to the garage I stopped at Vi's and who should I see there but Arn. "Arn's not looking well," I said. And that was the last time I saw poor old Arn alive.'

Mrs Pratt's father-in-law, or Arnold's father as she preferred to call him because it cut her out of the connection, had to be led away after this. Clinging to a thread of life at 91, he had been senile for the last 11 years and incontinent for longer. Mrs Pratt thought how lucky it was that she had sat him on a wooden chair.

'Why was it Arn was taken,' said old Mr Pratt.

According to his late mother Arnold had been one of the most delightful children ever born. He had been the wonder of the nursing home, the pride of the street, brilliant like all Pratts from the moment of birth which took place after a short labour of only an hour and a half, yet another mark of his consideration and brilliance.

He shot out of the world more quickly but with less warning the previous Thursday, felled by an aneurism in front of the refrigerator. He was holding a chicken sandwich in one hand and a glass of beer in the other and had been in the middle of saying, 'Haven't you collected my drycleaning yet, Louise.'

'Did he say anything?' A Pratt aunt's voice trailed away into her handkerchief.

'Before he died? Oh yes,' said Mrs Pratt. 'He said, "Haven't you collected my drycleaning yet, Louise."'

'And you hadn't.' The reproof was unmistakable.

Her cheerful tone was an error and would be added, she knew, to her list of crimes — disliking boiled lollies, saying, 'Isn't it a beautiful day' at Arnold's mother's funeral, saying Gloria's husband was too good for her and suggesting as a gift for Aunty Vi's golden wedding a sharp tap on the head with a hammer.

Wasn't it just like Arnold to think of his drycleaning, they said, at a time like that. Arn was that tidy.

Mrs Pratt stared at her shoes. All she could think about was how Arnold sorted through the rubbish bin to see what she had thrown out. How when she had two dishes of eggs in the refrigerator, one fresh and the other hard-boiled, he used to put them all in one large bowl because it looked tidier. How, thought Mrs Pratt, do you tell a fresh egg from an unshelled hard-boiled one?

His detailed neatness and his relatives had nearly driven her crazy. She thought of the time she lay on the carpet crying and saying she wished they had poison in the house so she could drink it and die.

Arnold had said, 'I'll just hang up your coat,' and after that she got up and cooked lunch. Arnold liked a cooked lunch and he liked coats to be hung up.

When they were newly married she begged to be taken away. This would have solved the problem of the relatives, but not the neatness. Arnold, obdurate, would not move.

'But I was born here,' he said. 'What would Mum say, and Aunty Vi, and what about Uncle Colin?'

In a fit of cold wildness Mrs Pratt packed some things and went on the bus, all one day and part of the night in a bitter frost, to see her mother.

'I hope you don't want anything,' her mother said. 'Buggalugs hasn't left much. I've been trying to keep it quiet but you might as well know he's gone off with some woman from up Nelson way. He's booked up stuff all over town and took my best clock. Just put the kettle on, will you? And get some wood in. Don't use any of the good stuff, that's for visitors. Get that mucky barky stuff. Good job you come really. The place hasn't had a good do through since you left.'

Mrs Pratt returned to Arnold and in time there came to her an obscure philosophy which she possessed secretly like the thorny shell of a crepuscular sea creature placed in an inner pocket.

Gradually she learned to snatch a little of what she called life within the framework that Arnold's obsession with neatness imposed, and learned to wear the yoke of his requirements with grace. She avoided his relatives when she could.

Only once did Mrs Pratt reveal this to Arnold and that was the afternoon a Pratt approached her in the library.

'How dare they,' she shrieked at Arnold the moment he stepped in the door that evening. 'They've got everywhere else. The library is mine.'

It was ridiculous. The library was a public place. As for relatives — she knew that when you married a person you had to bother with his family. It was simply that Arnold was all she could cope with.

Big Arnold, that plump and pouting puffin, had taken a step or two back at this belligerent stating of her territory by his uncaged canary.

In time quietness came upon them but never peace and that difference between quietness and peace is what their ease cost. Meticulous neatness was what he required and meticulous neatness was what he received. That was the bargain. Affection, interest and animation she saved for the cat, the birds in the garden and successive spiders named Albert who lived by the bathroom door.

'Why did you marry me, Arnold?' she asked him once.

'Don't ask silly questions.'

'Do you love me, though?'

'Not now,' said Arnold. 'Later.'

She supposed they meant different things by love and her spiky shadow on the wall that day seemed to lengthen, to assume the characteristics of a number in a sociology text dealing with the children of disturbed homes who seek what they lack in any marriage, and do not find it.

So ran Mrs Pratt's thoughts after Arnold's funeral.

'He was a wonderful man,' said Arnold's Uncle Colin, jammy bun in hand. 'Only 64. Hardly more than a boy. He was a prince among men.' He thrust forward his cup. 'Fill her up again, there's a good girl, Myra, and give me a bit of that cake over there.'

Someone gave Mrs Pratt a cup of tea with milk and sugar added — she disliked milk and sugar in tea — and a large ragged piece of cake on a saucer. Arnold would not have liked that, she thought. Arnold would have liked a proper plate.

It was time now to do a particular job that had weighed upon her all day, had weighed upon her heavily since Arnold sank down in front of the refrigerator.

'It'll do her good to have a good cry,' said one of the cousins. 'Have you had a good cry?' This last remark was addressed towards Mrs Pratt in a louder voice than was necessary as though Arnold's death had deafened her.

'Have a good cry,' they urged. 'Go on.'

Mrs Pratt did not care to reveal herself to the Pratts. If there was anything to cry about it was the wasted years and she had wept over those as she wasted them. If tears were to be shed now she would shed them for her lack of grief, for the invasion of her kitchen by the Pratts, the inspection of her dish cloths and for the fact that an unknown woman in an orange coat had looked in her wardrobe.

'He certainly done you proud,' she had said, fingering Mrs Pratt's grey fur jacket with the lucky sixpence in the upper left-hand pocket. 'He'll have left you a bob or two. You'll be sitting pretty.'

Mrs Pratt stood up. She must do the job.

'Goodbye,' she said. 'I am going to say goodbye to you all now.'

Goodbye? They turned questioning faces towards her.

'Goodbye. Permanently,' said Mrs Pratt. Her arms lay by her sides, the thumb and index finger on each hand linked to form a circle to induce calmness. This idea had come from a book. Mrs Pratt read a lot of books.

'We'll say goodbye now and we'll come back again tomorrow, first thing.'

'No, thank you,' said Mrs Pratt. 'I am going to say goodbye to you all now permanently. Now that Arnold is no longer here my link with you is severed.' How carefully she had mouthed the words as the clock in the hall struck one in the morning, then two, three.

'This's Arnold's house. We'll come if we like. We've got a right.'

'Goodbye,' said Mrs Pratt, the cracked record approach according to the book but like all instruction books it did not mention the party getting rough, the soufflé sinking or still being unpopular after reading *How To Be Popular*.

They said they knew what was best, she was upset and did not know what she was saying.

'Goodbye,' said Mrs Pratt.

She had never liked them.

Arnold's mother's wedding cry of 'So my son's married a nothing' was replaced in time by 'I've got no time for her' and 'She hasn't got our sort of appetite.'

If her dislike had been a see-saw it would have rocked on their gargantuan eating habits. It would have bounced on their custom of never saying thank-you, of never congratulating a living soul on good fortune. It would have rested on their collective stupidity which was such that they regarded as lovably quotable an aged Pratt's habit of saying 'Everything have its season' as if this were a vividly Confucian remark instead of the ungrammatical cornerstone of Mrs Pratt's dislike.

In her life their season had come and now it could go.

'We've really got to be quite fond of you, sort of,' said one of them now. 'In our own way, over the years. You're quite a dag, that way you've got of talking.'

'Goodbye,' said Mrs Pratt.

As they crushed underfoot the golden leaves of autumn all down the front path they said what she needed was nourishment.

'If she was a needle,' said Myra Pratt, 'you couldn't thread her.'

They said they would be back in the morning to go through Arnold's things and when would Arnie's house be going on the market because Uncle Charlie was quite a good land agent and could do with the commission.

'Don't forget that Uncle Colin's the same size as Arnie in most things,' they said. 'Except shoes.'

They thought Arnold's footwear might fit Gloria's husband.

'Not that he's much chop,' they added, Pratt-fashion.

On a westering wind their voices came, dully now, through the trees.

'She shouldn't of cut back Arnie's roses so hard.'

'Look what she's done to his Lisbon lemon.'

'What about Arnie's new raincoat?'

'Did you ask her about his golf clubs. The new ones.' She supposed that was from a thinner, sporting Pratt nephew.

They jammed themselves behind the wheels of bottle-green or chocolate-brown motorcars and revved the engines with glutinous throbs, children like dumplings spilling over the back seats and the exhaust pipes giving off a brownish haze which could have been vaporised treacle.

It was strange, thought Mrs Pratt, that they reminded her constantly of food. Even their clothes were often patterned with currant buns or peppermint sticks, or had foreign writing on which said 'Le Fromage', 'Déjeuner, s'il vous plait' or, for variety, 'Champs Elysée' which they thought meant being good at sport.

Mrs Pratt shut the front door and went to telephone the builder who had always done any alterations to the house.

'I would like you to come as soon as you can,' she said in the pedantic little voice that had been her arcane refuge from Pratt encroachments. 'I want you to make the front fence higher.'

How high did she want it, he asked.

'I don't really know,' said Mrs Pratt. 'But it must be higher than a person.'

They agreed on six feet.

'And I require a new front gate,' said Mrs Pratt. 'A gate like a door, with a doorknob and a lock so that when my friends are coming I can unlock it and otherwise I can lock people out.'

After that she meticulously cleared away all signs of occupation by strangers in what was now her house — it was easy as it just meant sweeping up drifts of sausage roll crumbs — and then she went to bed.

In the ensuing days the Pratts called often with that particular brand of persistent inexorability often possessed by the thick-headed. She did not answer the door.

A voracious reader, she gave up her usual diet of novels which for the most part dealt with the implications of life and death, public and private responsibility in satirical but wickedly funny vein. She waded through murder mysteries at the rate of two a day because they present death, waste, spite, destruction and misery in cheerful guise within bright covers and they warmed her.

Spreading herself a little through the house now, she ate her meals off a tray where she could watch the birds. Often she ate only an apple or a banana. Arnold had liked all meals to be large and cooked, served at the table.

She used Arnold's garden twine and began to keep it in the kitchen instead of the garden shed. Her coat was rarely hung up.

Occasionally she would open Arnold's wardrobe which still contained all his clothes and she would say, 'Good morning, Arnold. Wind from the north today, always a bad quarter,' or 'Well, goodnight, Arnold, I'm off to bed now'.

Irreligious and unspiritual, and unbeliever in most things except the unquenchability of the human spirit, she nevertheless clung to the idea that it was a trifle rude to toss out all Arnold's things. What if some essence of Arnold remained?

Mrs Pratt gave up trying to explain to her friends that she left Arnold's possessions in their usual places out of politeness, not morbidity.

'Now you promise that next time we come you'll have done something about those things,' her friends would say and Mrs Pratt, gently promising, would chide herself the next minute for mendacity.

Arnold had, after all, fed and clothed her all those years and she was used to him. A sort of affection came to her for Arnold when she realised that he took refuge in the minor details of life to avoid greater issues like triumph, aspiration and glory.

'Oh,' he had said when she told him this. Just 'Oh,' and he went off through the house holding a broken black shoelace and never said another word about the lack of spares in the shoe cupboard.

Her friends thought she should go away for a holiday.

'To forget,' they said, though she did not wish to forget her life. It was the only one she had had, and she had done her own odd best to ornament it.

'I might go on some sort of a trip,' she said experimentally to the builder who had by now begun work on the fence and the gate.

The builder nodded, and handed to her the day's offering, a 1900 sovereign in mint condition.

He collected coins and often brought one from his collection for her to see.

'And what would you think of this,' he would say, handing her a spade guinea or a Georgian penny. She often thought he presented the coins in lieu of conversation for he was an exceptionally silent man. She actually preferred them to greetings and remarks which were always over so quickly. The coins could be looked at, mulled over, put away and got out again, looked up in books, rather like a constantly revised conversation and more satisfying.

'Very interesting,' she used to say at the end of the day and he would pop the coin back in his pocket. That was all, but she sensed he knew she had looked it up in books and had found out its history in the course of the day like wonderfully satisfying silent chit-chat.

'I wouldn't mind going somewhere,' she told the builder, 'that reminds me of nothing. Where the people are not like people I have ever known and where nothing is at all familiar.'

The builder drank his tea and the day's coin felt warm and heavy in her hand, friendly even.

'I think I might try China.'

'There's an interesting place, now,' said the builder. 'China.'

Her friends stoutly maintained that the Sunshine Club tour of the world would be better.

'You'd see everything,' they said. 'Seventeen countries in 38 days, and a cooked breakfast supplied throughout. You couldn't even read the notices in China.'

Notices did not interest her, she said. No language was necessary to see butterflies and animals or to look for the plaited nest of the humming bird.

What she wanted to do, people said, was do Honolulu, have a look at Paris, mow through the Continent and have a peep at Greece for a couple of days.

'And don't forget the Dark Continent,' said the readers of geographical magazines. 'Don't forget Mother Africa.'

'What I'd like to do with you,' said a large woman at a cocktail party, 'is to dump you down in the middle of Renaissance Italy.'

Mrs Pratt gave an imitation of pretended interest, but in her own mind her purpose became clear. She wished to go to China, and she would go there.

Her packing was accomplished behind closed doors and with the velvet curtains drawn so it would never be known that all she did was toss a few bits and pieces in a little bag. Arnold would have made her pack again with more things in case of this or that.

Addressing Arnold's wardrobe for the last time before her departure she said, 'Au revoir, Arnold. I am going for a little holiday in China. I will not lose my traveller's cheques. I will watch my handbag like a hawk and I will not overspend.' That was the sort of thing Arnold liked to hear.

A peculiar blitheness came over her as she tripped, like a 47-year-old child of five summers, out over the tarmac to the aeroplane. She feared her radiant joy would scorch the steps to the cabin.

An image of the myriad towers of a fabled land glittered and trembled in her mind like a brilliant mirage as she was borne through the starry sky towards China.

It seemed that her whole life, which had been made up of chaos with flashes of joy, was now being weighed down on the side of joy.

(1984)

JOY COWLEY

The Woman Next Door

Six, perhaps seven, the child of the photograph, solid against the blur of a city, unsmiling in black and white.

She was old enough then to have learned that black and white were the non-colours, the everything and nothing that had no place in rainbows. She also knew that God was white and the Devil black, while the in-between tones, the greys of the street in the photograph, belonged to War.

And the child knew about War. It lay all the way between everything and nothing and covered the city so that no matter where one went there was no escaping it. It was a grey smoke that filled the air they had to breathe.

At school she watched the boys draw aeroplanes that resembled ducks, laying eggs in flight, and she would feel the metal disc, named, numbered, on the string about her neck, and look up at the sky above the playground.

In the home the blinds were secured when sirens sounded, cups rattled on their hooks when trucks rolled past. Every morning the newspaper was unfolded over the kitchen table, plates covered with grey pictures, and above the toaster there was a voice that said, 'This is the BBC London calling. Here is the news.'

The child learned much by remaining silent through mealtime conversations but she never discovered who had thrown stones through Mrs Gessner's front windows. No one seemed to know. No one seemed particularly interested. Nor could she find out where Mr Gessner had gone. Certainly he wasn't fighting with the soldiers, for one day someone, an aunt, uncle perhaps, someone had said, 'Well, what would you do if they told you to go over and shoot your relatives?' And a grey sort of silence had settled in the room.

Their neighbour had not appeared to be disturbed by the breaking of the windows. While the workmen cleared the fragments of glass and put in new panes, Mrs Gessner carried on working in her garden. The face under the straw hat was flat and expressionless. The unlaced boots never hurried. Up and down the rows, day after day, those broad, freckled hands pulled weeds from the flowerbeds.

The child didn't speak but she often watched. She would lie in the grass on her own side of the fence and press her face against the palings, thrilled by her own daring. Dirty Hun, they'd said at school. Watch out or she'll get you. Spy, spy, string her up high. She would watch every movement and when it seemed likely that the brim of the straw hat was going to tilt in her direction she would put her head down and crawl backwards until she was behind her Grandfather's bean frame, and she would stay there until the squat figure had moved away.

But nothing happened to her. Nothing. After a while the children at school lost interest in the story about the sounds of breaking glass in the middle of the night, and the mystery woman next door took on an ordinariness that defied the child's imagination. It did not seem right that a spy should put out tins of dripping for the birds or scratch down the back of her dress with a knitting needle. The child grew bolder. It was no longer satisfying to hide in the grass and stare. She came out into the open, walked along the fence, sometimes stood still and leaned on it. She met the woman's eyes, smiled when she smiled, even said hello.

Promise not to tell a living soul, she said to anyone at school who would listen. I talked to the spy.

Once she accepted a bunch of dahlias from the garden and was thrilled to find two earwigs in the petals. She took them to school next morning in a bottle and everyone looked. Oh yes, they were German earwigs, all right.

Then the child's father was killed. The man in the photograph on the mantelpiece was drowned at sea and everything about the child's house changed. It became quiet. People walked in it as though they no longer knew the way, and they talked in tired voices. Sometimes they would not leave the child alone. Sometimes they forgot she was there. The grey of war sat at the dinner table with them and curled up on their plates, making everything taste like the dead earth under houses.

The child took to playing in the garden next door.

Years later she would not be able to remember her first visit but soon she was crossing the fence so regularly that Mrs Gessner cut down some of the palings to make it easier for her. And because the child was older now, and in a new class at school, she no longer felt the need to confide in other children or relatives, for that matter.

On warm afternoons she would sit under the apple tree by a mound of green fruit, or wander along the borders popping fuchsia buds, or kneel on the path urging snails to compete on a brick raceway. Mrs Gessner used to bring out the canvas chairs and they would sit, the two of them, drinking milk and eating biscuits with currants and lemon in them.

Then there were the days when they went into the house and the cool dark kitchen with its smells of apples and firewood and caraway seeds, and the child would climb up into the rocking chair, wriggling into a nest of cushions, while Mrs Gessner brought out the music box. It was of dark wood, carved, with a lid which framed trees and dancing deer; and when the lid was opened it was easy to tell why the deer danced like that, for from the emptiness of the box came a song of little bells, the same tune over and over until the lid was closed and Mrs Gessner was wiping the box on her apron and smiling, ya, is beautiful? Is beautiful? and the child was holding out her hands, begging for the music again.

Perhaps she talked to her family about the music box. Later, she was unable to remember that either. But it seemed that the family, slow with grief, had dragged their thinking to the gap in the wooden fence. As an uncle nailed up the boards, they took the child before her grandfather who wanted to know how long she had been going next door. How long was long? Weeks? Years? She didn't know. Then Grandfather talked about King and country and the child's father. He talked to her seriously as though she were already grown up, the way he spoke to her uncles, only kinder. He had steel-rimmed glasses, and grey hairs growing out of his nose. She knew that she would give her dead father a pain that was much worse than drowning, if she ever went next door again.

Some time after that, Mrs Gessner moved away from the street. The child didn't see her leave. She came home from school and was met by Grandfather who gave her a brown paper parcel. Inside was the music box. The woman left it for the little girl, he said. She meant you, he said.

The child didn't know what to say. She felt as though she had been caught doing something wrong.

You know what your father would want you to do, Grandfather said.

Of course she knew. And as she put the music box on the fire, the aunts and uncle put their arms round her and told her she was a real little heroine, and that pleased her; but most of all she was pleased that she had made her father, who was living with the angels, very proud of his daughter.

(1985)

FRANCES CHERRY

Waiting for Jim

You stand, heels digging into the shag-pile and stare at the door. You would recognise the gouges, scratches, fingerprints ten years from now. Your eye travels along the skirting-board looking for other familiar things. You wonder if you could write them down from memory. Then you realise you've forgotten. It can be done. How amazing.

Jim has closed the front door and is swaying and bumping down the hallway. You take a breath and move back. Loosen fists to hands. Let them go. Limp Limp . . .

He peeps round the door. 'Sorry-I'm-late. Something-came-up . . .' He enunciates every word with care.

'Don't worry. They're not having dinner till eight.'

There is a silence while he stands there. Staring.

You begin to feel more confident. 'I've put the sauna on for you. Thought it might relax you. After such a long day . . .'

'Oh . . . Thanks, love,' he says, as if he can't quite believe it.

'Come and sit down. I'll get you a drink.' You feel the swish of your skirt against your thigh as you walk to the drink cabinet. Not often you wear decent, going-out clothes. You remember that time when you were a schoolgirl in uniform going home on the tram. Later, by coincidence, you caught the same tram back to town but this time dressed in good clothes, going-to-town-on-a-Friday-night-clothes. Feeling as different from that irresponsible schoolgirl as could be. *And* the conductor didn't recognise you. Funny how you've never forgotten that occasion.

'Ice?' You open the already prepared ice-bucket.

'What's all this for?' he says, taking the glass when you hand it to him.

'Well, as I said,' you turn to pour yourself a gin and tonic (and so he won't see the insincerity in your face), 'you've had a long, hard day . . . Not everyone has to work such long hours as you . . .' Watch the sarcasm — it'll be the downfall of you. You swing round and smile and sit in the chair beside him. 'We're going out to dinner. Nice to have a drink before we go. Relaxing . . . do you like my new skirt?'

'Yeah . . . Yeah . . .' He sips at his drink. Well, it's hard not to in this environment with a nice tall crystal glass in his hand. He does it well. Good at shaking his glass so that the ice clinks against the sides. A pretty sound. You don't mind it.

There is a long silence and then he says, 'Where're the kids?'

You clench your fists and stare at him for a moment. Why does he never listen? 'I told you.' And the little voice inside you says, keep calm, don't do anything wrong now, it's going to be all right. 'They're at Mum's.'

'Oh yeah . . .'

'How was work?'

'Think we've got that contract sewn up with old Withers.'

'Have you noticed the flowers? They're out of our garden.'

He looks up, feigning interest. 'Great.'

How nice he is. How polite. You should do this all the time. It would save so much trouble . . . If you were nice to him . . . All the time . . . When he came home with all his excuses and lies . . . To think that you could ever have been afraid, felt that steel band tighten around your chest. Why don't you be nice? Go along with him. It seems so easy — as long as you keep the anger down. Way down. Further down. Till it almost comes out of your feet . . .

You stretch your leg out and look at your elegant nyloned foot in the pointed high-heeled shoes. You should have been like this so long ago. You've known. Who cares about him? Why let him affect you? Spoil your life? You can run your own life. Completely.

You look across at him and see he has finished his drink. You jump to your feet, swoop the glass out of his hand. 'Have another.'

'Thanks love.'

He'll be nicely done.

You help him strip his clothes off. Arms behind his ears like a child. Go in with him, pour more oil on the hot rocks. He sits there staring into space, towel wrapped around him to soak up all the juices . . .

You close the door and stand for a moment. This is the bit where you have to think of the children and yourself. No more tension and fear. That's all there is about it. You reach up and push the bolt into the socket and walk into the bedroom.

There's your face in the big round mirror. Does it look the same, or does it have a wide-eyed look of fear? You practise smiles . . . Hello Leonie, hope I'm not late . . .

'Hello Leonie, hope I'm not late.'

'Joanna! Of course not. Where's Jim?'

'Oh-ah. He was late home so I decided to come ahead of him.'

'Good on you.'

'Actually, he was a bit under the weather . . .'

'You mean, had a few too many?'

'More than few.' You walk with Leonie down the hallway.

'Oh Joanna, I'm so sorry. You must be quite upset.'

'Oh, I don't know,' you feel yourself sigh. 'He does it all the time.

I'm used to it.'

'Still,' Leonie says, going ahead into the bedroom and showing you the white brocade bedspread covered with coats, 'I'm sure you must be.'

You take your coat off and lay it with the others. Then take a comb out of your bag and do your hair, studying your face in the mirror, and Leonie behind you.

'You are looking nice,' Leonie says.

'Oh — I bought this ages ago.' You smile at her twisted mirror face.

'It's lovely.' Leonie stares at you for a moment and then rushes towards you and crushes you to her sweet-smelling bosom, pats your back. 'I do understand. My first husband was an alcoholic.'

You are astounded. 'Really? I didn't know you'd been married before.'

'For seven years. The children aren't Ralph's, you know.' She smiles.

'Oh — I — had — no idea — He's very good with them . . .'

'He's wonderful. So there's hope for you yet.'

You decide not to say anything. You put your comb back in your bag and smile.

'Come and have a drink and meet the others,' Leonie says.

They stand and sit in various parts of the big room. You feel suddenly afraid and can't think of a thing to say to anyone. You keep your eyes on Leonie's back as she walks up to Ralph and asks him to give you a drink.

'What'll you have, Joanna?' Ralph says.

'A gin and tonic, thanks.' He is such a nice sensible man. Good-looking, too. If only Jim was like that. But then, you don't have to worry about Jim anymore. Can you believe it?

'Where's that husband of yours?' Ralph says, as he turns back with the drink.

'Oh, I came ahead. He was late home.' You turn to the room, look round for a corner to stand in. Until you've got your bearings and feel you can talk to someone. You know that in a minute, as soon as she sees you are alone, Leonie will come and introduce you to people. You would like to be invisible so you can watch them, listen to them. People are so interesting. You look at the pictures on the walls. Good prints. Nothing original. You'd like to have some original paintings. Money in them, too. He should have known that. Good one for making money.

There are flowers on the sideboard. Freshly picked today, do you think? Or would she have bought them? You turn to the window and look at the garden. There are shrubs there but no flowers that you can see. Of course there could be some in the back garden. Should you go to the kitchen, look through the window or go to the back door and see? Before it gets dark? Can you leave the room without attention?

'Come and meet some people,' Leonie says, holding her hand out. Are you supposed to take it? You smile and don't lift your hand to hers.

'Monica, this is Joanna, we're on the P.T.A. together. Her husband runs Odman's building and trucking business.'

That's something they'll have to stop saying. 'Hello,' you say, 'what does your husband do?' May as well say that. After all women are only what their husbands are. See how she likes it. See how they all like it.

'Oh, he's a teacher. That's him over there.'

'My husband should be along soon,' you say. As if you're nothing without him. 'He had to work late.'

'I s'pose he's quite busy? In a job like that?'

Is she being nice? 'He's home late every night.'

'At least I don't have that complaint.'

What complaint do you have, you wonder.

'Excuse me,' Leonie calls. 'Would you like to come through now?'

There are little cards on the table with everyone's name on. You are to sit next to an older man with white hair, and on the other side an empty chair.

'I hope you don't mind us starting before Jim gets here?' Leonie says.

'No, no, that's okay,' you say. 'Shall I ring him? Maybe he's fallen asleep?'

'I will,' Leonie says. 'You stay there.'

'Who's s'posed to be sitting here?' a girl across the chair says.

'My husband. He had to work late.'

'What a shame. He's missing a lovely meal.'

'Yes.'

Leonie comes back. 'He must be on his way. There was no answer.'

'Oh that's good,' you say, and almost believe he's coming.

You concentrate on your fish cocktail so no one will talk to you and have a little inside talk with yourself. You are feeling quite calm, quite together. And you don't regret a thing. It'll take time before you can get used to social occasions like this. They were your thing, so there's no reason why they can't be again. Once there's only yourself to think about. Don't have to worry about him. For instance if he was here now what would he do? You lift up your eyes and look around the table. He'd be holding forth so that no one else could get a word in. Probably put his hand on the knee of the girl next to him. Begin to spill his drink as the evening wears on and then start to put you down. Jokes jokes. Terrible jokes that no one thinks are funny, except him. Nothing will stop him. No matter what you say. Even when you get quite clever and throw them back at him.

'Hey,' Ralph calls across the table. ''Bout time your old man was here.'

'I think he's on his way.'

'He's taking quite a while,' Leonie says. 'Shall I ring again?'

'It's all right, I will.' You push your chair back and walk carefully out of the room.

In the hallway with the door closed it is reasonably quiet. You lift the receiver, dial the number and wait. And then suddenly your heart begins to beat faster. What say he does answer? But the phone goes on and on ringing.

You put the receiver down and go into the bathroom. It is still the same face in the mirror. Small and smooth. You splash a little water on and dab it with a towel.

(1986)

KERI HULME

The Knife and the Stone

Every morning before it was light, just before the alarm went off, she woke with a jolt. Not from a bad dream: it was as though her body had a prescience of pain and responded with a sudden hurtful wakening.

This morning was no different.

She lay quiet a moment, feeling her heartbeat slow down to normal. It is today.

She sighed. Shuffled off the eiderdown, shuffled into her work-clothes. Stood a moment by her warm disordered bed, touching it with one finger, her mind a blank. Then, like every morning, she went straight to the lavatory. Her bowels never worked until after breakfast but it was her father's belief that everyone should empty themselves on rising. And her mother was listening.

She banged the seat. The noise echoed. She stood a moment, not thinking. Letting whatever was around imprint itself. The stink of Jeyes fluid and excrement. One hinge off the door ever since she could remember. The old map showing English ley lines. Ahh! said the Guests.

Hand-adzed walls!

Rain-stained walls.

She touched them, briefly.

Five minutes after she'd risen, she was stoking the range. Like every morning. The rata-chips caught alight: the coal dust flared. Ten minutes to boil the kettle. She hated the range.

She set out milk-jug and honey-jar, china spoon and tea-mug on the wooden tray while waiting. She hummed, automatically, a tuneless wavering no-song. 'You have no idea how much it means to me,' her mother had said, often, 'hearing you cheerful and busy at dawnlight. It's only then I know I have survived another night, that another day has truly come.'

She picked up the tray with care and carried it, still humming to herself, into her mother's lair.

The room is dazzling with lights her mother never turns off. It is crammed with boxes piled with scraps of materials, with large pots and huge pale dusty plants. It is foetid. Full of blood-stink, like old menses or meat on the turn. Incense-smoke eternally spirals, boring into the blood-cloud. Today, as well, there is the rank sweetness of lupins, bunches of them jammed into the Ali Baba pots.

She drew a deep breath.

Past the harsh stares of the bed-lamp, side-lamp, signal-lamp. Past the duelling flickers of the thousand fragments of mirror sewn into the canopy over her mother's bed. Concentrating on the intricate stepping needed to carry a laden tray through the maze.

The breath ran out by the bedside.

Her mother smiled at the sound. With her pallor and enormous grey eyes, she looked a nocturnal carnivore. Her smile menaced.

'My darling daughter.'

Never, thank you.

'You had good dreams, my bantling?'

Never, how did you sleep?

'Yes mama dear.'

Another smile.

'Alas, no visitors,' said her mother.

What a menace you are, Maeve! laughed the Guests. An Aldis lamp. Imagine if some ship sees your flashes . . . Maeve the wrecker!

Her mother answered dreamily, 'Imagine if some starship sees them, and we have visitors . . .'

'Maybe tonight, mama.'

'The blind hope of youth,' said her mother and sucked at the mug of tea.

She put the tray down carefully. She thought, No more mama.

So charming, some of the Guests found it. How charmingly old-fashioned, said one, with a lop-sided smile. Natural word, said her father then. Better than you lot with your Mum and Mummy. Bloody old dead gyppos. He'd barked with laughter.

You can call me my given name now, said her mother a year ago, but o how I shall miss being your mama.

She waited for the next cue.

'Your father will be home soon dear one. Back from the wearying sea. Perhaps you could have something ready for him?'

My mother is mad. She knew that wasn't true. She sounded mad, with her artificial stilted language. She looked mad in her scrambled light-ridden den. She was frighteningly sane.

Today, she said.

'I'll put something on for him.'

As I've put something on every morning since I was eight. Mainly the same sort of something. Last night's spuds, chipped and fried. Two fried eggs, two onions carved into rings.

And he'll say

'There you are,' said her father, and

'Good. Breakfast,' and

'There's about a case on the lawn.'

That last could change.

Sometimes he'd stamp in, snarl over breakfast, grunt after every mouthful of tea, then rush into her mother's bedroom and slam the door.

On that kind of day she could steal back into her room and strip off her work-clothes; have a proper wash in water now warmed by the range. Get rid of the stinks. Then, no sneers from whoever sat next to her. Gidday Fishy, how's it goin' Gutbucket? Life okay down on the dope estate, giggle giggle.

Unless it was Mark. If it was him next to her, he'd grin his hesitant badteeth grin and whisper, Today, your eyes are like *pure* Marmite. Or something equally fatuous.

Which was worse, she wondered, turning the eggs and onions and chips with precision, which was worse?

If there was nothing, They sulked or did something horrid. If there was a case, it was bad because there was time to process it but not enough time to get properly ready. Inevitable scales on her hands, a feeling of slime all over her. Yet the times her father came in jubilant, shouting Hey a dozen cases! Hear that! We're riiccchhhhh! the rich sounding like coarse cloth tearing — those times were probably worst. It meant taking the day off, because a dozen cases took her hours. It meant her father could do the full round, paying something off the grocery bill, a bit off the petrol account, even some to the hardware store. But then he'd waltz into his favourite pub and drink his way into instant friendships. He never seemed to see the sly nudges, Could be on to a good thing here Mac, that she felt on her skin as though it were raw and they were hard knocks. And later, buying a crate or two of beer, a quart or two of vodka — 'Vodka my girl!' he'd roar. 'No congeners, remember that!' — he'd collect the drink friends and they'd all come rolling home. And he'd stand in the front door yelling You're Guests in my home, everything's yours my Guests! his dark face suffused with a purple wash, his lips loose and wet. And he'd take his dobro off the wall and twang it; sing old and pseud songs and the Guests would sing along. And some would vomit and some would wander curiously around, admiring or puzzled, and some would lie in a stupor on the livingroom cushion pile. And sometimes, her mother would limp out, swathed in one of her quilts, her face glowing, the blood aroma trailing heavily after. The singing would gather a mellowness, the bottles lower more slowly. She would have finished making tea for the drunker Guests by then. She would steal away to bed before her father noticed her, because otherwise he would come lurching and whispering God I love you girl love you girl, fumbling, delving

The jubilant times were very much the worst, she decided, sliding breakfast onto the three plates.

Yet, some times, rare times, she would get safely to bed by herself, and wake, she never knew how much later, and hear the end of the party. Her mother's thin perfect soprano winding like a flute above her father's velvet baritone, the dobro a sure melancholy underlining third voice. The songs were real, unknown to her. They were beautiful. She would cry, at the way the good dreams had come to die, and crying, sleep.

She ate quickly, as she did every morning. About a case, waiting on the lawn. She picked up her knife and stone and went to meet them.

The stone was a wedge of fine-grit sandstone, white and worn. A gift, like her first knife. One Guest, reeled in like all the rest, stayed until morning. He watched her awkwardly using the butcherknife. He didn't say anything. But when she had finished half the case, he'd gone inside and brought out a tableknife. He took the whetstone out of his pocket and beckoned to her. Warily she came. Still not talking, he broke most of the plastic handle from the knife. He bound what remained with tartape so it fitted edgeless and easy in the hand. He honed the blade to razor thinness, razor sharpness, after snapping it in half. He showed her how.

He took one fish out and demonstrated the right way, carve, scoop, flick, slice. He was slow and deliberate. Then he handed her the knife and the stone, and went back inside to finish off the remaining crate. He was a noisy drunk but he never touched or spoke to her. She still thought of him with love.

She also thought, bitterly, My fifth knife.

In the case on the lawn they waited, their murky golden eyes bulging in the heavy deeps of air. The slime was running out of the plastic slats.

Think of us as a team, her mother had said two years ago, picking her words with care. Don't *respond* to those ignorami at school. We are an elite, a tiny chosen venturing band. Do you remember the Company of the Nine Walkers? No? She had sighed. I never understood why your heart didn't thrill . . . let it be. We are heart people, special, tied by love, supports each for the other. If Gareth had lived . . . she sighed again. Not to mind (a brave smile). We are the team. Your father fishing our daily bread and maintaining the house. Myself, labouring over these quilts for all our extras. And thyself my dear one the helpmate, doing the little things to assist each of us. *Being* the reason it is all done for.

Hi team, she said, to the knife and the stone. We're the winning side, you know that? Couldn't be anything else because he always checks his nets even if he has to crawl to the boat. And look at the other side.

Flat, sticky, and already defeated. Among them, occasionally, a stargazer; rarely, silver-bellied eels, and most rarely, a glorious coral-fleshed salmon fresh run from the sea. But those he took care of. His ruined hands took infinite care boning them. He soaked them in brines of his own composing. He nursed them through the drying stage, gauzed against fly-strike. He travelled long roads in the battered van, selecting manuka and silver pine for sawdust. He hovered nervously while they smoked. He sold the beautiful results and bought records and grog. Any spoiled results he ate for breakfast.

She never ate fish, least of all them.

First cut, just below the belly fin, slip through a vertebra and sever the spine. Out the other side in one smooth slice to arrive just above another scarlet-edged fin, in line with the gill case.

She remembered little of before. Before she was eight. Before Gareth died. Before the close warm world fell apart. She did remember the night they brought her father in, howling, bleeding, cursing, bleeding. Drunken, he had lifted the outboard motor from the water. Drunken, he had slipped, knocking the gear from neutral to fast forward. Drunken, he had slipped further, and grabbed the prop. Healed to grotesque stumps and scars, he'd growled at her, 'That fiddly work is woman work. In the old days, that was the proper way. We men do the catching. You women clean it up. That's what you're for.' He'd handed her the boning knife and yelled at her until she had learned, clumsily, to carve up flounders. Second cut, quick flash to the anus careful not to rupture any sacs of roe. Then hold up the slimed thing and quickly slit down the other side to the arsehole again. Arsehole was Mark's word. Right in the arsehole from my old man, slight emphasis on the 'my'. His tall thin body twitching, as normal. The locker bay was crowded. They had their heads close, together.

Why? she had asked. Why tell me?

Because. He had brown eyes too, but not as dark as her own. Because I know about you. His eyelids flickered, a similar beat to his twitching body. Now you can destroy me if you want, he said. He shrieked out in a hun yell REVENGE. No heads turned. Mad Mark at it again.

The momentum of the cut and the weight of the newly-severed head made it fall, dragging the guts neatly behind it slop into the gut bucket. Slice: the lower intestine freed. Chop the tail off in one fluent cut. Throw the bloody thing into the wet bucket, ready for later washing.

I know it's not easy but we make do, crooned her mother. We're not rich in material terms, but we make do. We planned for this when we were not much older than you are now. O the sun and flowers of being sixteen! We planned a good place out away out of the corrupt system, a clean strong place for strong new people. If Gareth . . . her voice became throaty. But you're strong, she keened, fondling her daughter's arm, wiry but strong. And so rich in your mind! Far more rich than we were at your age, poisoned by the garbage they taught *us*.

She remembered hearing a Guest burst out, O you've given her such riches but you've sacrificed so much! Her mother had looked out the windows, over the beam of the Aldis light. We have riches too, she said strongly. Natural food and holistic medicine and freedom from city pressures. Strong Guestly murmurs of support. And we have a *good* child. God yes, said another one, you want to see my little monster fat and pasty and deathrays all day long and god the language! Yes! Yes! Yes! they top each other's monsters as her mother's smile grew wider, tighter.

Am I rich in my mind?

I have words for every colour under the sun. Weird gobbets of knowledge from weird Guests. I can hate. I can gut. I know all about dead and dying flounders. The fibrillation, the strange and beautiful fluidity of their rippling fins as they try to gain purchase on air. The mottling of their skins, mosaics of rust and olive-green and sepia on the back; mushroom and grey and terracotta and lemon-blotched cream on the underside. The pout of their lips as you hit their heads with the hammer.

She did that surreptitiously to the livelier ones. Her father sneered, 'Afraid they'll bite? You're bigger than them.'

She knew all about the occasional parasites, pinholes in the white flesh with black writhing cupheaded worms extruding. Sealice pecking away like bloated pink slaters. Colours, she thought, colours.

The pale yellow granular roe. Faintly blue gluey strings of slime. Grey blurred crabs in the anus tubes. Green fragments of annelid worms in the guts. Matt rusty liver. Pink veined coils. The delicately irridescent inner skin. The brilliant viridian of the gallbladder.

Today, she was halfway through the case.

It's not really work, said her mother to her complaint last week. You cannot, my sweet, truly call it hard labour now can you? I remember working twelve-hour days, on my feet all that time, waitressing for slobs. And your father, immersed to the heart in the gore at the freezing works, a sensitive singer breaking apart with all that pain. But we earned the money for here that way. That's work my girl!

Now she thought,

Every morning for the last eight years. Unless nothing has been caught. Maybe a day a week. 300 days a year. 2400 days. Normally an hour of blood and guts, sometimes much much longer. In the wind. In the rain. In the frost. In the sandfly hordes of summer. 'Allergic to sandflies? But she was *born* here,' exclaimed a Guest, a hundred years ago. 'Surely she'll grow out of it?'

Not so far. The bright welts keep coming, each marked with a watery red centre. The sandflies know her hands are full. They feast with impunity.

Cover yourself with treacle, said Mark. They'll have a bloody hard job biting through that.

Then he said, I have a cousin who can get us out.

Her heart had seemed suddenly huge, forcing the air from her lungs.

I have a cousin with a fish-shop in Auckland. Don't wince. There is a restaurant attached, and a flat attached to the restaurant. I can cook in my poofy way. You can process. He will send the fare.

He said, carefully,

If you want, we can make it?

She whispered.

I can't hear that, said Mark.

I said, it has got too hard. And your teeth are horrid.

Long lean body, long lean hands, long lean smile, all suddenly beautifully still.

Tomorrow then, midnight eyes.

She had shivered.

Why don't your friends ever come? she asked her mother yesterday. She remembered the afternoon light fighting through the lamps: her mother's hands stitching polygon to polygon: patchouli incense at war with the omnipresent reek of blood. Her mother gave a high sharp bark of laughter. 'O dear heart, we are friends of all the world! The house positively *vibrates* with our friends. Our hospitality is acclaimed far and wide — my darling sweetsullen child, you must have noticed!'

Slither. Cut. Scarlet floods or slow upwellings or a cold dark ooze. Slice. Slap of body in the water. Heads with eyes unchanged piling up amid the coiling innards.

It was time to cleanse them; scrub off the outside blood and slime, and force out the inside jellied clots from the secret cavities by the spine. A final inner sluice. Marketable goods.

As on every morning, she came to the last one.

She looked at it a long time, not thinking of anything.

Then she staggered to the porch with the basket of cleaned gutted fish, left it covered with a sack.

She scrubbed down the gutting block and the fish case. Slow cold-drowsy blowflies lifted away reluctantly from the streams of water. She picked up the shovel and the gutbucket and went to the burying-ground. The tin banged against her leg: the wire handle creased her palm painfully. She dug the hole, emptied the tin savagely down it, stared at the mound before covering it over.

Then she hurried inside. Washed her hands, pulled comb through her hair. She watched her father pull off his boots, awkward and slow, and tramp into her mother's room.

She picked up her heavy schoolcase.

On impulse, she took the knife and the stone and slipped them into a side-pocket.

She thought, I don't have much to offer. A body and a baggage of words. A hate. A knowledge of how to gut things. But it must be better.

'I'm late,' she called to the shut bedroom door.

This morning, she didn't say goodbye.

(1986)

KERI HULME

While My Guitar Gently Sings

            and the words drain into the music
            and the music drains silently, west

There is dust on my guitar, thick grey deadening dust.
    Dust, on my guitar.
    You remember the day you came home with it?
    'Hey girl!'
    yelling up the path,
    'hey girl, I got it!'
    And me sulking out by the lav, wild because I've had to get the tea on, again; round up the boys for their baths, again; feed the chooks and the pig and the house-cow, again, and all the time I wanted to be alone and quiet down by the creek, listening to friendly water and wind.
    I won't come in until you're inside, until you've skidded your shoes off your swollen feet, and are sitting down with a cup of tea Maki's made you.
    'Hinewai,' you reach a hand, 'don't be sad. Now you can sing all your troubles away!' My big mother, throwing her head back and laughing at my sulks. 'Real joygerm eh?' she says to the boys, winking. Then she picks up the long box. 'My girl, here it is.'
    And I take it in a grabby way, tear off the paper — then go more slowly, unpicking the cellotape, because I can feel you've got something good, not a Woolworth job.
    I look at you a moment.
    And that was the first time I remember *looking* at your face. Not just seeing Mum. Your lips are curved in a thick grin. There are dark shadows under your eyes. Rusty grey hairs already at the corners of your head. Aue, my mama is not young, still unwrapping tissue tenderly from the box and then further thought is drowned in Aaaaa!
    The varnish is rich golden: the wood like tawa, pearly-grained and blonde. The belly is some close heavy black wood, like ebony. Ibanez is the name above the neck.
    'E mama,'
    Breathing hard, just touching the silver strings.
    'Now watch her break it at a party,' you giggle, 'watch e Maki?' Maki is pouting because I've got the present and he hasn't, just for a change. You throw a pretend slap at him. Maki ducks, giggles back, and then Hone and Tara start in too, and I watch sneering, as you and the boys tussle on the floor.

I never did say thank you for my guitar.

E mama, taku whaea —

I am sitting in the dark.

Everyone else is asleep

There is too much smoke in the air, cigarette and that other soft cat & pine scent. Kohatu they call it now. I used to say pot.

Somebody has spilt beer on the chair I'm on and my pants are damp.

I'm not drunk or stoned. I'm gone past that.

I'm wretchedly sober.

The blue and white telegram, there.

The dusty guitar here, ready to hand.

I am smoking again, despite the clogged air. The small red eye pulses, in breath, out breath. You remember that, first of all, you never smoked anything but roll-your-owns? Tasman Gold Cut, and Zigzag rice papers. And you had this neat way of being able to roll a thin tight cigarette without looking at what your fingers were doing.

I never could. I've tried with pot and tobacco and everything leaks out either end. But then, when you went to work at Smith-Bonds, you took up tailor-mades.

'Cheaper nei?' you said, laughing your deep gutty laugh. 'I don't have time to make them, just time to pay for them!' Another belly laugh.

And you smoked them, two packets and more a day.

I hated that. Your fingers always smelt of smoke, each time you touched me, or gave me anything. And your breath smelt of smoke, kissing me good night. And your long black plait of hair, fallen over one shoulder to tease my face, reeked. You went round in an aureole of smoke.

And it got so fast into your lungs. You'd wake up in the mornings with this smoker's hack, and any fast stuff, like running up the hill home, or rounding up Nig Horse, or wrestling with the boys — why did you never wrestle with me? — and you'd get this breathless wheeze. 'Jeeze Hinewai, don't smoke, you get just like your fat old mother!'

Rocking with laughter because you never knew yourself as old or fat or breathless. I am nobly big, your eyes flashed, and just for this moment my lungs are playing tricks on me.

I only started smoking three years ago, with the band, I don't like it all that much. The taste can be as foul as the morning-after smell, but it keeps my fingers busy and after a while, my mind . . . stills.

Sometimes it must have been like that for you. Do you remember that night I woke up with period cramps and came into the kitchen, ready to groan and carry on and gouge some sympathy out of you? And stopped, because you sat so still in the chair before the fire. Your legs stuck out, propped on a stool. The only things moving were the flames and the smoke from your cigarette.

When you looked up, you didn't smile, you didn't make a joke. You said, so quietly
'I wonder where your dad died?'
And I forgot the ache in my young womb and crept back to bed. Because I swear to this day you spoke without opening your mouth. As though the thought that was always in your heart had grown to loudness out of the depths of your pool of peace and quiet.

We all wondered, time to time, what had happened to Dad. He was a possum-hunter and used to stay for days in the bush. But the last time, the days grew into a fortnight. After two months, the search parties stopped. Everybody said, 'He's great in the bush, Tom Kura, but nobody can last this long.'

Nobody even found his bones.

Not even his dog came home.

You wept. You stopped weeping. Went out and found your job, and worked days at the factory, nights round the house, weekends looking after the fences and the paddocks of our shrunken farm. And all the years it took us to grow up, you never wept again.

It's your laugh, e Mama. I keep hearing your laugh.

Loud, and so warm.

I always envied that great ability of yours to warm people. Shake them into smiles and laughter. Didn't matter their age. Some could be as old as blind Miratawhai, who was supposed to be a hundred and ten. You snuggled up to her the day she came to our marae, 'E kui, ka nui te pai nei?' Nothing specific, just isn't this good? And the old old lady's face, so laced and ridged with wrinkles, webbed out into a sensible smile. And her crooked hand crept into yours, and this creaky voice, made whispers by age, says 'Mokopuna.' Claims you as grandchild and she's never seen you before and hasn't spoken to anyone for a decade.

Some could be as young as that Samoan kid, Falasi. I never liked Fa'. Never thought of him as a brother. He was just this stubby heavybrowed kid, who never smiled at me, you brought home one night.

'E hine, look! They've cut him — look there. And there.' And you cuddled him, crooned over him, evening after evening, until his hurts healed and he would smile his dark slow smile as soon as he heard you yell from the hill path, 'Hey kids! Your mother made it through another day!' Raucous with laughter, roughing up the boys, grinning to me, 'Ah my Hinewai! You done all these jobs again!'

Fed the chooks and the pig and milked the house-cow and bathed the boys or harried them to the bathroom, when all I wanted to do . . . you knew it. Weekends, when I'd sneak away to the creek and play my songs, you never sent the boys to look for me, to rouse me back to the work. Just cackle when I mooned back to the house. 'Guess what fellas? The eels didn't get your sister *again*!'

He he he. Off I'd go, sulk into the bedroom, while the boys roared round the house and you roared right along with them. Fa' had fitted in by then. The boys protected him from the sneers — 'Hey coconut!' and fists at school until the stubby little kid grew so hard and solid and fast with his fists that it was a moot point who was protecting who. They never hurt him with words, just joked with him over his cloud of hair and his love of kilts and his hatred of the cold. Strange little brother Fa' grew stronger than them all. They still go visit him in Auckland. The last time I saw him was by accident, when I went bail for Colin, the drummer of the band. He was the constable taking down the details. He said, 'Hinewai, Sister. Kia ora e 'Wai,' in that heavy masculine voice of his and then, flatly, 'What is your relationship with the prisoner?'

Did you like it that Fa' became a cop?

Or that Hone is the newsworthy voice from Black Power in Wellington?

Or that Tara has a wife and two children in Christchurch, a child in Westport, a child in Gisborne, a child in Taihape, and twins in Porirua, and you've never seen any of the last five?

I know you hated it when Maki crashed his bike, from 80 miles an hour to a full bleeding stop against the side of the bridge in Whangaroa.

You and I were the first ones there, you cradling his bleeding head and me retching over the side of the bridge. I can't stand blood. I never watched when you killed the pig each year, but there would be the excited crowding boys all leaning over the sty wall and drooling. 'E lookit that!' BANG! the old .270, and you always got them in the head (said the boys) so there was this thin trickle of blood from bullet-hole and mouth (said the boys) from the head that had a moment ago been alive and grunting. Maki sometimes says 'pig'. Most of the time, he drools. The nurses and attendants, you wrote in your last letter, say he smiles among the drool sometimes. So he might be happy, you thought.

That was your big thing, remember? That we all be happy.

I know you didn't like it when I said Whangaroa was too small. That I didn't want to go and work in Smith-Bonds, packing stockings into bags or ironing them or sorting them or having anything at all to do with them. I said,

'I am seventeen and Whangaroa is the arsehole of New Zealand and I am too bright to slave away in that bloody factory, or just marry some farming oaf and have a tribe of kids.'

And you laughed till you nearly cried.

'*That's* what you think of your mum eh!' Because you had been seventeen when you married my farming oaf father. Then you said, seriously, 'Hinewai, brains are important and you have a lot of fat in that head of yours. But heart is important too, and you think hard about all the good things we got in our place.' And you enumerated all the ones that were so important to you, from the marae at the heart of the village, to the bones, dead in the cemetery and live in every second house. 'Who do we know in the city?' you kept asking. 'Why do you want to go there?'

Because nothing here makes me happy, I'd snapped back, not even my creek any more. I want to make something of myself, I said, drawing myself up so proud, I want to be (first thing that came into my head) a teacher!

Well, it might have taken one week of that first term e whae, one week for me to decide that I didn't want to be a teacher at all, but after all your work — talking to So & So who was president of the Maori Women's Welfare League, and to So & So who was in the Wellington rununga, and So & So who was with Maori Affairs — and after all your saving (overtime for my trainfare and new clothes, all the money you had in the bank for my first year's board) — aue! I couldn't back down immediately.

I quit after a year. But I didn't say anything to you. Not even when the train came to take me back, six weeks later after the holidays were finished supposedly. You hugged me and tangled over me, big gruff greying woman stinking of smoke and cheap lipstick. 'E, I'm so proud of you, my girl, so proud! We're all proud.' Then, throwing your big head back, the glint coming back into your eyes, 'Even those damn eels down in the creek are proud! You be happy, Hinewai.'

Easier said than done.

I worked in a downtown Woolworth's first; a Lambton Quay hamburger bar second, and a Cuba Street massage parlour, third. By that time, I was six months gone and neither knew nor cared who had been the father.

I've my mother's height, but not her strength or bulk. I hid the baby under my heart as long as I could, hid it all the glaring drunken weed-rotten nights, but it had to slip down, lower and lower. And sadly, it did not, she did not, stop outside my womb, but imperceptibly kept on slipping down, lowering her spirit back into mother earth. She lived 24 hours, tiny, hairless, yellowed.

E mama, I never told you. I could not tell you.

Hone came to Wellington and found me, at the end of a long bent trail from the Teachers' Training College. He was angry first, and then weeping second, and at last, practical and stern. 'You're eldest, tuahine. You can't live like *this*,' sweeping his hand round the tacky flat, messed with bottles, smeared with the sloth of grief, 'we won't let you.' He picked up my guitar. Play me a song, he ordered. And wild at him, sick of weeping, I played. And Hone grinned.

'I know just the band, the scene, the sound.'

And he did. Skilful little brother, two weeks in the city, already the big organiser, already in the know.

E Ma, did we chop up all your strengths between us? Tara has your fertility, your deep but easy love. Hone, your quick knowledge of people, your organising ability. Fa' somehow has got hold of your disciplined acceptance of life, your insight that 'this is the way things are, so I'll make the best of it.' Me, I have your music and way with mood and language. And Maki had your . . . who knows what Maki would have done, could have been?

It is strange.
    Here in the smoke-stained dark, my hands have found my guitar. I am rubbing the dust, sweeping it carefully gently away. Assuring the instrument that my neglect is not its fault. Pat pat stroke stroke and another little dustball fluffs away . . .

But I do know one thing Maki would have been good at, something you have great knowledge of — kawa. Marae protocol. The old people's way of doing things right.
    I was never interested in the past, only what happens to me, now.
    You remember that old witch Granny Hawe taking me out and whacking me because I pranced across some bloke's legs?
    'You can't do that, you take all the mens power from him. He's no good if we take his power from him. And those mens in there, they're very high persons. We have to be careful eh?'
    Wallop.
    I remember the words and I remember the sting, and I still hate all that shit, men being tapu, and women being noa. Don't eat here; don't put your head there. Don't hang your clothes higher than the men's; never get up and talk on the marae.
    'Our women don't talk out front,' you said. 'Arawa women speak only from behind their men.'
    And you wonder why I went city?
    But Maki used to love hui. He'd hang in there, listening with all his soul. He learned our whakapapa way before I did, and I have an ear that leads straight to my memory. He sucked up kawa — sucked up any kind of Maori knowledge. And then, and then
    The second to last time I came home, you recall I wouldn't go to that hui? Aue, I know you recall. You lost your good temper and yelled at me all kinds of rude names and swearing, taureka and sloven, 'pokokohua and bitch. 'I spent months getting this together, all the old people who know the waiata! It's a big thing for us, a big thing for *you*, and now Miss High and Mighty you *thing* won't go! Aue, what did I do to have such a daughter?'
    And I smiled back from my bed where I was lying, nestled in against Colin. I smiled a slow smile, a sneering smile at my big ranting mother, but my lips trembled. And you said then, quietly, painfully,
    'E hine, sometimes I think we live in different worlds.' Stopped a minute, shaking your head, rubbing your heart-place. 'You in one world, me in quite another. It's my fault, Hinewai. When you were growing, I wanted a place of sun and water and song. Not the mud and the bush

and Tom's heavy silence. The farm. The thick animals.'
 My smile trembled to a stop.
 'Different worlds, my Hinewai . . .'

It rings. Te ao tawhito, te ao hou. Different worlds . . . a slow minor chord and suddenly the strings sing so softly, my fingers play so easy — suddenly the stale smoke and the damp chair and the crowded dark are another world away.

You used to wear this glistening lipstick of shocking red that nobody had used for years. The last boyfriend I brought back, last time, saw you dressed to the nines for another hui and whistled at you. He didn't know then you were my mother. 'God what arse! God what class!' he crowed, genuinely applauding. 'She's the only woman in the world could get away with that!'
 I was shuddering. There you were, six feet tall and nearly sixteen stone, your eyelids lacquered green and your mouth crimson and your nails varnished shellpink and your brown skin a glowing background for this preposterous flaunting of colour. And while your feet were swollen over the edges of those narrow Pakeha shoes, you stood ebulliently, head thrown back, mouth full of that generous warming laughter, because you liked him coming straight out with what he thought and you were amused by my shrinking response. Go broadside into the world, Hinewai, you are grinning —

When Tara first rang me, I didn't believe him. He and his Pakeha wife came round then, and like Hone years before, first ranted then wept. There were no more bands by then. I grieved now for my dead music, and I still grieved among bottles. Tara said,
 'You've got to come home. She's asking for you. We're going in the morning so let's clear this up' the same sweep of arms as Hone, batting savagely against the clutter and debris 'and we all go together.'
 I shake my head numbly, whisper I can't.
 'But she's crying for you,' says Tara.

E whae, it is your laughter, loud and so warm, your laughter I keep hearing.
 When the telegram arrived this morning, I knew what it was without opening it.
 I did not scream.
 I did not tangi.
 I stood a moment in hopeless greyness.
 Then yelled.
 'I need a party!'
 It became a chant, She needs a party, Let's have a party! Party! All

the groupies and opportunists, the streetwalkers and transvestites, the city underbelly: my mates, my friends. Knowing the need, not needing to know what prompted it. Rowdily starting to make a party. The chant was the seed, and the seed grew and swelled into a roaring peoplemass that drank and sang and fought its way through all that day, and then, this night. Now, the party is dead. Someone is moaning in their bitter dreams. Someone else is snoring. And I am alone in the dark.

Different worlds, e mama. You are gone into the night, and I sit here, clutching the neck of my guitar, tears falling in tiny beads of sound. By now, you will have found Tom: by now, you will have met your secret grand-daughter. By now you will know all the disgrace and emptiness of my noisy crowded life. If I had any of your strength and generosity I would be packing up now, getting ready to catch the train, the bus, getting ready to hike, anyway back for the tangi. Doing all the proper things as befits the eldest child, as befits the daughter of my mother.

E Ma, I am sorry.

And you are sitting there, a tall slim woman with no grey in your hair, no lines on your face. Your arms are folded round your knees: you look at me hunched weeping in the dark and you smile a marvellous smile.
 'Be happy, Hinewai. Sing for me, my daughter. Play!'

And I am.

(1986)